I0670095

SPY HIGH

Book 9 of the NEVER SAY SPY series

Diane Henders

SPY HIGH

ISBN 978-1-927460-22-1

Copyright © 2015 Diane Henders

PEBKAC Publishing Inc.
P.O. Box 67, Station Main
Qualicum Beach, BC   V9K 1S7
www.pebkacpublishing.com

All rights reserved. No part of this book may be used or reproduced in any manner whatsoever without prior written permission, except in the case of brief quotations embodied in critical articles and reviews. For information, address PEBKAC Publishing Inc.

NO AI TRAINING: Without in any way limiting the author's and/or publisher's exclusive rights under copyright, any use of this publication to "train" generative artificial intelligence (AI) technologies to generate text is expressly prohibited. The author reserves all rights to license uses of this work for generative AI training and development of machine learning language models.

This book is a work of fiction. Names, characters, places and incidents are either the product of the author's imagination or are used fictitiously, and any resemblance to actual persons, living or dead, business establishments, events or locales is entirely coincidental.

First printed in paperback January 2015 by PEBKAC Publishing Inc.
v.8

Books in the NEVER SAY SPY series:

More books coming! For a current list, please visit
www.dianehenders.com
Or sign up for my New Book Notification list at
www.dianehenders.com/books

Humour by Diane Henders

Since You Asked...

People frequently ask if my protagonist, Aydan Kelly, is really me.

Yeah, you got me. These novels are an autobiography of my secret life as a government agent, working with highly-classified computer technology... Oh, wait, what's that? You want the *truth*? Um, you do realize fiction writers get paid to lie, don't you?

...well, shit, that's not nearly as much fun. It's also a long story.

I swore I'd never write fiction. "Too personal," I said. "People read novels and automatically assume the author is talking about him/herself."

Well, apparently I lied about the fiction-writing part. One day a story sprang into my head and wouldn't leave. The only way to get it out was to write it down. So I did.

But when I wrote that first book, I never intended to show it to anyone, so I created a character that looked like me just to thumb my nose at the stereotype. I've always had a defective sense of humour, and this time it turned around and bit me in the ass.

Because after I'd written the third novel, I realized I actually wanted other people to read my books. And when I went back to change my main character to *not* look like me, my beta readers wouldn't let me. They rose up against me and said, "No! Aydan is a tall woman with long red hair and brown eyes. End of discussion!"

Jeez, no wonder readers get the idea that authors write about themselves. So no, I'm not Aydan Kelly. I just look like her.

Oh, and the town of Silverside and all secret technologies are products of my imagination. If I'm abducted by grim-faced men wearing dark glasses, or if I die in an unexplained fiery car crash, you'll know I accidentally came a little too close to the truth.

I hope you enjoy the book!

For Phill

Thank you for being my technical advisor and the most tolerant husband ever. Much love!

To my beta readers/editors, especially Carol H., Judy B., and Phill B., with gratitude: Many thanks for all your time and effort in catching my spelling and grammar errors, telling me when I screwed up the plot or the characters' motivations, and generally keeping me honest.

To Rick and Sandy H. at Hand Crafted Images: Your talent makes my covers extra-special, and your sense of humour makes photo sessions fun even for a camera-hater like me. Thank you!

To Steve A. and the staff at The Shooting Edge: Thank you for lending us your excellent facilities for our cover photo sessions. You guys rock!

To everyone else, respectfully:
Canadian English is an unholy hybrid of British and American English, so I apologize if spellings in this book look odd to you. But if you find typos, please send an email to errors@dianehenders.com. Mistakes drive me nuts, and I'm sorry if any slipped through. Please let me know what the error is, and on which page (or at which position in e-versions). I'll make sure it gets fixed as soon as possible. Thanks!

CHAPTER 1

A distant shout made me jerk my head up to listen. A moment later I identified both the voice and the name it was calling.

Shit!

Snapping a glance around the forest, I dodged off the gravel path and dashed through the undergrowth to my favourite giant cedar tree.

Thank God I hadn't been spotted. Yet.

I ducked behind the tree and squashed through the large crack into its hollow trunk, hunching over awkwardly in the damp cedar-scented dimness. Even the thumping of my heart couldn't drown out the calls of my pursuer.

"Storm! Hello-o-o! Storm Cloud Dancer, where are you?" Aurora Peace Rain's strident voice made me wince and cower deeper into my hiding place.

Her calls got louder and I suppressed a groan. What the hell had I been thinking? If she caught me hiding in here, how would I explain myself?

"Storm!"

She must be standing right on the other side of the tree. If she came around it, she'd see my legs through the crack.

"*Storm!*"

Shit, and if she kept screeching like that, the damn tree was likely to split under the vocal assault.

The swish-thump of boots tramping through

undergrowth sounded nearly on top of me and I squeezed my eyes shut.

If she caught me I'd tell her... um...

My eyes popped open as inspiration hit. I didn't have to look like a deranged chickenshit. I'd just say I was communing with the Earth Spirit in here. Anywhere else in Canada that would be good for a VIP ticket to a psych evaluation, but here on the commune they'd probably be thrilled.

She gave one more ear-piercing call before her footsteps faded, and her next shout came from farther away.

I let out my breath with a whoosh and slid down to crouch on the damp ground, giving thanks for the size of the trees here in the British Columbia rainforest.

God, I needed to get back to my secluded Alberta farm. After four months of living a communal lifestyle my nerves were scraped raw. I cast a sheepish glance around my cramped refuge before thumping my forehead against my drawn-up knees.

How pathetic. Hiding like a coward just because I couldn't bear Aurora's voice. She was actually quite a nice kid... well, twenty-something. But her enthusiastic expositions on the benevolence of the Earth Spirit had gotten old after the first week. And that voice of hers, my God.

I leaned my head against the rough wood behind me and drew in a deep breath. Letting it out slowly, I debated how long to stay hidden. Aurora's calls had faded into the distance, but there was no telling whether she'd come back this way. I'd wait a little longer.

After several more minutes of crouching in silence my legs began to rebel, and the confined space made my breathing accelerate even though the opening was only a foot away. What if something happened? What if the tree somehow shifted and trapped me inside?

I drew a deep breath and let it out slowly. Don't be stupid. That couldn't happen. Just stay in here a little longer...

Claustrophobia won at last and I was about to make my escape when the distant crunch of footsteps on gravel made me hunch down again.

Dammit, she was coming back.

Moments later I realized it wasn't Aurora when I heard quiet male voices over the footsteps.

Well, fine. In a few minutes they'd be past. The commune was all about tolerance and understanding, but that didn't mean I wanted to be known as a forty-seven-year-old woman who hid inside hollow trees like a kid.

Besides, there was no need to give away my hiding place. I might want to use it again.

I settled back to wait.

The footsteps got louder and a snatch of conversation drifted to my ears.

"...think it'll be soon?"

"Mesker will tell us when."

"Aw, come on..."

That voice sounded familiar. I frowned, trying to place it.

It went on, "...you're his right-hand man. You must know."

I jerked upright with recognition, nearly cracking my head on the inside of the tree.

Orion Moonjava.

A pause, then the second voice spoke again, sounding smug. "Soon. Maybe even this week."

The voices and footsteps were fading and I eased my head out the crack to peek at the two figures receding along the path. Orion's broad shoulders, wavy brown hair, and buns of steel were easy to identify, but I didn't recognize his short, slightly-built companion. All I could see of him was black hair, baggy camo pants, and military-style boots.

The smaller man spoke again, his words drifting back to me so faintly I could barely identify the words. "I can hardly wait to get rid of the filth."

Orion laughed as they disappeared around a bend in the path and their voices dwindled.

Heart pounding, I withdrew into the safety of my tree again.

If I wasn't on a covert mission I'd probably dismiss the conversation without a second thought, but it was my job to be suspicious. And the words 'get rid of the filth' had sent a shiver down my spine. I hoped he'd been talking about the mud on his boots.

Or maybe I'd heard him wrong.

Feeling antsy, I squeezed out of my hiding place and stood hesitating. Should I follow them and try to overhear more?

But that likely wouldn't work. If I walked on the path they'd hear my footsteps on the gravel, and if they caught me skulking along in the undergrowth I'd rouse their suspicions in return. Orion thought I was just a bookkeeper, and I wanted to keep it that way.

But dammit, this was the second thing about Orion that had made me uneasy.

"Storm!"

I jumped at the sound of Aurora's call and flung a wild glance toward my tree, but it was too late. She'd spotted me.

"There you are!" Her voice assaulted my ears even from several yards away as she jogged up. "There's a phone call for you," she panted. "Where were you? I've been looking and looking."

Hoping to limit our encounter, I broke into a jog toward the main building. "Thanks, Aurora," I threw over my shoulder. "If I run maybe I can catch them before they hang up."

I should have known better. She caught up easily. And short of making it an obvious race, I couldn't shake her. Hell, she could probably outrun me anyway. I was in good shape, but so was she. And she was about twenty-five years younger.

I settled into a steady jog and resigned myself to my fate as she began, "Hasn't the Earth Spirit given us a lovely day today? It's so nice to get a break from the rain..."

I kept jogging, nodding grimly and trying not to wince while her monologue battered my eardrums like machine-gun fire.

When we panted up to the main building and ducked inside I sucked in a breath of relief at the sight of the old-fashioned telephone receiver dangling by its curly cord.

"Oh, good," I interrupted Aurora's soliloquy. "Looks like they're still on the line. Thanks for coming to get me."

"You're welcome, Storm!" Her voice rose in enthusiasm and I took an involuntary step backward.

"Talk to you later, then," I said, and hurried over to snatch up the receiver.

Aurora gave me a sunny smile and departed, and my "Hello?" wafted into the receiver on a sigh of relief.

"Is this Aydan Kelly?" The voice of my best friend made my heart lift.

"Nichele!" I clutched the receiver, grinning. "How the hell are you? It's so great to hear your voice!"

"Aydan, finally!" Her squeal of delight would have made me yank the receiver away from my ear if I hadn't just been subjected to Aurora's jackhammer voice. "Girl, I can't believe I'm finally getting to talk to you! Where were you? You sound like you just ran a mile!"

"I damn near did." I sucked in a few deep breaths, trying to control my panting. "I was on the other side of the commune. Sorry you had to wait so long. Talk to me while I catch my breath."

She launched into her usual exuberant chatter and I leaned against the wall, still grinning. This was going to take a while.

CHAPTER 2

"...secluded raincoast paradise, my ass!" I jammed the receiver between my chin and shoulder, the better to wave my arms while I paced and vented to Nichele. "Secluded, yeah, it's 'way out in the sticks; and 'raincoast' is no exaggeration. But 'paradise'? Ha! If there's really a hell, it's not fiery-hot like everybody thinks. It's cold and wet and gloomy-"

The curly cord jerked taut and I barely managed to catch the receiver before it hit the floor.

"This shitty old phone!" I stuffed it back under my chin.

"Why don't you just use your cell phone?" Nichele asked, her words blurred by the crackling of the bad connection. "It's such a pain to call you on the land line. Nobody can ever find you and they're lousy at taking messages. We've talked, what? Twice in the last four months?"

"Yeah. Sorry about that. I'd use my cell if I could, but the commune doesn't allow them."

"How would they know?" Nichele scoffed. "If they can't even find you, they can't possibly know if you sneak a cell phone in there."

"Yeah, but..." I paused, ransacking my brain for a plausible reason besides 'I can't use it in case some bad guy tracks its signal and comes to kill me'.

"Um, I just don't like to go against their rules," I mumbled, and changed the subject. "Anyway, I can't believe I fell for that 'paradise' bullshit. I knew damn well how rainy the west coast of Vancouver Island is in winter. If I have to listen to the pitter-patter of raindrops on canvas one more day I swear I'll go insane."

Nichele's giggle danced above the static.

"Yeah, laugh it up," I snarled, my acrimony only half-feigned. "I haven't been completely dry in months. There's mould growing in my underwear drawer, for shit's sake!"

"Girl, if you've got mould in your underwear it means you're not getting enough action," Nichele teased. "Why haven't you found some artsy hippie-type guy who's into all that tantric sex stuff? And anyway, I thought you said Hellhound and Hot John were going to come out and visit you." I could imagine her grin and bouncing eyebrows. "You can't tell me the two of them weren't enough to burn the mould off your panties."

I smiled in spite of myself. "Your fascination with my sex life is downright twisted."

"What sex life?" she demanded. "Somebody should pay attention to it, 'cause you obviously aren't."

"Mm." My smile faded. "John was here a couple of months ago..."

"*Really?*" Nichele's squeal coincided with a moment of clarity on the line and I jerked the receiver away from my ear, wincing. The static promptly returned, making me strain to hear her next words. "Oh-em-gee, he is soooo hot! Why would you even need underwear if he was there?"

"He was convalescing," I protested. "He was in pretty rough shape because he'd fallen on some ice and broken a rib a few weeks earlier."

The cover story left a bad taste in my mouth. It wasn't fair to make Kane sound like an accident-prone wimp, but revealing that he was really a secret agent recovering from a gunshot wound would tend to negate the 'secret' part.

She interrupted my thoughts with a lascivious purr. "Anybody with a bit of imagination can work around a broken rib."

"Yeah..." My word floated out on a sigh. "But we didn't get a chance to try. He'd only been here a few hours when he got a call saying his dad had been taken to the hospital with chest pain, so he left right away and flew out to Winnipeg. His dad had stents put in and he's fine now, thank God, but by the time things settled down John had to go back to work instead of coming here."

"But you'll see him when you get home, right?"

I held in another sigh. "Probably not. We aren't working together anymore and he has to travel a lot for his new job. I haven't heard a thing from him in over a month. I don't even know where he is."

My gut clenched. He could be anywhere in the world, in danger I'd never know about unless I got a call that began with the words 'We have bad news'.

"So, um... what about Hellhound?" Nichele inquired cautiously. "You're not going to spoil what you've got with John by sleeping with Hellhound again, are you?"

"There's nothing to spoil. John and I are just good friends..." The half-lie sounded feeble, but I forged on regardless. "...and I told you, I don't know..." I bit off the word 'if'. "...when I'll see him again. And I haven't seen Arnie since I left in December. We've talked on the phone a couple of times, but he's been too busy with his P.I. cases to come out here." I kept my tone light, hiding my twinge of hurt.

Apparently I hadn't hidden it as well as I'd hoped. Nichele snorted. "Well, fine. Forget those losers, then. Why not sample the herd there?" A wicked grin lurked in Nichele's faux-innocent tone. "Aren't any of those skinny granola-fed guys up to it?"

I glanced around the corner to be sure I was alone before lowering my voice as I slid down the wall to sit on the floor. "Finding somebody who's interested isn't the problem. They all are. They've got this sixties-style free love thing going on, and everybody sleeps with everybody else. By now every man here has made a pass at me including Skidmark, who I'm pretty sure has lived here for seventy years and been stoned the whole time."

"*Every* man?" Nichele's voice rose to a squeak of revulsion. "Your *uncle* propositioned you? *Eeeeuwwww!*"

"No, no!" I amended quickly. "No, of course Uncle Karma didn't, and all the other guys just asked nicely and it was no big deal when I turned them down. But still..."

"Yeah, still. Skidmark? Eeuw." She giggled again. "Why do they call him that? You mean, like, he has skidmarks in his underwear?"

"Jeez, Nichele! I don't even want to think about his underwear! Until this moment I was perfectly happy believing everybody calls him that because he's the closest thing to a mechanic they have out here in the middle of Bumfuck Nowhere. Funny, though, he's the only one who doesn't have some hippie-type name. Everybody else is Flower this and Rainbow that."

"I still think it's hilarious that you have these freaky-deaky relatives you didn't know anything about until this year. 'Uncle Karma and Auntie Moonbeam'. What a hoot! I'd love to come out and meet them!"

"No!" I converted my yelp of dismay to a calmer but still discouraging tone. "You'd hate it here. It's really primitive. We only have power four hours a day and we get hot showers on a twice-a-week rotation, so just about everybody reeks of body odour. And anyway Karma and Moonbeam aren't really my aunt and uncle. They're cousins of my aunt, but they were close friends with my mom before she died..." I let the lie trail off before I could dig myself in any deeper.

"That's so weird." Nichele sounded dangerously pensive. "I was at your place pretty much every day when we were kids. They must have visited if they were that close to your mom, but I don't remember them. And I know I'd remember wacko names like that."

Shit, shit! Time for a distraction.

I hurriedly reintroduced the apparently-fascinating topic of my sex life. Or lack thereof. "Um, one of the guys here is kind of interesting..." I let the sentence trail off tantalizingly.

Thank God, she took the bait.

"Oooh, Aydan, that's awesome! What's his name? What's he like? Tell me, tell me!"

I drew a silent breath of relief. "Everyone calls him Orion Moonjava. I don't know what his real name is; Moonbeam gives everybody a new name when they arrive at the commune and she's such a sweetheart that everybody just plays along." I bit my tongue. That wouldn't help discourage Nichele's visit. I returned to my distraction. "Anyway, Orion's probably too young for me, but-"

"How old is he?" Nichele demanded.

"I don't know, maybe mid-thirties? Or maybe a little older, but it's hard to tell. He's in really good shape."

"Mid-thirties isn't too young. Half your age plus eight years, that's the rule. So thirty-one-and-a-half is your bottom limit."

"There's a rule?" I massaged my blossoming headache with my free hand.

"Of course there's a rule. Now dish, girl! And please tell me he doesn't reek of B.O."

"He doesn't reek of B.O.," I parroted obligingly before reeling off the description I'd provided in my secret report to Charles Stemp. "He's about six-foot-one, brown hair, green eyes, athletic build; maybe one-seventy-five, one-eighty pounds. He sounds just as Canadian as the rest of us, but every now and then there's a turn of phrase or a funny... I don't know... cadence or something in the way he talks that makes him sound British."

Which was why I'd flagged him in my security report. He just didn't quite fit in with the back-to-the-earth types around here. And now I'd overheard that odd conversation...

Nichele's voice interrupted my thoughts. "Oooh, British! I loooove a man with an accent! Is he hot?"

I diverged from my official report. "Smokin', and he's been flirting with me ever since he got here in January. But like I said, he doesn't really have an accent."

"But he's young and hot and interested and you're turning him down?" Her voice rose to an incredulous crescendo. "Girl, are you *nuts?*"

"Probably."

I was definitely nuts. And I was also under orders to observe Orion Moonjava without engaging him, but I couldn't tell Nichele that.

"Well, if you aren't going to give Mr. Smokin' Hot Brit an entry visa and you hate it there, why don't you just come home?"

I crossed my fingers to dilute my lie. "I can't yet. The commune is in the middle of an audit. They're hippies, not bookkeepers, and their books are a total disaster. I'm trying to help them but it just keeps dragging on and on."

"Aydan, that's a load of crap and you know it!"

My heart stopped. Oh shit, how had she found out it was all a cover story? Had Dave blabbed? Shit, *shit*!

Before I could blurt out anything incriminating she went on, "You were supposed to be back by the end of February. It's nearly the middle of April, and I don't care if you're getting a free vacation in their so-called paradise; they're taking advantage of you. They never bothered to say boo to you for forty-some years of your life, and now all of a sudden they want to be your favourite aunt and uncle until you solve their financial woes? Tell them to stick it."

I drew a secret breath of relief and tried to keep the tremor of adrenaline out of my voice. "I'd love to, but I can't." I hoped the sincerity of my desire to escape was sufficiently concealed by my fake concern. "They're really nice people..." At least that part was the truth. "...and I just can't abandon them in the middle of this mess."

Nichele's voice softened and I could hear the smile in her words. "You're such a pushover. But if it makes you feel any better, there's still a foot of snow here in Calgary and we're freezing our asses off. You couldn't start your garden anyway."

"Thanks, Nichele, that'll keep me from screaming for one more day." I glanced up as a wrinkled apparition in a rainbow tie-dyed caftan floated around the corner. "Aunt Moonbeam needs the phone so I have to go now. Take care, and say hi to Dave."

"I will, and you take care, too. And have a little taste of Britain. Seriously, girl, I mean it. You're cranky as hell. You need to get laid."

"You are 'way too interested in my sex life. Pervert."

Nichele's giggle dissolved in the click of the disconnect as I hauled myself upright to replace the phone in the cradle.

Moonbeam's sweet face crumpled into concern. "Oh, Storm Cloud Dancer, I didn't need the phone. You didn't have to hang up on your friend."

"That's okay, we were done." I hesitated. I knew there wasn't much hope, but I had to try. Again. "Storm Cloud Dancer is such a mouthful. Why don't you just call me Aydan? Or Storm like everybody else does?"

"Oh, no, dear, the vibrations are all wrong. With your aura, you need a name that emphasizes your artistic expression. In numerology that's a three, so you need C and L and U."

"Are you sure about that aura thing?" I asked as deferentially as I could. "I haven't painted in thirty years and I wasn't any Picasso back then. I don't write poetry or play a musical instrument or anything. I couldn't carry a tune in a bucket. I can't even draw stick people."

"Well, of course. That's exactly what I mean." Moonbeam nodded as though we were in perfect agreement. "By the way, I didn't mean to eavesdrop, but did I hear you call me Aunt Moonbeam?"

"Um." I tried to suppress the guilty flush that warmed my cheeks. "I... um, didn't want to explain to Nichele why I was here so I kind of... fibbed a bit. I told her you and Karma were my distant aunt and uncle. I'm sorry."

"Oh." She hesitated. "That does explain the grayish overlay on your aura. It always indicates deception." Lines of concern furrowed her forehead. "But why are you concealing the truth from your friend? There's no shame in retreating from a trauma to heal, and a true friend would support you through the process."

"I, uh..."

Damn cover stories. I cast my gaze down to my toes, hoping I looked traumatized instead of guilty. "I'm not... ready to talk about it yet." I changed the subject. "I'm sorry if my lie bothered you. I'll call her back and confess if you want, but..." I gave her my best pleading big brown eyes. "If you could just play along as Aunt Moonbeam and Uncle Karma, I'd really appreciate it."

"Oh, my dear, it's quite all right. We'd love to adopt you. But please, it's Aunt Moonbeam Meadow Sky and Uncle Karma Wolf Song. Shortening our names..."

"...messes with the vibrations," I finished with resignation. "I'm sorry. I'll try to remember."

"You're completely forgiven." She hugged me, her arms remarkably strong despite their apparent fragility in the billowing caftan. She smoothed the hair away from my face with firm hands. "Please don't hold guilt, Storm Cloud Dancer; it makes your aura so murky." She gazed at me, her faded china-blue eyes focused somewhere beyond my physical form. "But your aura is much clearer now than when you came, thank the Spirit. And I notice you're sleeping better, too."

My flush returned with a vengeance. Goddamn tents; if you so much as farted in the night, the whole commune knew. My screaming nightmares were sheer humiliation.

I hid my discomfiture as best I could. "Yeah, it's been nearly two months since I woke up the whole camp. I'm sure everybody else is just as happy about that as I am."

"Oh, my dear, don't be embarrassed. Cosmic River Stone said you'd been through some terrible experiences. We knew you were coming here for healing, and I'm glad you're finding it."

Yeah, right; healing. And to secretly protect his parents and watch everybody else at the commune. I respected his expertise, but Cosmic River Stone, a.k.a. Charles Stemp, was a lousy, manipulative bastard.

"You're very dear to him, you know." Moonbeam's gentle voice interrupted my dark thoughts.

"Huh? Dear to whom?"

"To Cosmic River Stone, of course." At my strangled half-laugh-half-snort, Moonbeam's brow furrowed. "No wonder your aura has that gray overlay. You're deceiving yourself if you think he doesn't care for you. He has never sent a female friend to be with us before." Her expression grew dreamy. "How wonderful it would be to have grandchildren. Cosmic River Stone is a good man, you know, and his manager's position at the research facility is very secure. And he's only forty-three. Not too old to start a family-"

My bark of laughter made her start. I hurriedly hunched over, elbows on knees, hacking and gasping theatrically. "Sorry..." I choked. "Spit... down the wrong... pipe."

That seemed more tactful than falling to the ground and kicking my heels in helpless hilarity at the thought of Stemp and me together. Never in a million years; unless the profound desire to place my hands around his throat and squeeze counted as 'being together'.

Time to nip this in the bud. I straightened slowly, wiping my eyes and letting out a few last fake coughs.

"Oh, Storm Cloud Dancer, I'm sorry I upset you,"

Moonbeam cried, her face drawn in distress. She stroked my hand. "It was insensitive of me to say that. I'm so sorry. I should have known by the brown shadow in your aura around your uterus."

"Uh... wha...?" I croaked. I shook off my sudden sense of unreality and returned to the point I'd intended to make. "Ste... Char... jeez, *Cosmic River Stone* and I will never be a source of grandchildren for you. In the first place our office has rules against employee relationships..." I held up a hand to forestall Moonbeam's protest. "...and in the second place I can't have children..." My words slowed as I considered the fact that she'd apparently already known somehow. "...I've had a hysterectomy," I finished lamely.

"Oh." Her face clouded, and guilt prodded my heart in spite of myself. Then her luminous smile broke through again. "I'm glad that's all it is. I was afraid the shadow might have been some reproductive illness."

"Oh. Um, no, I'm fine." I backed away. "Well, nice talking to you. I'm going to... um... go check on the garden."

"That's a good idea, dear. Your aura clears so beautifully when you're in the garden. You have so much green in your aura, you know. I can tell you're deeply grounded in the Earth Spirit."

I smiled, nodded, and fled.

CHAPTER 3

Rattled, I strode along the path to the garden without appreciating the vivid greens of the rainforest as much as usual. I didn't believe in all that woo-woo stuff, but Moonbeam's diagnosis had given me a distinctly creepy feeling. What if there really were auras and she could see them? If grey meant deception it was a miracle she could see any other colour in mine, since I'd been spouting Stemp's cover-story lies for the past four months.

The sound of voices ahead jerked me to a halt near the garden clearing and I sidestepped into the thick undergrowth to listen. Aurora's brassy tones penetrated the forest silence, interspersed with a softer male voice. That would be Zen Earth Star, her more-or-less constant companion, though they didn't seem to be in a relationship. No more so than anybody else here, anyway.

Aurora let out a piercing laugh that set my teeth on edge. Damn, not again. Once a day was more than enough.

I turned and retraced my steps as quietly as possible.

Wandering down the path, I considered my options. I needed to wash a few clothes, but the idea of scrubbing them on the washboard and wringing them by hand didn't appeal. Better to wait until the power came on in a few hours and then jockey for position at the ancient wringer washer.

I wanted to report to Stemp, but I had to let the memory of his mother's matchmaking subside or I was likely to either laugh or gag at the sound of his voice; I wasn't sure which.

Working out was always an option. The gym was the only up-to-date part of the whole commune, and I'd made good use of it in the past few months. I was in better shape than I'd ever been, but I was still feeling the effects of the previous day's hard workout. Skip that.

Or I could re-read one of the tattered paperbacks from the tiny library. At least it was in the main building so it was dry and relatively warm, unlike my dank canvas tent.

I sighed and kept walking. God, I was going slowly crazy here. Surely it must be safe for me to resurface in my real life by now. After nearly four months all the bad guys from my last case should finally be behind bars.

A dark suspicion crossed my mind. Maybe Stemp was lying about the potential danger back home. Maybe he had decided to protect his secrets by warehousing me permanently out here, isolated from the rest of the world and slowly rotting away until I became just another bump under the moss of the forest floor.

I kicked at an inoffensive fern as I passed. Maybe I should just say screw it and leave against his orders.

A narrow offshoot of the path caught my attention and I turned down it, desperate for any form of novelty.

The faint trail wove through deep undergrowth, the soggy earth squishing under my hiking boots and the wet ferns soaking the legs of my jeans.

But at least it was silent and I could savour a few rare moments of solitude. I drew a deep breath of moist spicy forest air, feeling the tension easing between my shoulder blades.

After ten minutes of unhurried uphill walking, my equanimity was almost restored and I was beginning to wonder where the trail led. I hadn't met or heard another human being, but the trail showed signs of recent use in its squashed moss and the occasional broken fern frond.

I was debating whether to turn back when a thicket of bright green a few yards off the path made me pause. A couple of steps closer, my heart lurched into a rapid rhythm.

Shit, I'd stumbled onto somebody's marijuana crop. Bad place to linger unless I was looking for a neighbourly greeting from the business end of a shotgun.

I was turning to hurry away when a shout jolted adrenaline into my veins. My hand twitched reflexively toward my ankle holster, but I squelched the urge. The commune members might be a little naïve, but even they wouldn't believe a bookkeeper needed to carry a baby Glock.

Scanning the forest, I tensed at the sound of another yell, then relaxed when I identified the words.

"Skidmark! Where are you? Get out here, old man! You lazy, useless..."

The rest of the shouted insults were obscured by my sigh of relief. Not busted after all. Now I just needed to get my ass out of here before I really did get caught.

The pot garden was probably Skidmark's private stash, and at least now I knew where he wasn't. Better to head for the commotion and look innocent when he arrived than to get caught scurrying guiltily away in the direction I'd come. I fled up the path as quietly as possible toward the sounds of irritable impatience.

A few minutes later the verdant shade lightened as I approached a clearing, and I struck out into the undergrowth to circle it and approach from the opposite direction.

When I stepped out of the forest, a skinny dark-bearded young man jerked around to face me, his black brows knotted in annoyance. His camo pants and military boots looked familiar.

Orion's companion.

He cast a single glare at me before turning his back to rail at the trees again. "Skidmark! I need this truck now! Get out here!"

Thus soundly ignored, I took in the scene at my leisure. I had obviously arrived at Skidmark's automotive empire via the back way. Grass and weeds almost hid the gravel that paved the small clearing, and to my left a narrow gravelled track wound through the forest downhill to the main road. The commune's dilapidated 1970 Chevy one-ton truck sagged dispiritedly beside a moss-covered garage, and the other communal vehicle, a gigantic rust-pocked station wagon, slouched across from it.

The rodent-faced young man's complexion was reddening and cords stood out in his neck. "SKIDMARK! Curse you to a thousand hells, I NEED THIS TRUCK NOW!"

This didn't seem like a good time to visit. I began to retreat.

The crunch of my boots on gravel made Ratboy whip around to face me again. As he did, Skidmark shuffled out from behind the shed.

"Dude," he mumbled. "Be cool, man."

Ratboy spun, his fists clenching, and I took a couple of quick steps closer in case he attacked the older man.

I wasn't sure who might win if they actually fought. Skidmark was probably in his early seventies, but his arms were corded with ropy muscle. I'd seen him work out and I was pretty sure he could take Ratboy if he was sober.

But he wasn't. As usual.

Slack-faced, he swayed gently as he worked grubby fingers through his long grey beard as though searching for his own chin. In his other hand a twist of cigarette paper emitted a thin curl of smoke, and the sickly-sweet odour of smouldering marijuana drifted to my nose.

He raised the joint and blinked at it as if surprised to find it in his hand before offering it to Ratboy. "Toke?"

"No!" A sudden sweep of Ratboy's arm made me jump toward them, but he was only snatching the cigarette to fling it to the gravel. He crushed it under his heel, glaring at Skidmark from close range. "Fix. The. Truck," he ground out. "Now."

"I can have a look at it if you want," I offered, hoping to defuse the situation. "Those old trucks are usually pretty easy to work on."

Ratboy shot me a contemptuous look before deliberately turning his back.

Skidmark blinked again, his hand poised as though still holding the now-defunct doobie. His gaze tracked slowly to Ratboy's glare. "Fixing trucks is men's work," he mumbled.

Ordinarily I'd have responded to a comment like that with an insult of the unprintable variety, but the tension in their exchange stilled my tongue.

"Mm," I murmured noncommittally and fell back a pace, watching.

Ratboy gave a sharp nod and jabbed a finger at Skidmark's face. "Fix it. Or I'll have the woman do it."

Okay, that was enough to piss me off.

"Oh, I don't know," I drawled. "I don't think *the woman* will be able to do it after all. Men's work is much too complicated."

Ratboy barked an unintelligible word and strode away, his boots crunching angrily on the gravel.

Skidmark and I watched in silence while he marched down the road, his shoulders rigid. When he rounded a curve and the trees hid him from view, Skidmark yawned and scratched his head under the lank grey ponytail that dangled half-way down his back.

"He called you a whore," he translated helpfully.

I turned to stare at him and he smiled, his blank innocent eyes incongruous in his weathered face.

"Well, golly gee," I said after a moment. "Now my feelings are hurt and I'm going to go home and cry. What a little dickwad."

Skidmark wheezed what might have been laughter. Then he directed a puzzled frown at his empty fingers and mumbled, "Coulda sworn I rolled a bomber just before I came out here."

"Ratboy squished it," I reminded him, and pointed to the crushed cigarette.

"Aw, man..." Skidmark squatted slowly, eyeing the scrap of paper with intense concentration. "Bummer." He bowed his head as if in requiem. He stayed that way for so long I was about to bend down and make sure he was okay when he moved at last, reaching for the mangled joint. "Good roach..." he muttered, and brushed most of the dirt off it before tucking it into the pocket of his stained coveralls. "Smoke it later..."

He rose in slow motion and drifted over to stand contemplating the truck. After several minutes he sighed. "Need a toke," he said, and shuffled away.

I shook my head and wandered over to the truck. The

keys were in the ignition, and I popped the hood before sliding into the driver's seat.

The starter cranked over reassuringly, but the engine didn't even hint at catching. I grunted and slid down from the seat to go around the front. Poking my head under the hood, I eyed the greasy old V-8 squatting in the middle of its cavernous bay, festooned with grimy wires and half-perished rubber hoses. I sucked in a deep breath of burnt-oil scent and smiled. Likely an electrical problem.

After a brief visual inventory, I began to trace the ignition path. Examining the wire leading up from the ignition coil, I let out a 'hmph' of surprise when it dropped away from the distributor cap.

"Well, that'll do it," I muttered, and reconnected it.

Sure enough, the engine fired up on the first try, and I was basking in the satisfaction of an easy fix when it abruptly died.

"What the...?" I hopped out of the cab just in time to catch Skidmark carefully laying the wire in its original loosened position on the distributor cap.

"What the hell?" I demanded.

He straightened and took a drag from a fresh joint. After a long pause, smoke filtered through his beard as he mumbled, "Patience is a virtue, girlie."

My mouth dropped open in indignation, but then I caught the barest hint of a twinkle in his eye.

I snickered. "Ratboy's patience?"

"Don't know what you're talking about," Skidmark said, and offered me his cigarette. "Toke?"

"No thanks."

He nodded sleepily before taking another long draw himself. I stepped away from the eye-watering combination of pot smoke and body odour and was about to head for the road when he spoke again.

"So you're a girl mechanic."

"I'm not a mechanic. I just like working on cars."

"Huh." He squinted blearily at me. "Hey, you're really tall..." He blinked. "Are you a dude in women's clothes?"

"Yeah," I replied, deadpan.

He stared in silence for a long moment, his cigarette hand drifting up to his lips as though of its own volition.

"Far out..." he mumbled, and took another drag. After a long exhalation of smoke, his eyes narrowed as though an idea had braved the burned-out corridors of his brain. "Wanna go back to my place and screw?" he inquired.

"I just finished telling you I'm a man."

He shrugged. "So I'm into equal rights. Can l touch your ass?"

"No."

His shoulders jerked rhythmically, accompanied by the wheezing that served him for laughter. "You're a woman all right." He offered his joint. "Toke?"

"No," I repeated.

The distant crunch of approaching footsteps made me turn, my pulse kicking up a notch at the thought of another confrontation with Ratboy. My heart rate failed to slow at the sight of the man rounding the bend in the road.

Orion.

He smiled and waved, and I waved back while Skidmark stood blinking placidly in the mist that was beginning to gather itself into raindrops.

"Hi, Storm," Orion greeted me as he strode up. "Hi, Skidmark."

I managed a casual 'hi' in return.

Damn, it should be illegal for a man to have eyelashes that thick and dark. They framed moss-green eyes alight with intelligence, almost the same colour as the soft corduroy shirt he wore loosely over a brown T-shirt that showcased the hard contours of his chest and abs. He had been clean-shaven with close-cropped hair when he had arrived at the commune a few months ago, but now short whiskers accented a chin that might have been carved by Michelangelo and his hair fell in those soft waves that begged me to run my fingers through it...

My cheeks warmed when I realized he'd spoken while I was ogling him.

"Sorry, I'm brain-dead today. What did you say?" I stammered.

He smiled. "Word of advice: Don't stand so close to Skidmark. If you've been breathing that fug, you're probably half-stoned."

My brain snapped out of ogle-mode and into full alert. There it was again. A wholly Canadian accent, but 'fug'? Nobody used that word around here.

Stemp had enemies overseas. If someone was going to come after his parents to gain revenge on him, they might have some sort of British or European accent.

I forced a chuckle, and Skidmark emitted his wheezy laughter before offering Orion the much-diminished joint. "Toke?"

"Sure." Orion appropriated the butt and took a short drag before offering it to me.

"No thanks," I said for the third time.

Orion was handing the roach back to Skidmark when the sudden clamour of bells made me flinch and swear.

CHAPTER 4

"Jesus, not again," I muttered.

"Come on!" Orion seized my hand and dragged me into a full run. The pealing of the bells mounted to a frenetic crescendo, and I dug in my heels as we reached the first bend of the road.

"Hang on!" I pulled free of his grip. "You go ahead if you want, but they can honour the Earth Spirit without me this time. Moonbeam already hauled me out of bed in the middle of the night a couple of days ago. I'm all honoured-out for this week."

"Come on, Storm!" Orion grabbed my hand again and pulled. "Hurry up!"

Damn, he was strong. Dragged into a reluctant jog, I protested, "Hell, Orion, you're a smart guy. You don't really believe the ground's going to open up and swallow us if we skip some hokey ceremony, do you?"

He skidded to a halt. "It's not hokey! This is important! Why are we here if not to honour the Earth Spirit?"

"Honouring the Earth Spirit is fine if that's what you believe in, but these random rituals are bullshi..." My heart smote me as his beautiful eyes widened with hurt. I blew out a breath. "Sorry." I let him pull me into a run again.

When we panted up to the main building, Aurora Peace Rain was practically dancing with impatience beside the door.

"Hurry, hurry!" she brayed. "You're the last ones, and the Earth Spirit needs us!"

Clenching my teeth against the onslaught of her voice, I accepted the rolled-up mat she pushed at me and followed Orion into the darkened building. Weaving between supine bodies, I tiptoed to my designated spot, where I unrolled the mat and lay down.

Blissful humming rose from the commune members and I closed my eyes, trying without much hope to achieve the meditative state Moonbeam wanted. It hadn't happened in four months, so it didn't seem likely now.

I drew a deep breath and let it out slowly. Hell, even the little kids were lying perfectly still and humming along with their parents. Surely I could manage some form of meditation. What had Moonbeam said? Something about grounding my root chakra to the Earth Spirit.

But wasn't my root chakra somewhere down around my ass? So if I was going to ground it to the Earth Spirit, wouldn't it make more sense to sit instead of lying down?

But sitting on the Earth Spirit's face seemed a tad disrespectful.

Then again, dragging me out of bed in the middle of the night for a 'Spirit Calling' was damn disrespectful, too.

Maybe the Earth Spirit could just kiss my chakra.

My eyes popped open in defiance of Moonbeam's 'eyes closed' edict and I studied my surroundings without moving. The heavy hand-hewn beams above us were barely visible in the dimness cast by the heavy shutters shrouding the windows. The wall beside me radiated a damp chill, and I wondered what architectural madness had impelled the builder to pour a four-foot-high concrete base and then finish the building with wood frame construction.

A soft green glow swelled into the room, and I slitted my eyes to peer between my lashes, shifting slowly to get a clear sight line without disturbing my humming neighbours.

The raised dais at the front of the room always held a large copper gong suspended from a wooden frame, with a small table a few feet in front of it. But now green light pulsated from the heart of the large crystal that occupied the centre of the table.

While I watched, Aurora and her sidekick Zen rose from their mats below the dais and stepped up to the crystal, each pressing an ear against it from opposite sides while their hands stroked a complex pattern over its surface.

The green glow brightened, illuminating their exalted expressions, then abruptly extinguished.

Blinking to clear the afterimage, I barely saw Aurora and Zen exchange nods. Zen crossed to the back of the dais and struck the gong once.

As though animated by the mellow reverberation, the recumbent bodies stirred and sat up, looking expectantly toward the dais. I sighed and did the same. I knew what was coming.

"The Earth Spirit has spoken! Come; follow." Aurora's voice ravaged my eardrums like a jackhammer after the peace of the meditation.

Everyone rose and split into two groups, one behind Aurora, the other behind Zen. Two other leaders whose names I had forgotten brought up the rear, apparently to corral any stragglers.

Cold rain pelted down as we filed out of the building, and

I hitched my jacket collar up and muttered to Orion beside me, "Remember, this was your idea."

"Silence! We must honour the Earth Spirit with our silence."

Aurora had caught me. She gave me a severe look and I ducked my head, hoping I looked contrite and holding back the urge to reply, "I'll shut up if you will."

Instead, I bit my tongue and joined the rest of the mute group to plod off into the wet forest single-file behind Aurora. With superhuman restraint, I managed not to grouse about the stupidity of tramping the winding forest trails instead of taking the direct route along the gravelled road. After about fifteen minutes of hiking, our dripping crew filed into a large open field, meeting Zen's band as they arrived from the opposite side.

Like well-drilled soldiers, we split into groups under our four leaders and moved to the cardinal points of the field where we knelt in the sodden grass, still silent.

The icy wetness made my knees ache and the rain trickled in cold rivulets down the back of my neck. A raw breeze moaned through the trees behind me, cutting effortlessly through my soggy jeans. In front of me a bald man with a bushy beard shivered uncontrollably, and I blessed my long thick hair. It was soaking wet, but at least it provided a bit of insulation.

After what seemed like forever, Aurora and Zen must have received some sign from their beloved Earth Spirit. They released us with a joyous cry of, "The blessings of the Earth Spirit are upon you!"

The supplicants replied with an equally enthusiastic, "And upon you, too!" as they scrambled to their feet, though I could have sworn the bald man had actually said, "And fuck you, too."

Or maybe that was just me.

Shivering, I hurried for the road and made a beeline for the main building, jostling past the smiling and chattering commune members who seemed impervious to the bone-chilling rain.

Orion found me half an hour later at one of the big woodstoves in the communal kitchen, where I was reheating a pot of soup and huddling as close to the stove as I could get without actually branding myself for life.

His hair hung in dripping ringlets against cheeks ruddy with cold, and his green eyes sparkled with amusement at the sight of me.

"Are you just a bit chilly, then?" he inquired, grinning.

"Shut up." I licked the hot soup off the spoon before clasping it between my icy hands. Its warmth dissipated almost instantly, and I sighed and resumed stirring.

He touched the towel I'd wrapped turban-style around my head. "I like it. You look exotic."

"I look like I'm in the final stages of hypothermia. Which, by an amazing coincidence, I am." I scowled and licked the spoon again before lovingly embracing its tiny heat.

He moved a little closer, his eyes darkening. "You'd warm up a lot faster if you did that to me instead of to the spoon."

I hid my sudden breathlessness in a snort. "If I put these cold hands on you, you'd have indoor plumbing for the rest of your life."

"It's a chance I'm willing to take."

Those green eyes. Dammit.

His eyes crinkled at the corners, dark lashes lowering

over heat. "I'm up for shower rotation today. My slot is in an hour. You could share it with me." A slow blink, his eyes hooded with desire. "Nothing like a steamy-hot shower to warm you up."

Speaking of steam...

A curl of vapour drifted past my face. I stepped away from the stove just in case, but it was likely only wafting up from my suddenly-overheated nether regions.

I suppressed a sigh. After four months of peaceful cohabitation it seemed unlikely that Orion was a threat to Moonbeam and Karma, but still. I was under orders. And there was that niggling suspicion...

I leaned past him to grab a bowl. "Sorry, the power will come on in half an hour and I want to blow-dry my hair. And I want to wash some clothes while the power's on, too."

"Well, you know where I'll be if you change your mind." He gave me one last scorching look before withdrawing from my personal space to sink into a nearby chair. "I don't suppose there's enough soup in your pot for two?"

I glanced up to see if that was some kind of innuendo, but he was hungrily eyeing the saucepan on the stove.

"You're in luck."

He grinned. "It's not really the way I was hoping to get lucky, but it's almost as good."

I shrugged and ladled out soup. "You can get as lucky as you want. Any of the women and probably half the men would be delighted to share your shower."

"Not *any* of the women." When I glanced up, he was studying me intently. "You won't."

I sank into a chair and directed my attention to my soup before he could read my face. "So I'm a freak. Nothing personal."

"Are you... er..." He hesitated. "Do you *prefer* indoor plumbing?"

Soup shot into my sinuses and tears streamed down my face while I choked and groped for a napkin.

"Jesus!" I sputtered when my coughing subsided. "Don't do that when I've got a mouthful of soup! No, I like your plumbing just fine." My face heated. "I mean, as far as I know," I added hurriedly. "Not that I've been looking... oh shit, shut up! Isn't it time for you to go take a shower or something?"

Orion leaned back in his chair and laughed. "Not quite."

Hoping to fill my mouth with food so my foot wouldn't fit in again, I reapplied myself to spooning soup. Conversations from the other occupied tables rose around us, emphasizing our little island of silence.

Moonbeam and Karma strolled in looking warm and dry, their arms around each other and heads together in quiet conversation. I jerked my chin in their direction and muttered, "I didn't see them freezing their asses off in the rain."

Orion stiffened. "Moonbeam and Karma perform very important rituals when the Earth Spirit calls. Sometimes those rituals can be extremely uncomfortable, so please show some respect."

I clamped my teeth on my spoon so I wouldn't say anything I'd regret. Orion seemed like such a nice normal guy most of the time, but he turned into a total freak over this Earth Spirit thing.

Well, freedom of religion. If it was important to him and everybody else at the commune, I should respect their beliefs even if I didn't share them. And besides, his defense of them was reassuring. Maybe he didn't mean them any harm.

I swallowed my mouthful. "You're right, Orion, I'm sorry. That was rude and disrespectful of me."

His stiffness melted into a smile that made me want to apologize again just to see that deliciously edible dimple one more time. "You're forgiven, Storm. Thank you." He reached across the table and squeezed my hand just as Skidmark wandered into the kitchen.

In deference to the no-smoking-in-buildings rule, he wasn't actually carrying a joint, but the heavy cloak of marijuana scent preceded him by several feet. His thicket of beard and moustache twitched in a smile at the sight of Orion's and my clasped hands, and he wove unsteadily to our table.

"Sweet love..." he warbled in a key entirely of his own making. "Sweet, sweet love..." He swayed and caught himself by gripping the edge of our table. One of his eyelids drooped in a lascivious wink. "If you kids're gonna get it on, can I join in? Ol' Skidmark knows a thing or two 'bout lovin'."

Just in time to hear Skidmark's overture, Ratboy strode into the kitchen and froze, glaring.

Apparently Skidmark wasn't as far gone as I'd thought. When my gaze snapped over to focus behind him he spun with surprising agility to face the threat, then staggered with the sudden movement. I jumped up and seized his shoulders, steadying him.

Skidmark raised his voice in a tone that might have been dulcet if not for the rasp of too many decades of accumulated tar on his vocal cords. "Be cool, man," he cooed at Ratboy. "You're invited, too. You got such a nice tight little tushie. Tushie-wushie..." He squeezed the air with both hands as though fondling buttocks.

Ratboy went rigid. Then his face twisted in rage and he closed the distance to Skidmark in a couple of fast strides. Orion sprang to intercept him, but Ratboy had already spat in Skidmark's face.

"*Filth!*" Ratboy hissed, and stormed out.

"Aw, man..." Skidmark said plaintively. "You mean our date's off?" He appropriated my napkin to wipe the spittle off his face before drifting away humming, apparently unfazed.

I sank back into my chair and drew a deep breath, willing the tremors out of my hands.

Filth. Was it coincidence Ratboy had used that particular word? If not, it imparted a whole new aura of menace to the words 'get rid of the filth'.

"Are you all right?" Orion bent to clasp my hands between his own.

"Fine. I just... that scared me. That guy is seriously unbalanced." I seized the opportunity. "Who is he?"

"One of the renters."

I raised an eyebrow at him. "What's a renter? Is that some Spirit-thing, too?"

Orion laughed. "No, an actual renter. The commune has several acres of extra land they rent to various groups. That group has occupied the land for nearly a year."

"Why haven't I noticed them before?"

There was another layer to my innocent question. What the hell kind of secret agent was I, if an entire group of commune members had escaped my notice? How could I possibly have missed them in the nearly four months I'd been here? And if they were all as wacko as Ratboy, were they a threat to Moonbeam and Karma? And if Orion was friends with Ratboy...

I realized Orion had spoken while I was berating myself, and I shook off my self-recriminations. "Sorry, what did you say?" I asked.

"I said, they don't usually interact at all. Their land is separated from the rest of the commune by the river, and they generally only come over here to pick up food supplies once a week and occasionally to use the vehicles to go into Port Renfrew."

"Oh. That makes sense, then. I saw Ratboy up at the garage-"

Orion's burst of laughter interrupted me. "*Ratboy?*" he choked when he had regained some composure. "I'm glad Moonbeam named me instead of letting you do it."

I shrugged, grinning. "Well, he's a weasely little prick and I didn't know what else to call him." I returned to my line of questioning. "Why don't they just bring their own vehicles?"

"Moonbeam and Karma don't allow any vehicles except the commune's. Visitors have to be dropped off here, or if someone's making a supply run to town they can pick up visitors at the same time. Those are the only options." His lips twisted in a wry grin. "You don't want to count on the car or truck, though. They're so old they break down constantly."

I frowned. "I don't know; the truck sounded pretty good when it was running. Those old engines are nearly bullet-proof. And that big old boat of a station wagon probably has a decent engine in it, too. It'll be a gas-guzzler, but it won't be complicated. If Skidmark's any kind of a mechanic he should be able to keep them running."

"Uh, one problem with that," Orion said straight-faced. "Skidmark."

We both eyed the man in question as he shuffled toward the door. While Orion and I talked I had been watching Skidmark's antics out of the corner of my eye, and he seemed to have offended almost everyone in the kitchen. Some of the commune members laughed him off but others reacted angrily, and dark looks followed him despite the commune's stated policy of tolerance and harmony.

"Maybe I should go up and have a look," I said. "If Skidmark can't manage the vehicle repairs, I could probably do them. It'd give me something to do."

Orion chuckled. "Don't bother. Many have tried; none have succeeded. Skidmark will chase anyone away in short order. If his reek alone doesn't do it, he'll find some other way to offend you."

I rubbed a thoughtful circle over the frown lines in my forehead. "Yeah, I noticed he seems to like to stir the pot. But he just about boiled it over a few minutes ago with Ratboy." I turned my frown to Orion. "What's Ratboy's real name, anyway?"

Orion shrugged. "Nobody knows the renters' real names, just like nobody knows ours here at the commune." He shot me a mischievous grin. "Ratboy is good enough to go on with."

I held onto my best poker face. There was another expression that just wasn't quite... Canadian. And if they were friendly enough to wander through the woods chatting, why would he pretend he didn't know Ratboy?

Well, screw Stemp's orders; Orion had engaged me, not the other way around. I might as well take advantage of it.

"Hey, Orion, speaking of anonymity and all those good things, if you really want to..." I cleared my throat significantly. "...get to know me better... maybe we could do some basic hi-how-are-you stuff before we jump in the sack. I've noticed you sound British. Where are you from?"

If I hadn't been watching him intently, I might have missed the flicker of his eyelids.

"Oh, you have a good ear," he said easily. "I grew up in Bristol, but I've been here in Canada for ages. What about you?"

"Um, Saskatchewan," I said vaguely. "So how is it that you arrived at the commune after me, but you know all its inner workings already?"

A slight flush rose on his cheeks. "I asked," he said with one of his devastating smiles, and rose. "It's time for my shower. Do we know each other well enough yet?"

I laughed. "Nope. See you later. I'll try not to turn on the hot water for the washing machine at the exact moment you're under the shower."

He offered me a shallow bow, his dark brows arching sardonically. "You are too kind."

I indulged myself by appreciating his rear view as he left. Then I propped my chin in my hand, pondering.

He seemed so nice and normal compared to Ratboy. Why would they be friends? And if the renters kept to themselves, why would Ratboy associate with Orion at all?

I sighed. I'd just have to keep watching them.

Anyway, working on the commune vehicles sounded like an excellent idea. It would be good to have something to do; but more to the point, Skidmark's garage was at the top of a hill with a commanding view. I should be able to observe the renters from there.

And I wondered about Skidmark. When I'd grabbed his shoulders, his muscles had been tense and ready for action. He should have been a limp noodle if he had actually been as stoned as he appeared. And despite his bumbling and staggering, his tour of the kitchen had looked suspiciously purposeful.

Not to mention the fact that I was pretty sure I'd overheard him utter a blatant anti-gay slur at the table next to us, almost immediately after he'd made his apparently homosexual advance on Ratboy.

He was definitely stirring the pot, and not the cannabinoid variety.

And if he was trying to cause trouble for Moonbeam and Karma, he just became my problem.

CHAPTER 5

It was still raining when I left the kitchen building. I growled and twitched up my sodden collar. Fine. Might as well check in with Stemp before I got dried off.

Back in my tent I stood motionless, straining my ears. Stupid rain; I couldn't hear a thing except raindrops pattering on canvas. I hadn't seen anybody in the vicinity when I'd ducked inside, but I'd feel better if I knew nobody was coming up the path to catch me in the act.

I blew out a short breath and squatted to delve into the canvas bag I'd concealed under a blanket behind my cot. My fingers groped past the concealing towels in the duffel and did a quick count by feel beneath. Only two secured phones left. Damn. Stemp had promised to send more and they were undoubtedly waiting for me at the post office in Port Renfrew, but I didn't want to attract attention by requesting a trip.

It was beginning to look as though I'd have to, though.

The rustle of the tent flap made me jerk around to face the intruder, my hand flashing down to my holster. Then I let out a whoosh of adrenaline-laden amusement and extended my hand, palm down, fingers loosely curled. "Peaches, you little shit, you scared the hell out of me."

The heavily pregnant tortie-and-cream cat waddled over to rub her jaw against my knuckles, her whiskers turning up in a cat-grin.

"You're soaking wet, silly girl," I chided, and dug a hand towel out of the bag to blot her fur. "Why don't you stay in your nice dry cat house?"

Her purr rumbled under the towel and I grinned. Like all the commune cats, she seemed unconcerned by rain and more than willing to brave the moisture in exchange for human attention. After some cuddles and extravagant purring, I stopped her when she began to nose with interest at the towels padding the cat-sized cave of my open duffel bag.

"Sorry, Mom-To-Be." I picked her up carefully, supporting her hind legs and drooping belly. "You can't have your kittens in here. Go back to your nice warm cat house." I bundled her gently outside the tent again, using her as an excuse to make sure the coast was clear before securing my tent flap despite my guilt at putting a pregnant cat out in the rain.

But dammit, I couldn't shut her inside my tent while I was gone. The commune cats felt the same way about captivity as I did. And anyway, she'd walked all the way over here, so she obviously wasn't worried about getting wet. She'd just go back to the cat house in the main building, where she'd be warmer and dryer than I was.

I exchanged my soaked jacket for a more waterproof version and slipped one of the phones into my pocket before zipping up the duffel and stowing it under the cot again. Rising with a deep breath when my knees protested the damp cold, I pulled up my hood to saunter out into goddamn rain again, trying to look nonchalant.

My heart gave a guilty clutch when Orion emerged from his tent just a few yards down the path, and I willed my face into an innocent expression.

He offered me a jaunty salute with his towel. "Last chance."

"No thanks, I'm going for a walk. I need some, um... meditation time."

His brows drew together in concern. "You still look half-frozen. Why don't you get warmed up first? Maybe the rain will stop later, and if you wait a bit I can come with you. There's a cougar in the area, so Karma and Moonbeam want everybody to pair up."

Great, just great.

I forced a smile. "I'm not going far. And I'd rather go now while I'm wet anyway. I'll get dried off and warmed up when I can stay that way for a while." I made shooing motions. "Hurry up, or you'll miss your shower. See you later."

I was turning to leave when he snapped, "Wait!"

Startled by his tone, I spun. "What?"

"Where's your bracelet?"

"My br...?" I frowned at the empty spot on my wrist where it had been only moments before. Comprehension dawned. "Oh, it must have slid off when I was digging in one of my bags. I'll find it later. See you."

I made another attempt to leave but he blocked my way, his green eyes darkening with worry. "No, go back and find it right now."

"I'll get it later," I repeated through teeth that had clenched despite my best efforts.

"No, you need it." Orion peered earnestly into my eyes. "It gives us the protection of the Earth Spirit. Nobody can go without it." He pushed up his sleeve to display his own. "Surely Moonbeam and Karma told you that."

"Oh, for..." I bit off my impending epithet and plastered a smile on my face instead. "Yes, of course. Thanks for reminding me. I'll go and get it right now."

I turned, nearly tripping over Peaches as she wound around my ankles, and ducked back into my tent. Successfully resisting the urge to kick the stacked wooden boxes that served as my shelving unit, I dropped to my knees and shoved my hand back into the duffel to retrieve the stupid bracelet. Its hemp cord had broken, and I rose scowling at it just as Peaches padded in again and made a beeline for the bag. Outside, Orion scratched lightly at my tent flap, the commune's version of a knock.

I scooped Peaches up and shot a hurried glance at my cot to be sure the phone bag was completely concealed before saying, "Come in."

Orion pushed through the tent flap, his eyes anxious. "Did you find it?" His shoulders relaxed at the sight of the chunky wooden beads in my hand. "Oh, good. Put it on, then."

"It's broken. I'll fix it later." I showed him the frayed cord.

"No, I'll help you now. Here, hold out your wrist."

Resigned, I shifted Peaches to my other arm and obeyed.

Orion knotted the cord carefully, his brow furrowed with concentration. "There." He gave me that irresistible dimpled smile again, his fingertips caressing my wrist. The feather-light touch ignited nerves all the way up my arm and his voice deepened as he stepped closer. "How does that feel?"

Somehow I suspected he didn't mean the bracelet.

I gulped at the dryness in my throat. "Um... it's a little..." I swallowed again. "...constricting," I finished, and stepped back. "You'd better hurry. Your shower time is almost used up. And if there's a cougar around, you should take Peaches back to the main building with you." I transferred her carefully into the crook of his arm and tucked the hand towel around her.

He looked nonplussed for only a moment before his smile returned. "You're right. Enjoy your walk, and be careful. See you later."

He ducked out the tent flap and an involuntary sigh escaped me at the sight of that fine ass disappearing, unappreciated by my hands. Then I shook myself into duty mode and followed him out to hurry down the path before anybody else could accost me.

Striding toward the main road, I unzipped my jacket and flapped it a few times. God, either I was starting to get hot flashes, or else Orion's touch was enough to cause spontaneous human combustion. Tingly sensations in interesting areas of my body strongly suggested it was the latter.

Just my luck. Only I would get assigned to watch the hottest guy in the whole commune, but be forbidden to do anything more than that.

Hell, after four months of abstinence I was almost ready to reconsider the other men at the commune, and they were nothing to write home about. Nichele's crack about skinny granola-fed guys was a little too close to the truth. Some women might go for those fragile artsy-looking types, but my tastes ran more toward hard muscle and bulk. Like Kane and Hellhound.

Or Orion.

Yanking my wayward mind back to the job at hand with a sigh, I cast a casual glance around me as though enjoying the rainy landscape. In all the times I'd reported to Stemp I'd never met anybody else walking along the road to town, and nearly twenty minutes of brisk hiking had carried me far beyond where I might be accidentally overheard. But by now my paranoia had become ingrained. Funny how a year of dicing with death could do that.

My visual survey returned nothing more threatening than the usual dripping trees and ferns, and I pulled out my secured phone and pressed the speed dial.

"Stemp." He answered on the first ring as always, his crisp diction a welcome change from the drowsy tones of the commune's residents.

"It's Aydan." Neither expecting nor receiving a greeting, I launched into my report. "I've noticed a couple of things this week, and I'm not sure how relevant they might be. Orion Moonjava has started paying unusual attention to me, so I played along and asked a couple of questions."

I paused, expecting censure, but Stemp's silence encouraged me to continue, "I mentioned his accent and asked where he was from, and he seemed..." I fell silent again, recalling his response and trying to quantify it. "He seemed... uncomfortable. As if he'd been trying to hide it. I don't know why he'd do that; lots of people have British accents here on the coast. You know, 'British Columbia' and all."

Stemp didn't respond to my attempt at humour, so I went on, "Anyway, it just seemed odd. And then he seemed evasive when I asked him how he knew so much about the commune. But that might have been my imagination; it would be normal for him to want to know everything about it since he's so deep into this bizarro Earth Spirit thing-"

I bit off my words too late. Damn, Karma and Moonbeam were the high priest and priestess of the bizarro Earth Spirit thing. Nothing like insulting your boss's parents.

"Sorry," I added. "I didn't mean..."

"It's quite all right." Stemp's tone was as emotionless as always. "As I mentioned before, my parents and I have fundamental ideological differences."

"Uh, yeah..." I hesitated, wondering whether I should ask the question that was burning on my lips. I should probably just shut up about it.

Nope, I had to know.

"Uh, about that. Um... your mom is the sweetest person ever, but... do you think she can really see auras?" I asked.

I had expected him to dismiss the idea with contempt, but Stemp's momentary silence surprised me.

"I... believe... she perceives... a great deal," he said slowly. "If she chooses to name that perception 'aura', I'm not inclined to argue." A hint of humour warmed his voice. "She always knew when I was lying as a child."

His unexpected flash of humanity shocked a laugh out of me. "Most mothers do. But... what exactly did you tell her about me?"

His tone resumed its clinical detachment. "Exactly what I reported in the dossier I gave you. That you were a personal friend who had suffered a traumatic experience and needed a peaceful environment in which to recover."

"Did you tell her about my hysterectomy?"

"No, of course not. Even if it had been in your personnel file, which it wasn't, I certainly wouldn't provide that level of personal detail about any of my agents. Not even to my mother." His voice grew dry. "Especially not to my mother."

I knew that was the truth. He wouldn't give out the time of day without a signed affidavit and a need-to-know.

"Well, then, I'm feeling really creeped out," I said. "Because she said she could see it in my aura. So either she really reads auras or else somebody is feeding her personal information about me."

"What are you implying?" His usual detached tone had morphed into something a little cooler and stiffer.

I sighed. "Well, I seriously doubt she's a spy, and if she was, she'd be too smart to let something like that slip. So I guess I'm implying that your mother really reads auras."

A groan escaped me and I pounded my forehead with the heel of my hand. "I can't believe I just said that. I've been here far too long. When can I leave?"

"Soon. All the suspects from the Fuzzy Bunny case have finally been incarcerated and intel indicates the situation is settling down. No new threats to my cover have been identified, so presumably that means the danger to my parents is diminishing, too. If nothing else develops there at the commune, you may be clear to leave in a week or two."

"That's what you've been saying for the last two months." I scowled at a giant banana slug oozing along the shoulder of the road. Just as slimy as Stemp. "That audit cover is starting to wear thin," I added. "One of my friends from Calgary questioned me about it today. And what about my bookkeeping clients back in Silverside?"

"Your clients are well taken care of by the temporary bookkeeper I engaged. And I realize this has taken longer than we had originally hoped, but I truly believe we're nearing the end now."

"Thank God." I hesitated, balancing my heartfelt desire

to escape the commune against the guilt I'd feel if I didn't provide a full report and something bad happened to Moonbeam and Karma.

I sighed. No contest there. "There are a couple of other things."

"Yes?" His voice sharpened.

"I've discovered there's a group renting the commune's land across the river, and one of their members has me worried. He seems to have a violent temper. I've named him Ratboy because I don't know his real name. Orion doesn't know I saw him and Ratboy talking, and when I asked Orion about Ratboy later he acted as though he didn't know him. It just seems... off."

I repeated their conversation as close to verbatim as I could remember, and silence hummed on the line for a moment before Stemp spoke.

"But this is the first time you've noticed this Ratboy anywhere on the commune or near my parents."

"Yes. Orion has been around your mom and dad, but no more so than any of the other commune members. And his behaviour around them hasn't raised any red flags for me." I sighed. "I'll keep watching him, though. And one more thing: I'm suspicious of Skidmark."

"Why?"

"I don't think he's as stoned as he pretends to be. I haven't really paid much attention to him up to now, but I've noticed lately that he's making inflammatory remarks and getting people stirred up. I'm afraid he might be trying to sow discord and cause trouble for your mom and dad."

"I see." Stemp sounded thoughtful. "What sort of inflammatory remarks?"

"Racial slurs, offensive stuff about religion, gay-bashing

in front of the gay guys, homosexual come-ons to the straight guys..." I trailed off, dumbfounded by the unprecedented sound of Stemp chuckling.

When he spoke again, I could still hear the smile in his voice. "Skidmark is harmless. For decades he has been a constant irritant to everyone except Mother and Father. Sowing discord seems to be his sole raison d'être. That and partaking of cannabis at every possible opportunity. Throughout my entire childhood, I never saw him sober."

"You grew up on the commune?" Somehow I couldn't reconcile Stemp's suit-and-tie stiffness with Moonbeam's rainbow caftans and Karma's sarongs.

"Yes." The flat word was obviously intended to discourage further discussion. He changed the subject. "What else do you know about the renters?"

"Nothing yet, but Orion says they've been there nearly a year."

"That land has been rented to various groups since before I can remember, so that's normal. If they've been there that long they're unlikely to be related to our current concerns, but keep an eye on Moonjava and Ratboy just the same." Stemp hesitated. "And if Moonjava is engaging you, respond as you deem appropriate."

"Okay. By the way, do your mom and dad know about your... job?"

"No. They believe I'm a high-level manager with the oil and gas research division here at Sirius Dynamics."

"All right, that's what your mom said, but I wasn't sure if it was a cover story or what she really believed." Now it was my turn to hesitate. I really wanted to ask him one more thing. It was none of my business, but...

"Is that all?" I inquired, the three words invoking our

secret code.

No one else would have noticed the tiny edge of tension that knifed into Stemp's voice. "Yes."

We disconnected, and I turned to trudge back to the commune in the rain.

CHAPTER 6

When I arrived at my tent, I glanced at my watch. Now that I'd uttered the code words, Stemp would be waiting anxiously for me to contact him via the secret communication protocol he'd installed on my laptop. Not for the first time, I wondered how much trouble we'd be in if anybody discovered we were circumventing the official department reporting system.

Damn, the guy was paranoid. Even though his parents' existence wasn't a secret like his wife and young daughter overseas, he still forbade me to discuss any personal matters during my official check-ins just in case someone in the chain of command accessed the phone records.

I hesitated, debating. He'd be worried and expecting a report as soon as possible, but I was chilled under my still-wet hair and the power would only stay on a little while longer.

Screw it.

I hurried up to the main building to find an electrical outlet and blow-dry my hair, then back to my tent to change into relatively dry clothes before firing up the laptop.

I sighed as I watched the system boot. I didn't even like Stemp. I didn't want to be the repository of his personal secrets, and I especially didn't want the responsibility of being the only other person in the world who knew about his little daughter overseas.

As soon as I plugged the laptop into one of the burner phones to connect to the internet, the tiny white square began to blink onscreen. I pressed Alt-Shift and clicked on it, and the text window bloomed into existence.

The cursor zipped across it. "Report."

I immediately typed, "Your family's fine, don't worry."

I imagined Stemp's tension easing, and unwilling sympathy touched my heart. He was a ruthless bastard, but that single-minded dedication to his job was only exceeded by his devotion to his wife and daughter. He would have been worried sick waiting for my message.

But the first part of this wasn't about Katya and Anna; it was just embarrassing and I didn't want to discuss it over official channels.

I hesitated, my fingers poised over the keys.

Well, just say it.

I typed, "Your mom thinks you're in love with me because you sent me to the commune. I tried to discourage her but I don't know if I succeeded."

I waited for his response, half-wishing I could see his expression just now. Was he choking with laughter the way I had done?

When his reply appeared on the screen, it was as emotionless as Stemp's best poker face. "Understood. Continue to discourage."

This was where it got tricky. My fingers hovered over the keys again. Really none of my business.

But Moonbeam would be such a wonderful grandmother, and she wasn't getting any younger.

I drew in a deep breath and typed, "Your mom wants grandchildren. Are you ever going to tell her?"

The cursor blinked on the blank screen while moments stretched. I tensed at the crunch of footsteps on the path outside, but they didn't come as far as my tent. Must be Orion returning after his shower.

At last the cursor moved again. "Someday, I hope. Was there anything else?"

I typed "No" and the text screen vanished.

Flopping back on my cot, I stared up at the canvas ceiling. What must it be like to be separated from your wife and child for months at a time, unable to even mention their names? No photos, no phone calls, no childish scribbles taped proudly to the refrigerator. No spontaneous hugs and sticky kisses. No bedtime stories. No little voice calling him Daddy. Just an empty house and the constant fear that any message might contain news that would rip his heart from his chest.

My eyes misted and I closed the laptop and hurried out into the rain, suddenly needing something to do.

Tugging my hood up, I wandered aimlessly down the path. Same activity choices as earlier, minus one. I'd completed my report to Stemp so I was back to reading, scrubbing clothes by hand, or working out.

Or...

I smiled and headed uphill.

All was silent when I strode into Skidmark's gravelled clearing. The vehicles still sat where they had been parked, and the stream of rainwater from the gutters of the garage sounded like Niagara Falls.

I poked my head inside, gratified to find the work bay empty except for a few tools strewn on the floor. Perfect.

After a quick tidying, the bay was ready for use. I hauled the overhead door up and hurried out to pop the hood on the truck. Surprisingly, the ignition wire was secure on the distributor cap so I jumped back in the cab and fired up the engine.

I had just closed the garage door behind the truck when Skidmark staggered out of the woods to prop himself against the wall, his ever-present joint smouldering between his fingers. He surveyed me from half-closed eyes, and I braced myself for insults.

Instead he surprised me with a civil question, only slightly slurred. "Gonna work on it?"

I let out a breath I hadn't realized I'd been holding. "Yeah. I noticed you have a pair of valve-cover gaskets hanging on the wall over there and I thought I'd just pop them in and clean up the engine a bit. Looks like it's been blowing oil for a while."

Skidmark considered that with the aid of a deep drag on his reefer. "Yep," he said finally.

I turned away in relief and began gathering grimy tools from their scattered heaps on the blackened workbench before turning my attention to the truck.

Absorbed in the soothing mindless work and pleasant smell of grease and motor oil, I had almost forgotten Skidmark's sleepy presence when he spoke again as I bent over the engine some time later.

"Yeah, girlie. Bend over and I'll slip you my tool." His wheezy laughter made me smile in spite of the repulsive double entendre.

I straightened and eyed him with as much seriousness as I could muster. "Too bad marijuana destroys your reproductive system. By now you must have nuts the size of lima beans and you probably couldn't get your tool up even with that engine hoist over there." I nodded at the hoist in the corner. "Otherwise I'd totally go for it," I said straight-faced, and batted my eyes at him.

He wheezed laughter until he began to cough, clinging white-knuckled to the workbench until the paroxysm passed. "Far out," he croaked at last. "Girlie, you're gonna kill me."

"That's okay," I reassured him. "You'd have a heart attack and die anyway if I jumped your bones." A sense of inevitability filled me as Ratboy stepped through the door at the precise moment I uttered the words.

Of course. It had to be the one person in the whole commune with absolutely no sense of humour.

His face contorted with rage. "What are you doing, you filthy whore!" Fists clenched, he strode toward me.

In the instant it took for me to decide whether to blow my cover by pulling my gun or defend myself with the ratchet in my hand, Skidmark sent a trolley jack rolling in front of Ratboy with a well-aimed push of his foot. Ratboy tripped and went down in a flurry of unintelligible words that were probably violent invective.

By the time he regained his feet, Skidmark had a tire iron in his free hand, and I was gripping a breaker bar I had snatched from the jumble of tools behind me.

I dodged as Ratboy spat at me. "Whore!" he snapped. "Stupid, worthless whore!" He turned his ire toward Skidmark. "You said it would be ready by two o'clock! Why do you let this stupid-"

"...whore," Skidmark supplied helpfully.

Ratboy's eyes narrowed in fury. "You are..." he hissed a string of incomprehensible words in Skidmark's face. "Both of you! Have it ready by three o'clock! Or else!" He whirled and stalked out.

"Hey, be cool, man," Skidmark mumbled to his receding back.

I drew a deep, slow breath and laid down the breaker bar with a shaking hand, keeping it close just in case. "So..." My voice trembled slightly, and I swallowed to steady it before continuing, "What did he call us this time?"

Skidmark eyed me for a moment before sucking on his cigarette. Then he offered it to me, his hand as steady as ever. "Toke?"

"No. Not now, not ever."

He blinked. "'Kay. That's cool." He took another drag, but I noticed he didn't relinquish the tire iron in his other hand despite his apparent nonchalance. "Dunno," he added. He shrugged, yawning. "Defilers or something. That is one uptight dude."

I snorted, hiding my still-hammering heart. "Defilers of Dickwads. I like it. It sounds like a rock band. We should get T-shirts."

Skidmark wheezed amusement and began to drift toward the doorway.

"Not so fast."

He froze at the threat in my tone, then turned slowly to face me. "Aw, come on, be cool," he wheedled.

"I am not cool! I am pissed! Why the hell didn't you tell me you'd promised him the truck for two o'clock? I wouldn't have started this job if I'd known."

Skidmark blinked at me in silence. Then he sucked in a lungful of smoke and let it out again in a leisurely trickle. "You didn't ask."

Fighting the urge to pick up the breaker bar and introduce it to his kneecaps, I gaped at him in outrage.

I drew a deep breath, then another. Anger management. Thank you, Dr. Rawling.

"Fuck you, old man," I said at last.

He winked. "Any time, girlie."

My reassembly of the engine wasn't enjoyable. I rushed through the job, made sure everything was in working order, and vacated the premises by ten to three.

Wandering down the path behind the garage, I took slow breaths, trying to ease the tension from my shoulders. The rain had finally stopped, and when I discovered a bench perched at the edge of the hill I spread my waterproof jacket over its wet surface before sinking down on it.

The ground fell away steeply and the heavy clouds had lifted enough that I could see the entire commune spread below me, small figures moving around oblivious to my surveillance. A fitful ray of sun braved the clouds and I sought its warmth, closing my eyes.

Ratboy's enraged features filled my memory and my muscles tensed in reaction, my eyes popping open.

If I'd been alone, I could have shot him. Killed him without a qualm and stepped over his dead body on my way out. A bullet was an instant and permanent solution to problems like Ratboy.

I drew a shaky breath. God, how fucked up was I to even think that?

Below me the commune looked like a dream, gently wreathed in streamers of dissipating mist. Its peace and harmony seemed unreal and unattainable, a world I could no longer inhabit. What kind of sicko had I become?

The sound of footsteps made me jerk around to look behind me, my fist knotting around a heavy branch I'd picked up from the trail. A moment later I slouched back and closed my eyes again when the reek of pot smoke and body odour accompanied Skidmark's arrival.

"Fuck off, old man," I growled. "Unless you're standing there with a cold beer and an apology, you've got ten seconds to leave before I play a drum solo on your ribs with this stick."

After a moment of silence his footfalls receded, taking his foul miasma with them. I drew a long breath and returned to my dark contemplation.

Several minutes later Skidmark's stench assaulted my nostrils once more. I was about to snap at him when an instantly recognizable pop-hiss jerked me upright to see him extending a beer can dripping with condensation.

"Sorry," he said.

I stared open-mouthed for a moment, then accepted the peace offering, its blue metal icy-cold in my hand. Kokanee. At least the old goat had taste.

I took a long swallow, letting my eyelids drop closed as the bubbles performed their crisp dance on my tongue. A deep sigh escaped me. After four long months in the alcohol-free commune, my taste buds were in heaven.

"Don't tell," Skidmark warned. "Bad enough I gotta share my weed."

"If you didn't offer it to everybody, you wouldn't have to share," I pointed out after another long swallow. I fanned at a wayward tendril of smoke. "God, that's disgusting. Why would you even smoke that shit?"

He looked mildly affronted. "It's good shit." He sucked in another lungful. "It's medicinal. Need it for pain." He lowered himself to the bench beside me, smoke trickling through his beard. "Uptight dudes give me a real bad pain in my ass."

My lips twitched in spite of myself, but I didn't reward him with a smile. I jerked a thumb at the end of the bench. "Other side."

Skidmark got up and moved and I felt his gaze on me. When I slitted my eyes at him, he nodded at the branch. "Why? So you got a clear swing?"

"No." I took another swig and closed my eyes again, leaning my head back. "So you're downwind."

Wheezy laughter greeted that statement. Silence fell while I drank and ignored him, breathing evenly and easing the tension from my muscles.

After a long interval he spoke again. "You don't talk much. Why not?"

I shrugged without opening my eyes. "Why?"

I took a lazy swallow of beer, holding onto my relaxed state with deliberately slow movements. The can felt light in my hand. Almost empty. Maybe he had more.

I heard the soft hiss of his toke followed by silence, and I imagined his vacant expression and the smoke seeping out through his bushy whiskers.

"Aw, man, that's deep," he mumbled after a while.

I drained the can and extended the empty in his direction. "Beer me."

Nothing happened, so I wiggled the can. After a moment I opened my eyes to see Skidmark studying me blankly.

"I want another beer," I clarified, and pushed the empty can into his hand.

"You should stay away from that dude," he said without moving.

"No shit, Sherlock." I scowled at him. "Are you going to get me another beer or just sit there yakking all day?"

As if moving underwater, he set the empty can down and

withdrew cigarette paper and a small bag of pot from his pocket to roll a new joint, twisting the ends with intense concentration. Then he unhurriedly re-stowed the baggie and lit up.

He sucked in a deep draw before releasing the smoke on a breath so long I expected him to shrivel like a deflated balloon. Then he turned and blinked lethargically before inquiring, "You one of them bull dykes?"

I stared at him for a moment before replying. "Yeah."

"Far out..."

I waited.

Right on cue, a few moments later he began, "You wanna-"

"No." I rose, tired of him and tired of myself. "Do they call you Skidmark because you shit your pants?"

He wheezed amusement. "When you slam the brakes on the road to hell, the skidmark stays long after the tires roll on. Roll on, baby, roll on," he crooned before seguing into a dreamy off-key version of BTO's Roll On Down The Highway.

I left him sitting there, the thin smoke from his roach eddying in the still air while he slowly strummed nonexistent guitar strings.

Striding back to my tent, I swung my heavy stick at the ferns lining the path, half-wishing Ratboy would appear and get in my face again. When I caught myself fantasizing about bludgeoning him with my makeshift shillelagh, I laid it on the ground outside my tent and went in to gather some workout clothes instead. Probably better to work off my pent-up adrenaline constructively.

Though it wouldn't be nearly as satisfying.

Shaking my head at myself I made for the gym, leaving

my stick behind just in case temptation reared its rat-like head.

CHAPTER 7

I drew a breath of relief when I arrived to find the gym unoccupied except for Moonbeam, who was working out wearing yet another flowing tied-dyed caftan. Ducking into the change room, I gave thanks that she didn't expect the rest of us to dress like her. Having all that fabric hanging off me would drive me absolutely crazy.

Well, crazier.

I pulled my baggy sweatpants over my ankle holster and headed for the chin-up bar.

Moonbeam mercifully left me to my workout, and after nearly an hour I was drenched in sweat and feeling almost human again.

She finished her cooling-down stretches and rose from the mat, her lithe movements belying her wrinkled features. When she glanced in my direction I braced myself.

She padded over barefoot, her blue eyes seeming to look right through me. "You were very agitated earlier," she said softly. "I'm glad the exercise is helping. Do you want to talk about it now?"

I was about to brush her off when I realized this was a good opportunity to warn her about her tenants without arousing suspicion. "Actually, yes, I think you should know about this." I let out a breath and headed over to flop down on the mat.

She pulled out another mat and joined me, sinking gracefully into full-lotus position and eyeing me with concern.

"The tenants on the other side of the river..." I began. "I met one of them today."

"I presume there was conflict." Moonbeam gave me another unsettling inspection. "You had huge spikes of energy stabbing out of your aura when you arrived."

"Um, yeah." I shifted on the mat, wishing I could hide behind a psychic shield or something. "So anyway, I ran into this guy over at the garage. Short, maybe five-seven or so, and skinny. Black hair and beard, kind of rat-faced. I don't know his name so I've been calling him Ratboy..." I broke off at Moonbeam's scandalized expression. "Not to his face," I added hurriedly. "Sorry, but he just..."

I gathered my scattered thoughts and returned to the point. "Anyway, what I was trying to tell you was that he was really angry and aggressive to Skidmark and me. He called me a whore and I think he might have hit me if Skidmark hadn't been there."

"Oh, dear." Worry lined her brow. "Are you hurt, Storm Cloud Dancer?"

"No, he didn't actually hit me."

"I didn't mean physically hurt." Her gaze passed through me again. "Oh, dear. Almost as bad as when you first arrived." Her hands rose to stroke the air a few inches away from my arms and shoulders. "Please let Karma and me do some energy work for you. Your aura is too beautiful to sully with such destructiveness."

"Um..." I squirmed backward and stood. "Maybe later,

okay? I want to finish my workout."

"Of course. But please don't let this fester, Storm Cloud Dancer." She rose and hugged me despite my sweat-soaked clothes. "Promise you'll let us do a Spirit healing for you tonight."

I shot a glance over my shoulder, but there was no escape. And her concern was so sweet and genuine that I sighed and capitulated. "Okay. How about after supper? That'll give me a chance to get washed up and changed."

"Oh, good! Yes, please come to our tent around seven-thirty." She hugged me again and left.

Finished and cooled down, I had stopped by the main building to draw a bucket of hot water from the boiler of one of the wood stoves when Moonbeam poked her head into the kitchen.

"The mail's here, Storm Cloud Dancer, and there's a package for you from Cosmic River Stone."

"Oh, that's great!" Relief sent a wide smile to my face before I realized it might be misconstrued as excitement over a 'gift' from my 'boyfriend'. I hid my internal wince and hefted my bucket of water. "I'm just heading back to my tent to wash up, so I'll grab it after supper..." I trailed off as the inconvenient voice of duty reminded me that I shouldn't leave the package exposed to curious eyes any longer than necessary. "Never mind," I amended, and headed for the closet that doubled as a mail room. "I'll just take it now."

"Here, dear, let me help." Moonbeam hurried over to tuck the box under my free arm. "There you go. See you at seven-thirty."

I nodded and shuffled out, the edge of the box jammed

uncomfortably into my ribs while I tried not to spill the bucket along the uneven path to my tent.

"Hey, wait up, Storm! Let me help you with that." Orion materialized apparently out of nowhere and took hold of the box.

My arm tightened defensively around it. "No, it's okay, I've got it... shit!" Water slopped onto my sneaker and I relinquished the box to shake my wet foot vigorously. "Damn, I knew I should have put my hiking boots back on!"

Orion laughed and fell into step beside me. "You didn't have to fight me. I wasn't going to run off with it. Besides, even if I did, you know where I live." He dropped his voice to a suggestive purr. "There's a thought." He made a teasing detour toward his tent. "I could entice you into my lair by holding your parcel hostage."

"Bad idea," I said lightly, hiding the uptick of my pulse. "You wouldn't want to come between me and a care package from home."

"Oho!" He returned to the path and made a show of sniffing the box as we walked on. "Are there scrumptious edibles in here?"

"I'll never tell." I set the bucket down at the entrance to my tent and held out my hands. "Give."

He sighed. "You're a hard woman."

"And don't you forget it." I rescued the box from his grip and shouldered inside. When I returned for my bucket, he was already striding away.

At seven-thirty I presented myself at Moonbeam and Karma's tent, braced for yet another bizarre ritual and wondering what idiotic impulse had made me agree to it after successfully avoiding their offers for the past four months.

I sighed. Maybe the run-in with Ratboy had shaken me more than I wanted to admit. I had so desperately wanted to believe the commune was a refuge from the violence and evil of the outside world.

Well, grow up, Pollyanna. Safe havens only happen in fairy tales.

I squared my shoulders and scratched at the tent flap.

Moonbeam answered immediately, smiling and drawing me into the tent. "I'm so glad you've finally decided to let us help," she said. "We're all ready for you."

"Welcome," Karma agreed, his voice a deep drumroll in the barrel of his chest. "Please come in and make yourself comfortable." He gestured toward a blanket-draped table in the middle of the tent. Beside it, a smaller table held a pitcher and a trio of fat candles that provided the only illumination.

What the hell? Were they planning some outlandish sacrificial thing? I was *so* out of there at the first sign of goat's blood. Or my blood.

"Um..." I tried not to let my gaze dart around the tent, but I couldn't help tensing. "What... exactly... are you...?"

"Oh, I'm sorry, dear, I should have explained." Moonbeam patted my hand. "Don't worry, it's nothing invasive. We'll ask you to lie on the table and we'll be moving our hands above you, in your energy field. You'll be fully clothed and we won't touch you without asking permission. All you have to do is relax and try to release your negative energy."

"Okay..."

I sidled toward the table and hoisted myself up. As I lay

back, Karma tucked a pillow under my head while Moonbeam did the same under my knees.

"Are you warm enough, dear? Would you like a blanket?" she asked.

"Um, no, that's okay. I'm fine-"

My voice choked off in alarm as Karma removed his shirt, leaving him standing barefoot in nothing but his sarong.

Shit, I knew the commune didn't buy into the usual taboos about nudity, but there were some things about Stemp's father I just didn't need to know.

And from my vulnerable supine position, I suddenly realized how big he was. I was used to seeing him at a greater distance, and I had tended to focus on his piercing hazel eyes surrounded by their maze of laugh wrinkles, made even more striking by the way he kept his iron-gray hair sleeked back in a tidy ponytail.

But looming above me in the candlelight his powerful musculature made him look much younger, his age indicated only by the leathery texture of his skin. And that was 'way more skin than I'd been expecting to see.

He frowned down at me. "Does this make you uncomfortable? Would you like me to put my shirt back on?"

"Um... it's okay." I eyed him nervously. "But... you don't have to, um... get naked for this, do you?"

His booming laugh filled the tent. "No, I won't get naked..." He paused and cocked a mischievous brow in my direction. "Unless you ask me to."

"Karma Wolf Song!" Moonbeam's remonstrance was softened by her laughter. "The poor child is nervous enough already." She turned her luminous smile on me. "Don't mind him. It's just that you have such tremendous energy pouring off you, it will be hard work to deal with it all. We'll work up quite a sweat, you'll see." She paced slowly around me, her hands gliding through the air as though riding invisible updrafts over and around my body. "Merciful Spirit, Karma Wolf Song, feel this!"

Karma joined her at my feet and they waved their hands some more, exchanging a smilingly incredulous glance.

"You're tremendously grounded, dear," Moonbeam said, backing slowly away, hands outstretched. She stopped a couple of yards from my feet, still smiling. "All the way out here." She shook her head and gave Karma a rueful glance. "I hope you're ready for a workout, my dearest."

He nodded and they joined hands, looking deeply at each other before closing their eyes for several moments.

Feeling like a voyeur but too edgy to close my eyes, I concentrated on the canvas ceiling above me. When Karma and Moonbeam began to move I watched them from my peripheral vision, wondering what, if anything, I was supposed to feel And what they were feeling.

They worked in silence broken only by soft requests for permission to touch my ankles, hips, arms, shoulders, and head, and I slowly relaxed when nothing else happened. They certainly did seem to be working hard. Their hands moved constantly, sometimes stroking the air around me; other times making scooping motions as if to gather something undesirable and move it away. Sweat ran in rivulets down Karma's face and chest, and a fine dew of perspiration glistened on Moonbeam's forehead.

At last their movement ceased and they clasped hands again, heads bowed and eyes closed.

Then they disengaged, and Moonbeam moved to the

small table that held the jug. "You can sit up now, Storm Cloud Dancer," she said. "Slowly, though. Here."

She poured a glass of water and handed it to me, then did the same for Karma before pouring one for herself. They sank together to sit on the queen-sized mattress that formed their bed on the floor and sipped their water while I perched on the edge of the table and wondered what I was supposed to do.

"How do you feel?" Karma inquired.

"Um, fine." It seemed as though I should say something appreciative, but I didn't know exactly what. "Thank you for working on me," I added. "I feel more relaxed now."

At least that was the truth. I could hardly have gotten more tense than I'd been when they'd started.

"Oh, good." Moonbeam's smile told me I'd said the right thing. "Please rest there a few minutes and make sure you drink all that water. It will help cleanse your system."

I nodded and sipped obediently.

"So how long have you known Cosmic River Stone?" Karma asked in the easy tones of small talk, but I caught a tiny edge of something else behind his words.

"Um, not long." I eyed him, trying to gauge his reaction, but his poker face was as good as his son's. "I guess nearly a year," I added cautiously.

Moonbeam leaned forward, her hand finding Karma's in a grip tight enough to whiten her knuckles. "Tell us what he's like," she begged.

"Um..."

Shit, where were they going with this? I sensed a minefield ahead, but I didn't have a clue what would set off the explosives.

"I'm sure you'd know him better than I would," I

prevaricated. "We work together occasionally, but that's about it."

"No. We don't know." Moonbeam's voice sounded tight, but I couldn't tell whether it was anger or some other emotion. "Please..." Her voice broke and she swallowed before continuing, "Please tell us about him."

"Well, uh..." I racked my brain for something to say besides 'he's a manipulative snake-faced dickhead'. "Uh, he's, um, very dedicated to his work."

"Is he good at it?" Moonbeam eyed me pleadingly.

"Absolutely." At least I didn't have to equivocate on that. "He's excellent at his work. I couldn't imagine anybody else doing a better job."

"Oh..." Moonbeam's smile trembled on her lips. "Oh, that's wonderful. What else?"

"Well, he's, um..." Inspiration struck. "...very trustworthy. In fact, I'd trust him with my life."

And I did, every single day. If he leaked the secrets he knew about me, I'd be dead in short order.

Looking at Karma and Moonbeam leaning forward with their hands clasped like eager children, I cast about for some other small detail.

"Uh, he likes houseplants and he's really good at growing them," I offered. "You should see his hibiscus trees and cyclamens. A whole house full of plants and flowers."

"Oh, that's wonderful!" Moonbeam's eyes were bright with unshed tears. "He was always so close to the Earth Spirit as a child. I'm so glad he hasn't lost that connection. What else can you tell us?"

"Well..." I shifted uncomfortably. This was weird. "He's, um... a good neighbour. He plays cribbage with the elderly man who lives across the street from him, and they look out for each other." I frowned. "Why are you asking me? I'm really not that close to him."

She and Karma exchanged a glance, and Karma laid a gentle arm around her shoulders before turning to me. "We had a... falling-out. Decades ago, when he was eighteen. He left the commune and never returned."

"But you talk to him, don't you? You've visited him."

"We talk on the phone, but not frequently." Moonbeam's lips trembled. "Inconsequential things. Small talk, like strangers. We used to visit him whenever we could, but... several years ago..." Her voice faded into silence and Karma took over.

"He had been in a car accident and had to move shortly afterward," he said. "We went to help him, but... it was as though we were intruding. He didn't come out and say it, but..."

"But his aura was in turmoil," Moonbeam quavered. "Oh, my poor boy. He was so... so damaged. And the only time his aura calmed was when we mentioned leaving..."

"So we left," Karma finished. "And we haven't been back. We didn't want to upset him further. We keep hoping he'll find his way back to us..."

He trailed off and Moonbeam wrapped her arms around him, resting her head against his shoulder before turning to me. "Before he left at eighteen, we had argued about the Earth Spirit. He didn't... doesn't believe. All these years we've tried to tell him that we love him regardless of his or our beliefs, but..." She seemed to fold in on herself, looking her age for the first time since I'd met her. "...perhaps it's too late."

My heart wrenched. "Oh, no, it's not too late! He loves you! He wouldn't have sent me out here if he didn't!"

That hadn't come out quite right, but the hope in their faces made me forge on. "He said you're very dear to him. 'Despite our ideological differences, they are dear to me'. That's what he said."

"Oh..." Tears overflowed Moonbeam's eyes. "Oh, my boy..."

"And I know he was glad to have you there after his car accident," I went on recklessly. "I know that meant a lot to him."

I bit my tongue before I could blurt out that he'd actually been recovering from an attempt on his life and he'd just left the woman he loved an ocean away. No wonder he'd been in turmoil. He had probably been terrified that both Katya and his parents would be in the line of fire if his enemies found out he'd survived.

"I know he loves you," I repeated as firmly as I could.

"That's..." Karma cleared his throat and continued huskily. "You have no idea what that means to us. We thought... we used to send him little gifts and photos but when he moved, there was nothing of those things in his house. It was as though he'd erased us from his life."

"I'm sure he didn't want to do that," I insisted.

He had done it, though, to protect them. And he couldn't explain without breaching his cover. Sympathy for both Stemp and his parents tightened my chest, and I rummaged for any small crumb of comfort.

What could I say? They were right; except for his plants, Stemp's house had been barren. No personal items at all except...

I sucked in a breath, remembering the single thing in the house that had seemed out of character. "Wait... did you make him a dreamcatcher?"

Fierce hope kindled in Moonbeam's eyes. "Yes. Blue beads and an eagle feather."

"He still has it." My smile was so wide it hurt my cheeks. "It's hanging over his bed."

A different kind of hope lit Moonbeam's face, and I barely resisted the urge to smack myself in the forehead.

Shit. What possible reason could I give for being in his bedroom? I couldn't tell the truth about searching his house.

"We're not..." I began.

"It's all right, Storm Cloud Dancer, we're delighted." Moonbeam gave me a motherly smile.

"No, we're really not lovers," I repeated, cursing the heat rising in my cheeks.

"I wondered why you hadn't found a young man here after all this time," she mused. "It's lovely that you're being faithful to Cosmic River Stone, but I doubt if it's necessary. Monogamy is an unnatural state, you know, and Cosmic River Stone was never sexually inhibited-"

"La-la-la-la-la-la!" I shouted, clapping my hands over my ears before I could be scarred by any more unwelcome revelations. "Sorry, I can't hear you! La-la-la-la..."

I hopped off the table and made for the exit.

Karma's laughter penetrated my barrier of humming as he gently pulled my hand away from my ear. "Don't mind her," he said. "We won't pry. Moonbeam Meadow Sky sometimes gets carried away-"

"That's true, I do," Moonbeam interrupted. "But remember, Storm Cloud Dancer, regular sexual activity is normal and healthy, and it's particularly important to engage in it through menopause and beyond because-"

"Uh, yeah right, thanks, good session," I babbled as I backed toward the tent flap. "Thanks again for the energy work. I've got to go; I have to, um, do something... good night!"

I hurried out into the darkness.

CHAPTER 8

Scuttling away from Moonbeam and Karma's tent, I gave quiet thanks to the stroke of luck or benevolent Spirit that had provided a full moon with no clouds for a change. The sky had been softening into evening twilight when I had left my tent, and I'd forgotten to bring my powerful flashlight.

Moonlight barely penetrated the forest canopy but it was still bright enough to keep me from running face-first into a tree or tripping over the many roots that crisscrossed the path, so I didn't bother to extract the tiny LED light I always kept in my waist pouch. Instead I moved quietly through the darkness, regaining my composure.

After a few moments my discomfort over Moonbeam's too-frank sex conversation faded into amusement, along with a sneaking sympathy for Stemp. No wonder he had clashed with his parents at a young age. His rigid reserve was so diametrically opposed to their laid-back hippie ways.

My steps slowed. Or maybe he was so buttoned-up *because* of their hippie ways. The corners of my mouth twitched. Most kids rebelled against a conservative upbringing by seeking out a dope-smoking promiscuous crowd. I guessed it made sense that a child of dope-smoking promiscuous parents would do exactly the opposite.

Although...

I trailed to a halt, frowning at the silvery lacing of moon-drenched ferns beside the path.

Now that I thought about it, I'd never seen any evidence that Karma and Moonbeam partook of either free love or dope. They dispensed hugs and parental affection generously to all the commune members, but it never seemed to go any farther than that.

Hmmm. Interesting.

I filed that away for future consideration and set a leisurely pace, enjoying the silent moonlight. I had just reached the path that led to my tent when the clanging of the Earth Spirit's bells shattered the peace.

"Oh, for shit's sake," I muttered, and turned back toward the main building, my shoulders sagging.

A couple of commune members rushed by, beckoning me to hurry, but my feet dragged in stubborn resentment. Twice in a day? Screw this. I didn't see how anybody could know if the so-called Earth Spirit wanted a ritual, anyway. It wasn't like a bolt of lightning came down out of the blue.

I halted.

Wait a minute.

Who did decide when the Earth Spirit was calling?

I had assumed it was Moonbeam, but maybe I was wrong. And what 'rituals' did Moonbeam and Karma perform that were so uncomfortable, and why did Orion know more about it than I did if he was always humming in the main building with everybody else?

On impulse I stepped away from the main path and trod carefully through the undergrowth in the direction of Moonbeam and Karma's tent.

A flash of light made me freeze in the shadow of a giant

Douglas fir, and I pressed close to its deeply furrowed bark while I watched Moonbeam and Karma's flashlight illuminate their rapid exit from their tent. Following them as silently as possible, I trailed them down to the main path. They had just turned in the opposite direction to the other commune members when they encountered another bobbing flashlight and halted.

Straining my ears, I heard what sounded like a soft greeting before Moonbeam and Karma hurried on and the other flashlight continued its journey toward the main building. A patch of moonlight in the dappled shade illuminated Orion's broad-shouldered figure.

I shrank closer to the tree. He was probably looking for me. He seemed to have appointed himself my keeper, dragging me off to the ritual every time the damn Spirit bells rang. Well, he could go by himself this time.

While I watched, he hesitated at the junction of the path, then turned off the main trail and headed for Moonbeam and Karma's tent.

What the hell?

I followed him as silently as I could in the undergrowth. He should be rushing off to the ritual, not sneaking into a private tent.

And he was definitely sneaking. He paused outside their tent to cast a quick glance around as though making sure he was unobserved before ducking inside.

The glowing spot of his flashlight darted briefly around the canvas walls before settling into immobility as though he'd put it down. I held my breath, watching and listening with all my might.

Nothing. If he was searching their tent, he was doing it in absolute silence. A moment later the light moved again, flashing through the tent flap as he shouldered out.

"Storm!" His shout made me start guiltily and press closer to my tree. "Storm, where are you? Hurry, we have to go!"

The beam of his flashlight fingered through the forest and I scooted around to the other side of the tree.

Dammit, what the hell was he doing? Standing there yelling his head off, he didn't seem too concerned about being caught right outside Karma and Moonbeam's tent.

But then again, we'd be the only ones who weren't at the ritual by now. Well, except Skidmark. Come to think of it, I'd never seen him there, either. But he was probably too stoned to stagger down from his garage.

"Storm!"

Orion's approaching footsteps crackled through the undergrowth. Shit, what were the chances he'd take this particular shortcut? Now I was screwed. There was a miniscule chance that I could circle the tree while he went by on the other side, but it would be really embarrassing if he caught me.

I hissed out an irritable breath and stepped out of my concealment. "Over here, Orion!"

His flashlight blinded me and I flung up a hand to shade my eyes.

"Sorry." He aimed the beam downward and hurried over. "Storm, where have you been? Didn't you hear the Earth Spirit's call?"

I couldn't plausibly claim to have missed that cacophony, so I flung out the first excuse that came to mind. "I heard it, but..." I swallowed a growl as he gripped my hand and began to pull me toward the main building. "...but I'd forgotten my flashlight when I went to Moonbeam and Karma's and- ow!

Shit, slow down!"

I stumbled over a root and Orion spared a moment to steady me before dragging me on again. "...and the moon was so bright I thought I'd take a shortcut, but I got lost..." I continued. We gained the main path and accelerated into a dead run, and I abandoned my explanation to concentrate on sucking air instead.

A moment later gunshots froze my feet to the path, my hand twitching toward my holster.

"Fireworks," Orion panted. "Darn it, Storm, this is a special Calling! We hardly ever have fireworks. Hurry up, we're missing it!" He hauled on my hand again.

My heart vibrated in my throat as another barrage of reports exploded behind us, but he was right. That was fireworks, not firearms.

I sucked in a deep breath, trying to dissipate the tidal wave of adrenaline. "But we won't be able to see them; they're behind us..." was all I managed before he dragged me into motion again.

"Yes, of course! Hurry up!"

That made no sense at all, but I let him herd me into the main building anyway.

Inside, Aurora Peace Rain's eyes were wide with accusation, but she was mercifully silent as she pushed the mat into my hands and jabbed a finger toward my assigned patch of floor.

I hurried over and fell onto the mat to lie panting as quietly as possible while the other commune members hummed themselves into a blissed-out frenzy. Peeking through my lashes again, I saw that Aurora and Zen had lifted the glowing crystal down from the table to lie beside it on the floor. The fireworks continued at apparently random intervals, and I frowned and concentrated. It sounded as though they were being set off from different locations around the main building, and at varying distances. That would have taken quite a bit of advance preparation. And if Karma and Moonbeam were the ones setting them off, they'd have to rush from one place to another to do it.

Why bother? What was the point of fireworks if everybody was lying indoors with their eyes closed?

I sighed and gave up. This Earth Spirit thing was just plain weird, but whatever. Just go with the flow.

I hummed and tried to concentrate on my chakra.

It remained stubbornly elusive, and I returned to worrying over Orion's snooping. Even though Karma and Moonbeam's accommodations were decidedly spartan, Orion hadn't been in their tent long enough to search it thoroughly. And anyway, if he had been searching for something his flashlight beam would have been moving around the tent.

So what the hell had he been doing in there? Especially since he'd acted as though he was in such a hurry to get to this ritual.

The sound of the gong startled me out of my reverie and I sat up along with everyone else. The fireworks were still exploding sporadically, and I surveyed the sky as we fell into single file behind Aurora outside. Even though the reports sounded close, I couldn't see any sparkles up there. Maybe they were just setting off firecrackers at ground level. But firecrackers were usually rapid strings of explosions, and this rhythm seemed too sparse and uneven.

A chill tingled down my spine. That rhythm really did sound like weapons fire. A firefight, to be exact. Gunshots and return fire.

I shook off the thought. If there was one thing the past

year had taught me, it was the noise of gunfire. This wasn't it. The rhythm was right, but the sound quality wasn't. No echoing crack, no whine of ricochets, just the flat bang of explosive without a projectile.

I sighed and tramped through the darkness. Stop looking for danger where there isn't any. Think positive thoughts.

At least it wasn't raining, so our sojourn in the field wouldn't be quite so miserable.

Shivering on my knees a few minutes later, I defied the 'heads bowed' protocol to peep at the sky. I could see a few red and green spark trails in the sky, but they were disappointing. More like flares than fireworks. Probably cheaper. The commune likely didn't have a lot of spare cash lying around to splurge on fancy fireworks.

A roaring sound swelled from the trees around us and other heads popped up around me as brilliant spotlights flared. Blinded by the glare, I shielded my eyes and blinked away afterimages. Four spotlights blazed at the cardinal points of the field, one for each of our groups.

I squinted at them, first puzzled, then annoyed. Karma and Moonbeam must have turned on the generator just for this. What a fucking waste. I could have been basking in a hot shower instead of freezing my butt off out here.

The lights abruptly extinguished, and the leaders' shout of "The blessings of the Earth Spirit are upon you!" sounded slightly subdued.

"And upon you, too," I mumbled along with the rest, and hauled myself to my feet.

"I'll walk you back so you don't get lost again." Orion's voice in my ear made me spin to face him, clutching my chest.

"Jeez, don't sneak up on me like that!" I complained. "You scared the shit out of me."

"Sorry." His smile gleamed in the indirect glow from his downward-pointed flashlight. "I just didn't want you walking back alone in the dark. If the cougar is prowling around tonight, we should travel together."

"Mm." I fell into step beside him, wondering if I really was safer with him than with a large nocturnal predator.

Probably. But I wasn't quite as sure as I might have been before.

"You seem really comfortable moving around out here in the dark," Orion said conversationally. "Most newbies wouldn't part with their flashlights for anything, and they'd never forget them. Do you normally do a lot of camping?"

"I'm not really a newbie anymore," I objected. "But yeah, I've always spent a lot of time outdoors. How about you?" I nodded teasingly at his flashlight. "I see yours is glued to your hand."

He laughed. "I'm a city boy. I like the outdoors, but I always feel as though something's going to sneak up on me when it's dark."

I considered the irony in that statement and made no comment.

"You seemed a little spooked by the fireworks," he went on. "Do they bother you?"

"No, I like fireworks." I forced a laugh. "It's just that where I come from, if you hear that sound coming from the woods you'd better get your blaze-orange on before some hunter mistakes you for a deer."

"Oh. Yeah, I guess that'd spook, me, too."

"So what brings a city boy out here into the sticks?" I bantered. "Most city boys I know wouldn't venture anywhere there wasn't a four-star hotel."

"Oh, the Earth Spirit, of course," he said earnestly. "That makes it all worthwhile."

"How did you find out about the Earth Spirit, though? I'd never even heard of it until I came here." I peered at his dimly-lit profile, wishing his flashlight was a little brighter so I could read his reaction.

"I found it online," he said without hesitation. "I was searching for true meaning, and the Earth Spirit guided me here."

That sounded a little too glib. And a little too weird.

"And have you found it?" I prodded.

"Oh, yes." He glanced over at me, his eyes unreadable in the gloom. "What about you? You don't seem to even believe in the Earth Spirit. Why are you here?"

I weighed the pros and cons. If he was one of Stemp's enemies, maybe it was time to see what kind of a reaction I could get.

Watching him carefully, I said, "I'm friends with Karma and Moonbeam's son."

No reaction other than an interested nod that encouraged me to go on. Either he was an excellent actor, or he wasn't an enemy.

But if he *was* an enemy, he'd likely be an excellent actor.

Shit.

"That's nice," Orion prompted. "But it doesn't really answer my question."

I shook myself back to the situation at hand. "Sorry, I zoned out for a second there. Too tired after all this traipsing around in the middle of the night."

He chuckled. "It's only ten o'clock. Not exactly the middle of the night. So, you were saying...?"

Damn, he was persistent.

"Um, yeah. Well, I was pretty stressed out and Cosmic River Stone thought this would be a great place for me to relax and decompress. He asked Moonbeam and Karma if I could stay with them a while, and here I am."

"Work stress?"

"Um..." I stopped myself before I could fall into the trap of agreeing. Most people didn't wake up screaming every night because of too much paperwork at the office.

"It was more than that, wasn't it?" Orion asked quietly. "Do you want to talk about it?"

"No." I tried to temper the abruptness of my response by adding, "Thanks, but no. I did go through a bad time, but I've been having regular phone sessions with a psychologist and I'm better now."

"Oh, that would be the Dr. Rawling who phones every Wednesday."

"Uh, yeah, every second Wednesday now." Damn communal phone, everybody knew everybody else's business. "I didn't want to inconvenience anybody so I always tried to be there when he phoned for our appointments," I added. "But I guess I didn't always succeed."

"It must have been pretty bad, what you went through." Orion glanced over again, but I couldn't tell whether it was concern or prurient curiosity in his shadowed face. "You did a lot of screaming at night."

"Yeah," I said shortly. The path to my tent looked like a pale ribbon of salvation in the moonlight ahead of us, and I drew a breath of relief. "Well, thanks for the light. Goodnight."

I hurried to my tent and ducked inside without waiting

for a reply.

Sinking onto my cot with a long breath, I rested my aching forehead in my hands. I hadn't wanted to be reminded of my nightmares. Hadn't wanted to feel this fearful suspicion again. Had really wanted to believe this was a safe place and Orion was simply a handsome man with no hidden agendas.

Well, you don't always get what you want.

I sighed and dug another secured phone out of my bag.

CHAPTER 9

Weighing the burner phone in my hand, I stared at the moon-dappled canvas around me.

How long before I could leave my tent unnoticed?

Orion had said ten o'clock wasn't late, so how long would he stay up? And did he sleep soundly enough for me to sneak by without waking him once he did go to sleep?

If he had been anybody else in the entire commune I could have walked on by and pretended I was going to the latrine, but with my luck he'd offer to accompany me for 'safety'.

Maybe my report to Stemp could wait until morning.

I suppressed a groan and massaged my temples. Or maybe Orion was planning something tonight and delaying my report could mean the difference between life and death for Moonbeam and Karma. Or for me.

Christ, I hated this.

I shook off that unproductive thought. Focus.

Reporting to Stemp tonight wouldn't save any lives. He couldn't change anything from there. But if something did happen tonight and I ended up dead, at least my report might help him react faster and with more precision.

I thumped my forehead gently with the phone. Shit, stop

overreacting. Nobody's going to die.

So Orion had gone into Karma and Moonbeam's tent while they were gone, so what? It wasn't like I'd caught him stalking them with a weapon. And anyway, they might have asked him to go in and get something when they'd spoken to him on the path.

That must have been it.

I let out a slow breath, trying to release my tension along with it. There would be a simple explanation. This was nothing to worry about.

Probably.

But I didn't dare ignore it.

Growling under my breath, I shed my jacket and crouched to rummage in the duffel bag under my cot. A rustle from outside froze me in place, my breath stopping while I strained my ears. Was that human or animal? Or only the wind?

Long moments passed while I squatted immobile, listening. At last I decided it must have been my imagination and pulled out my lockbox, stopping to listen again before I thumbed in the combination.

When it opened, I withdrew my new shoulder holster and a spare magazine before relocking the box and stuffing it deep in the bag. I transferred my Glock and magazine to the shoulder rig and put it on, feeling reassured of a quicker draw if I encountered the cougar. Then I donned my jacket, tucked my big flashlight into the pocket along with the phone, and took my tiny LED light out of my waist pouch. After a few more moments of listening beside my tent flap, I eased outside.

The moonlit darkness was silent. No sound or light emanated from Orion's tent, but I didn't trust that to mean he was asleep. The man kept popping up where I least expected him.

Flicking my tiny light over the undergrowth, I stepped into the forest as quietly as possible, circling behind our tents and giving Orion's a wide berth. My back tingled with the sensation of being watched, but I couldn't tell whether it was nervousness at the thought of getting caught by Orion or fear of the cougar.

My pulse bounding at every night noise, I resisted the urge to draw my gun but I slid my hand inside my jacket for reassurance. The comforting feel of the pistol grip eased the jittery nerves in my stomach, and after nearly twenty minutes of stealthy movement through the forest I intersected the main road at last.

Walking in plain view on the road was probably more dangerous than sticking to the woods, but the moonlight and open space made me draw a breath of relief nonetheless. In the brighter open area my tiny flashlight had little effect, and I tucked it back into my waist pouch before moving cautiously out of the forest.

Every sense on alert, I strode along the shoulder of the road, my hand hovering near my gun. The trees seemed to lean farther over the road than usual, their branches reaching for me like dark skeletal hands. The blackness of the understory pulsed with menace.

I straightened my spine. Dammit, I *liked* being outside at night. It wasn't any more dangerous than the middle of the day when the forest looked soft and green and welcoming. In fact, I was probably safer now. Far less chance of meeting someone from the commune.

Less chance of meeting someone innocent, anyway.

Well, that thought hadn't been quite as reassuring as I'd

hoped.

Jeez, relax, already. Just enjoy the silence and moonlight.

When nothing untoward happened after several minutes of walking I switched to deeper belly breaths, easing out my accumulated tension. At last I withdrew the phone and punched the speed dial, still walking.

"Stemp." He sounded as wide-awake as if it had been the middle of the day.

"It's Aydan. I caught Orion sneaking into your parents' tent tonight when they weren't there. They might have asked him to; I saw them talking to him right before he went in. But I wanted to report it just in case."

"Did he spot you?"

"Not until after he was out, and he wouldn't have had any reason to believe I'd seen him go in." At least that's what I hoped. "And he's been asking a lot of questions under the guise of wanting to get to know me better. I've been asking a few in return and there haven't been any red flags yet, but... I've just got this feeling..." I broke off, imagining his expressionless face. "Sorry," I added. "I know that's useless. I'll keep digging."

To my surprise, Stemp said, "Your gut feeling is never useless. You have good instincts, and in our line of work that's sometimes the only thing that keeps us alive. Get close to Moonjava and find out whatever you can using any means you consider appropriate." A hint of dryness tinged his voice. "Within the scope of the law."

"Uh, yeah."

I was glad he couldn't see me because I was pretty sure I was blushing. I wasn't proud of the way I'd handled my last mission, but thanks to me Kane was alive and a major criminal organization was all but destroyed.

But maybe some important part of me had been destroyed in the process.

I jerked my mind back to the conversation at hand. "Should I ask your parents about it?" I asked. "If they told him to go into their tent, there's nothing to worry about."

Silence hummed on the line for a few moments. "True," Stemp said at last. "But if they didn't..." He sighed. "My parents tend to be... direct. They'd confront Moonjava, potentially causing an overt conflict and blowing your cover in the process. If Moonjava has been there nearly four months without attacking them, it means he's either innocent or he's planning something more complicated than a simple assault. So no; don't mention it to them, and continue to observe. I'll send you night-vision equipment."

"Okay." Something rustled in the undergrowth and I caught my breath, my hand flying to my Glock. Wishing I had night vision now while I peered into the blackness with my heart thumping, I lowered my voice. "We had a Spirit Calling with fireworks tonight. Why didn't you brief me about that? I nearly pulled my gun in front of Orion, and he noticed me twitching."

"I apologize." Stemp sounded as though he meant it. "I had forgotten about the fireworks. We only had them on a couple of occasions in the eighteen years I lived there."

There was no further sound or movement from the woods and I started walking again, casting nervous glances around me. "Do you know why they do it or how they decide whether it's fireworks time? And why do they set them off when everybody's in the building so we can't even watch them?"

"I have no idea." Stemp's emotionless tones dissolved

into uncharacteristic frustration. "As far as I can determine, the Earth Spirit is entirely a fabrication of my parents' imagination. When I questioned them as a teenager, their explanation was nothing but hyperbole and circular reasoning. The *Callings*..." He gave the word a sarcastic inflection. "...appear to be completely random, at whatever interval my parents arbitrarily decide, however inconvenient that may be. The use of fireworks also appears entirely arbitrary. We would go for months or years without them, then sometimes have them several times in succession."

"The ritual was a little different tonight, too," I said. "They brought the crystal down onto the floor in the main building, and they turned on spotlights and some kind of noise generator in the field afterward."

"Yes, those details are consistent with what I experienced as a child. Again, I don't know why, and my parents provided unsatisfactory explanations." He hesitated before continuing, "The maddening thing is that my parents are otherwise brilliant people. They each hold several academic degrees and doctorates in various disciplines, and the education they provide in the commune's school is second to none. It escapes me why they choose to waste their lives in pursuit of some imaginary deity, surrounded by drug-wasted losers and vapid directionless seekers of Truth and Meaning." I could hear the acerbic capital letters in his tone.

I'd seen Stemp remain completely unaffected in situations that would have made any normal man rant and tear his hair. If his parents annoyed him enough to express actual emotion, I definitely didn't want to get into it.

"Well, I guess as long as they're happy," I mumbled.

"Yes..." Stemp hesitated. "Is that all?"

I held back a groan at the invocation of the secret code.

Dammit, another clandestine session on my laptop tonight. All I wanted was peace, silence, and my bed.

"Ye- Wait!" I interrupted myself as a sudden thought occurred. "Hang on. Are you still there?"

"Yes, what is it?" His voice had returned to its usual clipped efficiency.

"I just realized what's been bothering my subconscious. You know how I said Orion seemed to know more than normal about the workings of the commune? Well, tonight when we were talking about the special Calling, he said 'we hardly ever have fireworks'. But I've been here longer than he has, and this is the first time we've had them. So how would he know?"

"An excellent question," Stemp said slowly. "Maybe he lived at the commune before."

"No, when I asked him, he said he'd found it online and joined because the Earth Spirit called him."

"The commune doesn't have a website. Newcomers hear about it strictly by word of mouth." Silence hovered between us for a moment. "It's possible he stumbled on someone's blog or made some other personal connection online," Stemp added, but he didn't sound convinced. His voice firmed into his usual crisp authority. "It seems your instincts are as good as ever. Continue to investigate, and keep me posted."

"I will." I hung up and turned to trudge back to the commune.

The return trip seemed longer. I strode along the ribbon of pale moonlight in the centre of the road, casting wary glances into the blackness of the undergrowth on both sides. A fitful breeze rustled the trees like a big cat moving stealthily through the undergrowth.

Several times I spun, certain I'd heard the padding of

lethal velvet paws on the gravel behind me, but nothing was there. At last the rough poles of the commune's gate traced straight moonlit lines against the dark forest, and I drew a deep breath and crept reluctantly into the blackness beside the road.

Moving a few steps at a time by the light of my tiny flashlight, then halting to peer into the darkness and strain my ears, I made slow progress. When I neared the encampment, I detoured warily around the scattering of tents, reassured by the snores emanating from several of them.

Near the path that led to my tent, I chanced a quick flash of light on my wristwatch. Past midnight. Surely Orion would be asleep by now. I could probably walk up the path. Even if he poked his head out and caught me, I could just say I'd been down to the latrine.

But if he was wide-awake enough to hear me coming up the path, he'd wonder why he hadn't heard me going down.

Shit.

I exhaled a quiet breath and stepped cautiously through the undergrowth, describing a wide arc around Orion's tent and easing my feet down to avoid snapping twigs.

When a sudden crack disturbed the soft night sounds, my breath stopped, my heart lurching into my throat.

That twig hadn't snapped under *my* foot.

Peering into the moon-dappled darkness, my pulse began to hammer at the sight of a black shape moving around my tent. I eased my hand onto my gun butt, praying my jacket wouldn't rustle. My need to breathe returned with a vengeance and I panted open-mouthed, trying to stay silent.

The black figure moved closer and the jackhammer in

my chest accelerated again when I realized it wasn't a cougar. This was a two-legged predator circling my tent.

The intruder paused to bow his head as if listening, and a shaft of moonlight slid across his cheek.

Orion.

What the hell was he doing sneaking around my tent?

Oh shit, had he searched it?

I did a rapid mental inventory of the incriminating objects inside. Could he have gotten into my lockbox? I had my holsters and spare magazine with me, but the boxes of ammo would be damn hard to explain. And I'd stowed Stemp's new box of phones in my duffel bag, too. Orion wouldn't know who I was calling or why, but a dozen burner phones were bound to raise some questions.

My mind hurtled through the possible ramifications while I strained my eyes against the darkness. A breeze rustled the trees, and the shifting moonlight glinted off something in his hand.

Shit, was that a weapon? My grip tightened on my Glock.

He stood motionless a few more moments before moving at last, creeping past my tent and avoiding the gravel path. Moments later he disappeared into his own tent, and the sudden glow of his flashlight illuminated the canvas from inside.

I drew a long slow breath, then another, standing completely still while my mind raced. If he had actually gone into my tent, he knew I wasn't there. Would he be watching and listening for my return? I could brazen it out and use the latrine excuse, but how long had he been out there? I'd have to claim a hell of a case of constipation if he knew I'd been gone for over an hour.

But if he had searched my tent, he wouldn't be listening outside it, would he? So he probably hadn't been inside.

But why was he sneaking around this late at night? There was no benign explanation for that. Either he was a creepy pervert who liked to whack off outside my tent while I slept, or else he was up to something more sinister.

I eased out a sigh. I would have actually preferred the 'pervert' explanation, but I was damn sure that metallic glint in his hand hadn't been his dick. Unless he had some truly extraordinary plumbing.

My dirty mind disgorged an inappropriate 'man of steel' joke but before I could let it distract me, the light in his tent went out. I tensed, frozen in the deep shadows of the undergrowth. A rustling sound from his tent ratcheted my heart rate up still higher. Was he coming out again?

When he didn't appear, I drew a slow breath. Maybe he was just going to bed. The chilly breeze ruffled my hair, sending me into adrenaline-laced shivers. Dammit, I was freezing. How long would I have to wait to be sure it was safe to move?

A few minutes later a light snore from the vicinity of Orion's tent freed me from my immobility. My paranoia reminded me that he might be faking it just to draw me out, but I ignored that. If he suddenly popped out in front of me, I'd deal with it. Anything was better than standing out here in the dark with the wind whistling up the crack of my ass and my feet falling asleep.

Hell, at least they were getting a nap. It was going to be a long time before I got any sleep tonight.

CHAPTER 10

It took nearly ten minutes for me to sneak the last several yards to my tent, stopping and listening with every step. By the time I closed the tent flap behind me I was shivering uncontrollably. I stripped and burrowed into my cot, but the damp chilly blankets only increased my frozen misery. Muttering curses, I quivered out again and pulled on sweats and a T-shirt before grabbing my laptop and retreating under the covers once more.

I pulled the blanket over my head to conserve heat and hide the glow of the screen, hoping I'd be able to hear any incoming threat over the chattering of my teeth. The little square began blinking as soon as I logged in, and I performed the Alt-Shift-Click sequence to activate the text window.

Too unnerved to wait for Stemp to initiate a message, I typed, "Orion was sneaking around my tent tonight. He seemed to be listening, but he might have been inside searching it earlier. I caught him outside when I came back."

The cursor scurried across the screen. "Did you confront him?"

"No. He didn't see me." I thought for a moment, then typed, "Along with the other gear would you please send me a waterproof storage box big enough for my lockbox and phones, and the smallest night-vision webcam you've got?"

"I'll courier it tomorrow. It should be at the depot in Port Renfrew the next day." The cursor hesitated at the end of the text for a moment before continuing, "Is that all?"

I typed 'yes', wondering what was coming.

Apparently he was having difficulty formulating his question. The cursor blinked in place at the end of the line for several moments.

I was about to ask what he wanted when it moved at last. "You said 'as long as my parents are happy'. Are they?"

It was my turn to hesitate. "Mostly, I think," I typed finally. "But they miss you and wish they were part of your life. I told them you love them and that seemed to help, but maybe you could call more often. Your mom was really happy to hear you had houseplants so that might be something you could talk about."

I stared at my words on the screen for a long moment, my finger hovering over the Enter key. Should I really offer personal advice to my cold-fish boss? Hell, who was I to advise anyone on family matters? My parents were both dead, I had no siblings or children, and my personal life wouldn't exactly win awards for wholesome normalcy. Maybe I should just say 'yes, they're happy' and dodge the whole thing.

Moonbeam's tear-bright eyes rose in my memory and I swore softly. Dammit, Stemp might tell me to butt out, but I had to try. And he must care about their happiness, or he wouldn't have asked.

I gritted my teeth and sent the message, braced for a scathing dismissal.

The cursor blinked innocuously.

It didn't move for so long I wondered if Stemp had dropped dead of apoplexy on the other end. Was he sitting there in a rage, trying to calm down enough to type one of his trademark emotionless responses? Or maybe he was composing an icy rebuke.

The cursor kept blinking, giving away nothing.

Or maybe my message hadn't gone through...?

I was considering re-sending it when the cursor moved at last, its short message zipping across the screen: "Thank you. I'll try that."

My jaw dropped as the text window vanished. Of all the responses he could have given, that was the one I had least expected.

I sat staring at the screen for several moments, but the connection had closed and there was nothing else unusual. No flying pigs, and I was pretty sure there would be icicles if hell had frozen over.

But... Stemp acting like a human being? I emerged from under the covers to check for flying pigs one more time.

My tent remained pork-free, and I shook off my bemusement and stowed my laptop under the bed. Burrowing back under the covers, I tucked my gun into its accustomed berth between my cot and the tent wall before squeezing my eyes shut and letting out a long breath.

Okay, relax. Sleep.

Yeah, right.

My tense muscles refused to ease and I lay wide awake, listening for the crunch of footsteps on gravel or the rustle of my tent flap. Or gunshots. It would be easy for somebody to fire a few rounds through a canvas wall.

Oh, for chrissake, shut up.

I hauled myself off the cot with a groan and quietly

relocated my wooden crates in front of the tent flap before crawling back into bed. At least if somebody tried to sneak in, I'd get some advance notice. That would have to be good enough.

My fingers crept over the edge of the cot to seek the reassurance of my pistol grip.

No, dammit, I refused to go to sleep with it in my hand. If I had a nightmare I might shoot some innocent person before I woke up enough to realize what I was doing.

I tucked my hand back under the covers and rolled over, yanking the blanket up around my ears.

Settle down. Belly breathe...

After a night of waking over and over at the slightest noise, the cheery sound of birdsong made me pry open an eye at last. Dawn-gray lightened the canvas, and I squinted at my watch.

Six-thirty.

"Shut up, you little feathered bastards," I growled, and jammed the pillow over my head.

A few moments later even its padding couldn't muffle the sudden din of the Spirit bells.

"For fucksakes! *Really?*" I demanded of the pillow.

It didn't reply, and I flung it to the floor and staggered out of bed to shift the wooden crates away from the entrance. With my luck Orion would-

"Storm!"

"...be right here to collect me," I finished my mental sentence in a cranky mutter before raising my voice. "I'm not coming! I'm sick!"

A moment later I gave quiet thanks that I'd worn my T-shirt and sweats to bed when he pushed through the tent flap, looking anxious. "What's wrong? Can I help?"

"No, thanks. I'm just not feeling well. I'll be okay after a bit more sleep."

"But what's wrong?" He eyed me for a moment, his eyes narrowing suspiciously. "You look fine. Are you just trying to avoid the Calling?"

I scowled and pulled out the heaviest hitter in my arsenal. "I have terrible menstrual cramps. Go away."

He paled. "Oh." A flush rose on his cheeks and he squared his shoulders, his lips firming. "You're lying, aren't you?"

"Clots," I ground out. "Giant slimy blood clots like pieces of raw liver..."

He clapped a hand over his mouth and fled.

My return to bed was sweet indeed.

I was drifting in the warm hazy limbo that precedes sleep when scratching at my tent flap roused me.

"Go away, I'm sick," I mumbled.

The rustle of my tent flap heralded Orion's arrival, his beautiful eyes wide with concern. "I brought you a hot water bottle," he murmured, and held it out.

I sighed. "Thanks, but I'm- *Jesus Christ!*" A deluge of icy water drenched me as he upended the bottle over my head.

"No, you're not," he said straight-faced, but the dimple flickered in his cheek.

I rocketed out of bed, bellowing the vilest insults I could summon on short notice, and swung for all I was worth with the soggy pillow. I scored a direct hit on the side of his head and was winding up for a second blow when he sprang and captured me in a bear hug, pinning my arms to my sides.

"You deserved that," he observed, grinning at me from close range. "For lying to me."

"Bullsh... I... you..."

He ignored my sputtering. "I was worried about you so I went to get Moonbeam. And she told me you can't possibly have menstrual cramps."

"Oh, for..." I tried to step away but he held me tightly, his grin changing from mischief to temptation.

His muscular body felt far too good against mine. And those stunning green eyes were heating up, evaporating the common sense right out of my head.

Before it could desert me completely I pulled free and took a couple of hurried steps backward. "All right, you got me. Yes, I was lying. I don't mean any disrespect to your beliefs or to the Earth Spirit, Orion, but I just don't believe in it the way you do and I don't see the point in participating in the rituals."

He sighed. "I wish you'd take part, though, if only to make Moonbeam and Karma happy."

That was a low blow. My conscience twinged.

"But they don't even come to the rituals," I argued. "They'd never know if I was there unless somebody told them. And anyway, Skidmark never shows up, either. That doesn't seem to bother them."

The corner of Orion's mouth twitched. "Skidmark isn't even capable of walking a straight line most of the time. I don't think you want to claim kinship with him."

"True." I seized the opportunity to change the subject. "Hey, you're the expert on the commune so answer me this: If Moonbeam and Karma don't mind Skidmark constantly smoking pot and offering it to everybody he meets, why do they prohibit any form of alcohol?"

Orion shrugged. "Marijuana is part of the natural world. If it grows from the Earth, it's a gift from the Earth Spirit for us to use. Alcohol doesn't grow from the earth."

"But it's made from fruits and grains," I began, but he was already shaking his head.

"Alcohol poisons our bodies and minds," he said firmly. "You've never heard of anyone going on a marijuana-fuelled rampage, have you? Alcohol makes people violent and dangerous. Marijuana doesn't."

"Alcohol doesn't change people at all," I argued. "It just removes their filters. If they're violent and dangerous to start with, then yeah, they get violent and dangerous. If they aren't, they don't. If somebody's shit-faced drunk, you just see what they're truly like."

Orion frowned. "But self-control is what separates men from animals. The Earth Spirit wants us to exercise self-control to live together in tolerance and harmony. Alcohol destroys self-control."

I sighed. "Okay, I'll give you that. But-"

"Storm." He stopped me with an upraised hand. "I know what you're doing. Stop stalling and let's go. We can still make it for the last half of the Calling."

I eyed him without much hope. "Do we have to? It's half over already."

Orion shook his head reprovingly, but a glint of mischief lit his eyes. "Well, there might be another way to celebrate the Earth Spirit's call."

The corners of my mouth tugged upward at his naughty expression. "Is that so?"

"Yes." He stepped closer, the dimple dancing in his cheek. "I could show you the ritual."

"I'm sure you could." My heart picked up the pace while

my mind accelerated into overdrive. I didn't trust him, but I had no proof that he was actually dangerous. And he was definitely hot.

He was inches away, his hands gliding over my shoulders and down my arms to lift my hands. Soft lips scattered butterfly kisses over my knuckles before he turned my hand to kiss my palm. Then his lips drifted to the inside of my wrist, his green eyes blazing temptation.

Oh, hell, *definitely* hot.

And Stemp had told me to get close to him. Shit, I was practically under orders to...

Orion's lips curved up at my indrawn breath as he kissed his way up to the inside of my elbow. My body called in a four-alarm fire, urging on my rationalizations.

What better way to encourage confidences than during pillow talk in a long, lazy afterglow? If he actually meant any harm to Moonbeam and Karma, he'd be more likely to let something slip when he was relaxed.

Relaxation was the farthest thing from my mind at the moment. His lips had found the sensitive spot near my collarbone, sending electric tingles to all points south. My hands traced the hard contours of his chest and he pulled me closer with a throaty murmur of satisfaction.

His kiss burned my lips while he shrugged off his corduroy shirt. His hands moved lower, pressing me against him while he deepened the kiss. Dipping under my T-shirt, his hot palms slid up my back while his tongue seduced mine.

He broke the kiss to nibble across my jaw toward my earlobe. Arching my neck to give him better access, I opened my eyes momentarily to judge the distance to the bed.

And froze, my already-pounding pulse leaping up into

heart-attack territory.

Nylon hand restraints.   Lying on the ground half-concealed by his dropped shirt. They must have fallen out of his pocket.

Oh, *shit!*

CHAPTER 11

"Storm?" Orion pulled away a fraction, his eyes dilated almost black. "What's wrong?"

"Uh..."

Dammit, suck it up. Jane Bond the Superspy would carry on as though nothing was wrong. Take him for the ride of his life, and end up with him wearing nothing but the hand restraints and spilling all his secrets.

"Um, I'm, uh..." I stepped back, my shaking legs barely holding my weight. The memory of nylon ties slicing into my wrists made me swallow hard, my heart rate rocketing into the stratosphere.

I drew a deep breath and pulled myself together, my voice only trembling slightly. "I'm sorry, Orion, I guess... I'm not quite ready for this."

"Oh." He frowned, and I calculated the distance to my gun behind the cot. I should be able to draw on him before he could grab the restraints...

"Oh," he repeated. "But... I thought... I'm sorry, then. I thought you fancied me. Sorry."

He looked so innocently disappointed that I almost second-guessed myself. But there was no innocent reason for anybody to carry a set of hand restraints. And there was that odd trace of an accent again.

"It's okay, don't apologize," I said, my wobbling voice almost under control. "I do like you, I just... I'm not quite ready for this."

"Okay." He turned away, stooping to pick up his shirt, and I thought I saw his back stiffen as he casually scooped up the restraints along with the bundle of fabric. He turned back to face me, smiling. "It was still a nice way to celebrate a Calling. Thank you."

I shoved an answering smile onto my stiff lips. "Thank you, too. For the celebration, and for taking no for an answer."

"Of course." He gave me a half-smile. "I guess, well... I guess I'll see you later?"

"Yeah, see you later." I nodded like a bobble-head, my smile plastic.

He withdrew with an awkward nod, and I tottered over to my cot and dropped onto it as though I'd been cut off at the knees. Several minutes of deep breathing restored my pulse rate to only slightly higher than normal. A few seconds after that, my brain kicked into gear again.

Stupid. I shouldn't have let my fear take over. This would have been a prime opportunity to get close to Orion and figure out what his game was.

A shudder chased itself down my spine. Or it might have been a prime opportunity for Orion to cinch those restraints around my wrists and do who-knows-what, completely unnoticed by the rest of the commune members while they hummed contentedly in the main building.

I sucked in a breath and let it out slowly. No point in second-guessing. Just do damage control.

After a moment of intent listening, I dropped to my

knees to rummage under my cot. Behind the duffel bag was a backpack I'd brought but barely used. Now seemed like an ideal time to remedy that.

Using a towel from my duffel as packing, I stowed all my phones and gun-related equipment in the bottom of the pack. Until I could create a hidden cache somewhere outside my tent, this backpack would have to be part of my body.

After some quick ablutions in the bucket of chilly water I kept handy for washing up, I got dressed and put on my ankle holster under my jeans. Strapping my heavy survival knife onto my belt, I rested my hand on its leather-wrapped hilt. It probably didn't make me much safer, but at least I felt better with its weight on my hip. My laptop filled the rest of the space in my backpack, and I shouldered the load and poked my head warily out the tent flap before emerging to hike down the path.

Trying to look casual, I scanned around me. Where had Orion gone? Did he have anyone else watching me? His ability to locate me was even more unnerving now.

I had just turned onto the main path when his familiar voice made my shoulders knot.

"Storm! Wait up!"

I turned, trying to look at least moderately welcoming, and he strode up from the direction of the main building. He eyed my backpack. "Going for a hike?"

"Yep, now's a good time to tell me to take a hike," I said too heartily.

He gave an uncertain chuckle before sobering. "Remember to watch out for the cougar. Do you have a signalling whistle with you? Or I could..." He trailed off. "I guess... you probably don't want my company."

"Not just now, but thanks for being concerned." I gave

him a smile, making sure I made my eyes crinkle as though I meant it. "I just need some time alone to think."

"Okay... well, be careful." He gave me a half-smile and turned away, and I hurried off in the opposite direction.

As usual I headed for the front gates and hiked briskly along the main road, my back tingling with the sensation of being watched. I chanced a nonchalant glance up toward Skidmark's eyrie but I couldn't spot the bench. Either it was too well concealed in the trees, or it didn't have a clear sight line to this part of the road.

My steps slowed as I thought back. How much of the road had I been able to see from up there? Dammit, I couldn't remember. I really needed to develop Kane's keen powers of observation and recall.

I sighed and hefted the backpack to a more comfortable position on my shoulders. That'd be the day. Kane was the best agent in the service, and I was just a civilian bookkeeper scrambling to learn.

Well, I'd better learn fast. Moonbeam's and Karma's lives might depend on it. And mine, too. I could start by breaking the dangerous habit of walking this road every time I called Stemp.

Glancing up at the brighter spot in the clouds that passed for the sun, I struck out into the undergrowth. At least I had good backwoods skills. I wouldn't get lost. That had to count for something.

After hiking for fifteen minutes, I intersected the river. I hadn't realized it looped so close to the road. Following its bank would be easy.

I hesitated, considering. Nope, too dangerous. The rush of its water would conceal the sounds of anyone sneaking up on me. Or any*thing*.

I glanced involuntarily over my shoulder, but the forest was devoid of any visible life except a squirrel cussing me out from the safety of a nearby tree.

"Easy for you to say, you furry little shit," I muttered, and angled away from the river until its sound faded to a whisper behind me.

After another ten minutes of walking, I still couldn't bring myself to talk on the phone. What if I'd been followed? I had been vigilant, but it wouldn't take much woodcraft for someone to remain concealed in this dense undergrowth. Orion could be only a stone's throw away, easily able to hear my voice in the silence of the forest.

I blew out a breath and sank down to sit on a fallen log. Moss squished and icy wetness soaked my ass. I sprang up and twisted to survey the dark stain spreading on my faded denim.

"Sure, fine," I muttered. "So now I look like I peed my pants. Perfect."

Well, I wasn't going to get any wetter. I blew out a breath of resignation and resumed my soggy seat.

Unslinging my backpack, I cast another glance around me. No threats appeared, so I plugged a phone into my laptop and fired up Stemp's communication system.

As usual, he was right on top of it. The cursor zipped across the screen. "Report."

I typed, "Sorry I can't call in. Someone might be listening. Orion is carrying nylon hand restraints. He tried to hide them and I pretended I didn't see them, but I'll need more equipment. Has the courier gone yet?"

"No. What do you need?"

"A trank gun, the silent kind. Some hand restraints. And do you have any locator/transmitter devices? I'd like to plant one on Orion so I can keep tabs on him."

His reply came back instantly. "What range do you need?"

Calculating, I stared up at the slivers of putty-coloured sky visible through the forest canopy before typing, "Probably no more than a mile. How big is the transmitter?"

"Only a few millimetres in diameter. It's self-adhesive, so you can stick it onto something he carries with him."

"Great. I'll look for the package at the depot tomorrow."

"No. Stand by."

I frowned at the blinking cursor. No? Dammit, I needed that stuff now. Hell, yesterday would have been nice.

After a short wait, the cursor moved again. "I can't send classified technology via common carrier. A courier agent will bring it. I can have someone in Port Renfrew by four o'clock this afternoon. Where do you want the dead drop?"

I blinked at the screen. Holy shit, he wasn't messing around. As far as I knew my 'mission' out here was completely unofficial, and I'd been surprised when he had provided me with secured phones in the first place. Now I was getting classified technology via courier agent? If Stemp was using Department resources for personal reasons, it was a risky move for him.

Well, whatever. He was covering my ass and I appreciated it.

I returned my fingers to the keyboard. "I'll bring the commune's station wagon. It's a rusted-out brown 1978 Ford wagon with fake wood panelling. I'll park at the internet café and leave the rear door unlocked so the courier can drop the package while I'm inside the café."

"Confirmed." The cursor blinked briefly before he added, "If you believe there is any danger to my parents, you are authorized to use deadly force if necessary."

Gulp.

My shaking fingers typed 'Acknowledged' and the text window vanished, leaving me staring at the blank screen as though it might reach out and bite me.

I had no doubt that Stemp would stand behind that command even if he didn't have the authority to issue it. If anything happened and I actually had to shoot somebody, he would take the fall, not me.

Several months ago, I had wondered exactly how far he'd go to protect his family. Now I knew.

I shivered and repacked my laptop in the backpack. Suddenly I was very glad Stemp considered me an ally.

My trip back to the commune was uneventful and considerably more pleasant in broad daylight. As I drew closer, I scanned the bluff near Skidmark's empire and finally spotted the bench. Nobody was sitting on it, and I relaxed fractionally even though I knew there were probably more observation points near it where a person could stand completely concealed.

Speaking of which...

My steps slowed in thought.

Time to pay a visit to Skidmark.

But first I had to make sure Moonbeam and Karma were all right. Stemp would kill me if something happened to them while I was messing around in the forest.

I turned my steps toward the encampment, wondering whether that was only a figure of speech. He would never lose control and kill me in a fit of rage, but I already knew he wouldn't hesitate to dispassionately execute anyone who posed a threat to his family. And I would definitely be a threat if he decided he couldn't trust me.

I picked up the pace.

When I strode back through the gates I accosted the first person I saw, a short grey-haired woman with a face like tanned leather. I couldn't remember whether she was called Primrose or Meadowlark, so I settled for a generic 'Good morning' before asking after Moonbeam's and Karma's whereabouts.

She shook her head regretfully. "Sorry, sweetie, I didn't set eyes on them at the Calling. I don't know where they'd be at. Might be they're in their tent or having a snack in the kitchen."

I hurried on, asking whomever I met and receiving similar replies. At Moonbeam and Karma's tent I scratched at the flap without getting a response, and turned toward the main building with my heart thumping a little faster.

The commune sprawled across at least eighty acres. They could be anywhere. It didn't necessarily bode ill that nobody had seen them, but after practically shadowing me for the past few days Orion was nowhere to be found either.

Dammit, I didn't like that combination one bit.

CHAPTER 12

A rapid search of the main building and kitchen did nothing but make my stomach growl and raise my anxiety level. No sign of Moonbeam, Karma, or Orion.

Turning away from the building, I pretended it was only hunger causing the hollow shaky feeling in the pit of my stomach. Shit, maybe I should have been following Orion instead of rushing off to report to Stemp.

What should I do now? How long should I search fruitlessly before sounding the alarm, and if I did need to sound an alarm, how could I do it in a way that wouldn't blow my cover with the other commune members?

I turned resolutely in the direction of the garage. One last possibility before I allowed myself to panic.

I drew a sudden breath of relief tempered with nervousness as I rounded a bend in the path and spotted Orion, Karma, and Moonbeam coming toward me. Thank God. I'd feel a lot better if Orion wasn't with them, but I'd take what I could get.

"Did you have a nice walk, dear?" Moonbeam inquired as they drew abreast. She eyed my backpack and survival knife. "Merciful Spirit, you look as though you're going to hike for a week."

"I did have a nice walk, thanks." I avoided looking at Orion. "And the backpack is only because I'm carrying my laptop with me. I thought I'd head into town and get some time at the internet café."

"Oh, I don't know if you'll be able to." Moonbeam's brow furrowed. "I think the truck has quit again, and the car hasn't been running for a couple of weeks now."

"But I just fixed the truck yesterday," I argued. "It was working fine at three o'clock."

"Oh, well, maybe I'm wrong," she said. "I don't know a thing about cars. Don't forget to write your departure time on the board in case anyone else wants to ride with you." She gave me her beatific smile. "We mustn't squander our gasoline or pollute the planet any more than necessary."

I nodded and was beginning to edge past when she laid a hand on my arm. "Actually, dear, I'm glad we ran into you. I was hoping we could have a talk."

"Come on, Orion, let's get some breakfast," Karma said in a slightly heartier voice than usual. He shot a significant look at Orion and the two of them headed down the path toward the main building.

I braced myself.

Moonbeam's china-blue gaze looked through to my soul and I fought the urge to confess every sin I'd ever committed. Damn, no wonder Stemp had such rigid self-control. If he'd learned to withstand that look as a child, even the most insistent interrogator wouldn't be able to crack him.

"You told Orion Moonjava a little fib this morning," she said at last. Her tone wasn't accusing, but shame heated my cheeks nonetheless.

"Um, yeah. I, um..." I let out a sigh, my shoulders slumping. "Yeah."

"Why, dear?" She gave me a searching look. "If you were trying to deter him sexually, it would have been better to simply be honest. 'Thanks but no thanks' is a much more respectful way to communicate your feelings, and in any case, having your period isn't a deterrent to a partner who-"

"No!" I barely resisted the urge to clamp my hands over my ears before she could enlighten me further. "No, it wasn't that, I, um..." Backed into a corner, I scrambled for an explanation. Heat rose in my face until I was sure my eyebrows were beginning to smoulder.

"Just be honest, dear," Moonbeam chided gently. "Your poor aura is almost completely subsumed by that ugly grayness."

"I was avoiding the Calling!" The words burst out before I could stop them. "I'm sorry, but I don't... believe..." The words stuck in my throat as I looked into those soft blue eyes. I took a deep breath and squared my shoulders. "I don't believe in the Earth Spirit the way you do, and the Callings are, um..." I stopped myself from saying 'a complete waste of time'.

"...not really meaningful to me," I finished instead.

"Oh." The single word was infused with such sadness that guilt twisted my heart.

"I'm sorry," I mumbled.

"There's no need to apologize for your beliefs, Storm Cloud Dancer," she said, but disappointment vibrated in her words. Her gaze looked through me again, and she reached up to lay a gentle palm against my cheek. "You're still not being completely honest," she said. "And I see fear in your aura that wasn't there before. Please tell me what's wrong. Did Orion Moonjava frighten you in some way?"

Goddamn it. I had enough trouble keeping a poker face

without any creepy aura-reading.

"No, of course not," I said, struggling to keep my aura under control, however the hell one might do that.

"Oh, Storm Cloud Dancer, don't be afraid." Moonbeam pulled me into her arms, rocking me and stroking my hair as if comforting a small child. "You're safe here. No one will harm you. Whatever evil touched you before, it can't reach you within our lands." She took my hand to touch the wooden beads of my bracelet with reverence. "Remember, dear, as long as you wear this, you're under the protection of the Earth Spirit whether you believe in it or not."

The sweetness of her concern touched my heart and I hugged her in return, her fine bones birdlike in my arms.

If Orion harmed her, I would kill him.

The matter-of-factness of that knowledge sent a shiver down my spine, and I manufactured a smile and put it on before releasing Moonbeam from the hug.

"Thank you," I said. "I'll see you later. And..." I touched her shoulder lightly, trying to find a way to warn her without blowing my cover. "Stay close to Karma, okay? You're hardly more than a mouthful for that cougar."

She chuckled. "You worry too much, dear. None of the Earth Spirit's creatures would ever harm me."

Successfully resisting the urge to tear my hair out, I smiled, nodded, and strode on down the path.

How the hell could I keep them safe when they trusted everybody? Even if I warned them, they wouldn't take me seriously. They had their wooden bracelets and their Earth Spirit to protect them.

I groaned and walked faster, welcoming the burn in my leg muscles while I powered up the hill to the garage. Next stop, Skidmark's lookout.

A few minutes later I sank down on the bench and stretched my legs out as though resting. Scrutinizing the view below me, I panned slowly from one side to the other, trying to memorize every detail.

Across the river, tiny figures marched in formation. Little glints from the marchers caught my eye and I sincerely hoped they were musical instruments for a marching band.

I snorted cynicism. Yeah, right.

Ratboy's army-style boots and misogynistic attitude likely indicated some wacko paramilitary group. They were probably over there marching with bayonets, pretending to be real men while true heroes like Kane and Hellhound quietly put their lives on the line without ever expecting thanks or recognition.

Straining my eyes, I squinted through the misty air but I couldn't see any structures other than a large tent in a clearing near their marching field. There had to be sleeping tents and latrines, but I couldn't spot them under the trees. Another long slash in the forest looked like some sort of target range. From my own target-shooting days, I recognized the foot-worn trails in the grass, widening around small structures that were probably backstops. I had never heard gunfire coming from over there, though, and I couldn't imagine Moonbeam and Karma willingly renting their land to that kind of group.

I hissed air out between my teeth. Maybe I was just too paranoid. That layout could be anything.

Shit, I should have asked Stemp to send binoculars. Too late now. The courier would already be getting on a plane.

Knotting my fists in my hair, I scrubbed my knuckles against my scalp in an attempt to rub away a tension headache that was starting too early in the day.

On our side of the river, small figures meandered along the commune's network of paths between the main building, garden, and encampment area. Tracing the pale lines of gravel, I identified Moonbeam and Karma's tent and rubbed a fist over the frown lines in my forehead.

I hadn't realized before how isolated they were. Down at the end of a twisting trail, they were nearly a quarter-mile away from the rest of the encampment. After living here most of their lives they probably valued their privacy, but that would also make them easy marks for an attack. Dammit.

Orion's and my tents were on the end of another long branch of gravel, easily identified by the large pond a hundred yards or so behind us. My forehead crunched into a frown despite the pressure of my hand.

When I had first arrived I'd been abjectly grateful for the distance and privacy until Orion's tent had been erected a couple of weeks later, but by then I'd been through the worst of the screaming nightmares. I hadn't spent much time in the rest of the encampment, and now I realized all the other tents were clustered together in a friendly village-type layout. Only ours were separate. And the gravel on our path shone brightly compared to the half-overgrown trails that made up the rest of the commune.

So I had been deliberately segregated. Gratitude warmed my heart. Stemp had said his parents understood the difficulties of recovering from traumatic stress, and that was obviously true. They had gone to considerable effort to make a private haven for me and offer comfort with no strings attached.

Guilt returned full-force. Okay, I'd get my ass to the Spirit Callings from now on and smile while I did it. It was the least I could do.

I sighed and returned to my scrutiny. To my right, the big field where we met for the Callings lay a few hundred yards off the road with an entrance at each end. I still didn't understand why we couldn't just march down the road to get to it instead of hiking twice as far along the winding forest trails, but I smothered that thought. Be respectful, dammit.

I spent the next several minutes memorizing the visible parts of the road and surrounding forest. Then I stood, stretched for the benefit of any hidden observers, and stepped into the trees behind the bench.

Scouting quietly through the forest, I identified several other viewpoints along the escarpment. One offered a wider view of the renters' land while another gave me a better look at the road, but none were as panoramic as the view from the bench.

Good to know.

I turned my feet toward Skidmark's garage at last, my stomach growling its displeasure. A glance at my watch showed it was nearing eleven o'clock, and a sudden glorious vision of a cheeseburger and fries flooded my mind.

If I went to town early I could hit the burger joint for a gut bomb instead of eating the mostly-vegetarian fare from the commune's kitchen. Drool nearly overflowed my mouth at the thought. After months of healthy eating, my grease and salt levels were critically low.

And if I went right now, I could have a beer, too. It would be okay because I'd be stone-cold sober by the time I had to drive back four hours later. My stomach emitted a whimper of eagerness.

And a milkshake for dessert. I hadn't had ice cream in four months...

I abandoned the path to crash directly through the undergrowth. Sugar, salt, fat, and booze: The four basic food groups. Ohmigod. Taste-bud orgasm, here I come.

When I panted into Skidmark's clearing shedding broken twigs and fern fragments, both vehicles sat in their usual places. The garage doors were closed and there was no sign of Skidmark.

Hurrying over to the station wagon, I tried the door and let out a small hum of satisfaction when it opened to reveal the keys in the ignition. I slid behind the wheel and twisted the key.

The starter turned over but the engine didn't catch.

Damn.

I popped the hood and strode around front to study the engine. Hoping for another simple fix, I checked the ignition wire, but it was secure on the distributor cap.

Fine, whatever. I could take the truck instead. Once I was in town I could contact Stemp and have him communicate the change to the courier.

Moments later my confidence evaporated when the truck's starter cranked over ineffectually as well.

What the hell? It had been running fine yesterday. Surely that dipshit Ratboy hadn't managed to undo all my good work.

I burrowed under the hood.

Like the car, its ignition wire was also secure. So Skidmark hadn't been messing with it this time.

Suspicion oozed into my mind.

Or had he?

Scowling, I traced the distributor wire to the first spark plug. The boot fell away in my hand, revealing an empty hole in the block. A hurried inspection revealed that all the spark plugs were missing, the boots simply resting in their cavities.

"Skidmark, if I don't get my cheeseburger and beer today, you are a fucking dead man," I muttered, and stomped over to the car.

Apparently originality wasn't his forte. Its spark plugs were missing, too.

I straightened and bellowed, "SKIDMARK!"

No reply.

A few more increasingly irritated shouts brought no answer, and I found myself feeling a moment of empathy for Ratboy. Maybe he'd needed a cheeseburger, too.

Well, fuck this. Skidmark probably wasn't walking around with sixteen spark plugs jingling in his pockets. If nothing else, it would screw up the gaps and he'd have to re-gap them all before he reinstalled them. Somehow I couldn't see him expending that kind of effort.

The garage door was locked.

"Asshole," I growled. "It's a fucking commune. Public property."

I examined the lock, but it was a sturdy deadbolt. The overhead door didn't budge when I tugged on it, either.

Whipped into junk-food-deprived indignation, I stalked around the building, studying it.

The windows were definitely the weak points. I couldn't justify breaking one, but...

A wolfish grin stretched my mouth as I examined the nearest one. Single sliding panes in a simple track system. Ha.

Carefully levering with the tip of my survival knife, I lifted the end of the pane out of the lower track. A moment later I got my fingertips wrapped around it and lifted it out. The window was only waist height, and I shed my backpack and climbed through the opening, my grin widening at the sight of sixteen blackened spark plugs lined up on the workbench with the ratchet drive and deep socket lying beside them.

You lose, old man.

I hesitated over the plugs for only a moment. The engines were both big V-8s so their gap specs were probably pretty similar. If I happened to choose the wrong set the car might run a little rough, but it would still get me to town and back with no harm to the engine. I tucked eight spark plugs carefully into my pocket, stowed the ratchet in another pocket, and climbed out again, replacing the window pane behind me.

A few minutes of work restored the plugs to their proper homes, and I gave silent thanks that sheer habit had made me lay out the wires in order when I'd removed them.

I paused, the first wire in hand.

Surely Skidmark wouldn't be devious enough to mix up the wires when he took out the plugs.

The old bastard wouldn't.

Would he?

I ground my teeth. Goddammit, if I was sabotaging an engine, I sure as hell would. With the wrong firing order the engine likely wouldn't run at all. Or if my luck was really bad, it could backfire, break a valve, and crater a piston and cylinder when the pieces fell in.

Muttering imprecations, I pushed the boots onto the plugs anyway. Only one way to find out.

When I slid into the driver's seat, I drew a deep breath, my fingers hesitating over the ignition. I'd hate to blow this poor old engine.

Cringing, I turned the key.

The starter caught immediately and the engine roared to life, idling as smoothly as a decades-old car was likely to run.

"HA!" I pumped my fist and hopped out to slam the hood and grab my backpack before returning to my triumphal throne behind the wheel. A black-smeared rag balled up on the floor of the passenger side indicated I wasn't the first person to undertake last-minute repairs, and I rubbed as much grease off my hands as possible before dropping the car into gear with a grin.

"Fuck you, old man!" I yelled out the open window, and stomped on the gas, flinging gravel across the clearing before rumbling off in a cloud of malodorous blue exhaust.

CHAPTER 13

Rattling along the gravel road with the window down, my hair swirled wildly around my head while I bellowed an off-key version of Jimmy Buffett's 'Cheeseburger In Paradise' over the roar of the rotted-out muffler.

My grin widened at the thought of Skidmark returning to the scene of the crime to find his carefully-sabotaged car gone. Ha. Let the old goat roll that up in his cigarette paper and smoke it.

Sudden realization halted my singing in mid-verse.

Shit.

Skidmark was deliberately sabotaging the vehicles.

Shit, shit, shit! What if he was working with Orion? What if he had disabled both vehicles so nobody could go for help when Orion attacked Moonbeam and Karma? What if something terrible was happening right this minute?

Had I just traded two wonderful human beings for a cheeseburger?

I slammed on the brakes, steering into the skid on the treacherous gravel. The car rocked to a stop at the side of the road in a shower of stones and I stared blindly through the windshield.

Stop panicking. Think.

I had covered nearly half of the twelve miles to town. It would take ten or fifteen minutes to get back to the commune. I had last seen Moonbeam around nine-thirty. I threw a worried scowl at my watch. Two and a half hours ago.

I swallowed hard, fear clutching my throat. What if Orion and Ratboy had been talking about attacking Moonbeam and Karma? Ratboy had said 'soon'...

Shut up. Think.

Okay, if they were making their move today, there was no reason to believe I'd get back there in time to stop them. And as Stemp had pointed out, they likely weren't planning simple murders. That meant they'd probably capture Moonbeam and Karma and hold them somewhere. Even with a trained team, eighty acres of dense forest would take a long time to search. Alone, with no thermal imaging or night-vision goggles, I didn't have a chance in hell of finding them before it was too late.

But the courier drop was still four hours away.

Four hours for Orion to do his worst.

The memory of torture-ravaged bodies rose and choked me. Fingers clenched on the wheel, I stared straight ahead and forced my shallow panting to slow.

Stay calm. Maybe Skidmark was just being a pain as usual. Maybe today wasn't the day for Orion to attack. Maybe Orion wasn't even planning to attack. Maybe he had some good reason for carrying those hand restraints.

Bullshit.

I abandoned that train of thought and tried again.

Rushing back to the commune only to find everybody fine was a waste of gasoline and nervous energy. And without the surveillance equipment, I was practically useless.

I had to go to town no matter what.

I drew a deep shaky breath and peeled my fingers loose from the steering wheel. Okay. Simple solution. Call the commune and ask for Moonbeam or Karma. If they answered, there was nothing to worry about. And I wasn't technically on the commune anymore, so nobody could object to me using a cell phone.

Heart hammering, I dug into my backpack and fumbled a phone out with cold stiff fingers.

And if nobody could find them, well, I'd just have a heart attack right here on the spot.

The sound of ringing on the other end of the line froze my fingers around the phone, its plastic case protesting my grip with a faint creak. When an unidentifiable male voice answered, it took two tries for me to force a voice from my constricted throat.

"May I speak to Moonbeam or Karma, please?"

"Hang on, I'll see if I can find them." A clunk signalled that the receiver was dangling from its cord in its low-tech version of 'on hold' while he went to search.

Long minutes ticked by. The thud-swish of my heartbeat in my ears accelerated, and I began to wonder about the state of my blood pressure.

Well, if something had happened to Moonbeam or Karma, it wouldn't matter. Stemp wouldn't let me live long enough to have a stroke.

"Hello?" Moonbeam's voice on the other end of the line released a small sob of relief from my throat.

"H-Hi..." I had to stop and swallow. "It's Ayd... Um, Storm."

Her voice went sharp with concern. "What's wrong? Where are you?"

I drew a breath and managed a normal tone. "Nothing's wrong. I'm in town but I realized I'd forgotten to ask if you needed me to pick up anything while I'm here."

"Oh." I thought I heard a breath of relief on the line before she spoke again. "Thank you, dear, but no. We got the mail yesterday, and we had a load of groceries last week. We really need very little. Have a nice time, and we'll see you later."

"Okay. Thanks." I hung up and toppled sideways onto the seat, panting and clutching my chest.

Jeez, I had to stop doing that. Getting myself all worked up over nothing. Dr. Rawling would call it catastrophic thinking.

I hauled myself upright again, trembling. But Dr. Rawling had never rushed into a butcher shop to find the man he loved hanging from a meat hook.

I shook my head and gave my cheeks a couple of not-too-vigorous slaps. So much wrong with that thought.

In the first place, it was inaccurate syntax or gender or something. I was pretty sure Dr. Rawling was heterosexual.

In the second place, I had no reason to believe Orion would torture Moonbeam and Karma. Hell, I didn't even know if he posed any kind of threat to them. Maybe those hand restraints were for somebody else entirely. Like me, for instance.

There was a cheerful thought. Not.

And anyway, Kane wasn't the man I loved. Well, okay, he was *a* man I loved. But not *loved*-loved. Not the get-married kind of love. And anyway, even if I wanted that, I didn't know if he was dead or alive right now.

"Shut up," I said aloud, and put the car in gear again.

My cheeseburger and beer were delicious, but they had lost some of their appeal. Even a thick chocolate milkshake failed to salve my nagging anxiety. At the internet café I plugged in my laptop and cell phone and pretended to work, watching the clock's hands crawl around the remaining couple of hours with agonizing slowness.

At last they approached four o'clock and I abandoned any pretense of productivity, staring blankly out the window at the parking lot. A fresh-faced young man wearing a bright scarf strode briskly from car to car, delving into his bulky shoulder bag for flyers and tucking one under each windshield wiper, but there was no sign of anybody carrying a box.

Four o'clock on the dot.

I frowned at the driveway, but no new vehicles drove up. Where the hell was the courier? Shit, I hoped the flyer guy didn't notice him when he arrived. Maybe the courier was delaying until the parking lot was completely devoid of people.

The flyer guy sauntered toward the station wagon, brochures in hand. He tucked one under the wiper of the SUV beside it, then casually swung open the rear door of the station wagon and deposited his bag inside. Pulling another handful of flyers from the bag, he strolled off, leaving the door open while he finished his advertising blitz and returned a couple of times for more flyers.

Then he closed my car door leaving the bag inside and strode away without a backward glance.

I sank my aching head into my hands.

I couldn't believe Stemp had entrusted me with his parents' safety. What a pathetic excuse for an agent. Hell, I hadn't even spotted the courier until he made the drop right in front of my nose. What obvious clues was I missing at the commune?

Trying to redeem at least some measure of professionalism, I dawdled over the fictitious document on my laptop for another twenty minutes to make sure nobody connected me with the flyer kid.

My lips twisted into a sour smile. Even if they did connect us, they'd probably think I was his mother helping him with his delivery job. If only I had one-tenth the deviousness in Stemp's twisty brain. He was the consummate spy; always calculating his moves three steps ahead of everybody else.

I sighed and packed up my laptop and phone. Maybe you just had to be born that way.

On the way out of town I made a discreet stop at the recycling depot and ditched the burner phones I'd used to contact Stemp. Moving over to the paper-recycling bin, I scanned one of the flyers before dumping them, too. They advertised a work-from-home internet marketing opportunity; exactly the kind of nuisance brochure people would glance at and promptly throw away. But no doubt it would be a valid website, at least for a few days.

Behind the concealment of the bin I examined the remaining contents of the courier's bag. My new gear was tucked neatly into a rugged-looking black plastic box in the bottom of the bag, and a quick survey of its contents made me breathe a sigh of relief at the sight of a typed sheet with 'Hi from Spider! Miss you!' scribbled at the bottom along with a smiley face.

Thank God, Spider had sent me a cheat-sheet with instructions for the night-vision webcam and headset. I made a mental note to do something nice for my favourite techno-geek when I got home.

There were binoculars in the box, too, along with a bird book. Built-in cover story. Thank you, Stemp. Some more burner phones were packed at the bottom, along with a spare laptop battery, the tranquilizer pistol, and a couple of magazines loaded with trank darts.

Giving quiet thanks that the rest of my team was more competent than I was, I took my spare phones, ammo, and holsters out of my backpack and tucked them into the waterproof box with the other gear before hitting the road.

About five miles out of town I pulled over and pressed the speed dial on a secured phone. When Stemp answered I said, "It's Aydan. I got the drop. Thanks, and please tell Spider thanks for the instructions, too. I just wanted to tell you I'm pretty sure Skidmark is sabotaging the commune vehicles. I know you said he's harmless, but it could be dangerous if anybody ever had to leave in an emergency."

"Are you sure it's intentional?" Stemp inquired. "Skidmark isn't exactly known for his intellectual prowess. And those vehicles were old and unreliable when I was a teenager."

"True, but yesterday I caught him purposely disconnecting the ignition wire on the truck, and today all the spark plugs were taken out and locked up in the garage. I don't know; it just seems suspicious to me."

"Very well." If Stemp had actually been human, I might have suspected that he'd sighed before continuing, "I likely have blind spots where the commune is concerned, so I'll defer to you. Shall I put Skidmark on the suspect list?"

"N... well, maybe..." I trailed off, thinking. "He's been there an awfully long time. You'd think if he was going to harm your mom and dad he'd have done it a long time ago... but..."

"But people change. And we both know better than to trust blindly." Stemp sounded weary. "I'll consider him a suspect."

"Should I tell your mom and dad what he's doing?"

It was his turn to hesitate. "Perhaps..." he said slowly. "If you can phrase it in a non-confrontational way. After all, Skidmark isn't a young man anymore. Decades of recreational drugs... It might be some drug-induced mental issue, or even dementia. Feel them out; see if they think he's changed in any way."

"Okay. I guess that's it, then."

"Very well. I'll wait for your next report."

About a quarter-mile outside the gates of the commune, I pulled the car over beside the road where I knew it would be invisible from Skidmark's bench. Extracting the waterproof box, I stuffed the empty courier's bag into my backpack and then stood studying my surroundings for a few moments.

A large rock jutting up beside the road made a helpful marker, and I struck out from it at right angles to the road, twenty long paces into the forest. There I halted and took stock. My hiding place didn't have to be perfect. The chances of somebody walking by it in the next few hours were slim to none, and I'd collect the box under cover of darkness.

I hefted it irritably. Another trip out into the damn woods in the middle of the night. But I didn't dare try to smuggle anything into my tent in broad daylight.

I sighed and selected a likely-looking fallen log. Digging my fingers into the moss at its base, I lifted the moist green blanket and stowed the box in the hollow it created. Then I draped the moss over top again and stepped back to survey my handiwork.

Good enough to pass casual inspection. I retraced my steps to the station wagon and slid behind the wheel.

A few minutes later I rumbled into Skidmark's clearing braced for a confrontation, but it was deserted as before. A quick inspection revealed that the garage was still locked, and I stood weighing the ratchet in my hand for a moment.

Then I turned back to the car, grinning.

If Skidmark liked playing with spark plugs that much, who was I to deprive him? I'd just put everything back in the garage exactly the way I'd found it.

The first spark plug turned reluctantly and I almost abandoned the idea. Normally I wouldn't take spark plugs out of a hot block. If I broke one off, it'd be a hell of a job to get it out.

But there was so much old oil on these ones, they came out slowly but surely. I transferred them one by one out of the socket's rubber insert and into the greasy rag, using it to keep from burning my fingers.

A few minutes of work gleaned all eight plugs, and I returned each empty boot to its allotted cavity and closed the hood. I was crossing the clearing with my rag full of spark plugs when the crunch of gravel under booted feet announced Ratboy's arrival.

When he caught sight of me a flush suffused his neck and his brows snapped together.

I took a rapid mental inventory.

Ratchet in my hand. Not an ideal weapon, but he'd

notice if I nailed him in the head with it.

Glock in my ankle holster, but nowhere to hide Ratboy's body. Oh, and shooting him would blow my cover. Technicalities.

Skidmark might come if I yelled for help, but I wouldn't want to count on that.

"You," Ratboy ground out.

His conversational gambit wasn't followed by 'whore', so I waited.

Apparently he was attempting reasonable behaviour. "Is the truck running?" he inquired tightly.

"No, Skidmark took the spark plugs out of it." I gestured cautiously with my greasy handful.

"You will put them back in now."

It wasn't a request.

I got a stranglehold on my temper and kept my voice even. "I don't have time just now. You go ahead." I proffered the rag in his direction.

His face went crimson. "You stupid wh-" He drew a breath, glowering. "How?"

I laid the rag and ratchet on the ground. "Eight wires. Eight plugs. Figure it out," I snapped. "And don't mix up the wires."

I turned back toward the car, ears open for the scuffle of gravel that would indicate an incoming attack. Instead, I heard the clink of ceramic and an exclamation that was probably a curse.

"Be careful, they're hot," I added.

I ignored the resulting torrent of incomprehensible invective and kept a close eye on him while I retrieved my backpack from the car, but he seemed to have decided to tackle the job instead of tackling me. When I left he was bent over the truck engine and the busy metallic chirping of the ratchet indicated he'd figured out where the spark plugs went.

Halfway down the road to the commune, I hesitated. I likely should have emphasized the importance of the firing ord-

A thunderous backfire made me wince.

Yep, should've explained the firing order. Probably not a good time to bring it up now.

I hiked on at a brisk pace, flinching when more backfires exploded behind me.

Come on, dumbfuck, don't keep torturing that poor engine. Surely by now you've figured out something's wrong.

Apparently he was a slow learner. The sound of backfires followed me all the way to my tent. At last they ceased, replaced by the sound of distant shouting.

I dropped my backpack on my cot, assumed my best innocent expression, and headed for the main building.

CHAPTER 14

I didn't dawdle in the kitchen. I had a feeling Ratboy might be a little cranky and I wasn't in the mood to find out for sure.

Moonbeam and Karma were eating at a table in the corner, and I exhaled relief at the sight of them as I slapped together a couple of sandwiches. Orion strode in just as I was packing up, and I offered him a noncommittal wave and headed for the door. When I glanced back, he was joining Moonbeam and Karma.

That didn't exactly reassure me.

But who knew, maybe he was just one of those people who couldn't bear to be alone. If he wasn't shadowing me, he'd latch onto them instead.

I really hoped it was that harmless. But I didn't believe it.

Casting a wary glance around me as I left the building, I took the winding path toward the garden. As soon as I was concealed from the building by a couple of bends, I stepped off the path and struck out through the forest toward higher ground.

When I discovered a vantage point that gave me a view of the main building, I found a moderately dry stump and hunkered down on it to wait. Munching my sandwiches, I watched the commune members coming and going from their supper until at last Karma and Moonbeam came out, Orion trailing them like a faithful puppy.

Or a hungry predator.

I pulled my jacket tighter around me to still my sudden shiver.

When they moved out of sight I rose and charted a parallel course, moving through the forest as quietly as possible and staying out of sight. I glimpsed them again at the fork in the path, where Moonbeam and Karma headed for their tent while Orion continued on alone.

Perfect.

I withdrew to watch as Moonbeam and Karma disappeared inside their tent. When they didn't reappear after several minutes, I found a fallen log and made myself as comfortable as its moist surface would allow. Keeping half an eye on the tent, I let my mind drift while I idly whittled a stick I'd picked up.

As soon as I could start using my new equipment, my surveillance would be much easier. I'd have to make a cache closer to my tent, though. Hiking a couple of miles every time I needed something wasn't practical.

And I needed to figure out how to get the tracer onto Orion. And where exactly I could place it.

I knifed a vicious gouge in the stick. Dammit, if I hadn't chickened out this morning, I could have had full access to him. Lots of excuses to touch him and plant the tracing device at the same time. Or I could have given him some fond little handmade gift and asked him to carry it with him and think of me.

Instead I'd driven him away, and it would be pretty

implausible to cozy up to him now.

I gouged off a few more chunks of wood, taking satisfaction in the razor-sharpness of my knife.

But would it truly be implausible to cozy up? Could I claim I'd had time to think and I'd changed my mind?

Orion had that slightly cocky air. He'd probably believe I found him irresistible. But if I went that route, I'd have to find a way to discourage him from following me around. He was persistent enough as it was. After we did the horizontal mambo he'd be damn near unshakeable.

Unless I turned out to be such a disappointment in bed that he didn't want anything more to do with me.

I sighed and turned up the collar of my jacket against the chilly breeze that always seemed to spring up around twilight.

I probably couldn't just lie there like a blow-up doll. If he was any good at all, my body would give me away. A hot tingle from my perfidious body reminded me exactly how good his lips had felt.

Nope, 'unresponsive' wasn't going to work.

I sliced off some more wood shavings.

Okay, ignore 'how' for now and concentrate on 'where'.

Where could I place the tracing device so it would stay on him at all times? Sticking it onto an article of clothing would only work as long as he didn't change clothes. If I stuck it to his wristwatch he might notice it. The device was tiny but not invisible, and wristwatches tended to get looked at a lot.

I whittled the end of my stick into a point, then rounded it off, squinting in the fading daylight.

What did he take everywhere with him, but wouldn't examine too closely?

I carved a notch in the stick, rounding it into a bead before beginning another notch farther down the stick while I pondered.

Then I bolted upright, stifling a triumphant cry. Wooden beads. Of course. He never let the Earth Spirit's bracelet leave his wrist.

My shoulders slumped as the corollary occurred to me. He never let the Earth Spirit's bracelet leave his wrist. So how the hell could I plant the transmitter on it?

I considered and discarded several other ideas including slipping the transmitter into a sandwich and letting him eat it, but that seemed unnecessarily risky. Who knew if the electronics could withstand stomach acid? And it would be bad if he bit down on it, or if it poisoned him.

And it would only work for a day or two. After that I'd be monitoring the latrine. A grin sneaked onto my lips. This too shall pass...

I sobered. No; the bracelet was still the best option I had so far.

Hauling myself to my feet with a sigh, I straightened my aching back slowly after my long immobility in the damp chill. First I'd look at the actual transmitter and see if I got any brilliant ideas. I couldn't tag him tonight anyway; it would be too late by the time I finished up and got back to my tent.

Another damn late night.

I stretched and rubbed my cold damp butt before hunkering down again. Three hours to kill, and then I'd make my move. Until then, this was the best place for me. I didn't want to encounter Orion until I'd decided whether to seduce him, and as long as Moonbeam and Karma stayed in their tent I'd guard them. Hard on my body, but easier on my nerves.

By the time ten P.M. rolled around, the moon was nowhere to be seen under thick cloud cover and my imagination had conjured so many cougars from the quiet sounds of the pitch-black forest that it had taken all the self-control I possessed to keep from fleeing pell-mell to the warm glow of Moonbeam and Karma's tent. Shivering, I coaxed my knees to unlock from their bent position.

I stuffed my icy fingers into my armpits for a few moments of warmth before withdrawing my little LED flashlight from my waist pouch. Time to pick up my equipment.

A quick flash of my light on the ground ahead; a couple of steps; wait; listen. Then do it again. And again. Moving with agonizing slowness, I worked my way around the encampment, freezing every time I heard a voice.

At last I made it to the road but the darkness was so profound my tiny light barely reached beyond my feet. I sighed and rotated my shoulders, trying to release the knots of cold and tension. I didn't dare leave my light on. A few small flashes of light might be dismissed as fireflies, but I didn't want curious eyes tracking a moving light source down the road.

When I thought I might be getting close to my cache at last, I dared to shine my light more frequently.

Nothing looked familiar in the blackness. Where the hell was my jutting rock? Had I passed it? How much farther should I walk before doubling back to try again?

But distances always seemed farther in the dark. I probably wasn't there yet.

Shit, why didn't I at least have a phone with a GPS? I could have just memorized the coordinates this afternoon and then walked directly back.

Stealthy rustling made me whirl to peer blindly behind me, my heart pounding, my tiny light devoured by the night. Resting my hand on my knife hilt, I clenched my teeth and walked on. Why the hell hadn't I taken my shoulder holster out of the box before I stowed it? I didn't dare carry my gun drawn in case someone with night vision was watching me.

Okay, I really wished I hadn't thought of that. Now my back crawled with the expectation of bullets as well as teeth and claws.

Abandoning caution, I kept my light on, its feeble glow barely illuminating the roadside.

Shit, what if its light didn't reach the rock? Was I doomed to shuffle along this godforsaken road until dawn?

I was about to turn back and try another pass when my light slid over the welcome contours of the rock at last. Gulping down a sob of relief, I took my twenty paces and dropped to my knees beside the fallen log.

My jaw cracked with the release of strained muscles when I opened my mouth to grip my flashlight between my teeth. After a quick re-reading of Spider's instructions, I selected the thermographic/night vision headset and secured it around my head.

The details of the forest sprang into visibility and relief turned my knees to jelly. I slumped down to sit trembling on the log despite its icy wetness. Thank God, at last a respite from the horrible sense of blind helplessness.

Flipping the headset switch, I briefly altered the view to thermal-only and drew my first full breath in what seemed like days. No large heat sources prowling in my vicinity.

Thank God.

Switching back to night vision, I leaned my elbows on my knees and let my head hang, easing out my tension in long shaky breaths.

When my heart finally eased its pounding, I drew a few more slow calming breaths before scanning around me one more time. The forest remained reassuringly unpopulated, and I repacked the box and tucked it under my arm before stepping out to the edge of the road.

My return trip seemed ridiculously short by comparison, the headset showing everything so clearly I felt as though I was walking in murky green-tinted daylight. I flipped occasionally to full-thermal mode, scanning around me and in the direction of Skidmark's bench, but no warm bodies showed themselves.

Inside the commune the occupied tents glowed in my viewer, and I circled confidently around the encampment to approach Orion's and my tents from behind. Both were cold and dark, and I stopped several yards away and lowered the box to the ground to stand thinking.

Where the hell could I stash the box? I hadn't considered the difficulty of creating a concealed cache until now.

If I was out in the middle of the woods I could simply dig a hole, drag a log over it, and walk away. But people wandered everywhere in the commune, not necessarily sticking to the paths. And with no corporate rat-race to preoccupy their minds, they tended to be observant. I'd be hooped if someone noticed disturbed vegetation and started investigating.

Hands on hips, I scowled around me. Rocks, trees, moss, and ferns.

Shit.

Okay, I could either put it so far away that nobody was likely to stumble on it, or keep it so close that nobody would invade my privacy.

Leaving it far away was just asking for trouble. If I needed this stuff, I was likely to need it in a hurry.

It would have been nice to bury it inside my tent, but the raised wooden floor prevented that.

Double-shit.

I paced in widening circles, searching for a place where I could easily conceal the signs of my digging.

No good options presented themselves, and I swore quietly. The fallen logs were either too big to move or too small to hide a hole. The open areas would show footprints and freshly-disturbed dirt, and the mossy areas would reveal the disturbance in a few days when the moss died after being uprooted.

Dammit.

I zigzagged back and forth all the way to the edge of the pond without finding an appropriate spot for a cache. The frogs fell silent as I approached and I trudged over to stand staring out over the dark water. After a few minutes of deep and futile thought I sighed and sank down on my favourite rock by the water's edge, clutching the box with mounting anxiety.

What the hell was I going to do? If I got caught with this stuff, my cover would be completely blown. If Orion caught me with it there was a good chance I wouldn't survive the encounter, and if anybody else saw it I'd be in deep shit for revealing classified technology.

A silvery vee disturbed the surface of the water, and the enhanced vision of my headset revealed a beaver gliding through the water on some nocturnal errand.

I sighed, the peaceful scene doing nothing to soothe my tension. Where could I...

Wait a minute.

The box was fully waterproof.

I scrambled down from the rock, my heart pounding with hope. Hurrying back the way I'd come, I flipped to thermal vision momentarily and drew a breath of relief when no heat signature showed in Orion's tent.

Thank you, technology.

Inside my own tent, I took the webcam and tracking system out of the box and tucked them into one of the big flap pockets of my jacket, then frowned at the rest of the gear. What else would I need?

More to the point, what could I keep hidden on my body at all times?

A couple more secured phones went into my pocket. Then I closed the box, making sure the lid was firmly seated on its rubber gasket, and exchanged my hiking boots for high-topped rubber ones before plodding back to the pond. After only a few minutes of searching I discovered the perfect hiding place: a fallen tree beside an overhanging rock.

Cringing at the icy contact of the water and the instinctive fear of putting my hands in a dark recess, I fought the buoyancy of the plastic box, forcing it down and under the rock and tree.

When I was sure it was firmly wedged, I rose and surveyed my hiding place. It seemed completely hidden now, but I was viewing it in the dark with night vision. Who knew what would be visible in broad daylight?

Still, it was the best I could do. And other people rarely came here. There was a much nicer view of the river on the other side of the commune.

I let out a breath and glanced at my watch. Ten minutes to midnight. Finally my day was done. I moved cautiously back toward my tent, trying not to step on any twigs and scanning frequently for heat signatures as I drew nearer. After all my caution, it would really suck if Orion caught me walking around wearing my night-vision headset.

There was no sign of him, though, and his tent was cold and dark.

Made it. Home free.

I ducked into my tent and had just removed my boots when a sudden thought made me straighten with alarm.

Orion was gone and it was the middle of the night. Where was he, and what was he doing?

Maybe he was sharing someone else's bed.

Or maybe he had night vision equipment, too, and he'd simply been waiting for me to abandon my post at Moonbeam and Karma's tent before making his move.

Shit, shit, shit!

I stuffed my feet into my hiking boots and ran.

CHAPTER 15

Heart pounding, I blessed my night-vision headset despite its thumping against my forehead while I dashed along the winding trail.

Near the turnoff to Moonbeam and Karma's tent, I abandoned the path to hurry through the intervening forest, panting through my mouth and trying to balance maximum speed against minimum noise.

As I approached, a steadily-mounting sound slowed my feet. What the hell was that?

A moment later I identified it.

Snoring.

I crept closer until my thermal imaging showed the warm glow of an occupied tent. Even at that distance, Karma's raucous snores rattled the forest, and a giggle of giddy relief escaped me.

Thank God.

And omigod, what a racket. No wonder their tent was so far from the rest of the commune.

I drew a long breath and let it out slowly as I faded back toward the path, a euphoric grin on my lips. My charges were safe.

And moving through the dark forest was so easy with

night vision. I felt great. Wide awake. Competent. Practically invincible. Look out, Jane Bond. Aydan Kelly will kick your skinny little ass.

I knew it was only an adrenaline reaction, but what the hell; I might as well take advantage of it. Until it burned out of my system I wouldn't be able to sleep anyway.

I turned toward Skidmark's hill. Time to check the layout of the renters' encampment.

On my way up, I trod cautiously beside the road instead of letting my boots crunch on the gravel. Other than my accidental discovery of the marijuana patch, I had never snooped around Skidmark's domain so I had no idea where his tent might be. If he caught me poking around up here I couldn't exactly claim I was going up to the bench to enjoy the view in the pitch darkness.

Several times I switched to thermal-only and scanned around me, but I saw only a few tiny glows that were likely slumbering squirrels. My euphoria mounted. For the first time in days I felt perfectly safe.

I pumped my fist, grinning in the darkness.

Perched on the bench a few minutes later, I surveyed the encampment across the river in night vision. Bathed in light, a single figure strode back and forth, gesticulating occasionally, but at that distance I couldn't make out much other detail.

I switched to thermal-only and frowned. Orderly rows of human-shaped glows were arrayed in front of the spotlighted figure. Okay, so it was a speaker addressing an assembly. But at one AM?

I rubbed my forehead where the headset was beginning to dig in. Maybe they had some counterpart to the unreasonable Earth Spirit that demanded attention at all hours of the day and night.

But their assembly was far more orderly than our haphazard gatherings. Rank and file were in perfect alignment and if I squinted and used my imagination the orientation of the glows looked like soldiers at parade rest.

I transferred my attention to the rest of the encampment, but thermal imaging revealed only a few hot spots stationed inside and around the main tent.

As I watched, the assembled company began to scatter at a leisurely pace. The movement reminded me of the way the Earth Spirit gatherings ended, with people drifting away in twos and threes. A steady flow trickled toward the main tent and a couple of other destinations that were probably latrines.

Gradually the activity settled down, the glows distributing themselves and becoming stationary as if retiring to their tents. Only a few stragglers remained.

Sudden interest straightened my spine. One of the glows had split off from the main encampment. As I watched, it crept across the landscape, giving the other glows a wide berth and heading toward the river.

Toward the commune.

I flipped to night vision, squinting in an attempt to locate the bridge. It was too dark to get a clear view at that distance, but I was pretty sure the glow was in the right vicinity.

I blew out a breath and switched back to thermal.

By now the intruder was definitely on commune land. Tension strung my muscles as the glow approached the far-flung heat signature of Moonbeam and Karma's tent, but it didn't turn in that direction.

Instead, it moved purposefully onward.

Toward my tent.

Sucking in a breath, I switched to combined vision. The intruder's glow wasn't on the paleness of the gravel path. Instead, it followed a parallel course. Sneaking along in the undergrowth, just as I had done.

Shit, had Ratboy decided to pay me a little visit and settle the score?

I watched, barely breathing even though he couldn't possibly hear me at that distance.

He slowed as he approached my tent and I imagined him creeping through the undergrowth, careful not to wake me. Then he stopped beside my tent.

Perched on the very edge of the bench, I stared until my eyes watered. What was he doing?

At last he moved, avoiding the gravel path as before. Then he went into Orion's tent.

What the hell was Ratboy doing in there? Was he looking for something to pilfer?

The heat signature moved around the tent for a few minutes, then settled into immobility.

I leaned slowly back on the bench, letting out a breath. That wasn't Ratboy. It was Orion, going to bed. I should have realized it right away by his lack of hesitation entering the tent.

So Orion had been lurking outside my tent again.

And consorting with the renters, even though he'd claimed to know nothing about them.

Before I could ponder the ramifications of that, the distant scuff of footsteps on gravel made me spin, then shield my eyes from the combined glare of heat and light.

Somebody was coming with a flashlight.

Lifting my headset for a brief unaided glance, I saw only

a few slivers of light glimmering through the trees. Whoever it was, they wouldn't have seen me yet. I repositioned the headset and hurried as quietly as possible into woods, cutting down the slope at a diagonal.

Looking back, I could see the light moving through the trees but couldn't make out its bearer. The bright spot stopped near the bench and the beam darted about for a few moments before going still. I eased behind the concealment of a big cedar and peeked out to see Skidmark backlit by the flashlight he'd laid on the bench. As I watched, he unzipped his pants and assumed a wide-legged stance.

Really didn't need to watch that.

I ducked back behind the tree before turning to creep step by step down the hill, placing my feet with care and keeping to the heaviest cover I could find.

When I neared our tents at last I took a parallel course to our gravelled path. The heat signature inside Orion's tent stayed motionless, and as I ghosted closer I heard a faint snore.

Easing out a breath, I crept into my tent and secured the flap behind me. Then I removed the headset from my aching head and fell onto my cot. My mind buzzed with adrenaline and unanswered questions.

What the hell had Orion been doing over on the renters' property? Was this the first time he'd gone over, his curiosity sparked by my questions? Or had he been visiting regularly, taking part along with Ratboy in some activity he didn't want to admit to me? It sure looked that way.

Damn, I had to figure out a way to get that tracer onto his Earth Spirit bracelet.

But how?

Seducing him would get me close to him, but then what

was I going to do? Ask him to hold out his wrist and close his eyes?

And if we were rolling around in the throes of passion, real or faked, it was going to be damn hard to hide the tracer on my own body in the first place and then transfer it without him noticing. Not to mention I couldn't carry my gun if I was planning to get naked.

I needed to somehow get him to hold still and close his eyes. And keep him from noticing that I was fumbling at his wrist.

My mind lit with a brief but delicious vision of a naked Orion, blindfolded while I tied his wrists to the bed. I shook myself back to reality. Not exactly plausible for a woman who'd been 'not ready for sex' to suddenly morph into a sultry dominatrix.

Though it would be fun...

Jeez, cut it out.

I tried to force my tired mind to focus, but it was no use. Maybe tomorrow I'd come up with some brilliant plan.

I hauled myself upright and bent to unlace my hiking boots.

Boots.

I straightened slowly, the idea curving my lips into a grin.

Like everybody else, he wore his hiking boots every day. As far as I knew he only had one pair.

My heart rate accelerated. Now was a perfect time. It was the middle of the night, and he'd been up late. He should be sound asleep.

And maybe, if I was really lucky, he might have left his boots close to the tent flap. I eyed my own tent speculatively. At least fifteen feet across. That was a lot of floor area to cover, and belly-crawling around Orion's tent looking for boots in the dark didn't appeal to me in the least. That'd be an interesting conversation if he woke up: 'What are you doing in my tent?' 'Um, sleep-crawling...?'

But maybe I wouldn't have to search in person.

My energy renewed, I fired up my laptop and plugged the webcam's remote port into it. Easing the tiny wireless camera out my tent flap, I panned over to Orion's tent, watching the view on my laptop. The resolution wasn't as good as my night-vision headset, but it didn't need to be. I only needed to be able to identify boots.

Next step: a camera boom.

A quick survey of my tent turned up nothing as long and thin as I needed. Blowing out a breath of annoyance, I donned the night-vision headset again and slipped out of my tent to head for the pond. A couple of slender branches of red dogwood fell to my knife, and I stripped off the leaves and twigs before retreating to my tent once more.

One last thing.

My sigh turned into a yawn, fatigue coiling into an aching ball between my shoulder blades. If only I could leave this until tomorrow night. But I didn't dare postpone it.

Extracting the tiny tracer device and its handheld tracking unit, I powered up the tracking unit and nodded weary satisfaction at the blinking red dot that overlaid its origin coordinates.

Fine; at least it was working.

I lashed the webcam to the tip of one of the dogwood branches with a short length of dental floss before gathering up my gear. Then I tucked the night-vision headset into my pocket and headed for my tent flap.

Showtime.

Creeping toward Orion's tent, my hands quivered with exhaustion and nerves. The glow of my laptop's screen lit the night around me. God, please let Orion be a heavy sleeper. If I got caught, this would be just as hard to explain as crawling around in his tent.

But at least I wouldn't get caught wearing the night-vision headset. I'd look like a sleazy pathetic voyeur, but not a spy.

I grimaced in the darkness. You know you're making the wrong life choices when your most fervent desire is to look like a pathetic sleazebag.

Lowering myself to a crouch outside his tent flap I eased my dogwood camera boom toward the opening. Inside, his snores continued in a gentle rhythm, and I tried to calm myself by matching my breathing to it.

One more inch...

The webcam slid under the tent flap and I surveyed my computer screen. Shit, I was looking at the floor. Carefully rotating the dogwood, I tried to get my bearings as the interior of Orion's tent panned by in grainy green and black.

His cot was against the opposite wall. He slept shirtless, his chiselled features relaxed, one muscular arm tucked under his head, the other draped across his chest. I tore my gaze away from the smooth curves of his biceps and continued to scan.

Dammit, where were his boots?

When I finally spotted them, I nearly let out a cry of triumph. Right next to the tent flap. Thank heaven for tidy bad guys.

Manoeuvring the camera carefully, I studied the boots. I'd love to tuck the locator under the insole. But that would mean I'd have to actually reach in and grab a boot. They were close to the tent flap, but not that close.

And I'd have to open the tent flap to pull one out. I didn't know about Orion, but I knew for damn sure that if it was me I'd wake instantly at the sound of rustling canvas.

I eased out a breath. Dammit.

Some more covert camera work revealed no safe place to stick my little tracing device on the outside of the boots. If he was tramping through heavy undergrowth, it would get wiped off.

My right leg cramped suddenly and I stretched my mouth wide in a silent scream, rising as quietly as possible out of my crouch to stretch the offending muscle.

Goddammit, I was frozen to the bone and every muscle in my body ached with tension. Time to finish up and get out.

Wincing, I hunkered down again and manipulated my camera one more time. At last an idea penetrated my exhausted brain. Those boots had nice padded tongues. And he'd left them loosened but still laced up. He'd never notice my tiny tracer tucked between the tongue and the eyelets.

Withdrawing my camera, I used the light of the laptop screen to illuminate my work while I split the end of my second dogwood stick and wedged the tiny tracer into it.

The tracer immediately began to ease out under the pressure of the moist wood. I pressed it back in again, watching and counting the seconds.

Ten seconds. I had ten seconds before it popped out of the stick, to be lost forever in the gaps between Orion's floorboards. And not only that, but I had to place it one-handed while I guided the camera with the other hand. Great. Fabulous.

I clenched my teeth and slid the camera back into the

tent, then did a trial run with the empty stick.

Yes, it was possible. But by no means easy.

A sudden cessation of snoring and the rustle of Orion's sleeping bag froze my heart in my chest.

CHAPTER 16

Paralyzed, I crouched helplessly outside Orion's tent, clutching my sticks and waiting to be discovered. Running was out of the question. If I made the slightest sound he'd get up to see what it was. I didn't even dare rotate my webcam to see what was happening.

Please, please, don't let him open his eyes and see the glow of my laptop outside his tent flap...

Eternity passed.

When the thumping in my ears reached deafening levels and my vision began to fade, I drew a breath at last.

Still no sound from inside the tent.

The cramp returned, twisting my leg muscles into a screaming knot.

At last the glorious sound of a snore ended my torment. Stifling whimpers, I carefully withdrew my sticks before rising to stretch out my leg, massaging the knot and hoping the sound of my hands rubbing denim wouldn't wake Orion.

He snored on reassuringly, and I steeled myself.

One chance.

Don't screw it up.

I inserted the camera stick again with shaking hands, laying it on the ground while I pulled the backing off the tracer's adhesive. Then I drew a deep breath and exhaled slowly. Just like shooting in a tournament. Master the adrenaline.

A couple more breaths slowed my pulse and steadied my hands.

Inhale. Exhale half-way.

I watched my hands tuck the tracer into its little notch and insert the stick smoothly into the tent flap. A quick peek with the camera, a little dip of the stick, and the tracer dropped into the crease beside the boot's tongue.

Staring at my monitor, I angled the camera this way and that, but I couldn't spot the tracer inside the boot. Either I'd succeeded in sticking it where I wanted it or it had fallen all the way into the boot. No way to tell.

At least if it had fallen into the boot, he likely wouldn't realize what it was. A small irritating pebble; a quick shake of his boot before he put it on; and that would be the end of my tracer. If I was really lucky I might be able to salvage it from the floor of his tent after he left and try again.

But in the meantime, I'd hope for the best and get my ass out of there before I got caught.

The short traverse to my tent felt interminable as I crept quivering through the cold darkness step by cautious step. Back in my tent at last, I stowed my gear, pulled off my boots, and fell into bed fully clothed.

An irritating sound nagged at the edges of my consciousness. I groaned and flapped my arm in the direction of my alarm clock, but I failed to find a clock or silence the noise.

"Storm!" Orion's voice bolted me upright, blinking

stupidly. "You're not sick again, are you?" There was probably good-natured teasing in his tone but the humour was lost on me, drowned out by the clanging of the Spirit bells.

"I'm fine," I mumbled. "Coming."

Staggering out of bed, I scrubbed both hands over my face to remove any traces of nocturnal drool. My tent was bright with daylight and a glance at my watch assured me that it was nearly eight AM.

Just over four hours of sleep. Fuck my life.

I pulled on my jacket and plodded out.

Orion's smile dissolved into concern at the sight of me. "Are you sure you're not sick?" he asked. "You look terrible."

"Oooh, flattery; thanks," I snarled. "I'm great. Fan-fucking-tastic. All I need is a nice brisk run on an empty stomach while the f-" I stifled a second f-bomb. "...while the Earth Spirit tries to explode my brain with those fucking bells."

I sighed. I should probably be proud that only two f-bombs had slipped out, and not as a description of the Earth Spirit.

"Come on," I added and jogged down the path, leaving him standing behind me looking uncertain.

A few moments later he caught up to run beside me. "Storm, are you mad at me? I'm sorry, I didn't mean to insult you, I just meant-"

"I'm not mad," I interrupted. "Just tired. Had a crummy sleep."

"Oh."

He didn't sound convinced, but he dropped it. We jogged the rest of the way in silence, and I accepted my mat from Aurora and headed for my assigned floor space.

The gong roused me from a bizarre dream involving tapioca pudding and a purple chainsaw, and from the disapproving looks I received from the other commune members I gathered I'd been snoring. Shuffling out behind the rest of the group, I tried to convert my expression from mutinous to apologetic.

As we wound silently through the forest, my foul mood began to dissipate. Shafts of sunlight filtered through the forest canopy, gilding the leaves and ferns. A riot of birdsong floated on the pearly air and the spicy aroma of cedar completed the sensory feast.

Drawing a deep delicious breath, I eased the lingering tension out of my shoulders and began to plan my day.

As soon as I was unobserved I'd check to see if my tracking device was working. If it was, I'd have one less thing to worry about. Then I'd take a nice innocent ramble through the forest with my binoculars and bird book, ending up at Skidmark's bench.

When we arrived at the field I filed obediently to my assigned quadrant. Kneeling, I continued my deliberations.

After I finished evaluating the renters' territory I'd continue my exploration and find some alternate routes to use while reporting to Stemp. I'd been lucky so far, but I wouldn't tempt fate by continuing to use the same route every time.

But first some breakfast.

My stomach growled at the same time Aurora brayed, "The blessings of the Earth Spirit are upon you". I mumbled the prescribed response and rose to wander back to the main building, still deep in thought.

After my report to Stemp was completed I wasn't sure what I should do. Continue to track Orion, certainly, but maybe I should search his tent, too. I blew out a breath.

If I was a real agent I'd have a plan already, along with contingency plans depending on what I discovered. Meanwhile, I'd better make sure Orion didn't have any reason to suspect me.

"Hey, Storm."

I managed not to jump when Orion spoke behind me. Damn, I wished he'd stop doing that.

I managed a smile. "Hi, Orion."

He fell into step beside me, studying my face with a worried frown. "I'm really sorry about what I said this morning. I didn't mean to be insulting."

"It's okay." I summoned a grin and bumped my shoulder against his. "You know what they say; the truth hurts." He smiled, shaking his head as if to protest, but before he could speak I added, "And anyway, I'm sorry I was so grumpy. I was still half-asleep. I feel a lot better now. I enjoyed this Calling."

His smile quirked into mischief. "I heard you enjoying the Calling in the main building. It sounded like you were sawing logs."

"Yeah, oops." I gave him a rueful smile. "I hope the Earth Spirit will forgive me."

"The Earth Spirit is benevolent. I'm sure you're forgiven."

We walked on for a while. When he spoke again there was a tiny undertone in his voice that made my paranoia spring to attention. "Maybe you didn't sleep well last night because you were hearing things outside your tent. I woke up thinking I'd heard something prowling outside. Maybe the cougar paid us a visit."

I managed a sickly smile. "Maybe. That's kind of scary,

to think it would come right up to our tents."

"Yes." His brow furrowed in concern. Or something that looked like concern. "I know you like roaming around in the woods, but maybe you should stay closer to the encampment for a while."

"Mm," I said, stalling. Inspiration struck. "I'm not too worried about it," I added. "I was talking to Moonbeam yesterday and she said I'm under the Earth Spirit's protection as long as I wear the bracelet. She said none of the Earth Spirit's creatures would harm her, so I'm probably okay. I'll just be extra-cautious."

Orion's furrowed forehead puckered into an outright frown. "I thought you didn't believe in the Earth Spirit."

I gave him my blandest expression. "I had a talk with Moonbeam yesterday and I feel badly about not keeping an open mind. I'm trying really hard to be more accepting and get to know the Earth Spirit the way she wants me to."

It was his turn to murmur 'Mm', and I got the distinct impression he wasn't pleased. As if realizing he'd given away his lack of enthusiasm, he turned a megawatt smile on me and squeezed my hand. "That's great, Storm, I'm really glad you're trying. You won't regret it. Finding the Earth Spirit was the best thing that ever happened to me."

I smiled back and seized the opportunity. "You said you'd found out about the Earth Spirit online. Where did you find the information? I'd like to read up on it a bit."

"Oh, uh..." He hesitated for only a moment. "I can't remember now, and I left all my technology behind when I came here so I can't even look up my browser history. You could try searching 'Earth Spirit commune BC' and see what you get." His smile brightened even more. "Or I could share what I know..." He trailed off, his gaze flickering down to his toes as though remembering our aborted make-out session. "Uh, or I know Moonbeam and Karma would love to talk to you about it."

"Thanks," I said. "Maybe I'll do that." The wheels turned inside my brain for a moment, and I added, "Actually, that's a great idea. I could spend more time with them and really get to see how the Earth Spirit works in their lives."

Not to mention it'd give me an excuse to stay close to them.

"Uh, yeah... Great idea." Orion's smile was distinctly anemic. "Well, uh... I guess I'll see you later."

"Yep, see you." I gave him a megawatt smile of my own.

He turned off on the next trail, and I strode toward the main building with a spring in my step. So far, so good.

Munching my granola and yogurt a while later, I eyed the other occupants of the kitchen and wondered if Moonbeam and Karma had eaten already. I had been hoping they'd come to the kitchen after the Calling the way they'd done the previous morning.

The temptation to peek at my little tracking unit was strong, but I didn't dare. As soon as I finished breakfast I'd find out whether my nocturnal skulking had paid dividends. And if not, I'd have to try to retrieve the tracer.

My heart leaped as Moonbeam and Karma strolled into the kitchen, affectionately entwined as usual. For a moment I wondered if they'd been 'celebrating' the Callings the way Orion had attempted to celebrate with me yesterday. That would be a good joke if their whole reason for conjuring the Earth Spirit was to get laid in privacy while the rest of the commune devoutly meditated.

As if sensing my cynical thoughts, Moonbeam turned her otherworldly blue gaze toward me. Flushing, I imagined a steel door rolling down between us and gave her a smile I hoped was innocent.

She smiled back, and the two of them collected their breakfast before making their way over to my table.

"Good morning," Karma greeted me in his rich bass. "Lovely day, isn't it?"

"Beautiful," I agreed. "Have you been out enjoying it?"

"Just for a short while," Moonbeam said. "After we finished the Earth Spirit's rituals."

"What exactly do you do when there's a Calling?" I inquired with my best show of interest. "I've been thinking about our conversation yesterday and I'd like to try to understand the Earth Spirit the way you do."

Not to mention I'd really like to know where they went during a Calling, just in case.

"Oh, Storm Cloud Dancer, that's wonderful!" Moonbeam leaned down to hug me. "I'm so glad you've decided to open your heart to the Earth Spirit."

"Why don't you join me?" I gestured to the empty chairs across from me. "We can talk about it while you eat breakfast."

"Thank you, dear, that would be lovely," Moonbeam replied, and they both seated themselves and dug into their own granola.

"Actually," Karma mumbled around a mouthful before swallowing and continuing with more clarity, "There's something we wanted to discuss with you anyway."

"Oh, not at mealtime, Karma Wolf Song," Moonbeam objected. "It's bad for the digestion."

I gulped my last mouthful along with a lump of trepidation. "It's okay, I'm finished. What did you want to talk to me about?"

"Well..." Karma shot a look at Moonbeam's perturbed expression before continuing, "There was a bit of a problem at the garage yesterday."

"Oh." I donned my best 'really, that's too bad, but nothing to do with me' expression.

"Yes, one of the renters..." Karma hesitated with another glance at Moonbeam. "The one you call Ratboy... apparently attempted to install spark plugs in the truck, damaging it in the process."

"Oh." Guilt flooded me as Moonbeam's Gaze of Truth locked with mine. "Um, I'm sorry, I think that was partly my fault," I mumbled.

"Ratboy indicated it was entirely your fault," Karma said. "Which I find difficult to believe since you were nowhere in the vicinity."

"That little..." I stifled my urge to enumerate Ratboy's many undesirable qualities and took the high road. "It wasn't entirely my fault, but I'm partly responsible. I told him to make sure he didn't mix up the wires, but I should have explained it more thoroughly." The guilt rose again. "Was there much damage?"

"Skidmark says he'll have to pull out the engine and overhaul it."

"Oh, shit. I'm really sorry." I clutched a couple of handfuls of hair in chagrin. "I'll pay for the damage and help him fix it. It's hard work to pull those big V8s and he'll probably need a hand."

"Payment won't be necessary, dear." Moonbeam patted my hand. "Our young friend should have asked for assistance, or at least clarification. But I do believe Skidmark would appreciate your help."

"I'll go and talk to him right away." I hesitated, my

remorse tempered by my sudden recognition of an opportunity to discuss Skidmark's sabotage from an oblique angle.

"Do you think he'll actually let me help?" I asked. "I got the feeling... um..." It didn't take much acting ability to look uncomfortable. "Um, I think Skidmark is a little..." I trailed off.

"What, dear?" Moonbeam's wise eyes looked through me. "Please tell us what's bothering you."

"Do you think Skidmark might be a little..." I stopped, then started again. "Have you noticed any changes in his behaviour lately?"

"No, dear, why?"

"Well, he just seems to arbitrarily, um... do stuff to the vehicles..." At their puzzled expressions, I blew out a breath. "I think he's intentionally sabotaging them. Or else he's getting a little... forgetful. Or something."

"Oh." Moonbeam and Karma exchanged a glance before Moonbeam leaned toward me, lowering her voice. "Please don't mention it, dear. He's done that ever since he came here as a very young man right after fighting in the Vietnam War. He gets extremely anxious if he's not in control of all the traffic in and out of the commune, so we simply pretend we don't notice that the vehicles never run unless he's just 'fixed' them."

"Oh." I sank back in my chair, my heart clutching. "Oh, shit. Poor Skidmark. I must have really upset him yesterday. I'm sorry. I won't fix anything again without asking him first. And I won't bring it up."

"That's very kind of you, dear." Moonbeam gave me her luminous smile. "Now..." She swallowed the last of her breakfast and rose. "You were asking about the Earth Spirit, and I know just the person to instruct you. Aurora Peace Rain!" She beckoned across the kitchen and Aurora hurried over. "Storm Cloud Dancer would like to learn more about the Earth Spirit." Moonbeam gave us both a smile. "Do enjoy your time together."

With that she and Karma withdrew, leaving me at the mercy of Aurora and her voice.

CHAPTER 17

Aurora was really a lovely girl, I told myself resolutely. All breathless sincerity, long silky hair, and fresh glowing skin.

And a voice like a fucking jackhammer.

I resisted the urge to flinch and cover my suffering ears as her exposition on the Earth Spirit reached a jubilant crescendo.

"And you know what the best part is, Storm? The best part is that the Earth Spirit is always here, and everywhere around us! As long as we're here on the commune, we're always protected by the Earth Spirit! Isn't that just the best thing ever?"

"Um, yeah..."

"And it's real protection, too, not just some abstract idea!" She leaned forward earnestly and I couldn't help scooting my chair backward. She raised her voice to compensate. "This is a true story! It happened just a couple of years ago. A little boy wandered off into the woods and his parents didn't realize he was gone until much later. It was windy and raining and he was only four years old, so he could have easily died of exposure. And guess what?" She gazed at me, her eyes alight.

"What?" My voice cracked with what I hoped she'd interpret as excitement.

"Moonbeam and Karma called to the Earth Spirit, and the Earth Spirit told them exactly where to start looking. The little boy had fallen into a hole under a log in the middle of the forest and we never would have found him otherwise, but we formed a search line where the Earth Spirit said and we found him fifteen minutes later!" Aurora's voice rose again in impassioned fervor.

My chair was wedged against the wall. Nowhere to go. "Wow," I croaked.

"And I know it might seem like some weird religion, but it's not a religion at all! The Earth Spirit isn't a god to be worshipped. You can follow any religion you want and still have the love and protection of the Earth Spirit. All you have to do is open your heart and you can feel it and practically *see* it all around you!" Aurora flung out her arms, her pretty features alight with rapture, her voice flaying my eardrums. "Can't you feel it, Storm?"

"Uh..."

She opened her mouth for a fresh assault and I flung up a hand in self-defence. "Wow, Aurora, thanks," I babbled. "That was really, um... inspiring. But you know what? I think I really need to go and commune quietly with the Earth Spirit by myself now."

"Oh, that's a great idea, Storm! The Earth Spirit is always honoured by your silence and attention!"

I rose and sidled away. "Yeah, I love silence. Really love it. So, um, see you."

I didn't quite turn tail and run, but it would have been dangerous to step in front of me. Ears ringing, I scurried outside and made a beeline for my tent.

Falling onto my cot, I clasped my aching head and closed my eyes, soaking up the soft woodland sounds. After several minutes of grateful immobility, I sat up at last.

God, what a nerve-shattering experience. Utterly pointless, too. Not only did I get separated from Moonbeam and Karma, but they also managed to avoid my question about their roles in the Calling ritual.

I blew out a breath of irritation and pulled out my tracking device. When I powered it on, my shoulders sagged with relief at the sight of the red dot and GPS coordinate display. The relative location indicated that Orion was northeast of me by about a quarter mile, so that would place him in the vicinity of the garage.

Hmm.

Now would be a perfect time to search his tent.

My pulse accelerated at the thought. Theoretically I'd be perfectly safe. I knew where Orion was, and ours were the only two tents along the path so nobody else was likely to come along and catch me.

But if Orion somehow found out I'd been snooping, he might get a little more assertive with those hand restraints.

Before I could conjure up any more frightening scenarios, I sucked in a breath, stuck the tracker in my pocket, and strode out of my tent.

Look decisive. Look like you have every right to be there. Do not look furtive.

Despite my mental admonitions I couldn't help peering guiltily around to check for witnesses before I ducked into Orion's tent.

I halted just inside, my heart hammering as though I'd run a mile. Everything was still as tidy as my camera had shown it the previous night, and I slipped out of my boots and placed them where Orion's had been to keep from tracking telltale dirt across his floor.

Padding around in my sock feet with the tracker clutched in my hand, I began a systematic search.

It didn't take long. Orion had about as many clothes as I did. A few neatly-folded T-shirts, a couple of pairs of jeans, some wool socks, and boxer briefs in various colours were tucked into the same wood-crate shelving as mine. A couple of jackets had nothing in their pockets but gloves. I found no hand restraints. No phone or laptop or electronic equipment whatsoever. A duffel bag under his cot held towels. A sparse selection of toiletries and a washcloth completed my discoveries. Five minutes later I was back in my own tent, gulping air and shaking like a leaf.

My very first clandestine search ever. Now I was a real spy.

I snorted. I'd found nothing incriminating or even interesting. There had been practically no risk, and I was on the verge of a heart attack anyway. Jane Bond would have laughed in my face.

Well, to hell with Jane Bond. For the past year I'd been backed into a corner again and again and forced to react. This time I'd taken the initiative. That was something to be proud of.

After some more bracing self-talk and a few deep calming breaths, I focused on my next objective: Skidmark's bench.

Guilt twisted my guts. Skidmark. Survivor of a war nobody wanted to acknowledge, fighting the demons of post-traumatic stress long before there was any help or even understanding available. And I had shattered his carefully-constructed safety zone.

And one of the commune's vehicles was wrecked because of my shitty attitude, too. I felt like the lowest form of scum.

Hauling myself to my feet, I scooped up the binoculars and bird book. I'd visit Skidmark first, apologize, and see when he wanted to tackle the truck overhaul. After that I could carry on with my plans for the day.

My feet dragged while I climbed the hill to the garage. I wouldn't blame Skidmark if he was furious with me. He'd tried to protect his peace of mind by locking the garage and I'd broken in like a lousy criminal, shouted abuse at him, and stolen his car. The previous day's triumph tasted of bitter shame now.

When I rounded the corner into the clearing, my heart sank even farther at the sight of Ratboy's glowering face. Before I had trudged halfway across the gravel he was in full cry. "I need that truck, damn you to a thousand hells! This is all your fault! Filthy stupid whore! You will fix the truck immediately..."

I tuned out his insults and headed for the garage. Skidmark was nowhere to be seen so I shouted his name, then turned to find myself unpleasantly face-to-face with Ratboy.

My disregard obviously hadn't improved his humour. His face was contorted with fury as he bellowed invective at me from close range.

"Fuck *off*, you little prick!" I snapped, and detoured around him.

I didn't quite make it.

He spat in my face.

The wet shock shattered the fragile barrier between reason and rage. My body coiled and released with mindless efficiency and the crack of my palm against his cheek sounded like a rifle shot. His head snapped sideways and he reeled back a step. Then his face darkened and his hands clenched into fists.

"Hey, Storm! Where are you?" Orion poked his head around the corner of the garage. "Oh, there you are."

Ratboy froze in mid-step toward me. He thrust his face close to mine and snarled, "You will pay!" Then he turned and stalked away, jostling Orion as he pushed past.

"What's going on here?" Orion demanded.

I shrugged, trying to hide how much I was trembling. "Ratboy had a bit of a tantrum over the truck." I scrubbed my sleeve across my cheek, barely suppressing my gag reflex at the slimy wetness.

"Stay here." Orion turned and jogged after Ratboy, who was already halfway to the bend in the road.

At the sound of his footsteps Ratboy spun, his fists rising, but he relaxed when he recognized Orion. When Orion reached him they spoke for a few moments, Ratboy's hands slashing the air angrily while Orion made conciliatory gestures. Then Ratboy turned his back and strode off despite Orion's entreaties, and after trailing him for a few paces Orion let his arms fall to his sides in defeat.

Alerted by a familiar whiff of body odour and marijuana, I turned to see Skidmark approaching from behind the garage, reefer in hand. He ambled over to stand beside me. "Man, that is one uptight dude," he mumbled. "What'd you do this time?"

"Apparently I forced him to wreck the truck. All my fault."

Skidmark wheezed amusement. "Damn girl mechanics."

Orion strode up, frowning. "You shouldn't have hit him, Storm. The Earth Spirit wants us to live in tolerance and harmony."

Jerk.

I stared at him for a moment, fighting the urge to tell him exactly what he and the Earth Spirit could do with their tolerance and harmony. Since I couldn't summon a civil response I drew a deep breath and turned to Skidmark instead. "I'm sorry about the truck. I should have stuck around to make sure Ratboy did it right. When can I help you repair it?"

Skidmark sucked a lungful of smoke. "No sweat," he mumbled after a moment, smoke wisping out along with his words. "This afternoon."

"I'll be here." I picked up the bird book I had dropped in the attack, shaking small stones out of it and smoothing the bent pages. Tucking it under my arm, I indicated the binoculars around my neck. "Well, if you don't need me until later I'm going to go and do some birdwatching."

Skidmark nodded without interest and drifted toward the garage, trailing a streamer of smoke like an underpowered locomotive. Orion stood in awkward silence for a moment, then smiled and said, "Enjoy your birdwatching. See you later."

I nodded and headed for the bench.

Sinking onto it, I eased out a long, slow breath. Then drew in another. In. Out. Nice and slow. Calm.

After a few minutes of belly breathing, I thought I might be able to hold the binoculars steady enough to see something besides a wildly-vibrating blur. Focusing on the renters' camp, I pressed the image stabilization button and studied the layout across the river.

The trees were so thick I couldn't see much more than I had with my naked eyes. The field I had thought of as a firing range turned out to be some kind of obstacle course. The well-trodden areas contained various types of walls and barriers and a couple of mannequins dressed in combat fatigues.

I spotted some tents whose locations I'd guessed based on the heat signatures the previous night, but the main tent was featureless and the rest of the encampment was hidden by trees.

I lowered the binoculars with a sigh. That wasn't helpful.

"See anything interesting?"

Orion's voice made me start violently and corkscrew around on the bench.

"Goddammit!" I clutched my chest in an attempt to keep my heart from jumping out. "Stop sneaking up on me like that!"

"Sorry." He smiled and came over to sit on the other end of the bench. "You were a million miles away."

"Yeah, I guess I was." Wondering how long he'd been standing there, I decided to play it safe. "I was just sitting here trying to calm down." I gave him a wry grimace and hefted the binoculars. "I figured when I'd stopped shaking enough to focus on something big like that tent over there, I might have half a chance of holding the focus on a bird."

Orion nodded. "I'm sorry, I should have asked if you were all right. I didn't mean to sound critical before."

"I'm fine." My words came out sounding a little more clipped than I'd intended.

"That's good." He hesitated as if searching for a topic of conversation. "Those are nice binoculars," he said after a moment. "May I try them?"

"Sure." I unslung them from around my neck and handed them over.

Peering through them, he focused on the renters' tent as I had done. "Nice," he said as he lowered them. "Those image stabilizers make all the difference, don't they?"

"Yeah."

He passed them over, and I stood and added, "Well, I think I'm ready to ramble. See you later."

He rose hurriedly. "Storm, wait." When I eyed him, he shuffled his feet, looking uncomfortable. "I just... be careful, okay? I didn't like that crack Ratboy made about making you pay. Maybe you should just lie low for a while."

A little late for the 'concerned' act, buddy. Maybe you should have tried it earlier instead of sucking up to Ratboy.

I shrugged. "I'll be out in the woods where nobody can find me. The only places I've ever run into him are up here at the garage and once at the kitchen. I should be pretty safe."

He let out a breath. "Okay. Be careful."

I nodded and strode down the path, my back tingling with the knowledge that his gaze was following me.

The gravel crunched under my boots, increasing my unease. Last night I'd heard Skidmark coming long before he got within visual range. I would have heard Orion today if he'd been using the path, or even if he'd been walking casually through the undergrowth.

So he had deliberately sneaked up on me.

A shiver coiled down my spine and I quickened my pace.

CHAPTER 18

When I was a good distance away from the garage, I abandoned the path and struck out into the woods. Safely concealed, I peeked into my pocket to check the tracker. Orion's red dot showed he was still in the vicinity of the garage.

Why would he keep hanging around there? He hadn't given any indication that he had any interest in vehicles, and the garage certainly wasn't the most attractive part of the commune, nor its social hub. The only other people who seemed to spend any time there were Skidmark and me.

And Ratboy.

I unslung my binoculars and scanned the trees for the benefit of anybody who might be watching me.

Dammit, Orion and Ratboy were definitely much closer friends than Orion was admitting. So if Orion was a threat to Moonbeam and Karma, Ratboy might be, too, along with who-knew-how-many of their cronies from across the river. Casting my mind back to the previous night, I visualized the rows of coloured glows I'd seen through the night vision goggles.

At least five rows, with probably six or seven people in them. So around thirty new suspects to worry about.

I gulped. If they were enemies, I was in deep shit.

Realizing I'd been standing staring through the binoculars at nothing, I replaced them around my neck and wandered on, trying to look casual.

Maybe tagging Orion hadn't been such a great idea after all. Maybe I should have tagged Moonbeam and Karma instead so I'd know where to find them at all times.

But that would be practically impossible. They weren't nearly as predictable as Orion with their footwear, and I couldn't think of any other place to put the tracer.

I let out a sigh and kept walking, stopping frequently to peer through the binoculars.

By the time I got back to the commune's encampment I had mentally mapped several new routes to follow while making my clandestine reports to Stemp, and my stomach was growling.

Plodding toward the kitchen, I flinched at the sound of Aurora's voice behind me.

"Hey, Storm, did you enjoy your meditation?"

I turned and summoned the best smile I could manage under the circumstances. "I did, thanks." I held up my binoculars. "I saw some birds, too."

"Oh, really? I love bird-watching! What did you see?"

"Um..." I racked my brain for something plausible. "I'm just getting started with birding. I saw, um... some robins and chickadees?"

"Oh, yes, we have chestnut-backed chickadees here, they're so cute! What else?"

"Some little brown birds..."

Aurora brightened. "Did they have creamy yellow around the tips of their wings?"

"Yes," I lied cautiously.

"Oh, those will be the pine siskins. Did you go down to the river? I've seen an American Dipper there in the shallows several times. And you must have seen the juncos foraging on the ground, they're all over."

"Um, yeah, they're the ones with..." I hesitated, hoping she'd fill in the particulars.

"Black heads and brown bodies, yes!" She smiled so brightly I could almost forgive her strident voice. "And the woods are full of red-breasted nuthatches, too; you must have seen some."

"Yeah," I agreed, making a mental note to look up nuthatches in the bird book.

"Oh, that's so exciting. I love it when the Earth Spirit shares its little creatures with us, don't you?" I flinched in spite of myself as her voice rose in enthusiasm.

"Uh, yeah." I turned away, trying to look nonchalant. "Well, I guess I'd better-"

"Oh, wait, Storm, there was a phone message for you." I turned back reluctantly as she continued, "A Nichele Brown called. I couldn't find you so I wrote her number down and left the message for you on the bulletin board by the phone."

"Okay, thanks." I backed away. "I'd better go and check it right away. It might be urgent."

"I think it might be." Aurora's big blue eyes were wide. "I saw three other messages for you up there, too, all with her name and number on them."

"Oh." My heart lurched. "That doesn't sound good. I'll go call her right now. Talk to you later." I turned to hurry away, throwing a 'thanks' over my shoulder.

By the time I got to the phone in the main building, my pulse was racing from more than just my brisk walk. Nichele wouldn't call me four times in a row unless something was really wrong.

I swallowed hard. Oh, God, don't let it be Dave. Visions of his highway tractor crumpled somewhere beside the road made my mouth go dry. With all the miles he covered, he was bound to be involved in an accident sooner or later even though he was the best driver I knew. It was just the law of averages.

Preoccupied with my frightening thoughts, I had dialled Nichele's number from memory and my blood pressure increased while the phone rang and rang on the other end. When her answering machine kicked in, I hung up the receiver, more worried than ever.

Then I realized it was a weekday and drew a deep breath. Stupid. Of course she'd be at work. I unpinned the messages from the board and checked the phone number.

Shit, that wasn't Nichele's work number. And it wasn't her cell phone, either.

Jaw clenched, I dialled the unfamiliar number and waited. After only a couple of rings, Dave's cheerful voice made my knees weaken with relief.

"Dave's Trucking, Dave speaking."

I managed to keep the tremor out of my voice. "Hi, Dave, it's Aydan. How are you?"

His reply held a note of tension. "Okay, I hope. Hang on a sec." The phone made a hollow sound as though he'd placed a hand over its speaker and his voice was muffled when he spoke again, obviously not to me. "Honey, it's the dispatcher. Just gotta go check, um... something. Sit tight. Be right back."

There was a pause followed by the sound of wind whistling over the speaker as he apparently stepped outside. "Aydan, shi... crap, finally!" he said in hushed tones.

"Nichele left four messages for you; didn't you get them?"

"I just did." My belly knotted. "What's wrong?"

"Well, nothing, I hope, but..."

"Just tell me, Dave! What the hell's going on?"

"Think I might've screwed up big, Aydan." I heard him take a deep breath. "I asked Nichele to marry me."

"Oh, shit!" The words popped out before I could stop them.

He groaned. "It's bad, isn't it? Shi... crap, knew I should've talked to you first!"

I backpedalled hurriedly, grasping at straws. "Maybe not, Dave. Was that her you were just talking to? Is she with you?"

"Yeah."

"Okay... well, it's not really, really bad, then. If it was really, really bad she'd have dumped you on the spot."

"Oh, shit!" His words came out in a groan, his despair evidenced by his failure to correct 'shit' to 'crap' for my sensitive ears.

"No, don't panic, Dave. You're on the road together, right? So that's good. She's with you and she's still talking to you. Where are you?"

"That's the bad part." He sounded defeated. "We're in Victoria. As soon as she found out I had a delivery out here, she said she'd come with me and I could take her up to visit you. You oughta see the size of her suitcase. Looks like she's leaving for good."

"She's coming *here*? Shit! Dave, I've got, um... some stuff happening here. It's really not a good time for a visit."

His voice dropped to a whisper. "You mean, like..." he paused significantly. "...*stuff*? Is it dangerous?"

"I hope not. But can't you talk her out of it?"

"Tried. You know what she's like." Worry vibrated in his voice. "Didn't want to fight her too hard in case I pushed her away. Well, further away."

I sighed. I knew all too well what she was like. If she had made up her mind to visit me, nothing would stop her. And I couldn't turn her away without blowing my cover.

Another big sigh escaped as I succumbed to the inevitable. "Okay, Dave. Don't worry, she always takes a giant suitcase even if she's just going overnight, and she loves her swanky condo in Calgary far too much to leave it. If she rode with you, it's a good sign, and I guarantee she won't want to stay here for long. If you can just hold out for a few days, she'll be begging for a ride home. Are you going to be in Victoria for a while?"

"Got another load going back to Calgary later today, but I'll tell 'em I've got engine trouble and they'll have to get somebody else."

"No, hang on, let's think about this." I thought for a moment. "What about after that? Where are you going to be?"

"Back in Victoria the day after tomorrow."

"Okay, how about this, then? Drop her off here and head out as usual. Just pretend everything's fine. It'll take a few days for her to admit she hates it here. By then you'll be back and she can ride home with you, but she won't feel pressured with you hanging around waiting for her. What do you think?"

Dave's voice sounded stronger. "I'll do it. Thanks, Aydan. How do I get to the commune?"

I gave him directions and hung up, my mind racing. Shit, now I'd have to go to Moonbeam and Karma and tell them I'd lied about an audit and ask them to support my story.

What if they wouldn't? They were so big on honesty; what if they told Nichele I was there to recover from some mysterious trauma? Nichele would freak-the-fuck-out and badger me until I told her something plausible.

And what if I had another run-in with Ratboy? He'd sounded pretty serious about revenge. If he attacked me I couldn't pull my gun with Nichele watching.

I groaned aloud as another thought occurred to me. Where would she sleep? Would she have to bunk with me? And if she did, how would I hide my concealed weapons when I was getting undressed for bed? And how could I sneak away to report to Stemp or keep up my surveillance on Orion and Moonbeam and Karma?

Shit, shit, shit!

Maybe I should phone Dave back and tell him I'd changed my mind and Nichele couldn't stay here after all. I could say... what?

Wild ideas rocketed through my brain. Some kind of contagious disease? A toxic spill that closed the road? No extra tents? A prohibition by the Earth Spirit?

Lame. And completely implausible.

I turned to thump my forehead against the wall.

"Storm Cloud Dancer, whatever is wrong?"

I turned to meet Moonbeam's worried gaze and groaned. "I'm an idiot, that's what."

"Merciful Spirit, dear, you're certainly not an idiot." Moonbeam took me gently by the arm and led me over to sit on the bench by the phone. She perched beside me and took my hand in both of hers, smoothing it with her fingertips in a soothing gesture. "Now please tell me what's wrong."

I hung my head. "You know how I lied to my friend

Nichele about you and Karma... sorry, I mean, Karma Wolf Song, being my aunt and uncle?"

She nodded, her brow furrowing.

"Well..." I drew a deep breath and poured out my story. "That wasn't all I lied to her about. I told her I was helping you with the commune's books while you went through an audit and I used that as an excuse for why I couldn't come home. I didn't want her to worry about why I'm really here. And now she's coming to visit me. She'll be here in a couple of hours. I don't want to tell her the truth, and I don't want to share my tent with her."

I studied my toes while Moonbeam sat in silence. "Oh, dear," she said at last. "That does put you in a spot, doesn't it? Why don't you just tell her the truth?"

"I can't!"

"Of course you can." She placed firm fingertips under my chin and forced me to meet her eyes. "Recovering from a trauma is nothing to be ashamed of. And if she's a good friend, she would be terribly hurt if you didn't trust her with the truth."

"I know, but..." I stared helplessly at Moonbeam, groping for a reason that didn't include 'I'm an undercover agent and she can't know'. "...but if I told her, she'd feel terrible, too," I finished. "And I can't bear other people's pity. If I told her, she'd never look at me again without feeling sorry for me. I just can't do it."

Moonbeam held my gaze for a moment before letting out a sigh. "I truly believe that is the wrong decision. Your fear is preventing you from realizing the joy of being completely loved and accepted in all your glorious imperfection."

"Please," I whispered. "Please don't tell my secrets."

"Oh, my dear." She drew me into a hug, her slim arms

strong around me. "Your secrets are yours alone. We'll play along while your friend is here. And we keep a spare tent available for visitors. Your friend can stay there. What is her full name, and how long do you think she'll be staying?"

Relief turned my spine to jelly and I slumped, letting out a long sigh. "Thank you. Thank you so much. I don't know how long she'll stay but I doubt it'll be more than a few days. And her name is Nichele Brown."

"All right, don't worry about a thing, Storm Cloud Dancer. Just enjoy visiting with your friend. But, dear..." She rose, her eyes troubled. "Please talk to your counselor about this. You need to learn to trust. You deserve the happiness and fulfilment of knowing you're loved for who you truly are."

Guilt heated my cheeks and I dropped my gaze to my toes. "Thank you. I will."

CHAPTER 19

At two o'clock, Dave's big highway tractor growled into the field beside the road. As soon as it pulled to a stop Nichele bounced down from the cab wearing her usual exuberant grin, but I could see lines of strain around her eyes.

"Aydan! It's so great to see you, girl!" She flung her arms around me in her customary bear hug.

"Great to see you, too!" I returned the hug, grinning in spite of my worry. Dave clambered down from the cab carrying Nichele's giant suitcase, and as he set it down and straightened I went over to collect a hug from him as well.

"Take care of her, Aydan," he muttered into my hair. "Call me if it gets dangerous."

"I will." I gave him a reassuring squeeze before stepping back and putting on a smile. "Hey, Nichele," I teased. "Are you sure about this? You're really out in the sticks here. There isn't even an internet connection." I conveniently omitted my own secret setup.

Nichele gave me a grin that didn't quite reach her eyes. "That's perfect. I need to get away from everything for a while." She turned to Dave. "Thanks for the ride. See you. Drive carefully." She gave him a quick peck on the lips before pulling away.

"I will." He hesitated, his brow furrowed with worry. "Call me when you get a chance. Or if you need a ride home."

Nichele smiled a little too brightly. "I will. Now scram. I want some girl time."

Dave nodded, opened his mouth as if to say something else, then closed it and turned to climb back into the cab. Nichele and I stood watching in silence until his truck was out of sight.

Then I turned to face Nichele. "What's up?" I demanded. "You hate camping. And I'm pretty sure your cell phone is surgically attached to your hand and you'll fade away and die without an internet connection."

Her face crumpled into misery. "He asked me to marry him."

"Oh." I kept my expression neutral. "So what are you going to do?"

"I don't know," she wailed. "Everything was so good between us. Why did he have to spoil it?"

"I doubt if he meant to spoil it." I hesitated, then dove in. "He's not like your dad, you know."

"No, I *don't* know! How do I know he's not boinking every floozy he meets along the road? Or if he isn't now, how do I know he won't start as soon as we're married? I can't live like my mom did. I can't just put up with it and pretend it isn't happening."

"Oh, Nichele!" I pulled her into a hug, my heart wrenching as she clung to me. "It'll be okay," I murmured. "Trust me, Dave's not like that."

"How do you know?" she demanded, pulling away to glare at me through tear-smudged mascara. "You don't! You can never know until it's too late!"

"Okay, you're right," I conceded with a sigh. "But look at it this way: You said everything was perfect up to now, but you still couldn't be sure he wasn't cheating on you while he was on the road."

"Yeah, but we weren't married. I could just dump him and walk away."

"Like you did with all those other guys," I said gently. "You never gave them a chance. Do you really want to throw away what you've got with Dave?"

"No." She sniffled and wiped her eyes, smearing her makeup even more. "But..." Her eyes brimmed up again. "I've *already* lost him. We can't go back to the way we were now. This will always be a huge ugly *thing* between us. Why couldn't he just leave it alone?" She swiped the tears away angrily.

"Maybe it doesn't have to be a big ugly thing," I argued. "Maybe it's not a yes-or-no question. You could tell him you need some time to get used to the idea. I know Dave loves you. He'll give you all the space you need, and I'd be willing to bet he'd never cheat on you."

"I don't know, Aydan. I just..." Nichele sniffled again before straightening resolutely and digging a tissue and a compact out of her purse. "Never mind. I'll figure it out. Oh-em-gee, I look like a raccoon! Here, hold this."

She pushed the mirror into my hand and set about repairing her makeup. When she was done she retrieved the compact and tucked it into her purse before looking up at me with a grin that only wobbled slightly around the edges. "Okay. Take me to meet your crazy aunt and uncle." She glanced around the empty field, frowning. "Is there a shuttle bus or something?"

I laughed. "Poor little rich girl. I told you you'd hate it

here. There's no shuttle bus or concierge or bellhop. If you brought it, you get to drag it to wherever it needs to go."

"Well, that sucks." She grabbed the handle of the suitcase. "Good thing it has wheels."

"Uh-huh," I agreed, eyeing the dense grass and uneven terrain. "Good luck with that."

After watching her struggle almost to the edge of the field, I relented and reached for the suitcase handle. "Here, let me do it. That thing's nearly as big as you are."

"Thanks." She relinquished it with a sigh of relief, rubbing her shoulder. "I was thinking about just leaving it here and walking back to get what I needed every morning. Is it a long way to the commune?"

"We're on commune land now, and we're pretty close to the encampment." I hoisted the suitcase over the remaining lumpy ground and onto the gravel road. "Come on, Moonbeam and Karma want to meet you, and they'll take us to your tent."

Nichele had apparently decided to shelve her personal worries, at least for the moment. Her usual sparkle returned and she chattered all the way to the encampment, bringing me up to date on our mutual friends and making not-so-subtle inquiries about the state of my love life.

When we arrived at the encampment she gawked unabashedly before asking, "So how does this work? I get a tent, but what about food and bathrooms and stuff?"

"Your tent will probably be in this area." I indicated the tents scattered around us. "In the main building there's a big kitchen with three wood stoves and you do your own cooking. You can take whatever you want from the iceboxes or the pantry and if you use the last of something, you write it on the grocery list. The showers are in the main building, too, along with the laundry and school and library, but you probably won't get assigned a shower slot. There's always hot water in the boilers of the wood stoves so you can wash up in your tent. The latrines are up by the main building, too."

"Wow, this is freaky." Nichele gazed around her. "It's like going back in time." She shot me a look. "It's 'way nicer than you said. These aren't tents, they're yurts. Raised wood floors and everything. And the weather's beautiful." She waved a hand at the blue sky and sunshine.

"Yeah, but this is the first day it's been nice," I grumbled. "And yurt or not, it's still a canvas tent. See how you like it once the fog rolls in and it starts raining."

"Oh, don't be such a grouch." She shot me a quizzical look. "No wonder you're cranky, sweating in that big jacket. Why don't you take it off? I'm comfy just like this." She indicated her crisp khaki shorts and scoop-necked tank top.

I surreptitiously wiped my forehead under the pretense of pushing my hair back. "I've spent the last four months freezing my butt off. I'm enjoying the heat," I lied. "And anyway, it's easier to wear it than carry it."

And the pockets were full of classified technology, but I couldn't tell her that.

Nichele shook her head. "You're nuts. Oh, look! Is that cat pregnant, or just super-fat?" She pointed at Peaches waddling down the path toward us.

"Pregnant. This is Peaches." I crouched to pet her, and her purr rumbled up under my hand. "One of the other cats had her litter a few weeks ago," I added. "The kittens are absolutely adorable. I'll show you later, but with your allergies you probably don't want to touch them."

Nichele sidestepped as Peaches came over to inspect her.

"Sorry, Peaches, I can't pet you. Why do cats always go to the person who's trying to avoid them?" She dodged Peaches again, eyeing her critically. "Oh-em-gee, Aydan, she's so fat! That can't be good for her. Don't they spay and neuter their cats here?"

"Yeah, but they keep a couple of females intact so they can maintain the population." I leaned down to give Peaches a quick chin-rub before walking on in deference to Nichele's feline-avoidance tactics. "They only let them have a couple of litters each, and then they'll spay them and choose a new female to breed."

"Oh, that's good."

I hid a smile at her satisfied expression. Even though she might not be fond of cats, Nichele's world-bettering crusades were legendary. I had no doubt that she would have been pushing for a spay/neuter program within minutes of arriving if she thought it was needed.

We rounded the corner and Nichele leaned over to whisper, "That's got to be your Aunt Moonbeam."

I grinned at the sight of the slight figure fluttering toward us in her rainbow tie-dyed caftan. "Yep."

Moonbeam gave us one of her luminous smiles, eyeing us as though amused by the contrast between my boots and baggy faded jeans and Nichele's crisp summer attire topped by perfect hair and makeup.

I made the necessary introductions and Moonbeam turned to study Nichele with the slightly unfocused gaze that indicated she was reading an aura. I imagined my steel door rolling down in front of me, feeling a little foolish for believing in it but too uneasy not to.

Moonbeam's smile brightened as she wrapped Nichele in a hug. "You have a lovely aura, dear. Welcome to our home."

Then she stepped back and reached into one of the folds of her caftan for one of the ubiquitous hemp and wood beaded bracelets. She gently captured Nichele's hand and tied the bracelet onto her wrist.

Looking deeply into Nichele's eyes, she said, "This bracelet gives you the protection of the Earth Spirit as long as you are here. Wear it always. From now on, you'll be known as Blaze Featherwind, the name the Earth Spirit has bestowed on you. Go forth in peace, tolerance, and harmony. The blessings of the Earth Spirit are upon you."

"Um... thanks." Nichele gave me a sideways look before turning a questioning expression on Moonbeam. "Am I supposed to... What's the right way to say I accept?"

Moonbeam smiled. "You don't need to say anything, but if you'd like, you could return the blessing by saying 'And upon you, too'."

"Oh." Nichele gave her a sparkling smile and an impulsive hug. "And upon you, too."

"Thank you, dear. Now I'll show you your tent, and at four o'clock Aurora Peace Rain will explain the rituals of the Earth Spirit to you."

To my relief, Nichele's tent turned out to be tucked into the village of tents, far from mine. At least I'd be able to sneak around without worrying that she'd hear me leaving my tent.

Once she had moved in I took her on a tour of the commune, excluding the garage and ending up in the kitchen for a snack.

Crunching the last of my apple, I glanced at my watch

and stood. "Sorry, Nichele, but I'm going to have to leave you on your own for a while. I'm due up the garage to help Skidmark work on the truck."

Nichele swallowed her last bite and rose with me. "I'll come along." She shot me a mischievous look. "I'm dying to meet Skidmark. And Orion. Your boy-toys."

I snorted. "Skidmark, a boy-toy? Yeah, right. Wait'll you see him. And smell him." I hesitated. I really didn't want her up at the garage in case Ratboy was there. "You probably don't have time," I added. "Don't forget you have to meet Aurora here in twenty minutes."

Nichele waved that away. "I have time. I can always jog back. I could use the exercise."

I narrowed my eyes at her. "Who are you and what did you do with my couch-potato friend?"

Nichele giggled. "I'm just trying to fit in. Everybody seems all healthy-granola here. It'll be good for me."

"Bad news about that fitting-in thing..." I made a gesture that encompassed her impeccably polished fingernails, perfect hair and makeup, and bountiful cleavage displayed by her snug tank top. "You stick out like a peacock in a chicken farm."

She pulled a solemn face, slightly marred by the impish twinkle in her eyes. "Buk-buk-buk!" She planted her hands on her hips and flapped her elbows, jerking her head forward in a creditable chicken imitation while she clucked. "Buk-buk-buk-*breeawk*!"

I laughed. "Okay, Chicken Little, let's go."

Striding along the path while Nichele chattered gaily beside me, I sent a mute entreaty skyward. Please don't let Ratboy be there. If he made a crack, Nichele wouldn't hesitate to take him on like a little terrier who thought she was a Rottweiler.

And where was Orion and what was he doing? Nearly four hours had passed since I'd seen him. That had to be some kind of record. The only thing that worried me more than having him pop up behind me was not having him pop up behind me.

What if he was making a move on Moonbeam and Karma? If I had to rush off to defend them, Nichele would surely follow me. Then I'd have three innocent civilians to protect. And if I had to pull my gun, it'd blow my cover sky-high.

I sighed and Nichele shot me a look. "You're really quiet. What's wrong?"

"Nothing." I summoned a smile. "Just figuring out my timetable between working on the truck and the bookkeeping stuff I have to do."

"Well, don't let me interrupt," Nichele said. "I need some time to think anyway. And you said Aurora was really nice, so maybe I can hang with her a while."

"Okay, thanks." I looked away quickly before she could see my guilty expression. I hadn't mentioned Aurora's voice.

CHAPTER 20

When Nichele and I arrived at the garage I drew a deep breath, equal parts worried and relieved by the sight of Orion and Ratboy standing on the opposite side of the clearing. At least now I knew where they were, but I'd really been hoping to avoid Ratboy.

Skidmark lounged in a chair against the garage, eyes half-closed and joint in hand. He looked up at the sound of our footsteps and brightened at the sight of Nichele's lush curves. Dropping the front legs of the chair to the ground, he rose and smiled so widely I actually glimpsed a gold tooth through his tangle of facial hair.

"Well, hello, Sugar-Loaves!" he greeted Nichele's chest. He turned his leer toward me. "See, if you dressed like that, guys wouldn't think you're a dude in women's clothes."

"Hello, pencil-dick," Nichele retorted. "If you kept your mouth shut, girls wouldn't think you have a teeny weenie."

Skidmark's eyes widened, his mouth falling open. Then he wheezed laughter until he doubled over coughing and staggered backward to fall into the chair, still convulsed.

Nichele shot me a look of concern while he hacked and gasped, but I shook my head. "Don't worry, he's fine. As fine as he ever gets, anyway. Meet Skidmark. Not that you'd want to."

At last the paroxysm passed and Skidmark sprawled weakly on the chair, wiping his streaming eyes. "Sugar-Loaves," he croaked. "You and her gotta be sisters. Storm here made a crack about my family jewels, too." He straightened and scowled with mock indignation. "You peeked."

I snickered. "Yep, I couldn't help myself. You're just that hot."

"That's the righteous truth." Skidmark nodded gravely before jerking his chin toward Nichele. "Who's the foxy chick?"

"Blaze Featherwind," I answered for her.

"That's 'ma'am' to you," Nichele corrected with a lift of her chin.

"Very pleased to meet you, ma'am." Skidmark offered her the half-smoked joint with a courtly bow. "Toke?"

Nichele grimaced. "No thanks."

Orion had drifted over during the exchange, and I did the honours. "Blaze, this is Orion Moonjava. Orion, Blaze Featherwind."

"Blaze," Orion murmured. "Lovely name. It suits you." He accepted her proffered hand and brought it to his lips, his eyes locked on hers.

"Oh..." Nichele blinked before retrieving her hand and offering a polite smile. "Nice to meet you, Orion."

His luscious mouth curved up, his green gaze full of hot sin. "The pleasure is mine."

If I hadn't known Nichele so well, I might have missed her instant of breathlessness before she straightened and gave Orion a cheeky grin. "You'd better believe it would be your pleasure. Too bad you'll never find out."

He laughed. "Too bad, indeed."

As they exchanged a few more words of banter, my attention shifted to Ratboy. He was still standing on the opposite side of the clearing, his gaze devouring Nichele, his lips twisted in a spine-chilling smile. I shifted casually to block his line of sight, resisting the urge to drape my jacket over Nichele's sexy top.

His cold black gaze met mine and fear tightened my throat as his teeth glittered. I might be able to beat him in a fight, but even though Nichele's small frame held the heart of a lion, she wouldn't stand a chance.

"...anyway, I've got to go and meet Aurora," Nichele was saying. "See you later."

I plastered a smile on my stiff lips. "Yeah, see you. I'll meet you for supper at the main building."

She jogged off, her considerable attributes bouncing under her tank top in a way that made Skidmark's eyes glaze over.

Ratboy's smile thinned to a razor edge and he shot a gloating look at me before following her like a jackal slinking after unsuspecting prey.

"Wait, Nichele!" The words burst from my lips as I ran after her. "I mean, Blaze." I threw a threatening glare at Ratboy as I passed him and caught up to Nichele. "I'll come with you," I panted. "I'm just going to grab a granola bar from the kitchen." I raised my voice to call back to Skidmark. "I'll be back a little later!"

He lifted his joint in a vague salute before returning it to his lips, and I faced Nichele's puzzled look as I fell into step with her.

"See the guy behind us?" I asked.

She turned to look as Ratboy stepped off the path to

disappear into the forest. "Yeah, what a creepazoid. I saw him up at the garage. What's his deal? Why didn't you introduce us?"

"I don't know his name. I call him Ratboy."

Nichele giggled. "Perfect. He totally looks like a Ratboy."

"Yeah, well, rats have a mean streak." She sobered at my tone, and I added, "Watch out for him. He's got a hate on for me, and he's exactly the kind of cowardly little dickwad to take it out on you because he knows we're friends."

Nichele tossed her head. "I'd like to see him try. I'll kick his weasely little ass."

"Yeah." I sighed. Just like a tiny terrier, all attitude and barely a mouthful for a big dog. "Just don't give him a chance, okay? Stick close to Aurora, and make sure you stay where there are lots of people."

"I can take care of myself, Aydan."

"I know." I made big pleading eyes. "Just do it for me, okay?"

She smiled and flung an arm around me. "Girl, you're such a worrywart. Okay, I will." Then she leaned in, lowering her voice and bouncing her eyebrows. "So that was Orion. Oh-em-*gee!* Holy hunka-burning-love, girl, why aren't you hitting that?"

I shrugged. "Why aren't you? He was hot for you, and you're always telling me you only live once."

"Aydan!" Nichele drew back, flushing with indignation. "I'm with Dave! How cheesy do you think I am?"

I grinned. "Just testing you." I sobered, looking her in the eye. "You know, there was a time not too long ago when you wouldn't have hesitated to jump him. The old Nichele would have had his clothes off by now."

She stopped dead, her cheeks paling. She stared at me for a long moment before dropping her face into her hands. Her voice came out in a terrified squeak. "Ohmigod, I'm in love with Dave. Ohmigod! Aydan, what am I going to *do?*"

"Hey, stop panicking!" I gripped her shoulders and gave her a little shake. "So you love Dave. Dave loves you. I'm not seeing a problem here."

"But I *can't* love him!" When she emerged from the shelter of her hands her eyes were wide and dark with fear. "If I love him it'll break my heart when he cheats on me and I can't, I just *can't-*"

"Nichele, for shit's sake! He won't cheat on you. That's why you love him!"

"No, I love him because I'm an idiot!" She hid her face in her hands again. "Oh, God, why didn't I just sleep with him and then dump him like all the rest? Ohmigod, I'm such an idiot."

"No, you're not." I pulled gently on her wrists, coaxing her hands away from her face. "You're not an idiot. You're a smart, beautiful, successful stockbroker with brilliant business sense. You know what you want and you go after it. And Dave is a hero who put his life on the line for you once already and he'd do it again in a heartbeat. He's one of the good guys, Nichele, and you know it. Don't second-guess yourself."

"He put his life on the line for you, not for me," Nichele mumbled, but she straightened, colour creeping back into her cheeks.

"For both of us," I corrected. "He didn't even know you then and he still risked his life to save you. You know I'm right."

She nodded slowly, then with more conviction. "I

guess... you're right."

"Of course I'm right." I nudged her with an elbow. "I'm always right."

"You're always full of shit." She gave me a wobbly grin.

"Well, yeah, that too. Why do you think my eyes are brown?"

After delivering Nichele safely into Aurora's clutches and extracting a promise that they'd stay in populated areas, I jogged back to the garage. Skidmark still lounged against the wall, and he still had a half-smoked joint between his fingers. I seriously doubted it was the same joint.

I came to a halt in front of him and surveyed his heavy-lidded eyes. "Maybe we should leave this for tomorrow," I suggested.

He yawned and scratched his crotch with luxurious satisfaction before carefully stubbing out the joint on the sole of his boot. Then he tucked the roach into the breast pocket of his grimy coveralls and rose with another cavernous yawn.

"'S cool," he mumbled. "Let's do it."

I followed him into the garage with trepidation, but it turned out he was as good a mechanic stoned as most guys were sober. We made passable progress even though he moved at a dreamy pace punctuated by drags on the ever-diminishing joint, which he took outside to light and carefully extinguish after each toke.

We had been working in comfortable silence for some time when he spoke as I was removing the second-last head bolt on my side of the engine.

"Tell Sugar-Loaves to be careful. Guys get funny ideas."

I stopped turning the ratchet to lock eyes with him. "I

told her. And if any guy gets funny with her I'll rip his nuts off and feed them to him."

Skidmark raised both hands in a 'don't shoot' gesture. "Be cool. Just saying."

"Okay, I heard you." I returned my attention to the bolt.

"So you're some badass chick," he said conversationally. "Sugar-Loaves must be your little lezzy rug-muncher. Can I watch while you two get it on?"

I extracted the bolt and eyed him expressionlessly, hiding my annoyance. "I'm here to wrench. If you're going to talk, it'll cost you in beer."

"That's cool."

He wandered out the door and I turned back to the last head bolt, trying to regain the pleasant relaxation I usually got from automotive work.

It eluded me. Even though Nichele had promised to be careful, I couldn't help worrying about her. I didn't know where Ratboy had gone or whether he had any way of figuring out where Nichele's tent was, and I was nervous about Orion, too. I didn't like the way he and Ratboy had been standing together in quiet conversation when Nichele and I had arrived at the garage.

I glanced toward the open door but saw no sign of Skidmark. Maybe he'd decided to go somewhere else and smoke himself into oblivion. That'd be nice. I chanced a quick peek at my tracking unit and breathed a sigh of relief at the sight of Orion's red dot in the vicinity of the main building. He likely wouldn't try anything that close to the busiest part of the commune.

I tucked the tracker back in my pocket and bent over the engine again. I was staring morosely at a scored cylinder wall when Skidmark shuffled in again and held out a condensation-beaded can of Kokanee.

I straightened with surprise and accepted it. "Thanks." I popped the top and tilted the can for a long, icy swallow. "Ahhh! Oh God, that's good."

"That's what she said, girlie."

I narrowly avoided snorting beer out my nose. When I managed to gulp my mouthful, I turned to face Skidmark's grin. "Wiseass."

He emitted his wheezy laughter before sobering and jerking his chin at the damaged cylinder. "Damn kids. Don't know shit about engines."

I grunted agreement and took another drink before asking, "Is there a place in town where you can get it bored out and sleeved?"

He shrugged. "Just hone it here."

"Those scratches are pretty deep," I protested.

"Hone the burr off it; new rings; good enough." He withdrew a second can of Kokanee from the pocket of his baggy coveralls and popped the top. "It's not a Corvette."

My heartstrings quivered at the thought of my beloved '66 'Vette, safely tucked away in my garage at home. My beautiful garage, with my clean tools all neatly organized in their shiny floor-standing chest...

"I wish." My words came out on a sigh as I surveyed the filthy garage with its scattered heaps of greasy tools.

He chuckled. "Yeah." He took a long swallow of his beer before placing the can on the bumper and tackling the head bolts on his side. "So you seen the cougar yet?"

"No." I picked up the ratchet and began at the other end of the head.

"Thought you might have. You're always out in the woods." When I shrugged, he continued, "Thought I came close to seeing it last night. Heard something out by the bench but it was gone when I got there."

I returned a noncommittal grunt as I pulled out my bolt and moved to the next one, hoping he didn't notice the sudden tremor in my hands.

"Orion thought he heard it moving around outside his tent last night, too," Skidmark persisted.

"Yeah, that's what he said." I busied myself with the ratchet.

"Did you hear anything?"

"Nope."

Skidmark ceased his pretense with the head bolt and faced me directly. "Aren't you worried about it?"

I sighed. "I'm careful when I'm in the woods. Besides, Moonbeam says the Earth Spirit will protect me." I raised my wrist to display the beaded bracelet.

"You really believe in that shit?" Skidmark asked.

Surprised, I straightened to frown at him. "Don't you?"

"It's shit." He picked up his beer and poured a healthy slug down his throat, then let out a resounding belch. "If you think a bracelet's gonna protect you, girlie, you're dumber than I thought."

I frowned at him in silence for a few moments, bothered by more than his words. The thought that had been nagging at my subconscious suddenly surfaced. For the last several minutes he had actually carried on a coherent conversation. Gone were the disjointed ramblings of an old hippie stoner. He was even standing straighter, his gaze sharp on me.

That was the fastest recovery from a high I'd ever seen.

Impossibly fast.

So he wasn't as stoned as he'd been pretending to be.

As if realizing his mistake, he yawned, his eyelids

drooping again as he shuffled over to the door and lit up. Slouched against the door frame, he sucked in a huge lungful of smoke and blew out a stinking cloud. "Aren't you supposed to meet Sugar-Loaves for supper?"

I glanced at my watch. "Yeah. Do you want me to come back afterward?"

He waved his joint vaguely. "Tomorrow."

He drifted away on a cloud of pot smoke, leaving me to finish my beer in uneasy solitude.

CHAPTER 21

The evening passed quickly while Nichele and I laughed and visited, and I realized how thoroughly I'd isolated myself from everyone else at the commune. In four months I hadn't gotten to know anyone beyond the exchange of a few friendly hellos.

I eased out a sigh. It didn't matter. I was there to do a job.

"Hey, what's wrong?" Nichele asked.

I snapped back to the present. "Nothing." I cracked a huge yawn. "I just zoned out for a second there. I had a crappy sleep last night and I'm bagged."

"Oh." Nichele glanced around the abandoned kitchen, the propane lantern on our table casting the only light. "Has everybody gone to bed already? It's only ten o'clock!"

"Maybe not to bed, but back to their tents," I said. "We tend to go with the daylight rhythms here. No all-night clubbing for us."

Nichele laughed. "Not so much for me anymore, either. I'm getting old. I can only make it 'til two AM."

"Well, feel free to stay up as late as you want." I stood and stretched, rubbing my ass to regain the circulation after several hours of sitting in a hard wooden chair. "I'm going to call it a night, though. I'll walk you back to your tent."

"Okay." She bounced to her feet, then cast an uncertain look around the dark room. "Do we take the lantern?"

"No, the lanterns stay here. I thought Moonbeam gave you a flashlight."

"Oh." Nichele frowned. "She did. I forgot it in my tent. It was still light at supper time."

I shrugged. "I forgot mine, too, but I always have my little one. Come on." I extinguished the lantern and led the way to the door.

When we stepped outside the chilly evening breeze greeted us, and I zipped up my jacket.

"Oh, *jeez!*" Nichele's voice trembled, and I flashed the light in her direction. Her arms were wrapped tightly around her naked shoulders and gooseflesh pebbled her arms and legs. "It was so nice and warm next to the woodstove I didn't even think about a jacket."

"Well, haul ass then." I set a brisk pace toward the encampment.

"W-wait!"

I turned in time to see her stumble over a root. She regained her footing and hurried up, her arms still wrapped around herself while she shivered uncontrollably. I reluctantly removed my jacket and handed it to her, beginning to shiver myself in my sweatshirt.

"Th-thanks." She wrapped the jacket around herself, her teeth chattering. "Hey, what have you g-got in here? Rocks in your p-pockets?" she teased, and I forced a chuckle and walked on, praying she wouldn't pull out any of the 'rocks' for examination.

As I had hoped, she hurried to follow the faint illumination of my light.

"G-god it's c-cold out here. And d-dark." She glanced fearfully around in the blackness.

"Less t-talking. M-more walking." My own teeth were starting to chatter with a combination of nerves and cold.

When we arrived at her tent she shed my jacket and dove into her cot, burrowing into the blankets so only her nose and eyes showed.

I pulled on my jacket with relief and searched briefly for the flashlight Moonbeam had given her. When I found it, I placed it beside the cot. "Here, you might need this if you have to go to the bathroom in the middle of the night."

"If I d-do, I'll just p-pee the bed," Nichele quavered. "I'm not g-going out there again."

I laughed. "This was your idea, remember."

"I *s-so* suck! Why d-didn't you t-talk me out of it? You know I hate c-camping."

"Goodnight. Sleep tight." I withdrew with a grin.

As soon as I was clear of the main encampment I delved into my pocket for my night-vision headset and breathed a sigh of relief when my green-tinted surroundings sprang into focus. Switching to thermal-only, I turned a slow three-sixty. The occupied tents behind me showed as faint glows through the trees, but no other heat signatures appeared.

Alone. Good.

I switched back to night vision and hurried in the direction of Moonbeam and Karma's tent. For the past four hours I'd forgotten my mission, happily immersed in being no more than Aydan Kelly the bookkeeper and Nichele's best friend. Now worry tightened my throat.

Four hours. I hadn't seen Orion or Moonbeam or Karma once during that time.

Shit, how could I have been so careless? A top agent like

Kane would never forget his mission; would never let
personal distractions compromise the safety of his charges.
If something bad had happened I'd never forgive myself.

I quickened my pace to a trot.

No snoring disturbed the silence of the forest. My
stomach twisting into a cold knot, I switched to thermal-
only. Was that a faint glow through the trees?

Creeping closer, I let out a breath when the intervening
forest thinned and the glow resolved itself into two large
blobs and three small points. Moonbeam and Karma, safe in
their tent with their three fat candles burning.

Thank God.

Turning away, I massaged my thumping heart through
my jacket. So far, so good. I pulled out my tracking unit and
frowned at Orion's dot. Over in the renters' camp again.
What the hell was he up to?

But at least if he was there, Ratboy probably was, too. I
stood thinking for a moment. This was probably the best
time to go for a walk and report to Stemp.

I headed for one of my newly-discovered routes.

After about twenty minutes of walking, I scanned around
me one last time before pulling out a secured phone. Stemp
answered on the first ring as always.

"It's Aydan," I said quietly. "Your mom and dad are still
fine. Orion has been making late-night trips over to the
renters' encampment, and he seems to be associating with
Ratboy more frequently. I don't know if they were friends
before or if this is a recent development. I'll see if I can snap
a photo of Ratboy and text it to you, but for now here's a
description..."

I rattled off Ratboy's particulars before continuing,
"Skidmark is definitely hiding something. He pretends to be

a lot more stoned than he is. Your parents said he's a Vietnam vet and part of his stress reaction is to control access to and from the commune by making sure the vehicles don't run unless he wants them to, but I'm not convinced that's all there is to it."

"Interesting." Stemp paused as if considering. "Easy enough to verify the military record if we have Skidmark's real name."

"Do you?"

"No." He hesitated again. "I can't think of any plausible reason why you would ask my parents for his real name, and I doubt they'd tell you even if they knew. Mother is unreasonably attached to her own nomenclature."

"Yeah, and I don't think Skidmark will tell me. He didn't even give me a straight answer when I asked why they call him Skidmark. And there's no point in trying to photograph him and do facial recognition. He's all hair and beard."

"But he'll be receiving a military pension if he's a veteran," Stemp replied. "I'll have the analysts check Veterans' Affairs here and in the U.S. for pension cheques going to the commune's address or a post office box in town, cross-referenced with approximate age. That should narrow it down to handful of people at most. I should have that information by late tomorrow. Meanwhile, continue to observe. If Ratboy is spending more time on the commune, that group may be more of a threat than we had originally thought."

I sighed. "Okay."

"'Til tomorrow, then." The connection clicked closed in my ear.

At least I didn't have to stay up and connect via the laptop tonight. I yawned hugely. Good thing. I needed the sleep.

Retracing my steps, I fought to stay alert. The thought of my bed beckoned like a promise of paradise and I forced myself to keep checking for heat signatures every few minutes.

When I neared the encampment, I detoured once more to Moonbeam and Karma's tent. Reassured by the snores echoing through the woods as much as by my thermal display, I turned away smiling. I'd just check Nichele's tent on my way by, and then glorious sleep would be mine.

Stepping softly along the path, I studied the cluster of glows that formed the main encampment. None moved and I eased out a breath of contentment as I got closer. Everybody was snug in their beds, and soon I would be, too.

My veins turned to ice.

Nichele's tent was dark and cold.

CHAPTER 22

Heart hammering, I scanned wildly around me but saw no other heat signatures besides the occupied tents. I fought for calm. Maybe there was a simple explanation. Maybe Nichele had just gone to the latrine.

Not likely. I'd only been gone for an hour, and she had sounded pretty serious about staying in her tent.

Okay, maybe Orion had dropped by and she had succumbed to temptation and gone to his tent.

My fear mounted. Orion and Ratboy were friends. Oh, God, what if both of them had come for her?

Oh, God, oh God...

Stay calm. Eliminate the most likely possibilities first.

I turned and fled back along the path.

The latrines were all unoccupied.

Gasping for breath, I shot a desperate glance around me. Dammit, I needed a vantage point. Skidmark's bench would work, but I'd waste precious time getting up there and even more rushing back the way I came. Unless they were holding her at the garage.

Sudden realization hit me and I swore at my own stupidity and checked Orion's tracker. Still in the vicinity of the renter's camp. He could have come over and snatched

Nichele and taken her back there, but it seemed unlikely.

But I still had no idea where Ratboy was.

A squeak snapped my head around, but it was only one of the swings from the playground next to the building. As I watched, the empty seat swung back and forth in the night breeze, emitting another desolate squeak like the ghost of a child's laughter.

An idea dawned.

The kids had been playing when I'd passed by at suppertime, and the braver ones had found their way onto the dangerously pitched roof of the building. The admonitions of their parents ringing in my ears, I hurried for the climbing frame.

I was up to the top of it in a moment, reaching for the naked limb of the overhanging arbutus tree. I hesitated, hands locked on the branch. For the kids, the dangerous part had been leaping from the top of the climbing frame to catch the branch. It was an easy reach for me, but would it hold my weight?

Clenching my teeth, I lifted myself slowly from the climbing frame, my feet leaving the solid structure with reluctance. The branch deflected but didn't make any ominous cracking noises, so I swung my feet up and traversed to the roof like an ungainly sloth.

When my back contacted the roof I squirmed around to get my feet under me before crouching, my muscles quivering with effort and adrenaline.

Leaning forward and trying not to think about the drop below, I cautiously scaled the slope, my fingertips scraping the rough asphalt shingles in a fruitless attempt to find a secure handhold. When I reached the peak at last I sucked in a breath of relief and straddled it. Scanning again with thermal imaging, I panted as quietly as possible.

No distinct heat signatures were apparent near the garage, though there was a diffuse glow from the building. Probably accumulated heat from the day's sun. Orion's and my tents were both dark and cold.

To the north, I glimpsed scattered glows from the renters' encampment but nothing closer. A bright movement caught my eye as I panned around to the south, but the heat signature was close enough for me to identify a graceful neck and four slender legs tapering into cool blue tones. Only a deer.

Dammit, where could Nichele be?

I rose awkwardly to my feet and hands and followed the ridge to the transverse peak that housed the big fieldstone chimney. I had just shuffled onto the peak with shaking legs when a shrill voice galvanized my muscles into a spastic jerk that nearly toppled me off the roof.

"Get lost! Go on, *scat!*"

A flashlight beam raked the shingles beside me and I flung myself behind the shelter of the chimney, scrabbling for purchase on the slope.

"Scram! And don't come back!"

My heart gave a painful thump when I identified Nichele's voice. Her flashlight scoured the roof and I huddled closer to the chimney, shaking and trying not to hyperventilate.

Of course. She'd been cold and she hated tenting. It would be the most natural thing in the world for her to abandon her tent for a warm berth beside one of the woodstoves.

Nichele apparently decided that the animal on the roof had fled, and her flashlight disappeared back into the building.

Relief weakened my knees and I fought to stay upright, hugging the chimney like a life preserver. Gradually my heart rate slowed, but fatigue and nerves conspired to magnify the tremors of my legs. The chilly breeze swirled around me, tempting my overworked muscles to cramp.

The ground looked very far away, and I swallowed hard. All of a sudden I didn't appreciate the clarity of night vision quite so much.

How the hell was I supposed to get down from the roof? As soon as my boots scraped the shingles Nichele would come running out with her flashlight again. And I couldn't think of any plausible excuse if she caught me squatting up here like a constipated gargoyle.

A spiteful sprinkling of cold rain spurred me into motion. If I didn't move before the shingles got wet and slick, I wouldn't need an excuse; I'd just need a body bag.

Or worse, I'd need a full-body cast and an excuse.

I coaxed my quivering muscles into motion, bending double to walk my hands along the peak and follow with my feet as quietly as possible.

Head down, ass up like a particularly uncoordinated inchworm, I crept across the ridge to the junction and turned the corner onto the final stretch of the roof peak. Too afraid to look anywhere but in front of me, I sent a silent prayer skyward that there was nobody watching with night vision right now. A hysterical urge to giggle seized me at the thought, but a moment later the giggle turned into a squeak of terror when my foot slipped.

Sprawled gasping across the ridge on my stomach, my lips framed the words 'please-don't-look-please-don't-look', the supplication not quite audible in my panting.

If Nichele came out now, I'd be busted for sure. Just stay put, Nichele. Please-don't-look-please-don't-look...

Either the gods or Nichele granted my prayer. No flashlight burst from the building below and after long minutes of immobility I finally dared to move again, turning over to inch feet-first down the slope toward the arbutus branch.

Most of my body was below the peak when a movement in my peripheral vision made me freeze. Turning my head slowly and praying, I spotted Orion striding along the path, coming from the direction of the renters' land.

He wore night-vision goggles.

Paralyzed, I hunched on the roof, watching him survey the forest around him as he walked.

Oh God, if he looked up he'd see my head above the peak of the roof, topped with the damning night-vision headset.

My heart pounded so loudly I was sure he'd hear it. His gaze skimmed over the side of the building and I stopped breathing entirely, but he kept walking without a change of expression.

Thank God, he must have been using regular night vision. If he'd had thermographic goggles, my head would have glowed above the roof peak like a spotlight.

He vanished around the corner of the path and I sucked in a breath at last, shaking from head to toe. Goddammit, if I got off this roof and into my bed unscathed and undetected I'd consider it a miracle right up there with the parting of the Red Sea.

Which was actually quite apropos, since it was absolutely pissing rain by now.

I eased down the slope, hands widespread on the wet shingles, feet shuffling in tiny steps. When I reached the branch at last, I hooked my legs over it but my icy hands could barely grip the slippery surface where the tree had shed its bark in winter. I managed a short hand-over-hand progress before realizing I wasn't going to make it.

Stifling my yelp of panic, I let my legs swing down. My hands slipped off the wet branch an instant later and I fell for terrifying seconds. Then my feet thudded into the deep pea gravel of the playground, the shock rolling up my spine as I overbalanced to sprawl on my back.

Spread-eagled on the ground, I whimpered in sheer relief. The pea gravel had done its job, cushioning my landing. None of my body parts hurt excessively. Even my night-vision headset was still intact and operating, which was more than I could say for my composure.

I lay there quivering on my back until rain started to run up my nose. Then I hauled myself to my feet and tottered toward the path.

Halfway to my tent I stumbled to a halt.

What if Orion was lurking outside again? If he had the same kind of headset as I did, he'd be able to spot me as soon as I saw him. I could take off my headset and innocently approach my tent, pretending to have just finished my visit with Nichele, but a simple conversation with Nichele would prove I was lying.

Undecided, I shuffled my feet for a few moments before making up my mind. He probably already knew my tent had been empty late at night before, so it shouldn't make him any more suspicious of me tonight.

And his scan of the forest had been the casual survey of a man travelling from point A to point B with nothing on his mind but his destination. So whatever he might think I was doing during my nocturnal ramblings, he obviously didn't consider me a threat.

I'd probably gotten away with it tonight, but I couldn't keep running around half the night and still function during the day. There had to be a better way to keep everybody under surveillance. And dammit, if I was a real secret agent I'd know what it was.

Too bad I was only a bookkeeper.

Heaving a long sigh, I turned and plodded back into the forest on aching legs. I might be in far over my head, but at least I knew where to get some advice. And by the time I got back, Orion should be safely asleep in his tent.

After fifteen minutes of walking I sank onto a soggy fallen log with a groan. Soaked to the skin and shivering, I scanned for heat signatures before pulling out a burner phone.

My trembling fingers barely navigated the tiny keys. When I got the number punched in I hunched over, my free arm wrapped around myself while I counted the rings on the other end.

One. Two. Three.

"Come on, Arnie, pick up," I muttered.

Four.

Expecting his voicemail, I was about to hang up when a sleepy voice growled, "Helmand."

Hellhound's irritable rasp sounded like the sweet music of salvation. I hugged the phone closer, tears of exhaustion and relief prickling my eyes. "Hi, Arnie, it's me. Aydan," I added just in case he wasn't quite awake.

"What's wrong?" If he hadn't been awake before, he definitely was now. His words vibrated with tension.

"Nothing. I'm really sorry to call you in the middle of the night..."

His rush of released breath cut across my apology. "No problem, darlin'. Good to hear your voice." He chuckled, the deep rough-edged sound tickling my eardrum and bringing a vivid image of his bulky muscular body reclining on the pillows, warm lamplight softening the battered contours of his face. "Ya know how many dumbfuck salesmen I've talked to in the last four months?" he asked. "Every time I see 'private caller' on my call display I pick up in case it's you."

"Aw, thanks, Arnie." I drew an unsteady breath and swallowed the lump in my throat. "It's really good to hear your voice, too. I miss you."

His voice deepened to a caressing rumble. "Miss ya, too, darlin'. My bed's pretty damn cold right now. Wanna warm me up with some sexy talk?"

I tightened my arm around my shivering body. "More than you can imagine. But that's not actually why I'm calling."

His teasing tone vanished. "Somethin's wrong, ain't it? Tell me."

"Well..." I hesitated, then let it all pour out. "You know how I'm supposed to be protecting Moonbeam and Karma and it seemed like everything was okay?" I kept talking over his rumble of assent. "Well, now there are three guys I'm worried about, and in the meantime Nichele has showed up and one of the guys has a hate on for me and I'm afraid he'll hurt Nichele, but-"

"Hang on." His usual rasp had developed an edge. "This guy wants to hurt ya? Tell me who he is. Ya got your gun?"

"I've always got my gun," I hastened to reassure him. "I don't know his real name so I've been calling him Ratboy. I'm not too worried about him hurting me. He's just a weaselly little shit, but he could probably hurt Nichele. I'm just afraid he might be friends with another guy I'm worried about, Orion. If they're friends it could be bad because Orion had hand restraints in his pocket the time he was in my tent, and tonight I found out he has a night-vision headset-"

"Shit, Aydan!" A rustle and thump on the other end of the line sounded as though Hellhound had lunged out of bed. "An' you're there by yourself? Why the hell didn't Stemp send ya a team? Who's the third guy you're worried about?" Muffled thumps formed a backdrop to his words.

"This is all just a gut feeling," I protested. "None of them have actually done anything that looks threatening to Moonbeam or Karma so Stemp doesn't have any reason to send a team. The third guy's name is Skidmark and I'm pretty sure he's harmless, it's just-"

"Fuck that, Aydan. If you're sayin' some guy wants to hurt ya an' his buddy's sneakin' into your tent with handcuffs, that ain't harmless!"

"No, I didn't mean that, I just..." The thumps on the other end of the line had given way to the click of computer keys. I changed the subject. "Arnie, what are you doing? I didn't mean to call you up and worry you, I just wanted to ask your advice on how to keep an eye on everybody. I've got a tracking unit on Orion, but-"

"Ya want my advice?" He sounded grim. "Call Stemp an' tell him ya need backup, right fuckin' now."

"But, Arnie, I can't justify that and neither can he. I haven't identified any positive threat to his parents and even if I had, this isn't really an official mission. I'm supposed to be on admin leave and the only reason he can run it through the department at all is because there's a tiny chance our last op might have blown his cover. He's already pushing the limits by sending me secured phones and classified gear. If he throws a team at this and it turns out to be nothing, he'll be in deep shit."

"I don't give a flyin' fuck about Stemp's problems. If your gut feelin' is right an' ya end up gettin' dead, he'll be in really deep shit for losin' a good agent," Hellhound countered. "An' then I'd hafta rip his fuckin' head off, too." He paused. "Okay. I got the eight-fifteen A.M. flight, gets me in at ten-thirty. I oughta make it there a little after noon tomorrow. Gimme directions to the commune."

"Oh, no, you're busy with your P.I. cases, I didn't mean for you to-"

"Darlin'," he interrupted. "You're wastin' your breath, an' you're wastin' time. It's already done. Just gimme the directions."

I let out a breath, my aching muscles relinquishing their tension for the first time in days. "Thanks, Arnie. It's going to be good to have you here."

I had just disconnected after giving him the directions when the distant clanging of the Spirit bells made me groan.

CHAPTER 23

"Fuck, *really?*" I demanded of no one in particular as I jogged through the dark forest, my night vision headgear thudding my forehead while a burgeoning headache thumped my skull from the inside.

Deciding to use my breath to better purpose, I concentrated on pacing myself. I was probably a little less than a mile away from the commune, so if I kept up a good pace I should make it to the main building in ten minutes or so. Since everybody else would be waking from a dead sleep and throwing on clothes before running to the Calling, I'd probably arrive around the same time as the last of the stragglers.

That would look normal, except that my clothes were soaked and I'd be red-faced and sweating by the time I got there. But what the hell, everybody would be half-asleep anyway, and it was dark. They probably wouldn't notice. And it was still raining, so I wouldn't be the only one looking like a drowned rat.

I spared a moment of envy for Nichele. She'd be warm and dry in the main building, all set to meditate in comfort. I hoped she'd brought a jacket with her this time. She'd need it for our hike to the field.

I groaned at the thought of another hike and forced my legs to keep moving. God, if I lay down to meditate I might never get up again.

A sudden report made me duck and leap sideways. Panting with the extra exertion and adrenaline, I shook my head at my own idiocy and kept jogging, too winded to even swear. The fireworks continued in a sporadic exchange, getting louder as I neared the commune.

I glimpsed some distant heat signatures hurrying in the direction of the main building and halted to stuff my headset into my pocket. Orion likely wouldn't be wearing his, but I couldn't take the chance.

Slowed to the careful pace required by my tiny flashlight, I had almost regained my breath by the time I trotted up to accept my mat from Aurora. A few other people crowded in behind me, so I didn't even merit a disapproving look.

Spreading out the mat in my designated spot, I collapsed onto it, managing to stifle my moan.

A sharp elbow in my shoulder made me jerk into sitting position, staring wildly around the dim room. "What?" I snapped.

"Shhh!" The man beside me gave me a dirty look. "You were snoring. Again."

"Oh." I sank back onto the mat. "Sorry."

"Shhh."

Suitably chastened, I stretched my eyes wide, fighting sleep. That worked for a few minutes, until a porcine snort from my own throat roused me from slumber again. I shook my head vigorously, digging my nails into my palms.

Do not fall asleep. Do not...

Snort.

I jerked awake again and chanced a sidelong look at my

neighbour. His eyes were tightly closed and he was humming determinedly, but a scowl knitted his brows together.

Do not fall asleep. Do *not* fall asleep...

At last the gong released me from my misery and I dragged myself to my feet, mumbling an apology to my neighbour. He shushed me severely for a third time, and I hung my head and shuffled out with everybody else.

Half asleep, I slogged along the winding path, mindlessly following the woman in front of me. In the field I sank to my aching knees and closed my eyes. At least it was harder to fall asleep kneeling in the rain. I phased in and out of awareness, not sure whether I was fighting sleep or hypothermia.

At last Aurora and Zen offered us the Earth Spirit's blessing in offensively cheerful tones, and I creaked to my feet. I was plodding across the field with my eyes half-closed when Nichele's voice chirped beside me.

"Well, that was freaky-deaky! How weird is it to get up in the middle of the night to hang with some wacko Spirit in the rain?"

"Too fucking weird," I growled. I pried open an eyelid to survey her in the reflected glow of her big flashlight. A bright yellow rain slicker enveloped her completely, framing her bright-eyed face and perky smile. She looked warm and dry and wide awake.

I came very close to hating her.

"Aydan, you're soaked!" She lifted a sodden lock of my hair and let it fall against my jacket. "You're going to catch your death of cold."

"That'd be a mercy," I mumbled. "Just shoot me now."

"You can't go back to bed like that." She frowned at me for a moment before her face cleared. "I'll get you fixed up. Come on."

It took all my willpower not to groan out loud, but I let her lead me back to the kitchen. I watched dully while she dragged a chair over beside one of the stoves and tossed a few sticks of wood on top of the glowing coals.

Then she pulled a blanket off the bed she'd made for herself beside the stove and held it up in front of me, stretching her arms wide.

"Strip," she commanded.

"Nichele..."

"Shut up and strip. I'll hold up the blanket and nobody will see you in the corner here." She glowered at me with all the authority of a tiny general.

Realizing protests were futile, I opted for damage control. "I have to pee first."

"Fine. Go and pee and then come right back."

"Yes, ma'am." I retreated, shivering my way out to the latrine and cursing steadily while I peed and, more importantly, removed my Glock and ankle holster and stowed them in my already-distended jacket pockets.

The pocket flaps barely closed and the jacket hung like a lead weight from my shoulders, swinging ponderously under its burden of classified technology and concealed weapons. Muttering, I took it off and draped it over my arm before re-entering the kitchen.

Nichele looked up from the steaming bucket she'd placed in front of the chair. "Good, now strip."

She held up the blanket again, and I carefully balled up my jacket around its cargo and laid it in the corner before stripping down to underwear and goosebumps.

Nichele wrapped the blanket around me. "Sit." She pointed to the chair. "And put your feet in that bucket."

I obeyed, then yelped and jerked my feet out of the scalding water.

"It's not that hot, it's just that your feet are that cold," Nichele reassured me. "Now get in there."

After a few more tentative dips I managed to keep my feet submerged, and she briskly towelled my hair before wrapping the towel around my head. "Better. Here, drink this." She handed me a mug of hot chocolate and added, "Stay put. I'll be right back."

Already feeling the warmth of the woodstove at my back and the heat rising through my feet, I nodded gratefully and sipped while she hurried out the door, flashlight in hand.

In a few minutes she was back bearing an object I couldn't identify at first. When she drew closer, I shot her a wary look. "What are you planning to do with that, give me a makeover? You know there's no electricity, right?"

"I know, silly." Nichele brandished her curling iron. "It's butane. It doesn't need electricity. And if you go to bed with all that long hair soaking wet, you'll be frozen again in minutes. This isn't as good as a blow dryer, but it'll dry your hair, so shut up and sit still."

I let her work on me in silence for several minutes, sipping the last of the hot chocolate while she wound locks of my hair around the barrel of the curling iron. Wisps of steam drifted around my head.

"You're enjoying this, aren't you?" I said at last.

She giggled. "Hell, yeah, girl. If I thought I could get away with it I'd give you a facial, too. And wax your brows, and-"

"Don't even think about it. This is embarrassing

enough." I cast a dark look at a couple of the commune members who were eyeing us with bemusement.

They mercifully vacated the kitchen, leaving us alone in the circle of light from our lantern, and Nichele carried on with her comb and curling iron.

At last she stepped back. "There." She applied a round brush to my new ringlets with expert twists of her wrist. "Oh-em-gee, Aydan, you have such beautiful hair. Why don't you spend a little time on it? I'd kill to have hair like yours."

"Your hair always looks beautiful," I objected.

"Yeah, because I spend an hour on it every morning," she retorted.

I appropriated the towel and extricated my feet from the bucket. "Well, take a picture, because this'll never happen again." I dried my feet and straightened just in time to face a blinding flash of light. "*Jesus!*" I yelped. "What the hell?"

"So I took a picture." Nichele hefted her phone, looking at me as if I'd lost my mind. "What did you expect?"

"Give me that!" I made a grab for the phone, but she danced out of reach, grinning.

"Nope. Blackmail photos."

"Okay, fine. I guess I owe you." I stretched, easing the knots out of my shoulders. "I feel so much better. Thanks." I eyed my wet clothes with distaste. "Maybe I'll just wear this blanket back to my tent."

"You should," she said seriously. "Drape your clothes over the stove and they'll be dry by morning."

I let out a breath. "You're one smart cookie, you know?"

"I know." She gave me a smug smile. "Leave your clothes here and get going. I'll put them on the stove and take them off when they're dry. Goodnight."

"Goodnight." I stuffed my feet back into my hiking boots

and scooped up my jacket. "Thanks, Nichele. You're the best."

Back at my tent I took exactly enough time to transfer my gear to a dry jacket and tuck my gun into its bedside niche before tumbling onto my cot, still wrapped in the blanket.

When I opened my eyes again, my tent was bright and the damn birds were singing at the tops of their lungs. I squinted at my watch and groaned. Less than five hours of sleep. Again.

Maybe I could just turn over and grab a few more zees...

No. Three lives might depend on me.

I dragged myself resolutely out of bed and checked Orion's tracker. Up by the garage again. What the hell was he doing there? I'd never seen him pick up a tool, and Skidmark certainly wasn't a big attraction.

But maybe he was meeting Ratboy.

I sank down to sit on the edge of my cot, frowning. Why did Ratboy spend so much time at the garage? He obviously had no automotive skills, and he and Skidmark didn't get along. And it wouldn't make sense for him to be meeting Orion there. If Orion was going over to the renters' land every night, surely they could do all the talking they needed then.

I blew out a breath and rose. Whatever. At least Orion was far away from the people I cared about, assuming Moonbeam and Karma were still in their tent or at breakfast.

I threw on some clothes and dragged a brush through my hair. The humidity had turned the previous night's ringlets into a dense frizzy mat, and I expended several minutes and some of my best swearwords untangling it. Then I checked Orion's tracker one more time to make sure he was still at the garage, and hurried off to the main building.

When I strode into the kitchen Nichele broke off her animated conversation to wave a cheerful good-morning from the table she was sharing with Moonbeam, Karma, and Aurora. I returned the salute with a smile. All present and accounted for. What a relief.

Grabbing some fruit, yogurt, and granola, I headed for their table and slid into the chair beside Nichele.

"Good morning, Ay... I mean Storm," she said. "Guess what? Uncle Karma was just telling me about their school, and I'm going to do a seminar on stock market investing tonight." She shot a bright-eyed smile at Karma. "This is going to be so much fun! And we'll have the electricity turned on, too, so I can show everybody the online stuff!"

Her enthusiasm brought a smile to my face as always. "That's great," I agreed. "What age of kids will you be teaching?"

"Not kids." Nichele took a quick sip of her coffee before continuing, "Well, the older students if they want to come. But it's for everybody. They're so progressive here! Nothing at all like the backwoods attitudes I expected!" She shot a contrite glance at Moonbeam and Karma. "Sorry, I didn't mean to be insulting, but with you being out here with no electricity I thought... well, you know."

Moonbeam gave her usual luminous smile. "Of course, dear, no offense taken. And we are looking forward to your talk tonight. We do try to offer our members the best educational opportunities whenever we have experts available. Storm Cloud Dancer gave us a wonderful bookkeeping seminar a couple of months ago."

"That's so cool!" Nichele's eyes sparkled. She turned to me. "Oh, by the way, your clothes are all dry, they're folded up beside the stove..." Without pausing for breath she transferred her smile to Aurora. "And I can hardly wait to talk to you some more about the Earth Spirit today; yesterday was so much fun!"

The two of them chattered busily, and I eased out a breath and applied myself to my breakfast. Nichele was in the thick of things as usual, making new friends and gobbling up new experiences with gusto. At least she'd have plenty of activities to keep her distracted and in the safety of a group. One less thing to worry about.

Karma and Moonbeam finished their breakfast and rose, and I gulped my last mouthful and stood, too.

"I've got some things to do this morning, so I'll catch you later, okay?" I said to Nichele, and received a nod and smile in return before she dove back into conversation with Aurora.

Turning to Moonbeam as we moved toward the door, I lowered my voice. "I'm sorry to keep springing people on you, but another friend is coming to visit me today."

"Oh." A hint of something coloured the word. It sounded almost like annoyance, but it was gone in a flash, hidden by gentle concern. "Oh, dear. I'm terribly sorry, but we're out of spare tents."

"That's okay, he'll sleep with me."

"Oh."

This time her intonation was easier to read.

Disappointment.

"I'm honestly not in a relationship with Cosmic River Stone," I said gently. "I'm sorry if you're disappointed."

Moonbeam sighed. "I have to admit I am disappointed, dear. I would have loved to have had you for a daughter-in-law."

"Oh." I swallowed the lump in my throat. "Well, thanks. I would've loved to have you for a mother-in-law."

"Thank you, dear." She gave me a quick hug before pulling away with a smile. "Now, tell me about your young man. What is his name, and will we be keeping up our pretense as your aunt and uncle?"

"No, it's okay. Arnie knows why I'm here. Oh, and that's his name, Arnold Helmand. But everybody calls him Hellhound."

"Oh. That doesn't sound auspicious... but the numbers tell the tale." Her eyes unfocused and she hesitated for a moment as though performing some mental calculation before her gaze sharpened again. "He must be quite creative and intuitive."

I managed not to let my mouth drop open. "Uh... yeah. He's a really talented musician, and he... um, probably understands me better than anybody I know."

Moonbeam's face relaxed into a smile. "He sounds like a wonderful person. And I'm so glad you feel safe enough with him to tell him the truth. I'm sure you'll be very happy together. Are you planning a wedding?"

"God, no!"

Moonbeam and Karma looked taken aback by my expression of horror, and I fumbled to explain. "Neither of us wants any kind of commitment. We're just friends with benefits, and that's how we both want it to stay."

"Oh." Moonbeam brightened. "So there would still be room in your life for a serious relationship."

"Um... in theory, yeah, but..."

She gave me a whimsical smile. "Don't worry, dear, I won't press. But a mother never gives up hope, you know."

"Uh, I think in this case maybe you should," I mumbled.

She patted my hand, unabashed. "We'll look forward to meeting your Hellhound. Is the station wagon running? How will you pick him up?"

"No, he said he'd get here on his own. When I told him vehicles weren't allowed on the commune he said he'd walk here."

Moonbeam's brow furrowed. "He does realize it's twelve miles from Port Renfrew, doesn't he?"

"I told him." I shrugged. "He's in really good shape. And he said he was looking forward to getting some exercise in our nice weather after all the snow they've had in Calgary."

"Very well, dear. Oh, and you may want to take a larger mattress from the supply room. Your cot is unlikely to be comfortable for two."

"Right, thanks." They began to move off, and I tried to keep my tone casual as I added, "So what's on your agenda for today?" They looked slightly bemused by the non sequitur, and I added in a burst of inspiration, "I'd like to bring Arnie to meet you later and I was wondering when would be a good time. He thought he'd be here around noon."

They exchanged a glance, and Karma smiled and replied, "The Earth Spirit has requested our service today. We'll likely be unavailable most of the day, but we'll look forward to meeting him at our evening meal."

"Oh. Okay, see you later, then."

They turned away, leaving me to worry about what 'unavailable' really meant.

CHAPTER 24

I wandered over to collect my clothes from beside the woodstove, deep in thought. What did 'the Earth Spirit requested their service' mean? No wonder Stemp had lost patience with the mysterious dogma.

I didn't know whether to be reassured or worried. On one hand it meant I needn't panic if I couldn't find Moonbeam and Karma, but on the other hand, all kinds of bad things could happen to them and I wouldn't know until suppertime.

And what did they mean by 'unavailable'? It wasn't like they were going to take their phone off the hook or refuse to answer email. They lived in a tent with no technology at all. Did they mean 'in their tent but not responding to visitors', or 'at some mysterious undisclosed location'?

I realized I was beginning to draw odd looks while I stood scowling at the stove, so I abandoned the kitchen and headed for the supply room.

Wrestling a queen-sized mattress from the main building to my tent provided my workout for the day. By the time I'd folded up my cot and made up the mattress on the floor I was drenched in sweat and beginning to curse the unaccustomed warmth of the sun on my tent.

I flopped down on the mattress and stared at the canvas ceiling. Wouldn't you know it; another nice warm sunny day. And I had to wear my jacket all day or risk leaving my secret equipment to be discovered in my tent.

Or I could sneak it back into my underwater cache, but I didn't really want to do that in broad daylight, and I didn't dare go without a secured phone just in case I needed to make an emergency call to Stemp.

Muttering imprecations, I put on my jacket and checked Orion's tracker one more time. His red dot was still in the vicinity of the garage, and I sighed. Might as well go up there and get some more work done on the truck. If it happened that Orion and Ratboy were both there, at least I could keep an eye on them.

The climb to the garage wearing my jacket did nothing to solve my sweat problem. Halfway up the hill I shrugged out of it and tied it around my waist by its sleeves instead. The bulging pockets bumped my calves annoyingly, but at least I wasn't sweltering anymore.

As I neared the clearing I slowed, listening, but heard nothing. When I rounded the corner and strode up the last of the grade I discovered I was alone. I poked my head into the garage and circled the clearing, but Orion must have left by another route while I was climbing the hill.

I stood frowning into space while I thought that through. First he had popped up everywhere as though he had been following me, and now he seemed to be avoiding me. Weird. He didn't strike me as the kind of guy who'd completely give up on a woman after failing to score on his first try, so he must have some other reason for lying low. Maybe my empty tent had aroused his suspicions last night after all.

Stepping into the garage, I untied my jacket and laid it in

the cleanest corner of the workbench. There was no sign of Skidmark, so I chanced a peek into my pocket to check Orion's tracker. My heart almost stopped at the sight of his dot superimposed on my origin point. He couldn't be more than a hundred yards away.

Pulse pounding, I stepped casually away from the workbench and crossed to the door.

"Hey, Skidmark!" I yelled. "Are you around?"

I hadn't expected an answer, but I strode in the direction the tracker had indicated, calling out again. "Hey, Skidmark!"

Standing in the forest where I thought Orion should have been, I turned in a slow circle, seeing nothing but trees and ferns.

Okay, he was definitely avoiding me.

I let out a few more yells while I circled the clearing, eyes peeled for any movement in the forest.

Nothing.

When I returned to the garage and surreptitiously checked the tracker again, the dot glowed in the same location.

What the hell? Why would Orion stand there watching and listening but evade me when I approached?

I stood undecided for a few moments before giving a mental shrug. It would make him suspicious if I kept returning to the place where he'd just been. If he wanted to show himself, he would. Meanwhile, I'd better look as though I had some reason to be here.

I picked up the ratchet and got to work on the engine, making sure I faced the door. Even so, the back of my neck prickled with the feeling of being watched.

A couple of hours later I'd almost finished stripping the

engine and Skidmark still hadn't appeared. I eyed the transmission bolts and decided against dropping the tranny by myself. It would be an easier job with two people, and anyway, there was just enough time to grab lunch before hiking out to meet Arnie.

I scrubbed off as much grease as I could and retrieved my jacket before heading for the kitchen.

Striding out the commune gates at noon, I stretched my arms above my head, easing muscles that had stiffened while I bent over the engine. The sun was warm on my back and the spicy scent of cedar wafted on a gentle breeze.

For the first time in days I felt my shoulders relax. No run-ins with Ratboy; no uncomfortable encounters with Orion; and Nichele and Moonbeam and Karma were all safe.

As far as I knew, anyway.

Worry niggled at the back of my mind, but I tamped it down. I might as well just enjoy the peace. It likely wouldn't last.

I had only walked a mile or so when a burly figure appeared from around a bend in the road. Clad in faded jeans and T-shirt, with a black leather jacket swinging from the pack on his back, he walked with the economical rhythm of a man accustomed to long marches. I hurried forward, smiling.

As the gap narrowed between us, I admired the flex and release of his bulky muscles with each stride. Soon I was near enough to make out his features, his beard and moustache failing to camouflage the long-ago-broken bones that formed a fearsome face belied by the twinkle in his eyes.

"Hey, darlin'!" He held out his arms and I dove into his

embrace.

"Oh, Arnie, it's so good to see you!" I planted a big smacking kiss on his lips before hugging him close, reveling in the feel of his hard bulk against me. "God, you feel good!"

"So do you, darlin'." He held me with his characteristic gentleness, and I snuggled safely into arms powerful enough to crush my ribcage.

"Mm. Come here," he murmured. He tilted my chin up and his lips met mine in a kiss that weakened my knees.

Slowly, softly, he tasted my lips as though relearning every contour. A small moan escaped me at the feather-light brush of his tongue, and desire coiled low in my belly. Pulling me closer, he continued his unhurried exploration, his tongue seducing mine while his palms traced down my back to curve around my ass.

I pressed against the stiffening bulge in his jeans, opening my legs to welcome his hands. The friction of our zippers sent sparkles of sensation directly to nerve endings that were already begging for his touch.

My hands roamed greedily over the hard planes of his chest, seeking down over solid abs toward the button of his jeans. His dexterous musician's fingers stroked a line of heat between my legs and I whimpered with need and rubbed the hard ridge straining his faded denim.

"Jesus, darlin'," he rasped against my lips. "If ya keep doin' that I'm gonna take ya right here in the middle a' the road."

"I could wait long enough to get to the side of the road." My voice came out hoarse and breathless. "Maybe a few feet into the woods. But not much more."

"Slow down, darlin'." His hands ceased their mind-melting work and slid up to my waist. "I wanna wait 'til I can take my time an' do ya right."

"Just a quickie to take the edge off," I coaxed. "I know you'll be ready to go again by the time we get to my tent." I dipped a finger inside the waistband of his jeans to caress the hot hardness pressing up to meet me.

"Ya sure, Aydan?" He trapped my hand against him and cast an assessing look around us. "Are we safe here? Any surveillance?"

I jerked my chin in the direction of Skidmark's bluff. "There's a viewpoint up there but this part of the road is hidden by the trees. And I've never met anybody else on foot out here." I returned my attention to the job at hand, stroking lightly. "Besides, you can't hike any farther with a hard-on like this. You'll get all chafed."

He growled low in his throat, giving me a toothy grin. "Well, where ya goin' in the woods all by yourself, little girl?"

I made big innocent eyes up at him. "My, what big..." I traced circles with my fingertip. "...teeth you have." He growled again, and I batted my eyelashes. "I'm going to my grandmother's house. Can you take me?"

"Darlin', I can take ya any way ya want." His mouth captured mine, his hands clamping on my ass to pull me to his hardness. I ground against him while he kissed me senseless before pulling away just far enough to make for the forest beside the road.

Pressed together, we stumbled into the undergrowth far enough to be concealed from the road.

"Have you got a condom handy?" I gasped, already pushing my jeans down.

He shoved a hand in his pocket. "Hell yeah. Figured I might need one in a hurry."

I bent to prop my elbows on a stump, legs wide.

He stilled and his hot gaze devoured me. "Jesus, darlin', ya make me glad I got a photographic memory. I'm gonna enjoy this one for a helluva long time."

"Enjoy it *now*," I urged.

He grinned and reached slowly for his zipper, teasing me with his unhurried movements.

Trembling with need, I watched over my shoulder while he rolled on the condom and stepped behind me. His hands glided down my back and over my ass, rounding my thighs and moving up to stroke exactly the right spot.

My tremors redoubled as tingling ripples of pleasure rolled through me. "Oh, God, Arnie..."

A moan burst from my lips when he slid slowly into me, then withdrew almost all the way before pressing in again, setting a leisurely rhythm of long sensuous strokes while his skillful fingers worked their magic.

Rosy haze obscured my vision and I let my eyelids fall shut, sensation expanding to possess my entire being. Little cries fell from my lips, my hips rocking back to meet him again and again while his fingers drove me to the brink of glorious madness. I quivered on the edge for a timeless instant, pleasure flooding every nerve before coiling back to implode into waves of ecstasy.

My body spasmed around him and he gripped my hips, accelerating to short hard thrusts that shattered me into another blinding orgasm, his panting mingling with my mindless cries.

He let out a raw-throated groan and slammed home one last time, iron muscles straining for a long trembling moment. Then his breath left him in a gasp and he bent over my back, wrapping his arms around my waist.

We straightened slowly and stood locked together

panting and swaying gently, his face buried in my hair, his arms tight around me.

As the heaving of his chest slowed, he turned his head to strew feather-light whisker kisses across my jaw. I sighed pure bliss and leaned into him, wrapped in his tender strength.

After a few minutes he gently disengaged himself and rolled the used condom into the tissue he'd taken from his jacket pocket.

I pulled up my jeans. "You must have been a Boy Scout."

He grinned as he zipped up. "Always prepared. Ya fixed that chafin' problem pretty good. Thanks, darlin'."

"My pleasure." A last stray ripple of orgasm shook me and I sucked in a breath, my eyes slipping half-closed. "Oh my God, was it ever my pleasure! I don't think I can walk." I propped myself against him, sliding my arms around his midsection. "Speaking of walking and chafing, I can't believe you went commando in jeans for a twelve-mile hike. Owie."

Hellhound shook his head, grinning. "Nah. I rented a street-an'-trail bike an' rode it all but the last coupla miles. I stashed it off in the woods in case we needed wheels."

I laughed. "Okay, now your badass image is completely destroyed. You voluntarily rode a little street-and-trail instead of a Harley?"

"Yeah, how fuckin' sad is that? Figured I better get somethin' a little more manoeuvrable than a hog, though. Didn't know what the situation was here." He planted a whiskery kiss on my forehead. "Can ya walk yet, darlin'?"

"If I have to."

I released him reluctantly and staggered for the road on rubbery legs. Hand in hand, we turned to meander toward the commune gates, the warmth of afterglow intensifying my enjoyment of the sunshine and birdsong.

"So fill me in," Hellhound said. "Gimme the whole thing, start to finish."

"Okay..." I let out a long breath and reached up to steal a kiss before laying out the events to date.

When I was finished, he let out a thoughtful "Hmph" and we walked in silence while I watched the wheels turn inside that incisive mind.

"So Skidmark's been here pretty much as long as Stemp's folks," he said after a few moments. "I can't see him as a big threat unless somethin's changed recently. But I don't like the timin' of this Orion guy showin' up at the same time you did. An' if he's gettin' chummy with Ratboy, that ain't good." He frowned down at me. "When ya were makin' out with Orion, how did it feel?"

Heat rose in my cheeks. "Well, he's not as good a kisser as you..."

Hellhound chuckled. "Thanks, darlin', but that ain't what I meant. Ya can tell me a sexy bedtime story later if ya like, but what I'm askin' is how he acted." His smile dissolved, his gaze searching my face. "Was he rough with ya? Did he try to push ya into it?"

"No, nothing like that." I grimaced. "Either he was a really good actor or those restraints weren't for me because it was... he wasn't rough..." My mind drifted back to Orion's hot lips and butterfly kisses. "Not domineering, just..." I trailed off into a frustrated shrug. "I don't know; just normal. He seemed really disappointed when I shut him down, but he didn't push me. Wouldn't you think I'd be able to sense if he had something bad planned?"

Hellhound blew out a short breath, his expression troubled. "I dunno. You'd think so. I know ya don't trust anybody, so I can't see ya missin' somethin' like that."

"Well, I was getting pretty desperate to get laid by then." I grinned and bumped my shoulder against his.

He laughed. "No shit. I thought ya were gonna eat me alive."

"I'll do that later," I purred.

"Darlin', I *really* missed ya," he said, grinning. "But before we get to the good stuff, gimme the grand tour. I wanna get the lay a' the land."

"Okay, we'll start at Skidmark's garage." I peeked at my tracking unit, eyeing the red dot. "Looks like Orion's still there," I added. "Maybe you'll get to meet all three of my suspects at the same time." I shot a look at Hellhound's backpack. "Do you want to drop that off at my tent first?"

Hellhound shrugged, the pack rising and falling on his powerful shoulders as if it was weightless. "Whatever. If the garage is on the way, let's go there first."

CHAPTER 25

When we strode into the gravelled clearing, Skidmark was back in his chair beside the garage. As we approached, he lovingly inhaled the last molecules of smoke from a roach so tiny I couldn't believe the embers weren't burning his skin.

Then again, between the yellowed calluses on his fingers and the marijuana high, it was probably a matter of 'no sense, no feeling'.

He squinted at us for a moment before pinching out the butt and slowly lowering the front legs of the chair to the ground.

"Christ on a crutch, that is one ugly dude," he mumbled. "Girlie, don't tell me you're getting it on with Frankendude here, or it'll break my heart."

I slid my arms around Hellhound and scowled at Skidmark. "You better believe I am. Watch your mouth, old man."

"Huh." Skidmark transferred his bleary gaze to Hellhound. "So she likes it rough and ugly, eh? I should've known. Tough bitches like her just want to be put in their place."

Hellhound gently disengaged himself from my grip and

stepped closer to loom over Skidmark. "How d'ya feel about smokin' your next joint through your asshole?" Hellhound inquired mildly. "'Cause that's how far down your throat I'm gonna shove it if ya make another crack like that."

Skidmark took in Hellhound's battle-scarred face and bulging arms sleeved in tattoos before raising both hands in a placating gesture. "Be cool, man. Just rattling your cage."

Hellhound regarded him expressionlessly for a few moments before replying, "If ya like livin', ya better be careful whose cage ya rattle."

Skidmark blinked and mumbled, "Hey, it's cool. I'm picking up what you're laying down, bro." He tipped his chair back again and his drowsy gaze tracked over to me. "You gonna introduce us, girlie?"

I scowled at him before turning back to Hellhound. "Hellhound..." I jerked my chin at the older man. "Skidmark." I took Hellhound's arm. "Let's go."

Skidmark's voice stopped us. "Hellbound?"

Hellhound's mouth twisted in a wry grimace. "Prob'ly."

"Hellhound, not hellbound," I corrected. I reached up to brush a kiss across Hellhound's long-ago-broken cheekbone and whispered, "You've done your time in hell."

Apparently Skidmark's hearing was better than he'd let on. His eyes sharpened to a shrewd glint as he eyed Hellhound. "How many?" he asked abruptly.

"What?" Hellhound's brows drew together.

"How many kills?"

Hellhound went expressionless again, crossing his arms over his chest. "What're ya yappin' about, ol' man?"

Skidmark nodded slowly, still studying him. "You know exactly how many, don't you?"

Hellhound regarded the older man with narrowed eyes

and said nothing.

The silence stretched until Skidmark nodded again and pulled out his baggie to roll a joint with his usual reverent concentration. Giving the paper a final twist, he offered the finished product to Hellhound, who shook his head.

Skidmark cupped his hand around the joint and the flare of the match illuminated his weathered features as he lit up, dragging luxuriously.

The smoke stayed gone a long time before trickling out in wisps as he spoke, addressing me with one eye on Hellhound. "There's three kinds of guys in the world. First kind won't kill no matter what. Call it principles or cowardice, it don't matter in the end. The second kind, he'll kill and be proud of his body count. Wackos, those guys. Kill 'em all and let God sort 'em out. The third kind, now..." He took another drag and shot a significant glance at Hellhound. "He'll kill in the line of duty, but he knows he's going to hell for it. And he does it anyway 'cause it's gotta be done. That's a brave man."

He leaned back, sucking in another lungful of smoke. "You know exactly how many, don't you?" he repeated.

Hellhound held Skidmark's gaze, poker-faced.

Skidmark nodded. "Can always tell; it's in the eyes. Sniper, right?"

For a barely-noticeable instant Hellhound stood as though carved from stone. Then he chuckled and shook his head. "Ya got a hell of an imagination, ol' man."

"Yeah." Skidmark gave him a crooked grin. "You wanna know how I know? Snipers're the only guys that know for sure. Us infantry grunts, we never really know how many." Skidmark toasted Hellhound with his half-smoked reefer. "See you in hell, son. Gonna be a good time; all my buddies'll be there."

I slid my hand into Hellhound's, lacing my fingers through his rigid ones. "I don't believe in hell. And even if there is such a place, he's not going there."

Skidmark wheezed out a laugh. "There sure as hell is a hell."

I squeezed Hellhound's hand tighter. "Hell is created by people, for people. And you don't have to die to go there."

Skidmark eyed me thoughtfully, his joint momentarily forgotten. "Girlie, you just said a mouthful," he said at last. "How many for you?"

I drew a breath to hide my surge of adrenaline. "You're nuts. And we have to go. I'll be back later to help you with the truck."

He waved the joint vaguely. "Tomorrow."

I led Hellhound down the path toward the bench. Just before we rounded the corner I glanced back to see Skidmark still propped against the garage, staring into eternity with heavy-lidded eyes while the smoke curled around his shaggy head.

"What the hell?" Hellhound muttered as we strode down the path. "How did he know?"

"He didn't. He's always throwing shit against the wall to see if any of it sticks. So far he's called me a male transvestite and a lesbian. Like he said, he was just trying to rattle your cage."

"Well, it worked," Hellhound said grimly. "If he's a vet he mighta noticed my PPCLI tattoo so he'd peg me for infantry, but nobody oughta be able to guess that close on the snipin'. He knows somethin'."

I hid my clutch of fear in a level tone. "I don't know how he could. He's never met you before and I've never mentioned you to him. And he wouldn't have any way to access your service records even if he did know your name in advance. I'm pretty sure he was just flapping his gums."

"Maybe," Hellhound growled. "But I still don't like it. An' what about Orion? I thought the tracker showed him around here, so where the hell is he?"

We emerged from the trail and I made a show of settling onto the bench, peeking at my tracker in the process. "Back at the garage. Looks like he's still avoiding us."

Hellhound sank onto the bench beside me and wrapped an arm around me, pulling me close and pressing his lips against my hair.

"Are ya sure the tracker's workin'?" he muttered. "Maybe he found it an' ditched it."

"Maybe, but it was working fine yesterday." I sighed. "I guess we'll find out. If it doesn't move for the rest of the day, we'll know what happened." I stood and spoke at normal volume. "Come on, there's a really nice view over the river from around the corner here."

I ushered him to the point that overlooked the renters' land and we stood with our arms around each other, ostensibly admiring the view.

Out of the corner of my eye I watched his gaze flick over the landscape, and I knew he'd be storing the layout of the commune and surrounding areas in his phenomenal memory. After a few minutes he turned to me with a smile.

"Pretty nice, darlin'. Let's walk down an' ya can show me the rest."

Hand in hand, we strolled back via the garage, but Skidmark had vacated his chair and there was still no sign of Orion. When we arrived at my tent I led Hellhound inside and checked the tracker again.

The red dot still glowed in the vicinity of the garage and my heart sank.

I flopped down on the mattress. "Shit, maybe it fell out of his boot. It's been in the same place all day."

Hellhound swung the pack down from his shoulders and joined me for a look at the tracker. "Well, like ya say, we might as well wait an' see." He eyed my wooden-crate shelves with a frown. "I got some gear in my pack that I don't wanna leave where somebody could find it. Ya got a cache around here anywhere?"

"Yeah, in the little pond I showed you from the viewpoint. I've got a waterproof box stowed under a log, but I don't know if it'll be big enough. What have you got?"

Hellhound glanced around the windowless tent and dodged the question. "Fuck, I hate bein' where I can't see outside. Let's go have a look at it." He rose and slung his pack over his shoulders again.

I was just getting up when my tent flap rustled. Our heads snapped around to face the incoming threat and Hellhound dropped into a combat-ready crouch.

The air whooshed out of both of us in laughter when Peaches entered, tail crooked in a question-mark as she made straight for Hellhound and wound around his ankles. She sang a little melody of purrs and trilling meows, and his laughter changed from surprise to delight. He leaned down, stroking her with a gentle hand, and she pushed her face into his palm and purred extravagantly.

"Who's this?" Hellhound inquired, his expert fingers rubbing a spot on her jaw that made her eyes slit in bliss. "Looks like somebody needs to go on a diet."

"This is Peaches." I smiled. "Careful, Hooker's going to be jealous when he smells her on you. And she doesn't need a diet, she only needs another week or two and she'll be skinny as a rail."

"She's gonna have kittens?" Hellhound knelt, cupping her bulging sides with the lightest of touches. "Hey, little lady." His rasp softened to a tender sing-song. "You're gonna be a momma-cat soon. Hey, little momma-cat."

She bunted his knee with her face before making her way determinedly up his thigh to press against his chest in the universal feline body language for "Pick me up and carry me, human."

Hellhound shot me a worried look, his hands hovering protectively near her. "What should I do? Will it hurt her if I pick her up?"

"No, just keep her supported, the same way you pick Hooker up."

He placed careful hands under her chest and hindquarters and tucked her close to his body, his brow furrowed in concentration. When he rose, cradling his purring passenger against his massive chest as though she was made of spun glass, I had to swallow a lump in my throat.

"Where can I take her where she'll be safe?" he asked.

I cleared my throat and stepped over to give Peaches a chin-scratch. "Just bring her along. We can have a look at the pond and then drop her off at the main building. There's a nice warm cat-house there for her and the other commune cats."

"Okay, good. Lead the way, darlin'." His gaze didn't leave the furry bundle in his arms, and as I went out the tent flap, his rough-edged croon followed me. "Hey, little momma-cat..."

He managed to tear his attention away from Peaches

long enough to evaluate my cache at the pond and nod approval. "Okay, that'll work. I ain't gonna get at it in daylight, though. Let's go drop off my little lady, an' then I wanna go for a walk an' scout the renters."

"Oh." I frowned. "I don't think we're supposed to go over there. When I got here Moonbeam and Karma were pretty clear about the extent of the commune's land."

Hellhound grinned. "Lucky I'm just a dumbfuck an' don't know any better."

I grinned back. "Damn tourists."

"Fuckin' right."

With Peaches safely delivered to the main building, we set off toward the river, hand in hand once more. On the bridge, Hellhound drew me to a halt about a third of the way across and pulled me into his arms to kiss me unhurriedly.

I sighed contentment and leaned into him. "I wish I didn't know you were just using this as an excuse to scope out the bridge," I mumbled against his lips.

He chuckled and guided me to the railing, where we leaned overlooking the river with his arm around my shoulders while he surreptitiously studied the structure below us. "Fringe benefit, darlin'," he murmured, and leaned closer to hide his lips in my hair. "This bridge could hold a fuckin' tank."

"Yeah." I dipped my head to let my hair swing down like a curtain between us and the renters' side. "They'd need to bring in supplies and stuff, so it'd have to hold a vehicle's weight. That's probably why Ratboy has been so cranky. They're probably waiting on the truck so they can make a supply run."

"Why wouldn't they just use the station wagon?"

"No idea." I hesitated. "Unless they need to bring in something that wouldn't fit in the station wagon."

Hellhound grunted agreement, then added, "How many guys d'ya figure are over there?"

"I don't know for sure." I leaned over for another kiss. "I saw between thirty and thirty-five in their assembly, but there might have been more in some other part of the encampment. And I don't know if they're all guys. I'm just assuming."

"Hm. Well, let's go see." Hellhound straightened and together we ambled across the bridge.

As we neared the other side, I scanned the forest without seeing anything but trees and ferns. My skin prickled with the uncomfortable recollection of the marchers and their glinting weapons. I really hoped those hadn't been bayonets.

We stepped off the bridge and strolled down the gravelled road, and I tried not to let my head swivel anxiously. My palm began to sweat in Hellhound's light clasp. If the rest of Ratboy's group hated women as much as he did, this might be a really bad idea for me.

Hellhound leaned down to brush his lips across my cheek. "Ya okay, darlin'?"

"Yeah..." My voice came out sounding unconvinced. "Maybe we should-"

"Halt!"

Adrenaline spiked into my veins as Hellhound and I wheeled to face the challenge behind us.

Oh shit, those were bayonets all right.

Two of them. One for each of the glowering men who were blocking the road back to the bridge.

The crunch of gravel yanked my attention in the opposite

direction in time to see two more armed men step into the road to box us in.

CHAPTER 26

Clinging to composure with all my might, I stared at the four bearded men surrounding us. Their bayonets gleamed in the sun, the dark abyss of each gun muzzle gaping behind the silvery threat.

Hellhound wrapped his arms around me, placing as much of his bulk as possible between me and the weapons. "Hey, now," he said mildly. "Think we got a bit of a misunderstandin' here. We're just out for a walk. Musta taken a wrong turn or somethin'. We'll just go back the way we came."

"You're trespassing," the nearest one snapped.

"Sorry 'bout that," Hellhound agreed. "We ain't from around here an' we didn't know. We'll just go now, an' we won't bother ya again." He began to ease us in the direction of the bridge.

The crunch of rapidly approaching boots on gravel made us all stiffen.

A moment later a tall man in a military-looking tunic strode around the corner. When he took in our little tableau his brows snapped together. "What is this?" he demanded.

Our captors didn't exactly snap to attention, but they straightened respectfully. "Trespassers," the spokesman rapped out.

"I see." The tall man scowled at us for a moment before bursting into laughter. The armed men exchanged a glance and regarded him warily. A moment later he stopped laughing as though a switch had been thrown. He waved a regal hand at the men, his mouth still smiling without diminishing the coldness of his eyes. "Good joke. Well done. Dismissed."

Our captors let out nervous laughs and shouldered their weapons to march away, casting uncertain glances back at us.

When they had disappeared around the corner, our rescuer chuckled again and slapped Hellhound on the shoulder with a display of teeth that fell short of a smile. "Sorry if you were scared. We're just running some war games today and we weren't expecting visitors."

His arm chummily across Hellhound's shoulders, he steered us toward the bridge, still holding onto his mirthless smile. "Here you go, then, no harm done. But you should stay on your side of the river. Our members take their sport quite seriously and I'd hate to see anyone frightened or... hurt."

"Yeah. Ya wouldn't want that." Hellhound's voice came out in a hard rasp, but I squeezed his hand warningly and he said no more.

"Sorry," I babbled, making no attempt to hide the quaver in my voice. "We're so sorry, we didn't mean to trespass. Thank you for coming to get us. We won't bother you again, I promise."

"No harm done," he repeated. "Have a good day." The cordial words were so incongruous with his chilly eyes that I might have laughed if I hadn't just narrowly avoided becoming a shish kebab.

"You, too," I piped brightly, and towed Hellhound across the bridge at a considerably brisker pace than we'd used earlier.

I kept up our hurried retreat until trees blocked our view of the bridge. Then I trailed to a halt and half-collapsed against Hellhound.

His arms enfolded me, strong and steady as ever, and he passed a gentle hand over my hair. "Okay, darlin'?"

"Yeah, I'm fine," I mumbled into his chest.

"Well, that was interestin'," he said reflectively.

"That's one word for it."

"So I guess ya were right, they're some kinda paramilitary club." I looked up to see him frowning, his gaze focused on the ghosts of the past. "I'll never figure out why the fuck anybody'd wanna pretend they were in combat," he muttered.

"Because they don't have a clue what it's really like," I guessed.

"Mm. They oughta join up for real an' do some good, 'stead a' marchin' around in the bush with toy guns like a buncha fuckin' overgrown kids."

"Yeah..." I suddenly caught his meaning and gave him a sharp look. "Wait, toy guns?"

"Yeah." Hellhound dragged his gaze out of the distance to focus on me. "Those carbines were just replicas."

"Shit." I drew a deep breath and eased it out slowly. "I didn't even look at their guns. I was too busy watching their bayonets. Don't tell me those were fake, too."

"Nah, they were the real thing. M9s. That's what the U.S. military used to use before they switched to the OKC-3S."

I attempted a grin. "How smart am I to pick a weapons specialist for a lover?" My grin didn't last long as the memory of the shining steel slipped back into my mind like a cold blade between my ribs. "I've never seen a real bayonet up close before. They looked like big survival knives."

"Yeah, ya can take 'em off an' use 'em for that. The OKC-3S looks a lot like a Ka-Bar knife," he replied absently, his brow still furrowed in thought. "Ya said they had dummies in their training field," he added. "So they musta been usin' 'em for bayonet practice."

"That's creepy." I shuddered. "God, I can't imagine stabbing somebody with a bayonet. Brrr."

Hellhound regarded me with bemusement. "Darlin', I watched ya shoot a guy's face off. Seven rounds, point-blank. I've seen ya kick an' punch an'-"

I waved a hand to silence him. "I know, but that was different." At his frown of incomprehension, I tried to explain. "I can shoot a person if I have to, but sticking a knife in somebody..."

I trailed off at the memory of my knife plunging into flesh. The heavy drag of the blade slicing through muscle. The spurt of bright arterial blood...

The horror gripped me as if it had been yesterday and I shuddered again. Only Stemp and Dr. Rawling knew about that. No need to share.

"I guess I'm just not the stabby-slashy type," I finished lamely.

Hellhound chuckled. "Okay, darlin', if ya say so."

The queasiness still clung to me like a clammy shroud, and I tamped down another shudder.

Time for a distraction.

I summoned a smile. "Come on, there's something I

want to show you."

A slow answering smile curved Hellhound's lips. "Sounds good. I'm ready to see anythin' ya wanna show me."

My next smile came easier, and I nudged him in the direction of the main building. "You're going to like my surprise, but sorry, it won't give you a hard-on."

His grin widened. "I dunno, darlin', it doesn't take much to do that when you're around."

"That's what I like to hear. I'll test that theory later." I slid an arm around him, bumping gently against him as we walked. "God, it's so good to have you here." My words came out on a long sigh. "It's been a hell of a long four months."

His arm closed around my shoulders. "Glad ya don't mind that I came."

"Mind? Are you kidding? I've been hoping for months that you'd come for a visit."

"Oh." His word held an odd intonation, and I halted to frown up at his unreadable expression.

"What do you mean, 'oh'?" I demanded. "Don't worry, I'm not asking you for a commitment or anything. I just missed you, that's all. Friends do that."

He smiled and dropped a kiss on my lips. "That ain't what I meant. I missed ya, too. I just thought..." He hesitated, studying my face. "I knew Kane was visitin' ya, an' I thought maybe... well, I didn't wanna show up an' mess up anythin' between ya."

"Arnie..." My heart squeezed and I reached up to cup his face in my hands. "Why do you always think you should take second place to John?"

"He's my brother, an' I owe him." He shrugged, avoiding my eyes. "But it ain't just that, I just... I don't figure I got the right to spoil things if the two a' ya can make a go of it together. I can't give ya a commitment. He can."

I planted my fists on my hips. "No, he can't. His job has to come first. Remember how he had to get married to maintain his cover at Christmas?"

"*What?*" Hellhound's incredulous bark morphed rapidly into indignant sputtering. "What the... That fucker! Got married an' didn't tell me! To who? Who the hell did he marry? Why didn't he-"

"No, no!" I waved him to silence. "No, sorry, he's not married. I didn't realize you hadn't seen that part of the mission report. Sorry. No. I mean, yes, he got married as part of his cover, but it didn't last a day. She tried to take us out with that death-ray thing and he had to kill her."

Hellhound gaped at me for a moment before erupting in a bellow of laughter. "Just like Captain Fuckin' Kirk! Never marry the captain; it's a fuckin' death sentence."

I grinned. "Yeah, something like that. Anyway, how many times do I have to tell you I don't want a committed relationship, with you or with anybody?"

He sobered. "Yeah, darlin', I know, but sometimes things change, an' I don't wanna be in the way if they do."

"Arnie..." I blew out a breath of frustration, trying to find a way to make him understand. "Look, do you think I'm the kind of person who'd cheat on a guy if I was in a relationship?"

"No!" He frowned. "Fuck, Aydan, ya wouldn't even ditch that asshole ex a' yours when he was abusin' ya. No fuckin' way you'd play around. Who the hell said that about ya?"

"You just implied it."

Hellhound scowled and shook his head, but I laid a

finger over his lips before he could speak. "Listen, Arnie. If I ever decide I want a relationship with John or anybody else, it won't matter what you do or say, you won't be able to come between us."

He stared open-mouthed for a moment. "Shit, I never thought about it like that."

"And in the meantime," I added, "I want you as a friend-with-benefits whenever you're available. If that changes, I'll tell you. Got it?"

A slow smile illuminated his face. "Hell, yeah, darlin'. I finally got it." His smile widened to a rakish grin. "An' I'm gonna *be* gettin' it. Right-fuckin'-on!"

I mirrored his grin. "Literally."

He laughed and pulled me into a kiss that made me forget my own name.

When I resurfaced, breathless, he smiled down at me. "So what'd ya wanna show me?"

"Uh..." I swam up through the tide of lust that had submerged me. "You mean besides my bed?"

"I'm good with that." He grinned. "But ya said it wasn't gonna give me a hard-on, an' considerin' I'm gettin' one just thinkin' about it, I'm guessin' your bed ain't what ya meant."

"Oh. Right. No, it wasn't, but I could be convinced."

"That's one a' the things I love about ya." He brushed my lips with his. "But now ya got me curious. Lead the way, darlin'."

"Okay." I grinned up at him. "You're going to like this. Come on."

As I led him toward the main building, he asked, "So ya ain't heard from Kane?"

"No, not since he was here in February, right before his dad went into the hospital. Has he called you?"

"Nah."

I let out a breath. "Shit, I was hoping he had." We walked on in silence for a few paces before I burst out, "Damn, I hate this. He could be anywhere; hell, he could be dead and we'd never even know. He thought it would be better if we weren't working together, but it really sucks not knowing."

"Yeah, I know, darlin'." Hellhound's arm closed around me. "But he's been doin' this for a long time, an' he's dropped off the grid lotsa times before. Try not to worry."

"I'm not really worrying, I'm just... I wish I knew, is all."

He nodded silently, and I shook off my mood as we rounded the corner behind the main building. Glancing up at his puzzled expression with a smile, I whispered, "The surprise is in that shed over there."

"What, that ol' piece a' shit?" He frowned at the dilapidated structure. "Looks like it's ready to fall down."

"Not quite." I put my finger to my lips and led him over to the door.

When I dragged it open, his jaw dropped and his face lit up.

"Aw..." he breathed, and knelt as if in reverence before the ledge containing a nest of wood shavings that cradled a gray-and-white mother cat with five multi-coloured kittens nestled side by side against her, their tiny paws kneading her belly while they suckled.

I sat in the shavings beside him, smiling. "This is Misty. She had her kittens about three weeks ago."

"Aw..." he said again, and lowered his voice to the same husky croon he'd used with Peaches. "Hey, Miz Momma-cat." He extended his hand slowly for her to sniff. She inspected it thoroughly, then offered her seal of approval with a whisker-rub.

He gently massaged her jaw and she slitted her eyes with pleasure, then stood and stretched in an exaggerated arch, stiffly extending first one hind leg, then the other. Deprived of her warmth, the kittens emitted a chorus of high-pitched mews, staggering and tumbling clumsily over each other in search of the missing milk dispenser.

Hellhound's brow furrowed. "Lie down, Misty," he urged. "Your babies need ya."

Misty seemed to think otherwise. She cracked her jaws into a cavernous yawn before picking her way over to the edge of the shelf and jumping down.

"Wait, come back!" Hellhound eyed her departing posterior with anxiety. "Shit, Aydan, we scared her off. She's leavin' them."

"No, she's not," I promised. "She's just taking a break now that the babysitters have arrived." He looked unconvinced, and I added, "If she was a feral cat she'd never let us near her kittens and she'd move them as soon as anybody discovered them. But she's so used to having people around, she knows we won't hurt them. She's probably just going to get a snack or something."

"Ya think so?" He turned a worried face back to the mewing kittens.

"I know so. Trust me, she does this every time I come to visit. Here." I reached carefully into the nest, gently grasping the nearest kitten by its scruff. It went limp as I lifted it, its hind legs and tail curling under.

Hellhound sucked in a breath. "Jesus! Aydan, stop! You're killin' it!"

"I'm not, I promise. And it's a 'him'. I think. It's hard to tell when they're this young." I tucked a hand under the little warm bundle for extra security while I transferred it. "This is how their mother carries them, and they're programmed to go limp like this when she takes them by the scruff. Hold out your hand."

Eyes wide, he complied and I lowered the small orange fluff-ball onto his palm. As soon as I released my grip the tiny tom uncurled, his spindly legs splayed across the uneven surface, his pipe-cleaner tail flailing for balance.

Hellhound tucked his hand to his chest, cupping his other hand around it to make a protective fence. The kitten mewed once before nuzzling close to Hellhound's warmth, and he extended a single fingertip to caress the small head and downy fluff of the body with infinite gentleness.

"He's so little," he breathed, his face full of awe. "I never knew they were so little. Hooker was full-grown when I found him."

"You should have seen them when they were first born and their eyes weren't even open yet. They looked more like mice than kittens." I fell silent, tucking a hand around the remaining kittens in the nest to silence their mewing while I enjoyed Hellhound's enchantment with the mote of life he cupped in his palm.

The spell was broken a few minutes later when Misty returned from her errand, chirruping a half-purr-half-meow as she hopped up on the shelf. Hellhound's little tom responded with a piercing mew, and as Hellhound leaned to bring him closer, Misty craned her neck to clamp her teeth gently but firmly on the kitten's scruff. Hellhound's mouth dropped open as she transferred the kitten back into the nest and curled herself around her brood again. After only a few moments of squirming and tumbling they rearranged themselves in a rapt row against her belly, and soon the silence was broken only by an occasional sucking noise.

"And visiting hours are over," I quipped, smiling. "See, I told you she wouldn't leave them."

"That's amazin'." Hellhound's gaze was riveted on the little furry family. "That's absolutely fuckin' amazin'. How do they know?" He turned a wondering face to me. "How the hell do they know?" He turned back to Misty and caressed her side with tenderness. "Goodbye, Momma-cat. Take good care a' your babies."

We rose and I quietly swung the door closed.

"Ya ain't shuttin' her in there, are ya?" Hellhound inquired worriedly. "She can still get out, right?"

"Yeah." I pointed to a hole in a rotten board near the middle of the shed. "She goes in and out through there. If we left the door open she'd probably move the kittens because predators could get in too easily."

"Oh. Okay, good." He nodded absently, his gaze still fixed on the shed, his mouth curved in a smile.

CHAPTER 27

As we came around the corner of the main building I turned to Hellhound. "I forgot to ask, are you hungry? I'll show you the kitchen, and we can grab a snack."

"Nah, I ate when I got off the plane a coupla hours ago, but I wanna see inside the buildin' anyway an' get the layout."

I led the way inside, pointing out the kitchen, phone, showers, laundry room, and storage. We were just coming out of the meditation room when Karma strode into the main hall.

"Oh, hi," I greeted him. "I thought you were going to be busy all day, but this is perfect. This is Arnie Helmand, or Hellhound if you prefer. Arnie, Karma Wolf Song."

Karma smiled and shook Hellhound's outstretched hand. "The Earth Spirit released us a little earlier than we expected. It's good to meet you-"

Moonbeam had entered as he spoke, and her gasp cut across his words. "Merciful Spirit, what a beautiful man!" she exclaimed, her eyes shining.

Hellhound and I both twisted to look behind us and found no one. When we turned back to face Moonbeam, I realized she was drinking in Hellhound as though worshiping at a holy shrine, her hands clasped in rapture. He cast another puzzled glance around the room before crossing his arms over his chest, frowning uncomfortably.

"Oh..." Moonbeam reached for him as if unable to prevent herself, her hands skimming the air beside his bulging tattooed biceps. "Oh, you are so beautiful!"

"Uh..." Hellhound shuffled his feet and his frown deepened. "Sorry, Miz, uh... ma'am... I think ya got the wrong guy." He leaned down to whisper in my ear, "Is she blind or somethin'?"

Moonbeam came back to earth with a little shake of her head. "I'm sorry, where are my manners?" She smiled and extended her hand. "I am Moonbeam Meadow Sky, and I do apologize for my impulsive behaviour, but you have the most beautiful aura I've ever seen." Her eyes unfocused again as she gazed up at Hellhound. "Silver and white and yellow, with streaks of that lovely sensual pink..." She sighed. "Extraordinary."

I tucked an arm around him, smiling. "He is."

Hellhound flushed and ducked his head as he took Moonbeam's slender hand in a careful grasp. "Pleased to meet ya, Miz Moonbeam."

I knew she was truly smitten when she didn't even correct him to use her full name. Instead she smiled and caressed his hand as though the contact was a gift beyond price. Then she dipped into the folds of her caftan to bring out another wood-beaded bracelet.

I had briefed Hellhound about the bracelet ceremony, so he stood patiently while she tied the hemp cord, carefully securing the short tails that remained after spanning the girth of his wrist.

She clasped his hand in both of hers and looked up at

him with unconcealed admiration that made him flush again.

"This bracelet gives you the protection of the Earth Spirit as long as you are here." She repeated the words of the ceremony with reverence. "Wear it always. From now on, you'll be known as Blessed Soul Dream, the name the Earth Spirit has bestowed on you. Go forth in peace, tolerance, and harmony. The blessings of the Earth Spirit are upon you."

"Blessed Soul Dream?" Hellhound's voice came out slightly strangled. When she nodded up at him with her ethereal smile, he cleared his throat, his face crimson. "Uh, thanks, Miz Moonbeam. Blessin's on ya, too."

As if to spare him further embarrassment, Karma spoke up in his hearty bass voice. "Well, Storm Cloud Dancer, have you been giving, er..." he hesitated with a sidelong glance at Moonbeam. "...Hellhound... the twenty-five cent tour this afternoon?" At my nod, he smiled and turned to Hellhound. "I hope you're feeling welcome."

"Depends on what ya mean by 'welcome'," Hellhound replied. "If ya like gettin' bayonets shoved in your face, then yeah, I got a helluva welcome."

Moonbeam gasped, and Karma wrapped a protective arm around her shoulders. "What happened?" he demanded.

"We took a walk over the bridge, an' these four guys jumped outta the woods an' held us up with bayonets," Hellhound explained. "Who the hell are those assholes... sorry, Miz Moonbeam, I mean, who are those guys?"

"Oh, Storm Cloud Dancer, I thought I had been clear about the boundaries of the commune," Moonbeam chided.

"Sorry, Miz Moonbeam, that was my fault," Hellhound said hurriedly. "I pushed her into it, but I wouldn't'a done it if I'd known it was gonna be dangerous. I didn't think there'd be armed guys runnin' around out here."

"Are you going to call the police?" Moonbeam asked.

"I don't know what we'd say if we did," I replied. "We were trespassing. And they weren't carrying real guns, so I don't think the police would do anything. I'm pretty sure it's legal to play war games on private land."

"Maybe we should call the police anyway," Moonbeam quavered.

A flicker of movement near the kitchen door caught my eye, and I glanced over to the now-empty doorway, trying not to distract Moonbeam and Karma.

Shit, had that been Ratboy? Several of the commune members were slim dark-haired men sporting beards, so maybe not...

I returned my attention to the conversation as Karma's arm tightened around Moonbeam. "We'll deal with it, my love," he rumbled. He turned back to Hellhound and me. "I'm very sorry that happened to you. That's actually what our meditation was about today. The Earth Spirit warned us that our renters were not living in the harmonious way of the Spirit, and after this incident it's obvious we'll have to evict them. Please stay far away from them. We'll ask them to leave as soon as possible."

"They might not take too kindly to that," I said. "We were barely across the bridge before they accused us of trespassing. We were lucky another guy happened along who seemed like their leader and he let us go. I don't think you should confront them. Send an email or a letter or something, and call the police if they don't cooperate."

"Thank you, dear, that sounds like good advice." Moonbeam exchanged a glance with Karma. "We'll write the letter tonight. But please, stay away from them. Such violent intent is against everything the Earth Spirit represents."

"We will," I promised.

"And speaking of the Earth Spirit," she continued, "I believe Aurora Peace Rain is helping Blaze Featherwind prepare for her talk this evening. Have you instructed Blessed Soul Dream in the way of the Callings, or should I arrange for Aurora Peace Rain to do so later?"

"I told him," I assured her.

"Very well then. We will need to meditate on the contents of our letter, so we'll take our leave now." Moonbeam hugged me and Hellhound in turn. "Spirit bless you, children."

"You, too," we chorused, and watched them leave arm in arm.

I hurried to the kitchen and peeked in, but it was deserted. I eyed the opposite door speculatively. It led to an outdoor deck with firepits that were likely used for cooking when the weather was too hot for woodstoves, but it would only be a short dash to the concealment of the trees from there.

"Whatcha lookin' at?" Hellhound asked.

"I thought I saw Ratboy."

He strode across the kitchen and stepped out on the patio, scanning the forest. After a moment he returned, frowning. "If it was him, he didn't hang around." Then he glanced around the empty room and leaned close to growl, "Fuck, Aydan, what the hell? A pink aura? An' *Blessed Soul Dream*? Don't tell Kane, or I'll never fuckin' live it down."

"I won't, I promise." I kept a straight face with an effort. "But she didn't say it was completely pink."

"Yeah, well, yellow an' white an' silver ain't much better."

He eyed me suspiciously. "Did she name Kane, too? What colour's his aura?"

"Um, yeah..." I made a stab at changing the subject. "Maybe you should think of it as chrome instead of silver. Nothing cooler than a chrome aura, right?"

"Nice try. Spit it out, darlin'. Tell me what she said about Kane."

I sighed. "Sorry, but she named him Sunstar Desert Hawk and said his aura was clear red."

"Fuck." Hellhound glowered at his boots. "Okay. Fine. She's just seein' what she wants to see an' I ain't gonna let it bug me." His scowl deepened. "Much."

"I don't think aura colours are supposed to be manly," I comforted him. "And, anyway, she's right." When he looked up, scowling as though he expected me to poke fun, I cupped his face in my hands and reached up to kiss him. "On the inside, you truly are beautiful."

He flushed and his face softened. "Thanks, darlin'." He kissed me back. "You an' her are the only people that'd ever think so, but thanks anyway." He blew out a breath. "So what else do I need to see?"

"That's about it." I led him outside. "There's the garden and a bunch of paths and the main encampment, but you saw the layout from Skidmark's bench. All the other tents are occupied so there's no point in going down there. I think there's only one thing left for you to inspect."

"What's that?"

"My bed."

He grinned. "Lead the way, darlin'."

As we strolled down the path hand in hand, Hellhound glanced around before dropping his voice. "So what d'ya think the deal is with Orion an' the renters?"

"I don't know. He doesn't seem to be into any of that paramilitary stuff, and he doesn't seem to hate women the way Ratboy does."

"Or he's just smarter about hidin' it."

I refused to shudder at the chill that chased itself down my spine. "Yeah. But I wonder what he'll do when they get their eviction notice. His tent is here, but he must be part of their group or they'd be on him with bayonets the instant he crossed the bridge."

Hellhound walked in silence for a few moments, frowning. "I dunno, darlin'; my gut says there's somethin' rotten here, but I can't figure out what it'd be. If those nutjobs've been there for a year, they were there before Stemp's cover breach so they shouldn't be after his folks. If Orion's part a' them, then he shouldn't be a threat, either, but then why's he pretendin' to be part a' the commune? An' I still got a bad feelin' about Skidmark, too."

I blew out a frustrated breath. "That's exactly what I've been struggling with. So you don't see anything I'm missing?"

"Not off-hand. As long as you're trackin' Orion, I think that's the best ya can do unless somethin' else changes."

"Shit." I stared gloomily at my feet. "So I'm stuck here, just waiting. Damn." After a few more strides, I added, "I wish Nichele wasn't here. I have a really bad feeling about this, and I don't want her in the middle of it."

"Ya think she'll leave soon?"

I cocked a jaundiced eye at the blue sky. "If the weather turns to shit like it's been for the last four months, she'll be gone before you can say 'five-star hotel'. But as long as it's nice like this, who knows? She's having so damn much fun with Aurora and she's so freaked out about Dave's marriage proposal, she might just decide to stay a while."

"But ya said Dave's back in Victoria tomorrow. If ya tell him it's dangerous here, d'ya think he can convince her to go?"

I kicked at a fir cone on the path. "He's afraid to try. If he pushes her..."

I trailed off, and Hellhound nodded understanding and slipped an arm around my shoulders. "Well, try not to worry, darlin'. Chances are nothin'll happen in the next few days an' she'll just get sick of it here an' take off. An' I'll stay, so there'll be two of us to watch out for her."

"Thank you." I halted to slide my arms around his neck. "Thank you from the bottom of my heart." I reached up to kiss him. "And other parts of my body are feeling pretty thankful, too."

His hands roamed down my back to cup my ass. "Yep, you're feelin' pretty thankful to me, but I better check everythin' out just to be sure."

"Oh, definitely."

Our next kiss was longer.

At last Hellhound pulled away, grinning. "This time we're gonna make it to your tent. Pushin' in the bush is all fine an' good, but I got things I wanna do to ya that're gonna take some time." He gave me a slow up-and-down look. "An' I wanna enjoy the view."

I pressed close for another quick kiss. "Me, too. All I got to see earlier was a close-up of the stump."

He clasped my hand and pulled me down the path. "Can't have that. This time I'll give ya a close-up of my wood."

Laughing, we ducked into my tent and I secured the flap behind us. I stole another quick kiss before pulling away to check Orion's tracker one more time.

"Ha! Look at this." I showed Hellhound the moving red dot. "It's working! He's moving around up by the garage."

He frowned. "Ya think we oughta watch for a while an' see where he goes?"

The dot halted, and I grinned. "Looks like he's not leaving yet. I think we'd better find something to do to pass the time while we wait for him to move."

"Good plan." He shrugged off his pack and flexed his shoulders with a sigh. "That's better. Now, where was I?" He pulled me into a kiss. "Think I was here," he mumbled against my lips. "Or maybe..." His whiskers traced a tingling path to my earlobe. "Here..."

I shivered and pressed closer, pulling the tail of his T-shirt out of his jeans to slide my hands underneath.

"Mmm. Or maybe here." He nibbled a trail of kisses down my throat, easing the neck of my sweatshirt aside to find the magic spot near my collarbone.

"Oh, yeah." My voice came out on a gasp. "Yeah, there!"

We moved toward the mattress, shedding clothes.

"Mm, hang on a sec, darlin'." Shirtless and barefoot, Hellhound released me long enough to delve into his backpack.

I grinned at the sight of the jumbo box of condoms he placed beside the mattress. "I love a man who comes prepared."

He returned my grin. "I never come any other way. No glove, no love."

I giggled and shucked off my jeans. "Cover your stump before you hump."

He snickered, wrapping an arm around my waist to pull me down to the mattress. "Wrap it before ya tap it."

"You can't go wrong when you cover your dong." I grinned and unfastened my ankle holster, reaching over to tuck it down beside the mattress.

"Mm, love that little red thong." He eased me onto my back and traced the edge of the thong with his lips. "Don't be a fool, sheathe your tool," he mumbled against my belly, his whisker-tickles making me squirm and giggle.

"Dress up your monkey before you get funky." I tugged at his jeans and he rose to pull them off while I skinned out of my underwear.

Reaching into the box of condoms, he extracted one and held it up with a wink. "Ya won't get sick if ya wrap your dick."

I let my gaze roam appreciatively over the muscular nakedness towering above me and my mind went blank. "I can't think of any more. Come here."

He grinned. "That's the line I was waitin' for."

He was just lowering himself to me when a wild shriek outside the tent made us both jerk with shock.

CHAPTER 28

"What the *fuck?*" Hellhound barked, lurching up to his hands and knees.

I drew a breath, trying to calm my pounding heart as another feral shriek ripped the air outside my tent. "It's okay." I reached up to pull him down again. "It's just a couple of tomcats squaring off outside. They've been battling it out over the ladies all spring."

Outside, spine-chilling growls rose and fell in a declaration of a fight to the death, or at least ignominious retreat.

Hellhound resisted my pull, his brow furrowed in concern. "Are ya sure? What if it's Peaches? What if somethin's got her cornered? She wouldn't be able to fight when she's so pregnant."

"I'm sure. It happens all the time-"

My words were drowned out by a cacophony of shrieks and growls, and Hellhound sprang up to drag on his jeans. "I gotta go check. Just in case."

As he shoved his feet into his boots the sounds of warfare faded as though the combatants were carrying the battle elsewhere, and I tried again. "They're just about finished. They'll be fine. Come back to bed."

"Hold that thought, darlin'. Be right back." He ducked out the tent flap, and his voice and footsteps faded as he hurried away. "Peaches! Is that you, little lady? Peaches..."

I blew out a breath of frustration mixed with fondness. Any other man would have ignored the feline battle and gone for sex without a second thought, but with Hellhound's soft spot for cats and his reverence for motherhood in any form...

I shook my head, smiling. What a marshmallow. One of the many reasons I loved him.

Apparently the tomcats had taken the fight elsewhere. Silence had fallen, but I could still hear Hellhound's voice calling faintly in the distance.

I tucked my arms behind my head and settled in for a wait. He'd probably scour the woods in case one of the cats had been hurt and was hiding somewhere.

A few minutes later the crunch of approaching footsteps on gravel indicated he was back already. I turned toward the open tent flap, surprised he'd given up so soon.

"Aydan?"

The voice outside made me bolt up in bed, a shock of recognition jolting through me.

"*John?*" I gasped.

Shit, shit, shit!

I sprang to my feet, dragging the sheet around me. In the next moment Kane ducked through the open tent flap, his grey eyes locking onto me like lasers, his muscular arms already opening to embrace me.

"You're back!" I yelped. "Thank God you're okay-oomph!" The breath squashed out of me as he crushed me in his arms and kissed me hard.

"Aydan. So... good... to see you..." he mumbled, devouring my lips between words. He pulled away a fraction, cupping my face in his hands and apparently noticing for the first time that I was naked and wrapped in a sheet. Heat kindled in his eyes and his lips curved up.

"Um, John..." I began, but he smothered my words with another kiss.

"I came straight here," he said against my lips. "I haven't even..." He began to trace a line of kisses down my neck, speaking between kisses. "Called in... to Stemp yet... and..."

"John..." I tried again.

"Mmhmm." He captured my mouth again before taking up where he'd left off near my collarbone. "And I'm staying... until-"

Hellhound ducked through the open tent flap, kicking off his boots and beginning to shed his jeans. "Hey, darlin', I'm back. Everybody's okay an' oh shit." He froze, pants around his knees, knuckles whitening on the denim.

Kane froze, too, his arms tightening possessively around me.

"Uh... hey, Cap," Hellhound said with a twisted smile. "Glad ya made it back okay, but your timin' kinda sucks."

He hoisted his pants and Kane was opening his mouth to reply when the sudden clamour of the Spirit bells made us all twitch.

"Oh, for shit's sake," I muttered and tried to pull away, but Kane's arms were still locked around me.

He opened his mouth again but hadn't managed a word before Orion's voice called from outside the tent. "Hey, Storm!"

"I'm not coming!" I shouted, wincing at the unintentional double entendre. "Go without me!"

"Don't tell me I have to dump ice water on you again," he sang out, and ducked in through the goddamn open tent flap.

Everybody froze all over again, and I barely resisted the urge to beat my head against the nearest hard surface, which happened to be Kane's shoulder.

Orion stood slack-jawed, his shirt open over a bare and chiseled chest. Fuck, wouldn't you know he'd pick this exact time to try to seduce me again.

Hellhound sprang protectively to my side, still holding his jeans up with one hand. "Who the hell're you?" he barked.

"Uh... Orion. Moonjava," Orion replied faintly, his gaze darting between Hellhound, Kane, and me. "And you are...?"

"Hey, Aydan!" Nichele's breathless voice sounded outside the tent.

"Don't come in!" I yelled.

"Hurry up, we're missing the Calling-" She burst in through the gaping tent flap. "Omigod-*omigod!*"

She clapped her hands over her eyes, then sensibly relocated them to clamp over her mouth instead, the better to check out the man-candy crowding my tent.

"OUT!" I bellowed, clutching the sheet to my chest along with the tattered remains of my dignity. "EVERYBODY GET OUT OF MY T-"

"Storm Cloud Dancer, whatever is the matter? ...oh." Moonbeam joined the throng, her question fading into a pregnant silence.

Time slowed to a crawl. My mortified gaze took in all the sordid details as if to create an extra-vivid memory to be revisited for future humiliation.

Me, wearing nothing but a sheet and a fiery blush, sandwiched between Kane's embrace and Hellhound's near-nudity and garnished with a half-dressed Orion. Discarded clothes littering the floor. My skimpy red underwear draped shamelessly on the mattress next to the giant box of condoms. Hellhound still holding up his jeans, the open zipper displaying his fine attributes to all and sundry. The air practically reeking of sex and testosterone.

"Somebody shoot me now," I muttered.

As if released from a spell everybody began to babble apologies and explanations while they made for the tent flap en masse, generating a fresh wave of apologies while they jockeyed for escape.

Soon only Hellhound and I remained, the bells of the Calling still jangling like sardonic laughter in the background.

I turned to him and opened my mouth but nothing came out.

He gave me a resigned shrug and did up his jeans. Then he shot a wicked glance at the mattress and waggled his eyebrows. Hysterical giggles seized me.

He began to laugh, and I lost it completely. Hooting and gasping, I collapsed to my knees to hug my aching midsection while tears of pain-wracked hilarity poured down my cheeks.

At last I sprawled panting on the floor, still twitching with feeble giggles. Hellhound knelt beside me and dangled the incriminating red thong between two fingers, and I would have dissolved into hysterics again if not for Moonbeam's reproving voice issuing from outside the tent flap.

"Storm Cloud Dancer and Blessed Soul Dream, your presence is still required at the Calling. Hurry up, now. I've sent the others on."

"We're coming," I gasped.

"Speak for yourself," Hellhound groused sotto voce. "I'm

just breathin' hard."

An explosive snort of laughter escaped me, and I clapped a hand over my mouth and jabbed a finger at the tent flap. He gave me an unrepentant grin and rose to don his T-shirt, boots, and backpack while I scurried around retrieving various articles of my clothing and trying not to giggle.

At last I managed to get fully dressed and strap my gun back onto my ankle. With my lumpy jacket tucked under my arm, I poked my head cautiously out the tent flap, but Moonbeam had left and the path was mercifully deserted.

Hellhound and I jogged to the main building and appropriated the two mats that had been left at the entrance to the meditation room before creeping guiltily to our assigned places.

Kane lay on the other side of the room, and I detected the gleam of watchful eyes under his lashes. Of course. He'd never lie unaware in a room full of strangers.

Nichele was peeking, too. As I lay down she mouthed, "O. M. G." and fanned her cheeks. I flipped up my middle finger and she let out a giggle that earned a shush and glare from my tight-assed neighbour.

The peace of the meditation was wasted on me.

My mind hurtled around my skull in a roller-derby of anxiety. Oh, God, what if this spoiled the lifelong friendship between Kane and Hellhound? Hellhound didn't care who I slept with, but maybe Kane had been lying four months ago when he'd said he was okay with not having an exclusive relationship.

I managed not to thump my forehead. Of course he'd been lying; I knew damn well he had. I had believed him because I wanted it to be true.

The memory of his possessive arms tightening around

me dragged a little groan of chagrin from my throat. Speaking of tomcats squaring off...

Dammit, I'd find a way to make this come out right. I wouldn't choose a lover at the cost of their friendship.

But maybe the decision was already out of my hands.

The gong roused me from my miserable contemplation, and I plodded out to kneel in the field with glum resignation.

This was going to get ugly; I just knew it. Maybe I should hide in the woods and wait for them both to leave. I could sleep in the shed with Misty and the kittens; sneak into the kitchen for provisions in the dark of night...

"The blessings of the Earth Spirit are upon you!" Aurora's unwelcome voice came far too soon.

By the time I got to my feet, Kane and Hellhound were vectoring toward me from opposite sides of the field and there was no escape.

If all else fails, pretend to be oblivious.

I plastered a smile on my face as they strode up and offered a hand to each of them. "Come on, let's go get some supper. I'm starving!" My voice almost cracked with perkiness and I suppressed a wince.

They exchanged wary glances and fell into step on either side of me. Bracketed by the two towering men, I felt as though I'd regressed to grade school. With a supreme effort of will I prevented myself from skipping and swinging our clasped hands.

Nichele caught my eye and I gave her a stare that promised slow and certain death if she came anywhere near us. She returned a smirk and a wink and turned away to chatter with Aurora, and I eased out a breath. She'd expect a play-by-play with excruciating detail later, but it was a small price to pay for her silence now.

"So, John, where did you blow in from?" I chirped.

"Victoria." He sounded decidedly terse.

I repressed the urge to say 'no shit'. It wasn't like there was any other way to get here.

I tried again. "Where were you before Victoria?"

His gaze flicked over the scattered commune members but none were in earshot.

"Classified," he grunted.

All right. Fine. Time for a different conversational gambit.

I lowered my voice. "We had an exciting afternoon..."

"So I saw." Kane's reply was distinctly edged.

A spurt of irritation dissolved my discomfort. "That's not what I meant, wiseass," I snapped. "Our excitement involved four guys with bayonets."

"What?" For the first time Kane met my eyes squarely, then glanced at Hellhound's scowl before returning his attention to me. "What happened?" Concern had replaced his distant tone, and I drew a breath of relief.

"It's a long story. A lot has happened since you were here last. You remember I mentioned I was suspicious of Orion..."

I paused long enough for him to nod before continuing, "...well, it turns out he's chummy with a group that's renting commune land across the river and they're some kind of wacko paramilitary group. I'm not quite sure what that means, but I have a bad feeling I might find out soon. That's why Arnie's here. I needed backup. So I'm glad you're here, too."

I squeezed his hand. "And I'm really glad you made it back okay from wherever you were. I was worried after not hearing anything for so long."

"I was undercover." He sounded curt and defensive, and I suppressed my eye roll and held onto my warm tone.

"I know, and I didn't expect you to call. I was just worried about you. That's what friends do."

After a moment of silence he sighed and turned to face me fully, the hard lines of his face easing. "I know. I'm sorry. I just..." He hesitated before finishing, "It was a tough mission. I didn't mean to take it out on you." He looked beyond me to Hellhound's stony profile. "I'm sorry. I was being a jerk."

Hellhound thawed immediately. "No sweat, Cap. Tough mission; been there."

"Thanks."

We fell silent as we caught up with the scattered groups of people straggling toward the kitchen. I garnered curious stares as people took in Hellhound's forbidding face and tattooed bulk on one side of me and Kane's square handsome features and eye-popping physique on the other.

I led them to one of the vacant tables and eyed the electric lights gratefully. "Good, the power's on. We can microwave our dinner instead of cooking on the woodstoves..." I trailed off at the sight of the lineup in front of the microwave. "Oh, hell, never mind. It's probably faster to use a woodstove. They're always hot."

"Can I help?" Kane inquired.

"No, that's okay. I'm just going to heat up some stew." I leaned closer to whisper, "I bought beef when I was in town the other day. Don't tell the vegetarians."

Both men chuckled, and I hurried to the icebox to retrieve the contraband stew. By the time I had unearthed buns and butter and cheese from the pantry and bowls and utensils from the long counter, the stew was bubbling on the stove. We loaded our dishes and silence fell again while we ate.

As soon as his bowl was scraped clean, Hellhound rose. "Thanks for dinner, darlin'." He leaned in to drop a kiss on my forehead and whispered, "I'm gonna go scout around a bit more. Gonna be at least two hours."

"Wait." I caught his hand. "You don't have to do that."

His gaze darted to Kane. "Yeah, I do."

I blew out a sigh and pressed his hand to my cheek before brushing a kiss over his knuckles. "See you later, then."

He nodded. "See ya."

As he strode out, Kane met my eyes with a bittersweet smile. "He's the best friend we could ever ask for."

"Yeah." I dropped my gaze to my bowl, concentrating on scooping up the last drops of gravy. "Did you get enough to eat?"

"Yes, thank you."

An awkward silence fell.

I jumped up. "Well, I'd better get these dishes done."

"I'll help."

Kane followed me to the counter bearing the dirty dishes and I focused on filling the dishpan, adjusting the temperature with intense concentration. We made short work of washing and drying the few dishes and I bustled around putting them away and avoiding his gaze.

As I was wiping down the table for the second time Kane laid a hand on top of mine, stopping the rapid circles of my dishcloth.

"Aydan, can we talk?" he asked quietly.

I bit my lip to prevent a sigh from leaking out. "Okay. Let's go back to my tent."

CHAPTER 29

I stalled for a few more seconds, wiping out the sink and hanging up the tea towel and dishcloth, but the earth didn't open and swallow me so I resigned myself to my fate and led the way.

As Kane and I strode down the path side by side, he reached for my hand and held it in a gentle grasp. When I glanced up at him, he smiled, and the tension in my shoulders eased. I drew a deep breath and slowed my pace.

"So. Tough one?" I asked.

"Yes." He walked on for a few paces in silence before adding, "I'm glad it's finished." He drew a deep breath of the moist cedar-scented air. "And I'm glad to be here. But I'm looking forward to getting home."

"I can imagine," I agreed. "Me, too."

"It has been a long haul for you, hasn't it?" Kane glanced around the deserted trail and lowered his voice. "What's happening?"

I briefed him quietly while we walked. We had just reached the path to my tent when a flicker of movement caught my eye on the main trail ahead of us and a moment later Moonbeam came into view. She smiled and beckoned when she saw us, and we waited until she drew abreast.

"Welcome back, Sunstar Desert Hawk," she said to Kane.

"Thank you. It's nice to see you again, Moonbeam Meadow Sky," Kane replied with his usual urbane charm, gaining immediate brownie points for remembering to address her by her full name.

Her smile brightened and she withdrew another bead bracelet from her caftan. I had a momentary vision of what the inside of that caftan might look like, lined with pockets like a bazaar merchant's tent; but I quelled the thought before I could giggle.

She tied the bracelet onto Kane's wrist and took his hand in both of her own. "The blessings of the Earth Spirit are upon you," she said softly. Her eyes took on the distant gaze of the seer, and her brow furrowed as she regarded Kane for a moment. Then she blinked her vision back into focus and stroked the back of his hand. "You are in better physical health than the last time I saw you. That dreadful shadow has faded from your ribs. But your poor aura..." She reached up to touch his cheek. "Please take time to let your spirit heal."

He offered her a small bow. "Thank you for your concern. I will."

"Good." She smiled. "Have a pleasant evening, my dears."

"You, too," we chorused.

Inside my tent, I secured the flap behind us and lit a couple of candles against the deepening twilight. Kane stood still and silent, and when I looked up, the lines on his face were carved deep.

For the first time I looked closely at him and realized that despite his superb muscular development he still looked thinner than before he'd been shot. The sprinkling of silver that frosted his short dark hair at the temples was beginning to spread.

My heart squeezed and I sought his tired grey gaze. Wordlessly, I opened my arms and he stepped into them, burying his face in my hair. We stood locked together for a long moment before he spoke, his voice taut with pain.

"There was a child," he said into the crook of my neck.

My heart stopped.

"A little boy," he added, the words barely audible.

I had to swallow hard and clear my throat before I could force myself to speak. "D-Did he... Will he be okay?"

"I got him out. He'll live." Kane's arms tightened around me, his voice scraped bare. "I don't know if he'll ever be okay."

"Oh, John." Tears stung my eyes and my words came out in a choked whisper. "I'm sorry." I rocked him gently, stroking his hair and murmuring soft nonsense.

After several moments he spoke again, hoarsely as though the words were being wrenched from him under torture. "That shouldn't happen, Aydan. It just... shouldn't happen."

"I know." I tightened my embrace, my heart breaking for him and for a little boy's shattered innocence. "I know."

He drew a deep shuddering breath and straightened. When I looked up at him his eyes were dry but his face looked carved from bone, seared brittle-white as if by heat fiercer than flame.

The phrase 'fires of hell' entered my mind unbidden, and I shivered.

"I'm sorry," Kane said quietly. "You didn't need to hear that."

"Don't apologize. Some things are just... too much to

carry alone." I laid a hand on his arm, feeling the tension thrumming in his muscles. "You're tied up in knots. Lie down and I'll give you a back rub."

He drew a breath as though glimpsing an oasis in a hostile desert. "Would you? That would be great."

"Of course-" The words got stuck in my throat as he stripped off his T-shirt, unveiling massive shoulders tapering down to a corrugated midsection. I'd forgotten just how spectacular his body was.

I tamped down the rush of heat and kept my hands to myself while he got comfortable face down on the mattress. Now was not the time. He needed the caring touch of another human being, nothing more.

Rummaging in my bag for something to use for massage oil, I discovered the little pot of face cream Nichele had given me for Christmas in her eternal but doomed hope of turning me into a girl. I had forgiven her because the gift had also included a delicious assortment of craft beers, but right now the cream was exactly what I needed. As I smoothed it on and began to knead Kane's back, a smile tugged my mouth at the thought of Nichele's expression if she found out how I'd used her gift.

At least it was being appreciated. Kane let out a long breath and the knots under my hands slowly eased.

On his upper back I worked carefully through the puckered network of scars that marked the devastating exit of the bullet that had nearly ended his life several years ago. On his side I avoided the still-reddened marks of the bullet wound only a few months old. In between, my fingers glided over other scars fading into near-oblivion, silent testament to a life risked over and over to save others.

In the soft glow of the candlelight I worked with my eyes

half-closed, ignoring the expanding ache from my arthritic thumbs while my hands searched out and soothed his taut muscles in a slow hypnotic rhythm.

I startled when Kane spoke, his voice muffled by the pillow. "Aydan?"

"Mmhmm?"

"I had really hoped we'd have some time to talk a couple of months ago, but I guess I'll just have to come right out and ask you now." He twitched his head on the pillow in a gesture that could have been resignation or annoyance. "Since we seem destined to never communicate unless there's some crisis or another."

I gulped, trying not to let my hands betray my sudden tension. "Uh... okay...?"

Keep the hands moving in gentle circles. Slow, easy rhythm. Breathe. Some little part of my mind yammered 'oh shit oh shit'.

Kane blew out a breath. "Aydan, when we were in Vegas before Christmas and I... got married..."

He hesitated. I wasn't the only one tensing up. I could feel the tightness creeping back into his muscles.

"I... felt as though that upset you," he finished. "Is that true, or was I just imagining it?"

I abandoned the pretense of rubbing his rigid muscles with my suddenly-wooden hands, and he turned over to study me. Since I had been straddling his hips to reach his back I ended up astride him, summoning blazing-hot memories.

I sucked in a breath. Maybe if I seduced him he'd forget the question.

Something in his expression told me he wouldn't, and he'd be hurt if I tried.

I dismounted and plopped down to sit tailor-fashion on the mattress beside him.

Just be honest. How hard could that be?

I met his eyes with a sigh. "You're right, I was upset, but..." I held up a hand to stop him from speaking. "...not because I wanted to marry you myself. It was just that you'd been going on about how much you wanted me and then as soon as your old girlfriend showed up I was nothing but chopped liver. As though everything you'd said had been lies..." I trailed off and addressed the mattress instead. "And when you begged me not to spoil it for you, that... It was like you didn't believe I was a good enough friend to be happy for you. Like even our friendship was a lie."

I summoned every ounce of my courage. "That... hurt," I whispered.

"I'm sorry." He took my hand, caressing the back of it. "I didn't want to hurt you. Holding onto my cover that day was the hardest..." He trailed off, the fresh and brittle pain twisting his face again. "Almost the hardest thing I've ever done."

"It's okay," I said hurriedly. "You don't need to apologize. It was okay as soon as I realized it was only part of your cover." I gave him a grin, going for the joke. "Mind you, it helped that you killed her a few hours later."

The strain melted from his face and he chuckled. "I'll keep that in mind, but I don't think it's a sustainable strategy for the long term."

"Mm. Probably not."

Kane tucked his arms behind his head and let out a breath. "All right. Thank you. That's all I wanted to know."

"That's all?" I eyed him warily.

"Yes, you can relax now." The corner of his mouth

quirked up. "I've seen you look less terrified under live fire."

I gave him a tentative smile. "Actually, I prefer live fire."

He sighed. "That's not funny."

"I'm not joking."

"You're not, are you?" He frowned at me. "For heaven's sake, Aydan; a firing squad over a simple personal question?"

"I didn't say 'firing squad'; I said 'live fire'," I grumbled. "Under live fire you still have a chance of surviving. I'd probably pick the relationship question over an actual firing squad."

"Probably?"

I picked up the tub of face cream and studied it. Almost empty. I moved some folds of the blanket aside, looking for the lid. "Bullet wounds heal," I mumbled at the mattress. "Or they kill you. Either way, it's good."

Kane's voice softened. "I didn't mean to sound critical. I know how your emotions were used to hurt you in the past. Thank you for trusting me enough to answer my question."

"You're welcome," I muttered, still searching for the elusive lid.

"Wait." The note of incredulous amusement in his tone made me stop rummaging among the blankets to look at him. He reached over to take the small gold-trimmed jar from my hand. "You used Christian Dior face cream on my back?"

"Yeah. So?"

He laughed. "So I assume you didn't buy it for yourself. This little jar probably cost over a hundred dollars."

"Oh, shit." I gulped down my chagrin. "Don't tell Nichele. I thought it was just a little stocking-stuffer and the beer was my real present."

"The beer?"

I nodded. "A dozen different bottles of craft beer from micro-breweries around Calgary. They were great."

He pulled a solemn face but his eyes sparkled with wicked humour. "I'll keep your secret, but it'll cost you." He rolled the little tub between his fingers and the wickedness spilled over into a grin that warmed places I'd been trying to ignore for the past hour.

"I've been having a lot of tension in my chest lately," he rumbled. "You could pay your debt by massaging it for me." He patted his hips, framing a breathtaking denim-clad package. "You can sit right here."

Apparently the afternoon's debacle with Hellhound and Orion wasn't going to be an issue, at least not tonight. Behind Kane's sexy smile I could sense his need to put aside the horror of his mission, if only for a little while.

"Hmm. Blackmail." I grinned and swung astride his ankles, leaning forward to place a hand on either side of his legs. "You do realize blackmail is illegal and now you're under arrest. I'll have to strip-search you..."

I dragged a slow fingernail up the inner seam of his jeans.

"...to make sure you don't have any..."

Higher, watching the hunger flare in his eyes.

"...dangerous weapons," I breathed as my fingertip glided over the denim-sheathed weapon in question.

"Ah..." His syllable floated out on a gasp and he tucked his arms behind his head again as if to prevent himself from reaching for me. Muscles rippled in his chest and abs. "Good idea." He sounded distinctly breathless. "You can't be too careful."

"Especially with a..." I bent down to brush my lips over

his stomach as I undid his button. "...hardened criminal..." My fingertips drifted lower and discovered exactly how hardened he was. "...like yourself." I eased his zipper down.

His reply was an inarticulate rumble. His eyes blazed, his gaze riveted on my mouth while I kissed my way unhurriedly down the valley between his washboard abs toward the landing strip of hair below his navel.

I had almost reached my goal when a low urgent voice from outside the tent flap startled me out of my absorption.

"Hey, Aydan! Cap! Are ya decent in there?"

I sat up and frowned at my wristwatch. Two hours on the dot.

"Trying not to be," Kane growled. "Can you give us a little longer?"

"Sorry, Cap." Hellhound really did sound sorry, but there was a tense note in his voice that made the back of my neck prickle. "We gotta talk."

Kane must have heard it, too. He did up his jeans and snapped, "Come in."

Hellhound slipped through the tent flap and secured it behind him. The look on his face made my prickle of apprehension turn into a chill.

"What? What is it?" I demanded.

He crossed the tent in a couple of strides and we leaned close to hear him mutter, "The bridge. It's got explosive charges under it. The whole thing's rigged to blow."

CHAPTER 30

"*What?*" I stared at Hellhound. "Why would anybody want to blow up the bridge?"

"I dunno, but the way those charges are placed, they ain't messin' around. An' it's a professional job. Nobody'd spot 'em unless they knew what they were lookin' for. By the cobwebs on 'em I'd say they been in place for a while so I gave ya the two hours I promised, but I didn't wanna wait any longer."

Kane pulled on his T-shirt with sharp movements, all the good work of my massage lost in the renewed tension of his shoulders. "There are only two reasons to blow a bridge," he said. "To destroy something on it, or to cut off a position for tactical reasons."

"Nothin' on it," Hellhound pointed out.

"And nobody from the commune ever goes across it," I added. "Except Orion, but I can't see somebody blowing up that huge bridge just to get rid of him. If there are thirty guys with bayonets over there, it would be easy enough to take care of one man without attracting attention with an explosion that size."

"So it has to be a tactical objective." Kane frowned at me. "What's on the renters' side of that bridge?"

"Nothing. No other access, no exit. I checked the satellite map online when I was at the internet café. That chunk of land has rivers on two sides and mountainous terrain on the rest. It might as well be an island. The only road to civilization goes over that bridge and through the commune to Port Renfrew. It would be stupid for the renters to cut themselves off."

"Unless they were lookin' for a place to dig in," Hellhound said slowly. "It'd be a fuckin' nightmare to try an' take 'em out once the bridge was gone. Hell, even with the bridge there. No good fightin' through a choke point like that."

"Access only by air; heavy forest cover and rugged terrain," Kane agreed. "So what are they hiding or protecting over there? Why would they want to cut themselves off from everybody else?"

"Maybe they're just one of those nutso doomsday cults," I offered. "Maybe they're getting ready to protect themselves from the zombie apocalypse."

Hellhound snorted. "Too fuckin' late for that. World's full a' dumbfuck zombies already."

I blew out a breath between my teeth. "Well, maybe Stemp can get the analysts to dig for some information on who that group is or what they might be planning. And I'll need to report the explosives, too, and see what he wants to do." I eyed Hellhound. "What do you think it would take to disable them?"

Hellhound shrugged. "Explosives ain't really my best thing, but I've done a bit. I could prob'ly disable 'em but I'd hafta get closer to see for sure."

Kane frowned at him. "Speaking of seeing, how did you spot them in the first place if they're concealed? It's dark out."

"Yeah." Hellhound patted his ever-present backpack. "I got some gear with me. Caught 'em with my night-vision scope."

I drew a breath of relief. "Good, you've got night-vision. What else have you got?"

"Thermographic, too, in a headset. My rifle an' scope. Sidearm. Climbin' gear. Survival gear. Camo. An' I got the bike stashed out by the road."

"You're brilliant." I shot him an admiring glance before turning to Kane. "John, I didn't even think to ask, how did you get here?"

He raised an eyebrow at Hellhound. "Great minds think alike, apparently. I rented a superbike and stashed it a few miles up the road."

I laughed despite the tension gathering in my shoulders. "Fabulous. I suppose you're fully geared up, too."

"Yes, but I don't have it with me. I made a separate cache out in the woods, away from the bike." Kane gave me a wry grimace. "I didn't realize the situation was heating up here. Stupid. I should have been prepared."

"Not stupid at all." I reached over to squeeze his hand, knowing he'd been focused on what he believed to be a safe haven after his devastating mission. "You didn't know what you were walking into so it made sense to leave behind anything that might compromise your cover."

He shrugged. "Be that as it may. I have my Sig with me, of course, but that's it." He scrubbed both hands over his face before eyeing me tiredly. "I suppose you'll be checking in with Stemp soon."

"Yes." I hesitated. "I don't have to tell him you're here if you don't want me to."

"It's all right." Kane's words were flat with resignation. "I'll hike out and pick up my gear, and while I'm out there I'll call in my report. I'll tell Stemp I'm staying here until the situation is resolved or until he gets a team out here to support you, whichever comes first."

"Thank you. I'm really glad you're here."

Kane looked slightly surprised, and I wondered if he had thought I didn't want him here. Or maybe he thought I'd feel threatened professionally if he attached himself to my mission without asking. Little did he know how abjectly grateful I was for both his and Hellhound's presence.

"Are you geared up, too?" Kane asked.

"Yes, I have night-vision and thermographic, my Glock and a trank pistol, a tracking unit for Orion..." My words faded into a burst of adrenaline. I hadn't checked on Orion for two whole hours. Jesus, I was such a shitty agent.

I whipped the tracking unit out of my jacket pocket and released my tension in a slow breath. "He's over in the renters' camp again." I tucked the tracker back in my pocket and went on, "...a night-vision remote webcam, binoculars, and a bunch of secured phones. Oh, and hand restraints and a couple of spare mags for the trank gun and my Glock, and a bunch of extra ammo for both."

"All right. How do you want to proceed?" Kane asked.

Shit, he was asking me? What the hell did I know?

"Um, I need to talk to Stemp first," I said. I glanced at my watch. "It's late enough now that we can move around fairly safely. Most of the members will be in bed. Nichele's presentation was supposed to last until nine-thirty..." I trailed off again as cold fear gripped my throat. "Arnie, did you happen to go by the main building?"

"Yeah, I checked to make sure she was doin' her talk in

there around eight-thirty," he confirmed. "An' I didn't see anybody around that looked like your Ratboy."

I sent quiet but fervent thanks skyward. "Okay, good," I said out loud. "So she should be safely holed up in the kitchen for the night by now and everybody else should be in their tents. I'll walk my east loop to check in with Stemp, and then I'll need to swing by and check on Moonbeam and Karma. John, do you need night-vision to find your cache?"

"No, I noted the GPS coordinates."

I managed not to grimace. Of course he had.

Hellhound spoke into the momentary silence. "While you guys're doin' that I'm gonna go have a closer look at those explosives, an' then scout for places where I can get a clear shot at the bridge an' around the main buildin' just in case those assholes decide to move. Don't like havin' all these civilians undefended."

"Okay, but don't go near the bridge," I cautioned. "If you can't see what you need with your scope, just wait until I have orders from Stemp. Remember Orion has night vision and he'll likely be coming back across that bridge sometime tonight."

"Don't worry, darlin', he ain't gonna see me."

"Okay..." I hesitated, wondering what I was forgetting.

"How many secured phones did you say you had?" Kane asked.

"A dozen."

"Let's each carry two," he suggested. "Since we don't have radios, we'll need some way to communicate if there are new developments while we're separated."

"And you're brilliant, too," I said gratefully. "Wait here and I'll go and get them from my cache."

"Where is it?" Kane asked. "Will you be long?"

"No, it's in the pond. I'll be right back." I pulled on my rubber boots and ducked out the tent flap.

Back inside the tent with my dripping box, I handed out the burner phones and we programmed the numbers into their speed dials. Then I tucked the tranquilizer pistol into my shoulder holster, strapped my survival knife to my hip, and pocketed a couple of sets of hand restraints before reaching for my own backpack.

Hellhound eyed me narrowly. "Expectin' trouble, darlin'?"

I sighed. "I don't know what to expect. And I don't want to leave anything suspicious in my tent in case somebody searches it, so I'm bringing everything."

I loaded the rest of the gear into my backpack, briefly considered my laptop, and then added it and the spare battery, too. At least if Stemp wanted a private conversation I could fire up the laptop out in the woods without having to trek all the way back here.

And Kane and Hellhound didn't know about my secret communication system, or about Stemp's family. I trusted both men with my life, but Stemp's little daughter's life was in my hands alone. What they didn't know, they couldn't be forced to tell under torture.

I shuddered at the thought of what Kane must have seen that had shaken him so profoundly. Whatever it was, I wouldn't let it happen to Anna.

"Ya okay, darlin'? Ya look like ya just saw a ghost." Hellhound's worried voice brought me back to the present.

"Sorry. I'm fine." I pushed a smile onto my lips. "So are we good to go?"

"Yes. When do you want to meet back here?" Kane asked.

"Um..."

I did a rapid mental calculation. Hike out, report to Stemp, possibly exchange a short conversation on the laptop, then come back via the kitchen to check on Nichele, and check Moonbeam and Karma's tent to make sure they were in for the night. I'd have to stop and visit for a few minutes if Nichele saw me. But maybe I could just peek in the window.

"An hour and a half," I decided. "Does that work for you guys?"

They both nodded and I shouldered my pack and turned for the tent flap.

"Hang on." Hellhound's voice stopped me.

I turned back. "What am I forgetting?"

"This." He drew me into his arms and kissed me.

It wasn't the chaste kiss he usually offered when Kane was present.

He didn't linger unduly, but he didn't rush, either.

"Be safe, darlin'," he murmured against my lips. Then he stepped back, meeting Kane's nonplussed gaze squarely. "Be safe, too, Cap," he rasped. "But I ain't gonna kiss ya."

Kane let out a bark of laughter. "Thank God. You be safe, too."

Hellhound grinned and ducked out the tent flap.

Kane turned to me and a wry smile twisted his lips. "Well..." He hesitated, then shrugged and pulled me tight against his body.

He definitely lingered over the kiss. By the time he released me I was breathless and my wobbling knees barely held my weight.

He cupped my face between his palms. "Be safe." He kissed me lightly again and turned for the tent flap.

"Uh," I croaked. "You, too."

I stood blinking at the flap for a moment after he disappeared through it.

Okay, that had been a little weird and awkward.

My lips turned up in spite of myself. But hell, if they were going to turn this into a competition, I could foresee only one winner.

Me.

My grin widened and I blew out the candles and left, securing the tent flap behind me.

CHAPTER 31

My smile didn't last long. Creeping along the moon-dappled path with my head swivelling like a manic owl, I felt as though at any moment Orion would pop out in front of me wearing night vision goggles and carrying a detonator.

Though heaven knew why he'd want to blow the bridge.

A trickle of fear oozed down my spine. What if the bridge wasn't the only thing rigged with explosives?

The fear gushed into an icy torrent. Oh, God, what if he'd rigged the main building, too? He could kill everybody in the commune with a single bomb. He could be on the other side of the river and still hear the damn Spirit bells ringing. He'd know exactly when everybody was gathered and he wouldn't have to be anywhere near it when it blew.

I yanked out a burner phone and punched the speed dial. The phone rang once before Hellhound's gravelly voice issued from the speaker.

"What's up, darlin'?"

"Arnie, did you check the main building for explosives?"

Momentary silence on the other end confirmed my fear.

"Shit," Hellhound rasped. "They wouldn'ta... Fuck! On my way! Call ya soon's I know." The line went dead.

Heart pounding, I stood on the dark path clutching the

phone. Should I call Kane, too?

A moment later logic asserted itself. No point. Hellhound was closer, and in a few minutes we'd know.

And there was no reason for Orion to blow the building immediately, so Hellhound should be safe unless the Spirit bells rang.

Oh, God, let him be safe.

I forced my trembling legs to carry me farther down the path. I might as well continue on as planned. I couldn't help Hellhound. I knew nothing about explosives. And if the building did blow, there would be nothing I could do anyway.

Shut up. It wouldn't explode now; that didn't make any sense. I'd just get my ass out to where I could call Stemp without being overheard. Hellhound would probably have a report for me by then and I could pass it all on to Stemp.

By the time I reached the outer limit of my trail's loop, my heart was pounding. No word from Hellhound. Surely that was good news. If he'd found explosives he'd have called me right away.

Or maybe he'd found so many he was still itemizing them all.

The phone's vibration made me jerk with nerves and I nearly dropped it in my rush to answer.

"What?" I demanded.

"Nothin'. All clear."

"Oh thank God." I hunkered down on the path, my legs shaking too hard to hold my weight any longer. "You're sure?"

"Pretty sure, 'less they're in the walls or somethin', but you'd hafta tear the whole buildin' apart to find out. An' they couldn'ta hidden anythin' in that concrete part on the bottom. It's like a fuckin' bunker."

"Right, and I can't see anybody having a chance to hide bombs inside the walls anyway," I agreed. "There are people in and out of there constantly." I drew a deep breath and eased it out. "Okay, thanks for checking. Sorry for the false alarm."

"No sweat, darlin', it woulda been a helluva lot worse if ya hadn't thought of it an' it turned out to be rigged. I'll get back to scoutin' my positions. What's your tracker say?"

I extracted it from my pocket and eyed the dot. "Orion's still on the renters' land so don't go near the bridge yet."

"Okay. Call me soon's I'm clear to move."

We hung up and I punched the speed dial for Stemp. At his crisp greeting I drew a deep breath and gave him as concise an update as possible. When I had finished, the line hummed with a few moments of thoughtful silence.

"I agree, there doesn't seem to be any tactical reason to blow the bridge except to allow the renters to isolate themselves," Stemp said. He hesitated, then continued, "Disable the explosives if it can be done without detection. I'll leave Kane and Helmand at your disposal for the rest of the week. After that we'll re-evaluate, and if the situation warrants it I'll assign a support team."

"Okay. What about the renters?" I asked. "Can you get the analysts to dig for any information about them?"

"Already done," he replied. "No paramilitary groups are claiming to operate in the vicinity, and my parents don't use a computer system so no records were available to hack online. If you knew where to look you might be able to find a paper rental agreement with some names, but I never saw my parents doing paperwork as a child so I doubt the records are kept in their tent or in the main building. I don't know where else they would be."

I sighed. "Okay. I'll start digging tomorrow. Any more information on Skidmark?"

"No. There are no military pension cheques being issued to anyone of the correct age and personal details anywhere around Port Renfrew."

"Shit."

"Indeed," he agreed.

"All right, we'll see if we can disable the explosives and I'll keep you posted."

I hung up and checked the tracker again, but Orion's red dot was still stubbornly planted on the renters' side. I was turning to trudge back along the path when my phone vibrated again.

When I answered, Kane's tense voice issued from the speaker. "I'm off the road about two miles out. Two five-ton moving trucks just passed here heading toward the commune. ETA less than five minutes."

"Outside vehicles aren't allowed," I said reflexively.

Kane must have dialled Hellhound and me simultaneously on separate phones, because Hellhound's slightly-muffled rasp spoke next. "I can get eyes on the main gate by then. Ya sure they were movin' trucks?"

"They were standard cube trucks and I could see the rental-company logos in the moonlight. Who knows what's inside, though. I'm not at my cache yet and I still have to report to Stemp. Unless you want me to come back now, my ETA at the main gate is about thirty minutes. Aydan, what are my orders?"

Orders? He expected *me* to give the orders?

"I don't know," I said. "I think it makes more sense for you to get your gear- ...oh!"

"What?" Kane snapped.

"Sorry, I just realized I forgot to tell you that there was a cougar in the area a couple of days ago, so be careful. But I suppose that's the least of our worries compared to bombs under the bridge."

"Thanks for the heads-up, but I'm not too worried about a cougar. They tend to look for smaller prey than me. And I don't know that there's any need to get caught up in an artificial sense of urgency about the explosives, either. They've clearly been there for some time. I don't like the timing of these moving trucks, but..." I sensed his shrug at the other end of the line before he continued, "Let's keep this connection open until we know where those trucks are going, but maintain radio silence unless reporting."

"Okay, I'm still about fifteen minutes out," I said. "I'm going to switch over to my hands-free, so if I lose you I'll call right back." I burrowed into my pack and fumbled out my earbud and cable. "Okay. There. Can you hear me okay?" I waited for their confirmations before breaking into a trot. "This path loops close to the river so I'll keep my eyes open," I added. "But the trucks will probably be gone by the time I get there."

After that I saved my breath for jogging, the phone clutched in one hand, the hands-free cable slapping annoyingly against my chin. My laptop dug into my spine through the backpack and the night-vision headset thudded my forehead.

I clenched my teeth and kept jogging, my embarrassing panting echoing over the open phone line.

A few minutes later Hellhound spoke in a barely-audible growl. "Got 'em. Comin' through the front gate an' it looks like they're headin' for the renters' side."

"Maybe they're moving out," I panted. "Skipping in the

middle of the night without paying their rent."

"Followin' 'em now." Hellhound's terse update reminded me I was supposed to be maintaining radio silence. I bit my tongue and kept moving.

"...An' they're over the bridge," Hellhound announced a couple of minutes later. "Lost 'em in the trees on the other side. Aydan, where's Orion?"

I halted to juggle the phone and the tracker. "Still with the renters."

"Well, if they're loadin' or unloadin' somethin' they'll be a while," Hellhound said. "I wanna find one more position around the main buildin', an' then I'll be ready to start scoutin' near the bridge whenever ya give me the all-clear."

"Okay, Stemp says to disable the explosives if we can, so I'll let you know as soon as Orion's back across the bridge," I agreed. "I'm almost at the edge of the commune, and I'm going to check on Nichele. I might have to close the connection for a while if she wants to visit, but I won't be long and I'll pick up if you call."

Murmurs of assent floated over the line, and I slowed my pace to a walk as I reached the part of the path that wound up and down through small gullies near the river. Bad idea to go dashing over a hill with all my gear on display only to run smack into one of the commune members.

And anyway, I needed to dry some of my sweat before I showed up to visit Nichele. It might be tough to explain why I looked like I'd been working out in the middle of the night.

Then again...

My steps slowed even more as a wave of mortification engulfed me. First she'd walked in on that orgy scene in my tent and then I hadn't showed up for her presentation. It would be far too easy for her to infer a plausible reason for my disheveled state. I suppressed a groan.

A moment later I was glad I'd suppressed it. The sound of nearby voices made me whip off my night-vision headset and click off the phone, stuffing both into my pocket.

Breathing silently through my mouth, I stood in the darkness waiting for my eyes to adjust to moonlight instead of green-tinged night-vision.

It sounded as though the speakers were mere feet away over the next rise, but maybe it was only the still night air carrying the two men's voices to me so clearly.

Shit, that sounded like Orion's voice.

Heart thumping, I inched my fingers into my jacket pocket. The rustle of fabric sounded loud in the silence and I froze again. Slowly, a degree at a time, I tipped the tracker up to face me.

"Did you take care of them?" The other voice sounded vaguely familiar, too. "She didn't call the police, did she?"

"Don't worry, the old folks are stashed where they won't cause any trouble."

My feet froze to the path. That *was* Orion. The red dot was practically on top of me.

The thunder of my heart nearly drowned out his next words. "I'll go and take care of them now. I won't be long."

"Curse you to a thousand hells, you were supposed have done it already!" That venomous hiss had to be Ratboy. "Hurry up! You'd better be back at camp by one o'clock or Mesker will finish us both!"

"Chill out. I'll be there."

The sound of footsteps drove my hand to my shoulder holster. No time to run or hide. In an instant they'd be over the rise.

My trank gun steadied on the place where they'd appear.

The footsteps faded.

Orion's words drilled into my brain.

He had Moonbeam and Karma.

He was going to kill them.

I jammed the night-vision headset back on one-handed, the fingers of my other hand tightening painfully around the trank gun.

I'd kill him.

If he had hurt them, I'd kill him.

My feet were already in motion, carrying me swiftly over the hill. I snapped a glance around me. The path branched to cross the road at this point. Ratboy's back was just vanishing around the corner to my right.

To my left, Orion slowed his stride, then stopped facing away from me, fumbling at his head with both hands. Probably putting on his night-vision goggles.

I dropped to a shooter's crouch, the open sights of the trank pistol clear in my night vision. An instant later the small flat report was swallowed by the dark forest.

Orion fell without a sound.

I stuffed the trank gun back into my holster and dashed to his crumpled body. Clamping both fists onto his jacket, I dragged him off the path, fury and fear giving me strength. Only a few yards away the terrain dropped off into another little gully. Snarling with effort, I wrenched his limp body to the edge and shoved him over.

The noise of his roll through the undergrowth brought me to my senses. No telling how far Ratboy had gone or when he might come back. Keep this fast and quiet.

I hurried down into the gully and crouched beside Orion's limp form. A quick survey of our surroundings assured me we were hidden from the path, and I glanced at my watch. Probably about fifteen minutes before the trank wore off.

I searched him rapidly. A small pistol in an ankle holster. One of the scary bayonets sheathed on his thigh. A radio. A flashlight. A tiny device in his ear that I would have missed if not for a moonlit glint as his head lolled to one side. A couple of sets of nylon hand restraints that I set aside for later use.

Ruthlessly, I stripped off his jacket and manhandled his entire body, checking every square inch and discovering one more small but vicious-looking knife in his boot. When I was positive he had no more weapons or communication devices on him, I sliced off the sleeve of his shirt for a gag and secured his wrists behind his back. Then I put his night-vision goggles on him and trussed his ankles with the nylon restraints. All his other gear went into my backpack.

Panting, I flopped down on the ground, clammy with sweat and fear. Damn, damn, damn! Why hadn't I found a way to tag Moonbeam and Karma? Now I had to figure out where they were. They could be anywhere in the forest. What if they were injured, succumbing to shock and blood loss?

A glance at my watch showed the trank should be wearing off any minute. Should I call Kane and Hellhound?

I eyed Orion's still form.

Maybe I didn't want witnesses.

Four months ago I had fooled a criminal into thinking I was torturing him with a secret weapon that had really been an ordinary depilator. He had told me what I needed to know at the cost of only a few leg hairs.

But I didn't have any beauty appliances with me this time. And I needed Orion to talk. Fast.

I squinted at my watch and my hands began to shake.

After eleven o'clock. In a little more than an hour, Ratboy would start to wonder why Orion wasn't back. And if he found Moonbeam and Karma before I did, they would die. I had no tricks up my sleeve this time. Nothing but brute force and urgency.

I would do what was necessary.

And if there was a hell, I would burn there for all eternity.

CHAPTER 32

Orion groaned and moved feebly against the restraints, and I locked away the last remnants of my humanity and sprang. Knotting my fist in his hair, I yanked his head back and pressed the flat of my survival knife against his throat. His eyes jerked open at the touch of the cold steel and I leaned close to growl in his ear.

"Keep quiet or I'll slit your throat. Got it?"

He stiffened and nodded, a bare fraction of an inch up and down.

"Good." I pulled off the makeshift gag.

"Storm, what-" he whispered.

I pressed the knife a little harder. He shut up, his rapid pulse vibrating through the blade and into my hand.

"Where are Moonbeam and Karma?" I demanded.

"I haven't the foggiest notion." His British accent was much more noticeable under stress. "Probably in their tent-"

"*The old folks are stashed where they won't cause any trouble*," I hissed. "Last chance. Where. The. Fuck. Are. They?"

"Why would I tell you that?"

"Wrong question," I ground out. "You *will* tell me. The right question is, 'how much do you want to suffer before you do'?"

He pressed his lips together, and rage overwhelmed me. I slammed my hand into his crotch, clamping down and twisting harder with each word. "If... you've... hurt... them..."

"*Wait!*" The word came out in a strangled squeak. Even in my night vision his face had gone white, sweat beading his forehead and upper lip.

I eased off a fraction and he gulped air.

"Where are they?" I snarled.

"You don't want to hurt them?"

"Why the hell would I want to hurt them? Now tell me where they are or I'll twist your balls off and shove them down your throat!"

"Let me explain!" He panted for a moment. "I promise they're safe. Please let go of my tackle."

"I didn't ask if they were *safe*! I *asked*..." I gripped and twisted harder. "...*where are they*?"

"I'll... tell... you..." The words grated out between his teeth. "Please..."

I eased off again, guilt prodding me despite my attempt to ignore it. Not having testicles of my own I couldn't exactly empathize, but I'd seen enough guys suffer a blow to the nuts to realize Orion was a hairsbreadth away from either puking or passing out. Or maybe both.

I gave him a moment to recover. When his breathing eased from jerky gasps to rapid panting, I leaned in again.

"I'll take you there," he said hurriedly before I could speak. "You wouldn't be able to find it even if I gave you directions." I eyed him in silence and he drew a deep tremulous breath. "Look, I know your real name is Aydan Kelly, and I'm pretty sure you belong to some branch of law enforcement. I do, too. I'm in the middle of an op and this is just a misunderstanding-"

"Shut up." I accompanied the command with a convincing squeeze, and he went quiet except for more jerky breathing.

Law enforcement. That would explain the hand restraints. Maybe he was undercover, investigating the renters.

Or maybe he was full of shit and setting me up for an ambush.

I gave him a toothy smile. "Okay, sure. I'm law enforcement. Now I'm going to read you your rights, so listen up."

A little of the tension went out of his body. Interesting.

"You have the right to remain silent..." I leaned closer. "...because if you don't I'll slit your throat. Vocal cords only, so you won't die. You have the right to take me directly to where you're holding Moonbeam and Karma, and I strongly recommend you exercise that right. You'll be pleased to know I grew up on a farm so I'm familiar with the technique for castrating large animals without any risk of them bleeding out."

He tensed up again. Imagine that.

I showed a few more teeth. "If you lead me anywhere Moonbeam and Karma *aren't*, I recommend you choose a place close to where they *are* because you're going to be extremely uncomfortable walking there afterward with your balls cut off. If you try to signal anyone in any way, they have the right to die instantly and I will make sure that right is exercised."

"You, on the other hand..." I paused and let my gaze travel the length of his body before glaring into his eyes. "If you double-cross me, or if you've hurt Moonbeam or Karma, you have the right to scream and beg for death. It won't do you any good because I won't let you die, but you can do it all you want. Are we clear?"

"None of that will be necessary." His voice was faint but steady. "I'll take you directly to them. No tricks. And please don't kill anybody."

His final sentence really made me wonder.

Not 'don't kill *me*'. 'Don't kill *anybody*'. It sure sounded like something a cop would say.

Or somebody who wanted to sound like a cop.

I hissed out my tension through my teeth. Only one way to find out. I let go of his crotch and stepped carefully around him, keeping the knife at his throat.

"Here's what's going to happen," I said softly. "See this?" I drew the trank pistol left-handed and moved it along his cheek so he could barely see the muzzle in his peripheral vision. Close enough so he could identify it as a gun; too close for him to be able to tell it wasn't a regular firearm.

He nodded very slowly and carefully.

"I'm going to cut the ties on your ankles. If you so much as twitch, I'll shoot you. Then I'm going to step back and you're going to get up and take me to Moonbeam and Karma at a nice steady pace through the woods, not on the paths. We both have night vision, so if we see anybody at all, we're going to stand nice and still and quiet until they pass. If you make noise, if you even step on a stick, I'll shoot you. If you try to run, I'll shoot you. If you make any sudden moves, I'll shoot you. And I won't shoot to kill, so don't think you can escape that way."

"I understand."

"Good." I took the knife away from his throat. "Roll onto your stomach."

He complied, and I cut the restraints on his ankles and backed away, sheathing my knife so I could transfer the trank gun to my right hand.

"Stand up."

He squirmed onto his knees and hunched there for a moment, breathing deeply, his hands flexing behind him in their bindings. I tensed, the trank gun trained on him, but he was apparently only taking a moment to recover. He clambered awkwardly to his feet and stood still for another couple of breaths.

"All right," he said evenly. "I'm going to walk in the direction of the garage. I'll do exactly as you said."

He moved slowly into the forest and I followed several paces behind, fervently hoping he'd do the 'take me to Moonbeam and Karma' part of what I'd said, not the 'force me to torture him' part.

I didn't even know if I could have tortured him while I was certain he was a criminal. Now that I was wondering if he was a cop...

But dammit, he could just be a really smart crook. Putting doubt in my mind; trying to get me to drop my guard so he could make his move.

I eased out a silent breath and willed my hammering heart to slow.

As we passed through the woods between the bridge and the main building I flipped momentarily to thermal vision to scan around us. If Hellhound was on his way to the bridge, what would he do if he spotted us?

I really didn't want a witness right now; and I also didn't want Orion to know I had allies just in case everything went to shit and he somehow got back to his buddies on the renters' side.

A few distant heat signatures flickered through the intervening tree trunks, but there was nothing close enough to be visible in night vision. Good. If I couldn't see them, they couldn't see me.

Orion kept moving at a steady pace. We left the main part of the commune behind and began to climb the slope to the garage, but instead of aiming toward the building Orion veered off to circle around the hill.

My arm ached with the strain of holding the trank gun at the ready. If we didn't get there soon, I'd have to switch hands. Nerves and the exertion of climbing made my knees tremble, and the trank gun wavered. Shit, was he just leading me on a wild goose chase until I got tired so he could overpower me?

I wasn't sure how he might accomplish that with his hands tied behind his back, but I was certain Kane could do it if he was in Orion's place. Who knew what skills Orion was hiding?

I steadied the flagging muzzle of the trank gun again and panted through my mouth so he wouldn't hear.

What if he was leading me into an ambush? This far from the main encampment, nobody would hear the sounds of a struggle. And Kane and Hellhound had no idea where I was.

The last of my rage-fuelled courage seeped away and my knees began to tremble in earnest. Who the hell did I think I was and what the hell was I doing? I wasn't Jane Bond, Superspy. Hell, Jane Bond would have been smart enough to tell somebody where she was going. I should call Kane and Hellhound right now-

Orion stopped and I nearly ran into him.

Fortunately he didn't turn to look at me as I blundered to

a halt. To my right the lush fingers of Skidmark's marijuana crop reached for the sky. Behind it an impenetrable tumble of fallen trees leaned against the hillside, overgrown with ferns.

"I'm going to move to my left now," Orion said quietly. "You'll need to follow closely."

I hesitated. I could tell him to stop right here; call Kane and Hellhound and wait for them to back me up.

But he was already moving, and I couldn't afford to let him think I was doubting myself.

In a couple of fast steps I closed the distance between us and clamped my fist on a handful of his hair, jamming my gun into his spine. He went rigid and I hissed, "One wrong move and you'll be paralyzed from the waist down."

"I understand." His British accent was very much in evidence. "Please stay calm. I promise this isn't a trap. There's a door hidden behind that log pile. Moonbeam and Karma are inside."

"Slowly," I grated.

We moved forward together, creeping step by step around the corner of the pile and ducking into a rough alcove formed by criss-crossed tree trunks. Even with my night vision, I couldn't see anything but tree trunks and dirt.

Orion stopped beneath the arch. "Aydan, there is a door concealed behind that large tree trunk," he said evenly. "That's where Moonbeam and Karma are. The control pad is above these logs. There's no other way to open the door. You'll need to either untie my hands or enter the code yourself."

"Yeah, right," I growled. "On the ground, face-down."

There was barely room for him to comply in the cramped space. He managed a crumpled semi-prone posture and I stood over him, debating.

I had no idea what to do next. No matter what choice I made, I could visualize some disastrous outcome.

I gnawed my lip, scowling. I could second-guess this decision all night long. If I entered the code myself there might be a booby-trap that would take me out and spare Orion because he was lying on the ground. Or he might use a duress code that would bring a squad of armed men down on me. If I freed his hands so he could enter the code himself I was wide open for an attack if he had any martial arts skills at all. I could probably trank him again if he tried anything, but that would only delay the inevitable.

And even if I waited for Kane and Hellhound, the choices were the same, only we'd all go down together. Not an acceptable risk.

"Don't move," I commanded, and trained the trank gun on Orion while I fumbled a phone out of my pocket and pressed the speed dial button.

"What's up, darlin'?" Hellhound asked, his rasp sounding clearly over the speaker in the enclosed space. Damn, I should have used the hands-free. Too late now, unless I wanted to put down my gun.

Not happening.

"Aydan?" Urgency filled his tone and I pulled myself together.

"I have Orion." My voice came out flat and harsh. "We're downhill north of the garage and he says Moonbeam and Karma are being held in a room concealed under a brush pile. There's a control pad in the logs overhead." I nudged Orion with my toe. "What's the code?"

"Five-one-niner-three-seven-seven," he recited without hesitation.

I repeated it to Hellhound, then added, "Hold your position there. I'll check in again in five minutes." I hung up on his protest.

Before I could lose my nerve, I punched in the code, then swooped down to yank Orion up by the hair as the door opened.

Warmth and light poured out, and my night-vision headset adjusted to compensate. I shoved Orion forward into the doorway, gripping his hair and jamming my body against the pistol I still held in his back.

A moment later the scene inside the room registered, and my grip on Orion slackened, my hand falling to my side to dangle uselessly.

"Shit," I croaked, and holstered my pistol.

CHAPTER 33

"Hello, dear," Moonbeam said, looking up from the console where she and Karma sat side by side, apparently monitoring feeds from multiple security cameras.

On the opposite side of the large control room, Skidmark pushed his rolling chair back from a desk, swivelling to face us and grinning widely enough to show his gold tooth.

"Ha! Told you she was law enforcement, Rand!" he crowed. "You owe me fifty bucks! Look at you trussed up like a Christmas turkey! So much for your fancy MI6 training. Ha!" He turned his grin on me. "Girlie, as soon as he pays up, I'm giving his fifty bucks to you to pay for the entertainment. That was the funniest thing I ever saw."

"Shut it, you old wanker," Orion/Rand snapped. He eyed me over his shoulder and wiggled his hands in their bindings. "If you please?"

"Sorry," I mumbled, and cut the ties.

"What happened to your shirt, Rand?" Skidmark was in full cry again. "You cut off your sleeve to use for a diaper when you shit your pants? Or is that a *nappy* like you Limeys say?"

"Now, Skidmark, dear," Moonbeam remonstrated gently. "That's really not fair. Storm Cloud Dancer is obviously not run-of-the-mill law enforcement." She turned her luminous smile on me. "Are you, dear?"

"You saw the whole thing? Explain!" I tried to sound authoritative but it came out more like a plea.

"Yes, we have surveillance cameras on the bridge and at intervals along the road inside the commune. Won't you sit down, dear? We'll tell you all about it." She indicated a desk chair.

"Uh... no... thanks, I'd rather stand," I lied, and leaned against the wall as close to the door as possible. "I have less than five minutes before my check-in, so let's make this quick."

"She told Helmand where the door was," Orion interrupted. "We need to do damage control. I'll start." He turned to me and extended his hand. "Ian Rand. MI6. Five Eyes," he added as if that should mean something to me.

I shook his hand warily. "Okay...?"

Karma's laugh boomed out. "Remember, Rand, she's just a bookkeeper."

"Oh, yes, that's very funny," Orion griped. "Ha, ha." Then he apparently recognized my genuinely blank expression. He frowned. "MI6," he said slowly. "The British Secret Intelligence Service."

"Yeah, I got that part," I agreed. "I watch James Bond movies."

He winced.

"Sorry," I added. "I just didn't get the four-eyes part."

"*Five* Eyes. The international intelligence alliance."

Obviously I still looked as confused as I truly was.

"The U.K., Canada, the United States, Australia, and New Zealand," he enunciated slowly. "Working together to monitor and neutralize terrorist activities."

My shock was wearing off, rapidly turning to fury. Dammit, had Stemp been jerking me around for the last four months? Surely he'd know about any joint operations like this. And he sure as hell should know that his parents...

My mind reeled.

His parents were agents. Fuck me.

"Why the hell didn't I know about this?" I demanded.

"I'm sure I don't know," Orion said, his accent sounding slightly snooty. "Five Eyes has been active since World War II, and has been widely known to the public since the late 1990s."

I shot him a glare. "I should have left the fucking gag on you. I meant... *this!*" I jerked a hand at the electronic equipment that surrounded us. "Why the hell wasn't I briefed?"

"Perhaps your security clearance..." Moonbeam began tactfully, then stopped, maybe reading something in my face. Or maybe in my goddamn aura.

"Oh," she said. "You have a very, very high security clearance, don't you, dear?"

I didn't reply to that, mostly because I didn't know how to without revealing much more than I wanted them to know.

"Well, that explains a few things," Karma said. "Your lovers came up in our system immediately; Kane's cover as a police officer and occasional petroleum consultant, and Helmand's as a retired army corporal turned private investigator. Then Rand dug into the classified records and discovered Kane's credentials as an undercover agent and Helmand's Special Forces weapons expertise. But no matter where we searched, all we found on you was Aydan Kelly, a.k.a. Arlene Widdenback and Arlene Cherry; bookkeeper, fraud artist, and part-time internet porn star."

It was my turn to wince.

"So we speculated."   Moonbeam took up the story. "Cosmic River Stone would have told us if he'd known about your, er... line of work..."

Wait, they were agents but they didn't know their son was the director of clandestine operations in Alberta?

I dragged my attention back to Moonbeam's narrative.

"...when you arrived so obviously traumatized, we first assumed you had been a victim of some violent crime."

"*They* assumed that," Skidmark butted in.   "*I* said if you'd been mugged or raped you wouldn't be wandering around in the woods alone at night."

"How did you know about that?" I demanded. "Nobody ever..." My voice faded as Karma pointed to a large video screen displaying a map of the commune. It was peppered with small dots, evenly distributed in the area of the encampment.   A few dots moved slowly, scattered in the vicinity of the main building and latrines.

The dots looked a lot like the one on the tracker in my pocket.

"You've tagged everybody." I stared at the screen. Sure enough, five dots were clustered at the garage. Right where we stood. Goddammit, now I knew why my tracker had shown Orion at the garage all day but I couldn't find him.

"The bracelets." I barely squelched the urge to shout. "You've tagged the fucking Earth Spirit bracelets. 'The protection of the Earth Spirit', my ass!"

A phone vibrated in my pocket.

"I have to get this," I said. "I've missed my check-in."

"You can't tell them about any of this," Moonbeam said urgently. "You mustn't blow our covers. Please!"

I stared at her for a moment, my mind spinning. Then I punched the Talk button.

"I'm here. I'm fine. Sorry I missed the check-in," I said.

"What's happenin'?" Hellhound demanded.

"I've found Moonbeam and Karma..."

Moonbeam shook her head, giving me an imploring look.

"They're fine," I added. "And Orion is cooperating. I'm questioning him now."

A moment of silence hovered on the line before Hellhound spoke. "Ya want help with the cleanup when you're done?"

"No cleanup this time," I assured him. I threw out the first idea that occurred to me. "Orion didn't want to kidnap Moonbeam and Karma but the renters forced him. He led me right to where they were being held and I'm figuring out what to do next. I'll call you when I have the whole picture." I changed the subject. "What's new on your end? Have you had a chance to try disabling those charges on the bridge?"

A sudden movement made me look up. Everyone wore expressions of chagrin. Moonbeam shook her head violently and Karma drew a vigorous finger across his throat.

Hellhound replied, "Nah, but now that I know you're okay I'll go check-"

"Uh, hold off on that for now," I interrupted. The almost-palpable relief in the room indicated I'd said the right thing. "I, um... I don't want you to get close to them until we know what the renters are up to. If they decide to blow them while you're down there..."

"They can't blow 'em if I disable 'em," Hellhound argued.

"I know, but I don't want to take a chance while those trucks are over there," I countered with no logic whatsoever. When he began to demur, I spoke over him. "Sorry, Arnie, it's..."

I nearly blurted out 'Stemp's orders', which would not only have been a lie but also would have outed Stemp to his parents if they didn't actually know what he did.

"...just a gut feeling," I finished instead. "Let me finish questioning Orion first."

"Okay, darlin'. I'll tell Kane. Check in again in ten minutes."

"Okay."

I hung up and glowered around the room. "Spill it. All of it."

Everyone began to speak, but Karma's deep bass won out. "The three of us..." He gestured to himself, Moonbeam, and Skidmark. "...began this commune in 1968, looking for..." He glanced at Moonbeam, and I got the distinct impression he was editing the story already. "...a peaceful retreat," he finished.

I did the math. That was the year Stemp had been born.

"We were joined by several like-minded people, and the commune has grown modestly in the decades since then," he continued. "The three of us had..." he hesitated again, choosing his words carefully. "...played various covert roles for the allies in Vietnam around the time the conflict with the United States was escalating. But even though we retired to civilian life and sought peace and solitude, we couldn't turn our backs on our obligation to our countries."

"They're Canadian; I'm American," Skidmark interjected.

"The rented land has served various groups over the past decades," Karma continued as though Skidmark hadn't spoken. "Due to its isolated nature it has been attractive to militia groups and occasionally to home-grown terrorists.

When we discovered the first terrorist training camp decades ago, we reported it through our old intelligence contacts. We were instructed to continue our surveillance role."

Well, shit. That explained why Skidmark wasn't getting a veteran's pension. He wasn't retired.

Karma was still speaking. "So far we have foiled three separate terrorist groups over the years. The current renters are the fourth."

"They're terrorists?" Adrenaline surged into my veins. "Shit!"

"Yes, and I need to be back over there in twenty minutes," Orion said. "This is big, Aydan. They're part of a group of terrorist cells who have been organizing across Canada, and they're planning a synchronized strike on all the provincial legislative buildings. Mesker, their leader, described the plan but he never disclosed a date, so we didn't know until an hour ago that they planned to strike tomorrow at ten AM Pacific."

Skidmark added, "But we guessed it'd be pretty soon when their arms shipment came in a couple of days ago."

"They're planning to take over the parliament buildings with replica guns and bayonets?" I asked.

"No." Orion frowned. "They have operational M4 carbines. They smuggled them in from the States across the Strait of Juan de Fuca a couple of days ago. The replicas were just for drills until they got the real weapons. They did their live-fire exercise last night during the fireworks."

My heart lurched into my throat to vibrate there. Thirty wacko terrorists with assault rifles and bayonets. Jesus Christ.

Orion turned to Moonbeam and Karma. "I'll tell them you're dead and there's nothing to hinder them pulling out tonight."

"Good," Moonbeam agreed. "JTF2 reports that their roadblock is in place and surrounded by ground troops. All you have to do is get the terrorists clear of the commune."

Orion turned to me with a slightly condescending smile. "I presume you're familiar with JTF2? The Special Forces counter-terrorism troops?"

"Yeah." I held my face expressionless. "I've worked with them a few times."

"Oh." He had the grace to look slightly sheepish. "Sorry." His expression faded into concern. "One more thing," he said. "All the terrorists are dangerous since they view the commune members as depraved sinners worthy of death, but Ratboy has a real vendetta against you. He's been bragging about how he'll make you pay, and I think he was on his way to look for you. You should probably stay here in the control room until we're clear of the commune."

"That little prick," I muttered. "I'd like to see him try."

Skidmark wheezed laughter. "Girlie, I'd pay good money to watch you take him apart. But you're gonna have to let this one go." He winked. "You wouldn't want to blow your cover."

"Yeah," I grumbled.

"I'm running out of time," Orion interrupted. "But before I leave, I need to know: How did you knock me out?"

I eyed him. If he didn't know, it meant he wasn't familiar with our classified weapons. Probably not up to me to enlighten him.

"Vulcan neck pinch," I said.

"Oh, very funny." His brow furrowed. "So, a new classified weapon, then. I don't suppose you'd fancy lending it to me for the evening?"

"Sorry, I can't."

"Pity." He shrugged off his dismembered shirt with a resigned arch of his eyebrow before pulling his jacket on again over his T-shirt. He gave me a pointed look. "Perhaps you could inform your team I'll be returning to the renters' side. This mission has been jeopardized enough. And I'd like my gear back, please."

"Hang on..." I rummaged through my backpack handing him bits and pieces. My stomach roiled at the thought of how bad this could have been. Hell, might still be. I passed over the last knife and added, "I'll call them right away. And I'm really sorry."

Orion finished stowing the last of his equipment and his smile came back, transforming him from a grim-faced agent to the carefree hippie I'd thought he was. "It's all right. I likely would have done the same under the circumstances." He eased his weight cautiously from one leg to the other. "I'll have some interesting bruises tomorrow, if I live the night."

Skidmark snickered, and Orion shot him a narrow-eyed look before returning his attention to me. "Just so you know, I would have made a better show of resisting if I hadn't been so pressed for time tonight." His mouth hardened. "And if I hadn't believed you were law enforcement, you wouldn't be standing here."

"Big words," Skidmark needled. "She had you, Rand. You weren't going to get out of it."

Orion shrugged. "Maybe, maybe not. But even if I couldn't, it wouldn't have mattered." His expression was grim again, his beautiful eyes hard as emeralds. "I wouldn't have broken. No matter what you did."

I swallowed. "I don't doubt that. I'm really glad it worked out this way."

"Me, too." Orion's face softened into a smile and he gave us a jaunty salute. "Well, I'm off. Cheers, all. See you on the other side."

As he vanished out the door I pulled out both my phones and pressed the speed dials. Hellhound and Kane answered simultaneously, and I rattled off, "The renters are terrorists, and they're planning a strike on the parliament buildings in Victoria tomorrow morning at ten AM. They're fully armed with real M4 carbines and live ammo. Orion is going back to the renters' side as a mole. Don't interfere with him, and don't engage the renters. We just want them clear of the commune. JTF2 has a roadblock set up to stop them down the road."

Their exclamations assaulted my ears in stereo, and I tried to reassure them without giving away any secrets. "We can trust Orion not to sell us out." I drew a deep breath and spoke over their continuing objections. "Yes, I'm sure... Look, my op; my orders. I can't tell you more now; I have to get back to Moonbeam and Karma. I'll call you as soon as I have them settled."

I clicked off both the phones and turned back to my deceptively-smiling hippies. "Why are we leaving the explosives on the bridge?"

"Those are mine, dear," Moonbeam said with a hint of pride. "Any time we feel one of the groups might be a threat I rig the bridge so we can contain them in an emergency if necessary."

I eyed the flowing rainbow-coloured caftan that disguised a ruthless professional agent. "So the Earth Spirit is bullshit," I said.

"Oh, my dear." Moonbeam gave me a sorrowing look. "The Earth Spirit is as real as-"

"It's bullshit," Skidmark interrupted. "The only reason we feed it to the members is so we can run the evacuation drills. Every man, woman, and child is conditioned to go to the muster point and follow their leaders immediately and without question as soon as the bells ring. If we have to get them out fast, there's room for four cargo choppers to land in the field, one for each group."

I stared at him, my jaw slowly dropping. "That's... fucking brilliant. And the fireworks simulate live fire so nobody will be alarmed if they hear it. And the lights and sound generators in the field simulate the helicopters..." The penny dropped. "So you only set off fireworks when you think there's an imminent threat of gunfire from the renters. And the lower walls of the main building are bulletproof. As long as everybody's lying down meditating, they're safe."

Three smug smiles greeted my deduction.

"So Aurora and Zen and the other leaders..." I began, still struggling to catch up.

"Just as brainwashed as the rest of 'em," Skidmark said, earning a reproving look from Moonbeam. "They think the Spirit talks to them through a series of tones the crystal makes. Each tone corresponds to an evacuation route. That way we can guide them via the safest route from the control centre here."

"Shit." I tottered over to a chair and sat down after all. "So why can't I tell John and Arnie about this? They have really high security clearances."

"You mustn't!" Moonbeam shot a look of alarm at Karma before returning her wide-eyed gaze to me. "Our cover is too deep. The only reason we revealed ourselves to you at all was to save Orion Moonjava."

Skidmark tilted his chair back, grinning. "If it was only

Rand's balls on the line we wouldn't have bothered, but we needed him to be able to walk for the op tonight."

"Skidmark!" Moonbeam frowned at him before turning back to me. "Of course we wouldn't have let you harm him. But if we hadn't been reasonably certain you were a covert agent yourself, we would have found another way to stop you."

"But if you're working with Five Eyes, John and Arnie could find out about you anyway," I argued. "They've got the clearances, so why-"

"We're not," Skidmark interrupted.

"What do you mean, you're not?"

"Five Eyes doesn't know we exist," Karma explained. "Nobody does, except one person in one small department of the B.C. government. We get cast-off equipment from other intelligence operations so there's no paper trail of resources to us. If we report a possible threat it gets filtered through that one person and leaked 'accidentally'..." He made air quotes around the word. "...so the Five Eyes analysts think they've found it themselves."

"But Orion is Five Eyes, and he obviously knows about you."

Karma smiled. "When Five Eyes 'discovered'..." More air quotes. "...the threat six months ago, they assigned Rand to go undercover in the terrorist group. We knew about him but he didn't know about us. But after you arrived, we couldn't protect you the way we protect our members because you wouldn't follow the drills. We knew things were heating up over there so we revealed our operation to Rand and swore him to secrecy. He convinced the terrorist leader that they should have someone planted here to watch our members, and Mesker agreed to let him pretend to join our commune. That's when we set up his tent next to yours."

I thought about that for a minute. Okay, so that explained why Stemp hadn't told me anything about his parents' secret life. He didn't know. But he probably knew about the Five Eyes operation right next door. So he'd manipulated me to come out and protect his parents while it was going on. No wonder he kept delaying my departure, the sneaky bastard.

And his parents wouldn't have any way to know he was directing clandestine operations in Alberta if they didn't have any official contact with the intelligence community.

God, what a tangled mess.

"Bringing me here was a hell of a risk," I said. "What if I'd just been a nutcase with a gun? What if I'd tried to kill you and Orion instead?"

"You'd be dead," Skidmark said with chilling affability. "And we'd report to the police how you'd been tragically killed by a cougar. Poor silly little girlie, always going off in the woods by herself even though she'd been warned about the big mean cougar. That's why we circulated the rumour about the cougar, so the members would back us up if we had to kill you. But we were pretty sure you were law enforcement. I had you pegged after that first run-in with Ratboy. And we figured guys like Kane and Helmand wouldn't be friendly with you unless-"

My phone vibrated, and I picked up to hear Kane's worried voice. "Aydan, is Nichele with you?"

My heart contracted to a small cold lump in my chest. My voice came out equally small. "No."

"She's gone."

CHAPTER 34

"She's gone?" I echoed stupidly. "She can't be. Nichele would never go wandering around outside in the dark. Did you check the kitchen and the latrines?"

"Yes." Kane sounded as worried as I felt. "She's not in her bed beside the stove or in her tent. Hellhound is stationed at a vantage point overlooking the main building, and he's been there for at least half an hour. He didn't see her leave, so she must have been gone before that."

"Shit, we've got to-"

Moonbeam pressed a button on the console and the din of the Spirit bells poured into my ear from Kane's end of the connection.

He swore, but my heart leaped with hope. "John, this is good! If she hears the Spirit bells she'll come running. She's been tight with Aurora since she got here."

"I hope you're right," he said. "But I hate the thought of all these civilians milling around while the terrorists are on the move. I'm at the main building now. I'll wait for you here and call you as soon as I see Nichele."

"I'm on my way. Tell Hellhound to stay where he is, okay? He'll be able to give us a birds-eye view."

I barely waited to hear his acknowledgement before

hanging up and hurrying to the console to study the commune map. The dots in the encampment churned like a stirred-up anthill, already beginning to stream toward the main building.

"Which one's Nichele?" I demanded.

"Here, dear." Moonbeam pointed at a dot halfway between the bridge and the main building.

It wasn't moving.

"Something's wrong." I jammed my night vision headset on and wheeled to run for the door.

"Stop!" Karma's deep voice halted me, and I turned to see him and Moonbeam pulling night-vision goggles from a locker as well. "We understand your concern for your friend, but our responsibility is to all our members, Nichele included. This Calling is part of our original plan with Rand. We want all our members behind bulletproof walls until the terrorists are clear of the commune. Moonbeam and I will be holding positions between the main building and the bridge in case they pose a threat to our members as they leave. You and your team can help if needed."

A flash of memory recalled Orion's affronted voice: '*Moonbeam and Karma perform very important rituals when the Earth Spirit calls. Sometimes those rituals can be extremely uncomfortable.*'

Yeah. Or life-threatening.

Despite the band of fear tightening around my throat, I forced myself to wait in silence while they collected an earpiece each. Skidmark turned to me, holding out a third.

"Here," he said gruffly. "Use mine." As I secured it in my ear he gave us a look that could only be envy. "Damn emphysema. There was a time when I could take out a little weasel like Ratboy with one hand tied behind my back."

To my surprise, Moonbeam stooped and dropped a kiss on what I assumed were his lips behind the tangle of facial hair. "You still could, dear," she said gently.

He wheezed his usual laughter, but his eyes were soft as he touched Moonbeam's cheek with his callused fingertips. "If the fight only lasted fifteen seconds and I had oxygen after."

"It wouldn't be the first time you took a man down in less than fifteen seconds," Karma said. "But we need you here."

Skidmark tilted his head in resigned acquiescence and turned back to the console to press buttons. "Radio check."

His voice sounded clearly in my ear and I said, "Mine's fine."

Moonbeam and Karma added their confirmations, and Skidmark nodded, his gaze already locked on the tactical displays. "Good and readable. Go."

Just before I ran for the door, I glanced again at the commune map. Almost all the dots were moving toward the main building.

Nichele's was terrifyingly still.

As we jogged down the hill, Karma asked, "Where are Helmand and Kane?"

"John is at the main building," I panted. "I don't know exactly where Arnie is, but he's in position with a full view of the main building."

"In position," Moonbeam repeated. "Does that mean he has his rifle set up?"

She wasn't breathing any harder than I was. I hoped I'd be in as good shape when I was her age.

If I lived long enough to be her age.

"I assume so," I replied.

"Tell your team to use firearms only as a last resort,"

Karma said. "We don't want to alert the terrorists that we're armed. We'll go directly to Nichele's last known position. Moonbeam and I will stay out of visual range. Get Nichele into the main building and join the meditation. Leave Helmand in place. If you and Kane can leave the meditation without arousing suspicion, do. We can use the support."

He delivered the entire speech in short sentences with deep breaths in between, but he didn't sound winded. Now I knew why the gym was the most up-to-date part of the commune.

I fumbled the phones out of my pocket and hit the speed dials. Hellhound and Kane picked up simultaneously, and I panted, "Is Nichele there yet?"

"No," Kane replied.

"Shit, shit!" I bit off the waste of breath. "I'm still a few minutes away. It took me a while to get away from Moonbeam and Karma. They're pretty shaken up."

Jogging beside me, they both grinned, looking thoroughly invigorated.

"Don't fire any shots unless you have to," I added. "We don't want to tip off the terrorists."

"Acknowledged. Almost all the members are here," Kane said. "Should I start searching for Nichele?"

"Yes..." I hesitated, wondering where to direct him. If I sent him in the direction of Nichele's dot, he might run into Moonbeam and Karma.

"I'll begin a search grid at the main building," Kane said. "When you get here we can divide up the area."

"Okay, thanks," I agreed with relief, and hung up.

We were nearing the main building when Skidmark's voice spoke in my ear. "Nichele's on the move. Heading for the main building."

"Oh thank God!" Relief turned my knees to water and I stumbled to a halt.

Moonbeam and Karma stopped on either side of me and we hunched over panting.

Moonbeam straightened first. "Well, Storm Cloud Dancer, we'll leave you to go on to the building. Karma Wolf Song and I have a commune to protect."

I eyed her curiously, realizing for the first time that I hadn't seen them arm themselves. "How exactly are you going to do that?" I asked.

"Oh, we both carry pistols at all times," Moonbeam replied cheerfully. "Loose garments are convenient. You wouldn't believe what Karma Wolf Song has under his sarong."

A devilish grin spread over his face and I protested, "Too much information!" and hurriedly changed the subject. "But I thought you said you didn't want gunfire."

"We're both experts in hand-to-hand combat," Moonbeam assured me with a smile. "Well, Karma Wolf Song is. I used to be. The arthritis in my hands bothers me quite a bit now, so the garrotte is my weapon of choice these days." She produced a lethal-looking length of wire with wooden handles from another recess of her caftan.

"Okay, now you're scaring me," I said with considerably more truth than I cared to admit.

"Go to your friend," she said kindly. "We'll start the fireworks as soon as the terrorists begin to move."

"Okay, good luck." I hugged them both and ran for the main building.

Nobody was there when I panted up, and I punched my speed dials. "John? Arnie? Any sign of Nichele?"

Two negative replies accelerated my already-pounding

heart.

In my ear, Skidmark said, "She's still moving toward the building, but slowly. Couple hundred yards out."

My earlier relief evaporated without a trace. "Oh, God, maybe she's hurt," I blurted, before remembering Kane and Hellhound didn't know I had inside information.

Fortunately it wasn't too much of a non sequitur and Kane replied, "Stay positive, Aydan. I'm searching a grid to the southeast, so why don't you take the northeast? Hellhound, do you have eyes on us from up there?"

"Got a visual on Aydan near the buildin'. Lost ya in the trees, but I still got your thermal... hang on! Just picked up a thermal north-northeast of Aydan."

At the same time Skidmark corroborated, "Go north-northeast from your position, you should run right into her."

Sucking in a breath that caught in my throat, I hurried forward.

"Take off your night vision so ya don't blow your cover, darlin'," Hellhound reminded me. "I'll tell ya which way to go."

I gulped and juggled the phones while I pulled off my headset and stuffed it in my pocket before placing a phone to each ear again. "Thanks. I completely forgot."

"That thermal's straight ahead," he reassured me. "Headin' right for ya... shit!"

Without my night vision I didn't immediately see what had caused his consternation.

Then Ratboy stepped out of the forest into the moonlight with Nichele's limp body slung over his shoulders.

My chest constricted on a sob of terror. Only a tiny whimper choked from my lips.

He let Nichele slither down, holding her against him

with an arm under her armpit and across her breasts. Her head lolled against his chest, her arms dangling, but her feet moved feebly as though she was trying to stand.

His vicious grin glinted in the moonlight, almost as brightly as the bayonet he held against her throat.

"I found your little whore friend," he sneered. His fingers dug savagely into Nichele's breast and she twitched and whimpered. "What is her life worth to you?"

"Anything you want." My voice came out high and tremulous. "Tell me what you want and I'll do it. Anything. Just don't hurt her."

"What's happening? Storm, report!" I barely heard Skidmark's demand, every cell of my being focused on Ratboy.

"Target acquired." If I hadn't known it was Hellhound speaking I wouldn't have recognized his voice in the flat distant tone of a killing machine.

"Hold your fire!" Kane's command issued from the other phone. "Wait and see if we can take him without alerting the others."

"Hang up the phones and drop them, whore," Ratboy said.

I clicked them off and let them fall.

"Storm, report!"

Just shut up, Skidmark.

"Tell me what you want," I begged Ratboy. "I'll do anything."

A sudden touch on my pant leg made me yelp and snap a glance downward. Peaches chirruped her little song of purrs as she wound around my ankles, and I nudged her gently back toward the building with one foot, my heart hammering.

She tried again, clearly annoyed by my lack of response. Then she abandoned me and waddled toward Ratboy and Nichele.

"Peaches, no!" I hissed. "Here, kitty, kitty! Come on, Peaches!"

Tail in the air, she stalked away from me without a backward glance. Sick horror seized me at the sight of Ratboy's expression.

"Here, kitty, kitty," he mimicked in a squeaky voice. He bared his teeth at me. "The kitty likes me." The bayonet stroked Nichele's throat, obscenely shiny against her skin. "The kitty likes me better than your little whore friend likes me. But which one do you like better? The kitty?" His voice hardened. "Or the pussy?" He jerked Nichele higher against him.

Her head was on his shoulder now. Hellhound wouldn't have a clear shot.

My entire body felt encased in ice, my lungs unable to expand despite the fierce battering of my heart against my ribcage.

"Just tell me what you want," I whispered.

"Here, kitty, kitty."

"*WHAT DO YOU WANT?*" The shriek tore my throat and I dimly heard Skidmark swear.

Ratboy smiled, his teeth silver in the moonlight, his eyes black empty holes. "I want you to pay. And here's what will happen to your little whore friend if you don't do exactly as I say."

He released Nichele to swoop down and seize Peaches by the tail, his bayonet flashing toward her.

Peaches twisted in his grip, screaming agony and defiance.

Ratboy's head exploded.

CHAPTER 35

An instant later the echoing whipcrack of Hellhound's rifle split the night, the sound arriving after the bullet had done its work. Peaches hit the ground on all fours and fled like a streak of furry lightning into the forest.

I dashed toward Nichele as Skidmark swore again in my ear, a short curse bitten off before he snapped, "Shots fired. Starting fireworks now."

The first explosion of the fireworks slammed more adrenaline into my veins even though I'd known it was coming.

"Storm, report!" Skidmark demanded.

"Ratboy kidnapped Nichele and Hellhound shot him," I gasped as I slid to my knees beside the two still forms. I wrenched Ratboy's body off Nichele, barely noticing the protests of my muscles in my haze of fear.

Nichele was drenched in blood.

My heart stopped.

My world stopped.

A high-pitched keening filled my ears.

My hands wouldn't work. Quivering bunches of useless fingers at the end of wooden arms.

I pawed helplessly at the blood.

Make it stop.

Oh God, make it stop.

Then Kane was there. Making a rapid examination before he laid her gently on the grass and turned to take my face between his palms.

I tried to push him aside. How could he leave her?

He gripped my wrists. Wouldn't let me go to her.

My best friend since childhood. The sister I'd never had.

I jerked and struggled in his grasp.

"Aydan, stop! It's not her blood! She's fine!" Kane's words finally penetrated.

My shrill keening faded to silence, my throat feeling like it was lined with broken glass. Unable to speak, afraid to believe, I stared at him.

"Come and see." His baritone was warm and soft, a blanket of comfort wrapping around me. Gentle hands on my shoulders guided me over. "See?" Kane used his sleeve to wipe the blood from her face. "She's not hurt. It's not her blood, Aydan. She's all right. Just drugged or something."

I slowly became aware of my surroundings again. Fireworks exploding in the night.

I should be feeling fireworks of joy.

Nothing.

"Aydan. Come on, Aydan." Kane patted my cheeks, smart little slaps that jarred me back to myself.

I sucked in a breath and collapsed in his arms. "Oh thank God! Thank God!" I trembled in his embrace for a long moment, hugging him fiercely before I pulled away.

"Okay," I said. I sucked in another breath and let it out slowly, forcing my mind and muscles back under control. "Okay. We need to get her inside and cleaned up. If she's drugged, she might not remember this."

Kane nodded and scooped Nichele up as though she was weightless. "Get your phones," he said as we hurried toward the building, and I detoured to where I'd dropped them.

One was vibrating. I fumbled it into my shaking hands and punched the talk button.

"Everythin' okay?" Hellhound's anxious rasp was nothing like the cold implacable voice that had dealt death only moments before. "Is Nichele okay?"

"I think so." I pocketed the other phone and forced my quivering legs into a jog toward the main building. "She was covered in Ratboy's blood and I panicked, but John thinks she's just drugged. Nice shot, by the way."

He didn't acknowledge the compliment. "How about Peaches? Did that asshole..." His question faded and the sound of his swallow came clearly over the line before he tried again, "Is she...?"

"She's okay, Arnie. She took off like a bat out of hell."

I ducked into the building, glimpsing Kane's back as he disappeared into the kitchen. By the time I arrived he had already laid Nichele on a blanket and was heading for the nearest boiler with a bucket.

"Are ya sure?" Hellhound demanded. "Cats crawl away an' hide when they're hurt bad. When I found Hooker he was hidin' in a garbage can, just about dead."

I dropped to my knees beside Nichele as Kane returned with the bucket and a couple of cloths. He handed me one and I tucked the phone between my chin and shoulder and went to work. Trying not to think about what I was wringing out of the cloth, I returned my attention to Hellhound.

"I really think Peaches is fine, Arnie. She sure as hell wasn't crawling. I think she broke the sound barrier heading for the forest."

Hellhound began to reply as Skidmark spoke in my other ear. "Terrorists are on the move. One truck is pulling out; the other's stopped just over the bridge. They're sending a party to check out that gunshot because Ratboy is missing."

"Shit!"

Kane's head jerked up. "What?"

Cover blown. I had to tell Kane and Hellhound about the incoming terrorists. And I'd have to reveal how I knew.

I stared at Kane, my mind rocketing through possibilities even while I spoke. "The terrorists are sending a party this way. They're investigating the gunshot."

Skidmark spoke again. "Eight hostiles incoming. Eight more with the truck by the bridge. The other truck is bugging out. Clearing the gate now."

"Shit! At least eight coming, maybe up to sixteen," I snapped, then shut up as Skidmark spoke again.

"Relay from Moonbeam; hostiles are not to reach the main building. Take no prisoners. I say again; intercept hostiles and kill them all."

"Roger that," I said faintly.

Kane and Hellhound spoke at the same time, their aggregated questions translating approximately to 'Aydan, what the hell?'

"Sorry," I said, sorting and editing facts as I spoke. "Orion is an MI6 agent. Five Eyes posted him here to infiltrate the terrorist training camp." I couldn't quite bring myself to lie to them outright, so I added, "I have radio contact. Our orders are to eliminate the terrorists before they reach the main building. No prisoners. But Orion's out there, too, so we can't just shoot at any old thermal signature." And I couldn't warn them about Moonbeam and Karma out in the woods.

Hellhound sounded affronted. "I never shot anybody I couldn't identify before an' I ain't plannin' to start now."

"I'm sorry, I know, I'm just..." I trailed off at the sight of Kane's face. "What? What is it, John?"

"Children." He stared at me with haunted eyes. "There are *children* in the next room..."

He was already lunging to his feet.

"John!" I seized his wrist. "John, stop!"

He froze, his eyes burning with frightening intensity in brittle skull-like features. Tension vibrated in his arm, sizzling through my grip like an electrical current.

"John," I said, holding my voice calm and even. "We won't let anything happen to them. Okay? We won't."

He nodded once, a short sharp motion that looked as though it might shatter his neck.

I had to keep him away from the woods. Eyes glazed, body vibrating with the need to annihilate, he looked as though he would steamroll over every living thing without a thought for his own safety until a bullet ended his rampage permanently.

He might recognize Moonbeam and Karma and Orion.

Or he might not.

"John," I repeated. "Look at me."

He drew a deep breath and focused on my face. The terrifying blankness in his eyes dissipated, but the hollow horror remained.

I put all the authority I could muster into my voice. "You're going to guard the children. Hellhound and Orion and I will deal with the terrorists in the woods. You'll be the last defence in case we fail. The concrete walls are bulletproof so stay low. Your orders are to hold the meditation room. Clear?"

He gave another sharp nod, looking like himself again except for those eyes. "Understood. Stay in phone contact so I know what's happening. Go."

I went, heart hammering.

"Kane okay?" Hellhound asked worriedly as I reached the door.

"I think so. For now. But if we let any of those guys through it'll be a bloodbath."

"That ain't gonna happen," he rasped. "Tell Orion he can engage 'em in the woods if he wants. We'll take 'em out if they try to cross the open space. I got it all covered 'cept for part a' the west side. Can ya find a high place where ya can cover the west?"

"I can get on the roof." I hurried toward the playground climbing frame.

"Too exposed, darlin'," he objected. "Can't ya find a spot with more cover?"

"No time. I have to hang up now so I can update John, and I'll call you back when I'm in place." I punched the off button without waiting for his reply and rapped out an update to Skidmark. Then I stuffed the hands-free earbud in my ear and pressed Kane's speed dial with trembling fingers.

"Kane," he snapped.

I held my voice as steady as I could. "Arnie is covering the north, south, and east sides of the building. I'll cover the west from the roof. I'm going up now, so don't worry if you hear me moving around up there. I'll keep this connection open so you know what's happening."

I pulled on my night-vision headset again, manoeuvring it around Skidmark's earpiece on one side and the phone's earbud on the other. Then I drew a deep breath and clambered up the climbing frame.

Balanced on top, my entire body rocked with tremors. When I reached up to grab the branch my arms felt like limp noodles. The roof looked very far away.

So did the ground.

Fireworks were still exploding intermittently and my guts twisted at the sound of an echoing crack. Was that a rifle shot or a firecracker?

I'd be an easy target while I made my sloth-like way along the branch.

If I could even hold on that long.

Shut up.

I clenched my teeth to prevent my heart from escaping and swung my legs up.

I barely made it. My hands gave out just after I reached the roof and for a heart-stopping moment I slid toward the edge. Scrabbling and flailing, I managed to stop inches away.

I lay plastered to the roof for a couple of long moments, my too-rapid panting whistling in my throat. Then I mustered the last of the strength in my shaking legs to creep up the pitch of the roof.

I knew Hellhound would be watching me in his scope, and I didn't care. Abandoning dignity, I gained the roof peak and inch-wormed along it as fast as my trembling body would allow. The chimney loomed like a bastion of safety.

Skidmark's sudden voice in my ear nearly flung me off the roof with the force of my twitch. Hyperventilating, I sprawled belly-down across the peak.

"Missed that," I gasped. "Say again."

"I say again; four hostiles down, twelve incoming."

The whole damn truckload.

"Shit! Shit-shit-shit!" I bit off my swearing and

redoubled my efforts toward the chimney. "Do they have night-vision?" I panted.

"Negative. Flashlights only."

"Twelve hostiles incoming," I repeated for Kane's benefit. "But they only have flashlights, not night-vision."

Thank God.

Not that it would matter out here. The damn moon was like a spotlight. Hellhound was right; I'd be almost as visible if it was daylight.

As if summoned by my thought, his rifle spat its deadly report. My overloaded adrenal system surpassed terror in a single bound and I scrambled mindlessly into the shadow of the chimney. Arms flung wide, fingertips locked in its mortar joints, I pressed my cheek against the rough fieldstone.

Below, one dark figure lay crumpled and unmoving at the edge of the forest.

"One more hostile down," I croaked for Skidmark's and Kane's benefit.

Five down. Maybe more if Moonbeam and Karma and Orion were still picking them off in the forest.

My pocket vibrated.

It took a couple of tries to convince my fingers to loosen their hold on the chimney. I crouched in as stable a position as I could manage and withdrew the phone, clutching it in both shaking hands. If I dropped it...

Wishing I had a second hands-free earbud and a third ear, I managed to punch the button and whisper, "What?"

"That's a good spot, darlin'," Hellhound muttered. "Ya can back me up if they all come at once, but leave 'em to me otherwise. I got a suppressor so they won't see my muzzle flash."

Great, that was something else I'd forgotten. With my first shot, I might as well send up a flare announcing my presence.

Fabulous. Fan-fucking-tastic.

But hell, the way my hands were shaking, I'd probably fumble my gun and drop it over the edge of the roof before I could fire it anyway.

"Okay," I whispered.

I didn't bother to add that I'd be lucky to hit anything at all.

"I love ya, darlin'." The connection clicked off and a moment later his rifle cracked again. Another dark figure toppled out of the woods, and a fusillade of shots and muzzle flashes erupted from where it had come.

Paralyzed, I held my breath waiting for the sound of Hellhound's rifle again. Had they hit him?

My mind refused to accept the thought.

"Another hostile down," I whispered.

I had a job to do.

Do it.

Jamming my back against the chimney in the deepest part of its shadow, I drew my Glock. Its familiar grip comforted my palm, and I touched the spare magazine in the holster for reassurance. Twenty shots. Only ten possible targets. Hellhound would take most of them.

If he was still alive.

I banished the thought. Concentrate on the job.

Summoning every mental tactic I'd learned in target-shooting tournaments, I drew a deep breath and let it out slowly.

Visualize the calm flowing along my arms; steadying my hands...

The men in the woods had stopped shooting. Hellhound hadn't fired again, either. Nothing moved.

The fireworks had stopped. They must have run out. The silence sent a shiver down my spine.

The indifferent moon sailed high above, riding a bright ribbon of cloud. I stared wide-eyed at the west side of the forest, the trees unmoving in the moonlight as though cast in silver.

Still as death.

Another long breath. In. Out.

My hands still trembled finely, but as long as I didn't go for a long-range shot I'd be accurate enough to hit a body-sized target.

A man's scream tore the air, a raw animal-like shriek. Icy-hot talons of primal fear plunged into my guts and wrenched them tight.

The sound cut off mid-scream.

"Seven down," Skidmark said.

Heavy silence fell again.

They must have realized their losses by now. Surely they'd retreat to the truck and pull out. Their objective was bigger than a few hippies in the middle of the woods.

I recalled Orion's words with a shiver. '*They view the commune members as depraved sinners worthy of death.*'

The moon sliced the clouds like a bright blade.

More long minutes of silence.

Then a nightmare of gunfire exploded from the woods.

CHAPTER 36

The shots seemed to come from all directions. Adrenaline searing my veins, I snapped a look around. Muzzle flashes from all four sides. I couldn't see any shooters.

Bullets thumped into the walls of the building but they didn't seem to be aiming for me.

Laying down covering fire, maybe?

A moment later it stopped. Behind me Hellhound's rifle cracked once, then again. And again. They must be charging.

A man dashed out of the west woods toward the building, firing toward the door.

Years of trapshooting instinct took over my hands.

Lead the target.

Smooth pull.

My Glock spat fire and I steadied the recoil, looking for my next shot. The man was down and motionless but I put another round into him just to be safe.

Answering fire spewed from the woods. A bullet thudded into the roof beside me and the crack-whine of a ricochet off the chimney made me yelp and duck.

My foot slipped.

Flailing for balance, I fell hard on my hip, jolting out a cry. More bullets battered the roof.

The slope claimed me.

Tumbling helplessly...

Kane's voice shouted in my earpiece, his words lost in the hellish din of gunfire.

I flung out frantic arms and legs, halting my tumble but not the deadly slide.

More bullets struck the roof above me.

My mind served up one last pointless thought with slow-motion clarity: Lucky the gunman wasn't a trapshooter.

I slid over the edge.

A desperate grab as the building sailed by. My left hand clamped onto the rain gutter only to be wrenched loose by my momentum.

I crashed onto the pea gravel of the playground and the world exploded in noise and bright flashes.

My lungs wouldn't work.

Drowning in pain...

Kane dashed from the door, firing over and over into the woods.

A long moment later I managed to drag in a breath, my lungs wailing with effort.

My brain caught up. Not shot. Just the wind knocked out of me.

Kane clamped an iron hand on my collar and dragged me backward. The earsplitting reports of his pistol above me dulled to heavy impacts in my overtaxed hearing.

Another wailing breath.

Through the doorway.

A crack and whine as a bullet ricocheted from the concrete beside us. Behind us came a thump and clatter as the bullet spent itself in the stack of stove wood.

Then we were behind the protection of the concrete wall.

Kane crouched beside the doorway, gun at the ready, gaze riveted outside. The muscles of his arms stood out in hills and valleys of stone.

I drew an easier breath. Pain subsiding.

Another breath.

Kane lunged forward and snapped off two shots.

"Got him," he said as though discussing an annoying mosquito. "Aydan, talk to me!" His voice sounded muffled and distant in my ringing ears.

"Two more down," I croaked for Skidmark's benefit.

Kane spared me a glance from the doorway, his taut face easing. "Thank God," he muttered. Then he spoke again, and I saw the phone earbud in his ear for the first time. "She's conscious," he said. "I don't know how badly hurt yet."

"I'm okay." I rolled over slowly, wincing. Miraculously, my Glock was still clutched in my hand, my fingers aching in a death-grip. The phone's earbud trailed from my pocket, and I reached in to hang up on my redundant connection with Kane. "Thank God I landed in the pea gravel," I mumbled. "How many did Arnie get?"

"How many down?" Kane relayed the question before replying, "Three."

"Three more down," I told Skidmark.

"Moonbeam took another out, but he got a piece of her," he replied. "One hostile still at large, likely retreating to the truck. Rand is hit. Karma is working on him. If there are any bodies by the west door, clear them now. I'll take the members out through that route in about five minutes. Tell Kane and Helmand to hunt down that last hostile and then start collecting bodies and dumping them in the truck. You stay there. Moonbeam's incoming; needs first aid."

I hauled myself to my feet, discovering I'd twisted my ankle in my fall. I limped over to prop myself against the wall while I relayed the message to Kane, blurting, "Orion's hit..." before remembering I was purportedly getting radio instructions from Orion himself.   "...uh, but he's still conscious," I added, hoping that was the truth.   "He says there's only one guy still alive, probably heading for the truck. He needs you and Hellhound to get the last guy, and then start moving bodies to the truck. We'd better move the ones outside the door right away.   Who knows how much longer they'll meditate in there and we don't want..."

I trailed off, thinking better of mentioning the children, but fortunately Kane was already barking instructions to Hellhound. He finished speaking and turned to me. "You're hurt. Stay here. Guard the members. I'll drag these two bodies into the woods so they're out of sight until we can move them to the truck. Where's Orion? We'll check on him before we do anything else."

Skidmark must have either overheard or anticipated the conversation. He was already speaking in my ear. "Rand's hidden under the south end of the bridge. Shot in the leg, probably a broken bone. He can't walk. Karma's stabilizing him.   Tell Kane and Helmand to concentrate on the last hostile and the bodies."

"He's hiding under the south end of the bridge," I relayed, editing as I spoke. "He's shot in the leg but he says he's stable and he wants you to concentrate on getting that last guy and then cleaning up the bodies."

Kane nodded, kissed me once hard, and lunged out the door in a crouch.

I held my breath, but no gunfire greeted him. In a few moments he had dragged the bodies out of sight and kicked fresh gravel over the dark stains they'd left behind. Then he vanished into the forest without a backward glance.

I drew a deep breath, visualizing a shield of protection around him and Hellhound.

Let them be safe.

Please let them be safe.

"West door is clear," I muttered to Skidmark.

"Signalling them to come out now," he replied. "Cover their six."

I limped to the door and slipped outside, flinching with the expectation of muzzle flashes and bullets.

All was silent, and I hurried across the open space to hide in the undergrowth facing the door. My ankle protested mightily for the first few steps before settling down to a sullen throbbing, and I drew a breath of relief. Probably not too serious.

I had just ducked behind a tree when Aurora and Zen came out the door followed by the members, their expressions beatific. The children filed out in an orderly row, their little faces grave with the import of the Calling.

A slow shudder worked its way from my head to my toes. Somewhere in these dark woods, a killer still lurked. A single shot, and a precious life could be extinguished.

And with an assault rifle...

My stomach clenched. So far I'd only seen them fire three-shot bursts. But what if they could go fully automatic? One deranged man could mow down an entire column of innocent people.

The last of the members filed silently into the woods, and I whispered, "They're in the woods now. Should I follow them and cover?"

"Negative." For the first time Skidmark's voice held worry. "Moonbeam is incoming. She won't say how bad it is, but she's moving slow. Take care of her, Storm." I heard him swallow, and suddenly he sounded like a frightened old man. "Take care of my lady."

The knots in my stomach tightened. "Tell me which way to go. I'll meet her."

His voice steadied. "Northwest, a couple hundred yards. I'll tell her you're coming so she doesn't try to take you out."

"Thanks," I muttered, and half-hopped, half-jogged northwest as fast as my ankle would permit.

I spotted the pale oval of her face first. Hugging her left arm, she picked her way unsteadily through the undergrowth. The flowing caftan was gone, revealing a slim figure clad all in black with a holster at her shoulder and a large knife strapped to her thigh. A moment later I realized the caftan had been sacrificed to wrap her injured arm. A slow dark trickle ran from her fingertips.

Already pinched with pain, her brow furrowed more at the sight of my unsteady gait. "She's injured," she snapped, presumably to Skidmark. "You said she was all right."

"I fell off the roof, but I'm okay except for my ankle," I explained, and offered her a hand.

She shook her head and tottered forward. "No, dear, I'm fine. Don't overtax that ankle."

"Let me see your arm."

"When we're inside, dear," Moonbeam insisted. "Keep moving."

I blew out a breath of frustration and limped beside her.

By the time we reached the building her face was paper-white, sweat glistening at her temples. I made for the west door but she stopped me with an outstretched hand.

"No; the north patio, directly into the kitchen," she commanded. "I don't want to bleed across the main hall."

"For shit's sake..." I began, but she was already navigating around the side of the building, swaying precariously and steadying herself against the wall.

I hurried after her. As we rounded the corner, my throat closed at the sight of a black empty space where one of the windows should have reflected silver moonlight like its neighbours.

Oh God, had the last terrorist broken in?

Nichele was in there.

I drew my Glock and ran, ignoring the pain in my ankle.

Ducking below the level of the windows, I scuttled to the door. Still crouched, I wrenched it open and snapped a glance around the room, my gun sights tracking across the woodstoves. Nichele still lay in the corner on her blanket, the abandoned bucket and cloths beside her. Nothing moved.

I switched to thermal, but saw only the angry glows of the woodstoves.

I nearly jumped out of my skin when Moonbeam spoke softly behind me. "Go. I'll cover you."

When I looked up, her pistol was rock-steady in her right hand. Her left dangled at her side. The dark trickle was faster.

Beyond fear, I switched back to night vision and hurried across the room. My lips and hands and feet felt icy; numb and tingling at the same time. Massive adrenaline overdose. Soon the uncontrollable tremors would start and then I'd be useless.

And if I had to fight the terrorist in that condition,

shortly afterward I'd be dead.

As if on autopilot, I ducked into the main hall, gun at the ready.   Scan and sidle to the next door.   The empty meditation room. Scan.

Then the storage room.

Moonbeam sagged in the doorway of the kitchen. Her gaze still followed me, but her gun dangled by her side as if the weight of the weapon was too much to support.

When I cleared the last room and turned back to nod at her, she slid slowly down the doorjamb to slump on the floor. A broad streak of crimson smeared the white wood, marking her path.

Heart clenching, I hop-jogged into the kitchen to snatch one of Nichele's blankets before hurrying back to wrap it around Moonbeam. She let out a half-sigh, half-moan, and I eased her down to lie flat. Grabbing the corners of the blanket, I towed her across the floor to the stove next to Nichele, avoiding the scattered shards of glass.

With a short but fervent prayer that the remaining terrorist was nowhere in the vicinity, I lit one of the propane lanterns. Even in its warm light Moonbeam's face was stark white. Her eyelids drooped half-closed, but her gaze still followed me while I dragged a chair over and elevated her feet.

When I unwrapped the caftan from her arm at last, my stomach twisted at the sight of a slice from wrist to elbow. Blood still welled from the wound, and I rapidly cut and folded the caftan into bandages and bound the pads of fabric tightly.

Her pulse was rapid but strong, and I drew a breath that might have been relief if I hadn't been so terrified.

"Aydan here," I said to Skidmark. "Moonbeam has a bad

cut on her left arm. It doesn't look as though any arteries have been cut but she'll need stitches and she looks like she's going into shock." As I spoke I dumped some wood into the stove and put the kettle on. "She's conscious so I'll get some hot chocolate into her but she'll need to go to the hospital as soon as possible."

Moonbeam plucked at my pant leg and shook her head feebly, but I gave her a stern look and she subsided.

"We can't get past that military roadblock," Skidmark said. "They're still shooting out there. Karma's a doctor. I'll tell him to get over there as soon as he's got Rand stable. Any word from Kane or Helmand on that last hostile?"

"Not yet." I swallowed a lump of fear. Apparently I had some emotion left after all.

Tremors were slowly taking over my body, beginning in my guts and rolling through my arms and legs. Moonbeam wasn't the only one who needed hot chocolate.

The mugs rattled like maracas in my hand while I dug out the spoons and powdered hot chocolate. Then I sat on the floor beside Moonbeam, shivering in the heat of the stove.

"Turn off the lantern," she whispered. "We're sitting ducks."

Dragging myself to my feet again, I turned off the lantern and put on my night-vision headset. I didn't dare sit down in case I couldn't get up again. Instead, I hovered over the stove until the water was hot enough.

Mug in hand, I knelt beside Moonbeam. "I'm going to lift you up enough so you can sip," I whispered. "Tell me if you feel faint."

"I'm fine." She struggled up on one elbow. "Sit back to back with me. That will prop us both up and help keep us warm."

I set the mugs on the floor and obeyed, hugging my knees to keep from overpowering her slight weight against my back. We sipped in silence for a while and my tremors began to abate, but they seemed to be transferring themselves to Moonbeam.

I drained the last sugary dregs from my cup and twisted to eye her over my shoulder. Her hand lay lax across her lap and when my body shifted she slid sideways as though unable to catch herself.

CHAPTER 37

"Shit!" I caught Moonbeam's shoulders and lowered her to the floor.

"I'm... fine..." she whispered, her eyes closed.

"Skidmark, where's Karma?" I demanded.

"He'll be there soon."

"Talk to me, Moonbeam," I urged.

"Moonbeam... Meadow... Sky. Please." Her lips turned up at the corners, her eyes still closed. "Vibrations, dear."

"Sorry. Moonbeam Meadow Sky," I corrected myself. "Keep talking. Tell me how the vibrations work."

"Just basic... numerology," she murmured. "Not proper... calculations. I only... dabble... with names..." Her voice faded.

"Moonbeam!" I patted her cheek, my heart thumping painfully. "Keep talking. Tell me about auras. Do you really see them or is that just part of your hippie schtick?"

Her eyes snapped open. "Yes, dear, of course I see them. I have since I was a child..." Her eyelids drifted down again. "Cosmic River Stone... always could, too."

I gulped and made a mental note never to lie to Stemp again. Just in case.

"He was... such a lovely child," she went on. "My dearest

boy... I always wanted... lots of children..."

She trailed off into silence again.

"Why didn't you and Karma have more children?" I prompted.

"Oh, he might not be Karma's, dear." She smiled without opening her eyes. "He might be Skidmark's. We were never sure."

"Uh..." I didn't quite know how to respond to that.

Fortunately she went on, her voice a dreamy singsong. "It was the 1960s. Free love... We were young... Thrown together in the jungle..."

When she didn't go on, I murmured, "Tell me about Vietnam, Moonbeam. You need to keep talking."

"Ah. Yes..." She peered heavy-lidded at me for a moment before her eyes slipped closed again. "No contraception, of course. I got pregnant..."

She fell silent and I was about to prompt her again when she continued, "I was eight months along... when I was shot."

Her voice wavered with emotion. "Emergency caesarian... in a filthy hut in the jungle... I got an infection, of course... nearly died..." A tear eased from the corner of her closed lids and trickled slowly into the hair at her temples. "Scarring... No more babies... for me." Her voice choked off.

My heart squeezed. "I'm so sorry," I whispered around the giant lump in my throat. I took her good hand and stroked it. "I'm sorry to make you relive it."

"It's all right, dear... It was... long ago..." Her breath eased out on a sigh and she went limp.

"Moonbeam!" I lurched to my knees, fresh adrenaline scorching my veins. "Moonbeam, wake up!" I patted the waxen cheeks desperately.

"Yes, dear?" she whispered.

"Oh thank God." I slumped back down on the floor. "You scared me. I thought you'd passed out."

"Still... here. Please... Moonbeam..."

"...Meadow Sky," I finished. "I'm sorry, I'll try to remember. How did you get out of Vietnam?"

"Airlifted." A smile tugged her lips, but her eyes didn't open. "When we got home... Skidmark didn't want a child... at the time... but Karma Wolf Song did... very much. We agreed... to register as Cosmic River Stone's parents. It was easier... with the citizenship... anyway."

Her smile widened. "We didn't know then... that Skidmark would... live his life here... after all." Her chest rose and fell in a deep sigh, her smile softening at the corners. "My dearest men..." Her hand went limp in mine. "If only..." Her voice faded so I had to lean close to hear. "...we could have... had... grandchildren..." The last word ghosted out on a faint breath and her face relaxed.

"Moonbeam! Come on, Moonbeam!" I patted frantically, but she didn't speak again.

Heart hammering, I fumbled for her pulse. It was still there, stronger than I had expected, but not so rapid now.

"Skidmark, where the hell is Karma?" I snapped. "We need him here *now!*"

"What's happening?" he demanded.

"Moonbeam's passed out."

"He's still with Orion. Helmand and Kane haven't shown up yet. I thought you said she was okay!" His voice rose in fearful accusation.

"Just send Karma," I begged.

Crouched in the dark silent room between the two unconscious women, I stroked Moonbeam's hair and patted her hands and face, feeling utterly useless.

I should have made her drink more hot chocolate. Too late now.

Oh God, if she died it would break Stemp's heart. And Karma's and Skidmark's.

And mine.

I rocked miserably beside her, fighting tears. Too soon for such a sweet woman to die. She was so full of life and love. She hadn't gotten to meet her little granddaughter.

Her hand was cold and motionless in mine.

No more blankets available.

I lay down and pulled her close, wrapping my jacket over her to share my body heat.

"Oh, Moonbeam," I whispered into her hair. "Don't go yet. Anna needs you. She wants to meet her grandma, I know she does."

The bang of the door and rapid footsteps made me jerk up, my hand flying to my holster, but Skidmark spoke in my ear at the same time. "That's Karma, don't shoot."

A moment later he barrelled through the door and dropped to his knees beside Moonbeam, his fingers already reaching for her pulse.

His brow furrowed. "Strong and steady," he muttered, sounding puzzled.

Moonbeam's eyes popped open, her lips stretching into a grin of sheer exultation.

"Karma Wolf Song, Skidmark, we're grandparents!" she cried.

My mouth dropped open and I rocked back to plop flat on my ass. "Wha...? You..."

Relief choked me for a moment before giving way to furious indignation. My mouth opened and closed a few times before I could get my voice working again.

"You played me! You... you... ruthless... cold-hearted..." Words failed me and I tried again. "...manipulative... conniving... *you're exactly like Stemp!*" It was the worst insult I could come up with on short notice.

"Like mother... like son," she said faintly, still grinning. "I'm sorry, dear." She drew a breath as though she couldn't quite get enough air. "I was hoping... you'd confess your love... for Cosmic River Stone... but a granddaughter... is even better."

She closed her eyes and panted for a moment, her cheeks still bloodless.

"She might have overacted a bit but she's not faking this," Karma said, concern wrinkling his brow.

"Of course... I am, dear," Moonbeam whispered. "I'm perfectly... fine."

"Shhh. Of course you are," he agreed. "Let's get some more fluids into you and get you out of here. Storm, if you could find it in your heart to forgive? And maybe make some more hot chocolate?"

My anger drained away at the sight of her white face and rapid breathing. "Of course." I hauled myself upright and plied the kettle.

Skidmark spoke in my ear. "They've secured the last of the terrorists at the roadblock. They'll be cleaning up for a while but it's safe to approach."

"Good," Karma said, and I realized Skidmark must have spoken to all of us simultaneously. "Rand will need to be medevacked," Karma went on. "I've stabilized him but he'll need surgery." He turned to me. "No word from Helmand or Kane yet?"

"No." Caught up in Moonbeam's drama I had almost forgotten the remaining gunman, but now fear slithered cold tentacles into my belly again. I hesitated. "I don't want to call them unnecessarily," I decided. "If they're stalking this guy..."

I trailed off. Or if he was stalking them...

Don't think about it. Deal with what you can control.

"Will you look at Nichele?" I asked Karma. "John thought she'd been drugged, and I'm worried about her. She's been breathing okay and she moved a bit when Ratboy hurt her, but she hasn't moved since we got here."

He nodded and went to her side, pulling out a small flashlight to check her pupils and closing his fingers over her pulse.

"She's definitely been drugged," he said as he rose to return to Moonbeam. "Without examining her more thoroughly I can't be sure, but I'd suspect an intramuscular injection, maybe haloperidol or something similar. Or he could have slipped an oral sedative into her food or drink. Her vital signs are strong so I don't think there's any reason for concern unless the drug doesn't wear off over the next several hours. But she won't remember much about this, if anything."

"Thank God." I finished mixing the hot chocolate and handed the mug to him before going over to kneel next to Nichele. "I'll get her cleaned up and back in her tent and maybe she'll think it was just a bad dream. She always used to sleepwalk as a kid so that might work."

Karma wrapped an arm around Moonbeam's shoulders, easing her into a semi-reclined position. I watched them for a moment, cuddled together while he fed her sips of hot chocolate.

My eyes prickled and I turned back to Nichele and picked up a cloth.

A few minutes later, Karma put the empty mug back on the table. "I'll take her back to our tent," he said, and picked Moonbeam up as though she was made of thistledown. "As soon as I have her settled I'll come back and take Nichele to her tent, too."

"Karma Wolf Song... I'm perfectly... capable... of walking," Moonbeam protested.

Karma winked at me over her head. "Yes, dear," he agreed, and made for the door. "But I need you to cover us, and you can't do that if you're trying not to pass out. Now pull out your pistol and let's go."

Her fussing and his fond answering rumble receded as they crossed the hall out of sight, and I turned back to Nichele.

Her face was finally clean but her hair was sticky with drying blood and bits of tissue I preferred not to identify. Her nice clothes were probably done for, but her shoes weren't stained. Small mercies. They probably cost more than my entire wardrobe.

I sponged busily, refusing to think about Kane and Hellhound creeping through the darkness. Refusing to think about the shots that might erupt at any moment.

My back crawled with the sensation of being watched by malevolent eyes.

A cold draft snaked through the broken window, coiling around Nichele's wet hair and clothes. She began to shiver but didn't open her eyes. I hesitated for a moment, then stripped her clothes off and wrapped her in both blankets, the clean one next to her skin and Moonbeam's blood-soaked one around it. Several rinses later I deemed her hair clean enough to wrap in a tea towel.

My hands trembled, icy with nerves and blood-tinged

water.

When Skidmark's voice sounded in my ear, I twitched so violently I nearly knocked over the bucket.

"Karma's just walking up to the west door," he informed me. He hesitated, and I thought I heard a smile in his voice. "So, a granddaughter? How old?"

"You can't know about her," I growled. "Nobody can. It could cost her life."

His voice went as cold and flat as Hellhound's had been. "Who wants to kill her? Tell me."

A shiver trickled down my spine. Emphysema or not, I wouldn't bet against Skidmark if it came to a fight for his granddaughter's life.

"Later," I promised as I dragged myself to my feet. "When I can talk to all of you together." I grabbed the bucket and pitched the bloodied water out the broken window just as Karma strode in and crouched beside Nichele.

"Lucky she's small," he grumbled. "I'm getting too old for this." He hoisted her into his arms without visible effort and stood. "Cover us."

I nodded and drew my Glock, my heart rate accelerating at the thought of leaving the bulletproof concrete.

Karma was already striding out into the main hall. I hurried after him, scurrying ahead to open the door for him only to wonder if I should go through first just in case.

I compromised by bumbling out beside him and nearly tripping us both.

Outside, the moon was obscured by gathering cloud. A chilly breeze cut through my damp jacket. Shivering, I limped beside Karma trying to look in all directions at once.

"Wait," I whispered.

He halted and I switched to thermal-only, scanning

while I turned a full circle. I drew a breath of relief when no heat signatures appeared and switched back to night vision.

"That's not regular night-vision is it?" he inquired with interest.

I wasn't sure if it was classified technology or not so I muttered, "Mm," and started walking again.

"So Moonbeam was right; you do have a very high security clearance," Karma said. "You have some fascinating toys."

"Yeah. Sorry I can't share."

"So am I, believe me."

We walked on for a minute or two before I stopped for another scan. Karma let out a breath and lowered Nichele to the ground.

Crouching beside her, he massaged his shoulders and muttered, "I really am getting too old for this."

"What, for sneaking around in the woods killing armed men with your bare hands half the night and then toting unconscious women around for the rest of it?" I inquired lightly. "Yeah, you're such a feeble old man."

His chuckle turned into a long exhalation as he reached for Nichele again. This time his straightening didn't look quite so effortless.

"Let me help," I offered. "I can take her feet."

"No; one of us has to cover." He hefted Nichele higher in his arms with a grunt. "Unless you can carry her by yourself. With a bad ankle."

I sighed. "Sorry. No."

By the time we reached Nichele's tent, sweat was pouring down his face and his panting was audible several paces away. He dropped to his knees beside her cot and lowered her into it, then braced both hands on the edge of the bed with his head hanging, the muscles of his shoulders trembling with overuse.

"Sit for a minute," I urged. "I'll get you a drink of water."

"No." He inhaled as though gathering himself for the effort, then rose slowly to his feet. "I have to get back to Moonbeam. Stay here and protect Nichele until Skidmark sounds the all-clear. Then meet us in our tent."

I reached for his hand and squeezed it. "Thank you."

Karma smiled his usual smile, but his eyes were weary. "You're welcome; and thank you for giving Moonbeam a reason to fight another day. She pretends hard, but..." He sighed, the wrinkles on his face deepening. "None of us are young anymore."

I grimaced sympathy, and he ducked out the tent flap.

My ears straining for any movement outside, I rooted through Nichele's giant suitcase and found her silk pyjamas. As I wrestled her inert body into them, I discovered exactly how many of my muscles were protesting the night's activities. Groaning quietly, I stretched and massaged my neck and shoulders before returning to my task.

At last I had her tucked in, her precious shoes under the cot. I was straightening clutching my aching back when a fusillade of shots froze me in place.

CHAPTER 38

My knees collapsed and I sat on the floor of Nichele's tent with a thump that jarred every sore muscle I owned. Holding my breath, I waited for more shots.

I was sure that had been a three-shot burst from an assault rifle. Maybe some pistol shots. From the other side of the commune, in the direction of the bridge.

Oh God, oh God...

Sparkling blackness at the edges of my vision convinced me to suck in a breath and drop my head between my knees until the light-headedness passed.

Straining outward with every psychic feeler I could imagine, I tried to sense Kane and Hellhound. Surely I'd feel it if one of them was hurt.

Surely I'd know if one of them was d...

Don't go there.

My hand hovered over my pocket.

Should I phone?

What if I phoned at exactly the wrong moment, distracting them in a life-or-death situation?

Which one was I willing to risk?

Paralyzed, I did nothing.

One of them would phone.

The gunman couldn't have gotten them both.

He couldn't have...

"Last hostile down." Skidmark's voice sounded in my ear like angel trumpets.

"Are John and Arnie okay?" I demanded.

"Unclear. Kane probably is. Rand's too out of it to report. I'm guessing Kane found him under the bridge and took his earpiece. Kane reported in but I couldn't respond to him without blowing my cover. He said the last guy was down, but that was all he said before he realized he wasn't getting a response."

"I'll call him." I fumbled a phone out of my pocket and pressed the button, but the screen was dark and dead behind its cracked face. "Shit, I fell on that one." I dug out the second. "Shit!"

"What's wrong?" Skidmark asked.

"I broke both phones when I fell off the roof. I must have landed on them." I probed gingerly, wincing. "That explains the massive bruise on my butt."

I dragged myself to my feet, my insides wobbling with the fear of what might have happened. "I'll go to the bridge-"

"Negative," Skidmark interrupted. "I'm giving the signal to Aurora and Zen to bring the members back from the field now. They'll come via the south where there are no bodies. Lucky everybody goes straight back to bed or to the kitchen after a night Calling, so that'll give Kane and Helmand time to pick up the rest of the bodies. We need to spread a cover story about the broken window and blood in the kitchen, and then we need to debrief right away. We'll only have a short time before Kane and Helmand get the bodies delivered and come back, and then you'll need to debrief with them."

"But I'll just check on them-" I began.

"Negative!" His voice softened. "Look, I know you're worried but our timing is down to the wire here. I need you to talk to any members you encounter and I'll do the same on my way over. The story is that a buck and doe spooked out of the woods because of the fireworks and jumped through the kitchen window. Moonbeam cut her arm trying to herd them back out the door. If anybody sees blood in the forest, it's because the deer got cut on the glass and ran. Clear?"

My mind went back to the innocent solemnity of the children's faces.

I drew a deep breath and locked my fear away. I couldn't change what might have happened by the bridge tonight. And both Kane and Hellhound would want to protect the children at any cost.

"Okay. Meet you at Moonbeam and Karma's tent then," I agreed.

Turning a slow circle in Nichele's tent, I surveyed it for anything that might give away the night's events. Her bloodstained clothes went into a bundle with Moonbeam's gory blanket. I blotted her hair one more time before bundling up the tea towel as well, hoping her hair would be dry enough to pass inspection by the time she woke up.

Leaden fatigue gripped me, and I forced myself to double-check. Then triple-check. At last, hoping I hadn't missed anything, I stuffed my night-vision headset into my pocket and the blanket-bundle under my arm and went out.

I had gotten as far as the main path when I spotted the first of the flashlights bobbing toward the encampment. I drew a long breath and marshalled my acting skills.

Aurora's penetrating voice carried clearly on the damp air and my heart sank. Damn. I'd been hoping to meet a member I didn't know so I could just drop the information and retreat.

No such luck.

"Storm!" Aurora's flashlight inspected me from head to toe. "What happened? Is that *blood* on your jacket?"

Goddammit, I knew I'd been forgetting something. My jacket looked as though I'd been working in a slaughterhouse.

I suppressed a shudder at the truth of that and plucked at the darkening stains, trying for a rueful smile. "Yeah, but don't worry, it's not as bad as it looks. A couple of deer got spooked by the fireworks and jumped through the kitchen window. This is partly their blood and partly Moonbeam's. She cut her arm on the broken glass when she was trying to get them out again."

"Oh, dear, I hope she's not hurt too badly..." Aurora trailed off and her smooth brow furrowed. "What were you doing in the kitchen? Why didn't you come to the Calling? And where's Nichele?"

"Uh..."

My fatigue-dulled mind ground into motion. If you can't come up with a decent lie, tell the truth. Or part of it...

"Nichele's in bed. I tried to wake her up for the Calling but she sleeps like a log. I got her halfway out of bed but she just kept falling back to sleep."

"Oh." Aurora dropped her gaze, and I could see the colour rising in her cheeks even in the reflected glow of the flashlight. "Oh, dear. That might be my fault."

"Huh?" Too exhausted to take advantage of this stroke of luck, I stood dumbly waiting for an explanation.

"We had a little celebration. After her presentation went so well tonight." Aurora gave me a shy glance as though expecting a reproof. "We... well, *I* sneaked some of

Skidmark's pot and we smoked a joint together. I didn't think it would hit her so hard."

"Oh." I did my best to suppress a smile. "Well, that explains it, then. Anyway, don't worry about the blood and broken glass in the kitchen. It's nothing serious."

"Thank you, Storm. And I'm sorry you missed the Calling." She flung her arms around me. "The blessings of the Earth Spirit are upon you."

Her clear eyes and bright smile brought a lump to my throat. This was what we were protecting. For this, the nightmares would be worthwhile.

"And upon you, too," I said, and gave her an extra squeeze. "Goodnight, Aurora."

"Goodnight, Storm. I'll go and clean up the kitchen now so nobody gets worried."

I drew a breath of relief as she hurried away, apparently forgetting that I hadn't explained what I'd been doing in the kitchen in the first place.

Mission accomplished.

I limped toward Moonbeam and Karma's tent, stumbling painfully over roots in the path. After spotlighting me on the roof like a second-rate karaoke singer, the fucking moon had completely hidden its face now that I could have used its light.

I could barely make out the pale ribbon of gravel on the path. My waist pouch and backpack with their respective flashlights were still in the control room where I'd forgotten them in my dash to rescue Nichele, and I didn't dare use my night vision with the commune members still moving around.

Right on cue, a drizzle began to dampen my hands and face.

Fine. Just fucking fine.

I plodded on.

At the tent, I scratched lightly and called, "It's Storm."

Karma's warm bass bid me to come in, and I ducked in through the flap, drawing an involuntary breath of relief at the welcoming glow of their fat candles.

"Oh, good, more blankets," he said.

"You probably don't want to use these," I warned. "They're full of blood."

"They'll be fine for this. We'll wash them in the morning." Karma relieved me of my load and busied himself tucking the bundle behind Moonbeam to prop her comfortably in their bed.

"Merciful Spirit, Karma Wolf Song, stop fussing," she protested. "I've been hurt much more seriously than this."

"Yes, and I want to make sure this doesn't become more serious," Karma replied.

"Shouldn't she go to the hospital?" I asked. "I'm no doctor but I'm pretty sure a cut that size should be stitched."

"And it will be," Moonbeam agreed. "Karma Wolf Song has a great deal of experience at suturing. He handles all but the most serious medical events here at the commune. Skidmark is bringing the medkit from the control room." She frowned at me. "You poor child, please sit. You shouldn't be putting weight on that ankle and you look utterly exhausted."

"Sit on the table," Karma said. "I'll have a look at your ankle right now."

Too tired to argue, I hauled myself atop the table and sat with my legs dangling while he carefully removed my boot and examined my ankle. After a few moments of wincing on my part, he had just finished declaring it a strain when a scratch at the tent flap announced Skidmark's arrival.

When he came inside, the stench of pot smoke nearly strangled me.

"Jesus," I choked. "Do you *have* to smoke that shit? It's fucking disgusting."

He grinned and tucked the extinguished butt into his pocket. "Yeah, actually I do have to. I met some of the members on my way over. It's part of my cover."

"But *now?*" I protested. "Seriously, you were giving us tactical directions while you were stoned out of your mind?"

The three hippies exchanged a conspiratorial look before they burst out laughing.

I stared at them for a moment, then sighed and gave in. "Okay, what's the joke?"

Skidmark tapped the pocket that contained the half-smoked joint. "This is extra-special shit. I've been developing this variety ever since I got here."

"Well, it sure smells like extra-special shit," I agreed sourly.

Skidmark withdrew the roach and held it up as though exhibiting a precious artifact. "It's not the smell. It's the THC content. The psychoactive part. This is damn near my life's work."

"Oh, great," I growled. "I can't tell you how pleased I am to know you were extra-high while you were guiding us between bullets."

"Not extra-high." He smirked. "Extra-sober. I've bred the THC right out of this shit. You'd get a better high smoking a chunk of rope." He bestowed a kiss on the joint and tucked it back in his pocket.

While I was staring at him open-mouthed, Moonbeam added, "Skidmark works very hard to determine everyone's hot buttons and secret prejudices by making inflammatory remarks and antagonizing people whenever possible. That helps us determine whether we're dealing with simple narrow-minded prejudice or borderline psychosis. The stoned-hippie image helps mitigate their reactions; though it's not always successful."

"Almost always," Skidmark objected.

"Except for those times when you get beaten within an inch of your life and spend a week in the hospital," Moonbeam countered disapprovingly.

Skidmark waved an airy hand. "Only because I let 'em. And that only happened once. Or twice." He narrowed his eyes at me. "That's how I pegged you for law enforcement. If two guys are getting ready to fight, most women won't go near 'em unless they're in love with one of 'em. When Ratboy came at me, you jumped toward us instead of backing away. You were gonna break up the fight." He winked and buffed his fingernails against his chest. "'Course I figured it was just because you were in love with me."

"Uh-huh," I agreed, deadpan. "It was all I could do not to jump you on the spot."

"You could do worse, dear," Moonbeam assured me with a fond look at Skidmark. "He's an expert lover. And his testicles are definitely larger than lima beans."

"Too much information!" I threw my arms around my aching head in a desperate attempt to ward off the mental image of a naked Skidmark. "Too much! Too much!"

Skidmark leered cheerfully at Moonbeam. "Kids. They always think they invented sex."

Karma eyed them both, smiling. "All right, you two. Time to get serious. We don't have much time. Skidmark, pass me the medkit."

Skidmark handed over the plastic-wrapped bundle he'd carried in, and Karma opened it to spread a sterile pad under Moonbeam's arm. A syringe and suturing materials were laid out next, and I transferred my gaze to the ceiling of the tent.

"I think I managed to keep your cover intact," I said. "Will you do the same for mine?"

"Of course," Karma said immediately, and the others echoed his assent.

"What about Orion... Rand?" I asked. "Can we trust him?"

"Yes, we think so, dear... ouch!" Moonbeam protested.

I didn't look to see what Karma was doing to her arm. I'd seen more than enough already.

"We checked him out pretty thoroughly before we revealed ourselves," Skidmark agreed. "He's got an exemplary record and high security clearances. Bit of a pretty-boy ego, but it doesn't seem to keep him from getting the job done." He wheezed laughter. "That reminds me, I have to go visit him in the hospital. He owes me another fifty bucks. He bet me he'd have you in his bed by now."

"Mm. A little overconfident," I murmured, opting not to reveal how close it had been. "Ask him not to mention me to Five Eyes."

"He won't," Skidmark assured me.

"Tell us about our granddaughter," Moonbeam burst out.

I sank my head into my hands. "You can't mention her. Ever. To anyone. Not even to Stemp... um, Cosmic River Stone. I shouldn't have said anything at all, and if something happens to her because of this I'll never forgive myself."

"But why?" Moonbeam sounded bereft.

"I can't even tell you that. The less you know, the

better."

"Please. Tell us something. Anything." Her desperate entreaty wrung my heart. "Anna," she begged. "You said her name was Anna."

"It was. It's not now."

Karma spoke up. "So her name was changed. Is she in a witness protection program?"

I dragged my head out of my hands to meet their eyes squarely. "Do you honestly want me to jeopardize your granddaughter's life just to satisfy your curiosity?"

They blanched, their hands finding each other to clasp tightly.

"No," Moonbeam whispered. "But... just one question. I have to know. Is she your daughter?"

"No."

She studied me, eyes unfocused in her aura-reading expression. Then her shoulders slumped.

"I see truth in your aura," she murmured. "I had so hoped..." She drew a deep breath. "Do you think we'll ever meet her?"

"I think if it's humanly possible, your son will find a way to make that happen."

She let out her breath, some of the sadness easing from her face. "Thank you. You may consider this conversation forgotten. So you and Cosmic River Stone are not-"

"No," I said. "Absolutely not. Never have; never will."

"But you respect him. And he obviously has high regard for you." Moonbeam frowned. "So how do you know what Cosmic River Stone has in his bedroom?"

"Dearest." Karma laid a hand on her shoulder. "Perhaps it's best to leave well enough alone."

I shifted uncomfortably. They were getting too close to

the truth. I wasn't sure what the repercussions might be, but if Stemp had concealed his true career from his parents, I was pretty sure he wouldn't thank me for giving them enough clues to figure it out.

Time to shore up this thin ice.

"It's all right," I said. "I can tell you that."

Now I needed to choose my facts carefully. All true, but...

"My cover identity is a bookkeeper at the same office as Ste... Cosm..." I began. "Sorry, I'm just going to call him Stemp. It's what I'm used to." Karma nodded encouragingly and I continued, "So we work together sometimes. And you're right, I do respect him. He's very good at his job." I studied them carefully, not wanting to miss any nuance of reaction. "Do you remember getting a telephone call from the police a few months ago?"

"Yes. Dermott, I believe the officer's name was." Karma paused his suturing to frown at me. "He was trying to find Cosmic River Stone. We researched Dermott and he checked out. When we asked Cosmic River Stone about it later he deflected our questions. Were you involved in that?"

"Yes." I projected my very best honesty. "It was an internal investigation and your son was under suspicion. I believed he was innocent but the police insisted on searching his house while he was out of town. I got the key from his neighbour, and I cleaned up a bit after the search. That's why I know what's in his bedroom."

"Oh." Moonbeam sighed and slumped against the blankets. "Well, thank you for taking his side. No wonder you mean so much to him."

Karma cocked an ear at a distant rumble. "There goes the truck. Let's wrap this up."

"Agreed," Moonbeam said. "So, Storm Cloud Dancer, will you stay here permanently?"

CHAPTER 39

"Will I what?" I stared at Moonbeam.

Beside her, Karma paused his suturing again to repeat, "We want you to stay. Permanently. Take over from us."

"In case you hadn't noticed, we're not getting any younger," Skidmark put in.

"Our members are our surrogate children," Moonbeam added. "We want to be sure they are protected and their way of life is preserved even after we're gone."

I scrubbed my hands over my face.

Too tired. Not grasping the concept.

"Let me get this straight," I said slowly. "You want me to stay here. Pretend the Earth Spirit is real. Live out in the middle of Bumfuck Nowhere in a tent in the rain with no hot showers or electricity for the rest of my life, on the off-chance that some terrorist group might just happen to rent the land across the river."

Moonbeam's face fell. "Well... I suppose when you put it like that..."

Skidmark blew out a breath and sank down to sit on the mattress by her feet. "That's what Rand said, too, when we asked him." He shrugged. "But he was a city boy. Never comfortable in the outdoors the way you are. We were hoping..." He trailed off.

"We had originally planned for Cosmic River Stone to take over the commune when he reached adulthood," Karma said. "We taught him everything we knew. Made sure he had the optimum education for a career in covert operations. He had the intellect, the temperament... he would have been a perfect fit. We were going to send him for advanced training and reveal the operation to him when he was ready, but..." Karma's shoulders slumped.

"Now he's wasting all that in a civilian management job," Skidmark said bitterly, but I barely heard him.

Shit, I'd been right. Stemp really had been born to be a spy.

I shook myself back to the present. "I'm sorry that didn't work out for you. But we're short on time and I have some more questions. Why didn't those nutcases just run back to their truck and drive away when they realized we were picking them off? And if you knew they were that much of a threat, why didn't you just blow the bridge and let JTF2 come in and clean them up?" I made fists in my hair and tugged, trying to release the knotted muscles in my neck. "And if Orion's not going to mention you in his reports, he'll have to mention John and Arnie and me. There's no way anybody will believe he took out sixteen guys using hand-to-hand combat and three different types of firearms, so how can you promise he won't reveal our involvement?"

"When we first began researching you, Orion Moonjava agreed not to mention you in any official channels," Moonbeam assured me. "We assumed if you hadn't initiated contact with him you weren't aware of his operation, and we couldn't imagine that you were undertaking any other sort of covert operation. The scope for that sort of activity is rather limited around here. So we decided that you were either in hiding, or else recovering as per your story. We researched your Dr. Rawling and discovered he specializes in PTSD, so your night terrors and regular contact with him supported the latter. Orion Moonjava will likely have to report that he had outside help, but your identity won't be revealed, nor that of Kane and Helmand."

"And to answer your first question, the groups were in radio contact," Skidmark added. "When the first truck got stopped at the roadblock they radioed their buddies here. They knew they were trapped so they tried to do as much damage as possible. Die a heroic death in combat." Skidmark looked as though he wanted to spit on the floor. "Scum."

"And we didn't blow the bridge because we expected them to leave together," Moonbeam finished. "Which I believe they would have done if not for Ratboy's absence."

"That asshole," I snarled. Now I wanted to spit, too.

"Well…" Skidmark rose tiredly. "Guess we're done here. In a couple of hours JTF2 will have everything cleaned up at the roadblock and by morning there won't be a sign that anything happened. Come on, Storm. You can pick up your gear from the control room."

I eyed his drawn face. "It's okay, I'll just let myself in and get it. You've had enough activity for one night."

He snorted. "All I did was walk down here from the garage. And you can't get back into the control room. I've already relocated the keypad and changed the code. If Helmand starts poking around there, all he'll find is a keypad that lets him into a little storage closet under that brush pile. We'll access the control room from a different door now."

I must have looked incredulous, because Moonbeam

smiled. "Remember, dear, we've been here for over forty years. We have to have backup plans in case our members find our access doors. The official story is that we maintain locked storage areas so our members can store any valuables they may want to protect."

I shook my head slowly. "You're amazing."

"Thank you, dear." She smiled. "Now go and get your gear. Soon you'll need to debrief with your men."

My heart clutched at the thought. Please let them be okay.

Cold rain was pelting down when we emerged from the tent, and I swore and dragged my night vision headset on before pulling up my hood.

Skidmark eyed the sky with approval. "Good. That'll clean up the blood in the woods."

I sighed and limped after him.

Climbing the hill to the garage our paces were evenly matched. I limped; he panted and wheezed while his lungs laboured to keep up with the exertion.

When we reached the garage, he gasped, "Wait here," and plodded off into the darkness behind it.

Leaning against the building under the relative shelter of the eaves, I drew a deep breath and let it out slowly, trying to calm my skittering heart.

I still expected gunshots and muzzle flashes. Every time the wind rustled in the undergrowth my muscles tensed.

And my worry for Kane and Hellhound pulsed through my heart like aching poison. Kane was probably all right. He had checked in with Orion's radio, and somebody had to be driving the truck. Orion couldn't drive with a broken leg, and Kane wouldn't leave unless the bodies had been collected. He must have been in good enough shape to be capable of that.

But I'd seen him push through and disregard injuries before. He'd finish the mission as long as he was conscious and capable of forcing himself to move.

But Arnie...

What if he'd been injured? Or even killed? Kane had no way of finding or contacting me. He'd finish the mission regardless, putting duty ahead of his personal feelings as he always did.

What if 'I love you' had been Arnie's last words to me? I hadn't even told him I loved him in return.

A twig snapped and my hand flew to my gun.

"Stand down," Skidmark said hurriedly as he emerged from the woods. "It's just me. Here." He held out my backpack and waist pouch. "They're just like you left them. I didn't look inside."

"Thanks." I accepted the waist pouch and strapped it on, then reached for the backpack. "I wasn't worried."

Mainly because I had all my classified gear in my pockets, but he didn't need to know that.

I frowned at the object in his other hand. "What the hell are you going to do with that?"

He hefted the metal detector tiredly. "Pick up the cartridges. Don't want the members finding them. Where did you engage?"

I described the approximate locations where I'd seen muzzle flashes and where I thought Hellhound's position might have been. Then I added, "But what if one of the members catches you? It's going to be pretty damn hard to explain why you're out in the middle of the night." I paused and checked my watch. "Hell, 'way too early morning, with a metal detector."

He shrugged. "Nobody'll ask. I'm a wasted stoner. I stink, I'm old and ugly, and I piss off anybody who comes near me. If I want to wander around in the dark and rain with a metal detector, nobody's going to give a shit."

For an instant I glimpsed a proud lonely man who had spent his life protecting people who gave him nothing but hostility in return.

He lifted his chin, his level gaze rejecting any sympathy.

I hid the contraction of my heart in a grin and planted my hands on my hips. "I know you're angling for a pity fuck. Nice try, but it won't work."

He let out a whoop of laughter and staggered over to prop himself against the garage while he coughed and wheezed. "Girlie," he gasped at last, "Any time you want to come back, you're welcome here. I'll even share my beer."

"I might take you up on that. You know, I just realized that was one of the things that was subliminally bothering me about you. I didn't see an icebox up here and I couldn't figure out how you kept your beer cold." He laughed, and I added, "Well, that and the fact that you seemed to go from stoned to sober in seconds flat."

He grunted. "I'm out of practice. Not used to holding my cover longer than it usually takes to piss people off."

I hesitated, then inclined my head in the direction of the garage and the half-stripped truck. "So... sabotaging the vehicles... is that post-traumatic stress? There's help available, if you want it."

"Thanks, but no. Just making it harder for the terrorists. We knew they'd need the truck to bring in their weapons so the longer we stalled them the better. And it kept you where we could see you." He gave me a not-too-intimidating scowl. "Trying to protect you was a pain in the ass. Wish we'd known for sure you were an agent."

I grimaced. "Sorry about that. But I'm glad you're not suffering."

"Nah." He gave me a shrewd once-over. "So what's your story? Why were you really here?"

"Uh..." My tired brain refused to disgorge any useful lies. "I really was just, um... recovering," I said lamely.

"Uh-huh." Skidmark surveyed me, eyes narrowed. "I bet your last op went south," he said after a long moment. "You went a little too far questioning some dirtbag and things got messy so they put you on admin leave until they could decide what to do with you. And if Rand says anything about how you manhandled him, it's gonna look even worse. You facing disciplinary action?"

"No," I muttered. "Just admin leave."

His gold tooth glinted in a grin. "Huh. Your boys covered it up for you, didn't they?" When I stared at him, he added, "Yeah, I caught that part where you said 'no cleanup *this time*' when you were telling them about questioning Rand." The smile disappeared into his beard as he studied me. "Girlie, don't look so sick. Sometimes we gotta do what's gotta be done. If we end up in hell for it, well..." He shrugged and extended his hand, his eyes solemn. "Proud to serve with you."

I accepted his handshake and choked, "Thanks." I cleared my throat and added, "Proud to serve with you, too." I nodded at the metal detector. "Let me know if you want help."

"Nope, just keep Kane and Helmand busy for the rest of the night." He leered. "You can do that, right? Can I come by and watch later?"

I grinned and shook my head at him. "Get out of here,

you old pervert."

He wheezed laughter and headed for the road.

As soon as he was out of sight I pressed closer to the building to stay out of the rain and unearthed a secured phone from the bottom of my pack. Stemp answered on the first ring as usual.

Holding back my need to rip a strip off him, I kept my tone dispassionate. "We had a problem here tonight. It turned out the renters were a terrorist group that planned to attack the Parliament buildings in Victoria tomorrow morning. Orion was an undercover MI6 agent named Ian Rand, working with a Five Eyes operation to monitor the terrorists here."

I paused, but he admitted nothing. Bastard.

"We killed half the terrorists," I continued. "JTF2 cleaned up the other half at a roadblock outside the commune. No civilian casualties, but your mom cut her arm on a piece of broken glass. Not life-threatening. The bodies have been removed and everything's cleaned up. None of the members realized anything was happening. Rand won't disclose our identities to Five Eyes. I haven't had time to debrief with Kane and Hellhound yet."

"Very well." His crisp response held an undertone of tension. "Is that all?"

I rolled my eyes. Gee, what a surprise. The secret code.

"Yes." I hung up and delved into my pack for the laptop.

When it booted, the tiny square was already blinking at the bottom of the screen. I activated the text window and the cursor zipped across it immediately.

"How is my mother?"

"Fine. It was a bad cut and she lost some blood, but it's sutured and she should be okay." My outrage spilled over and I added, "You knew about the Five Eyes operation!"

The cursor blinked for a moment before spitting out its response. "Unofficially. But that knowledge didn't negate the validity of your mission. I was genuinely concerned about reprisals against my parents as a result of my cover breach in our last mission."

Fingers shaking with anger, I typed, "Why the hell didn't you tell me? How dare you saddle me with the responsibility for your parents' lives without giving me the whole story? Who the fuck do you think you are, playing God-"

I stopped and drew a deep breath. Then I let it out slowly and deleted the last two sentences before pressing the Enter key to send the first.

The cursor scurried across the screen. "I apologize. Five Eyes doesn't share information with our department unless they need our help locally, but I secretly monitor the system for anything that may affect my loved ones. I couldn't request official support without admitting my unauthorized knowledge, and I didn't disclose it to you because Rand was so certain he could pull it off without affecting the commune members."

The cursor blinked briefly on the next line before scurrying across the screen to add, "Please believe that I would have informed you regardless of the consequences to myself if I'd had any reason to believe this would affect your safety or that of my parents. I am truly sorry it did, and I am profoundly grateful to you for protecting Mother and Father. If I could have been there in your place, I would have."

I stewed over that for a moment before typing, "Aren't there going to be questions about you sending me classified equipment?"

"No one knows, and the courier won't say anything. He

owed me a favour."

Another deep breath dissipated the last of my irritation, leaving nothing but aching fatigue. No point in being pissed off at Stemp. Ruthless manipulation was simply what he did. And I'd been known to get pretty ruthless when protecting the people I cared about, too. I couldn't blame him for that.

I exhaled slowly and typed, "Okay. I won't mention your knowledge."

The cursor moved again. "Thank you. Do my parents know about the terrorists?"

I hesitated. If Kane or Hellhound reported, they might mention Moonbeam and Karma had been 'kidnapped' by Orion. But Moonbeam and Karma likely wouldn't mention it to Stemp, their civilian son.

I blew out a sigh. Cover as many asses as possible.

I typed, "Yes, they were briefly kidnapped. I got them back uninjured but I had to tell them about the terrorists. They might not mention it to you because they won't want to worry you."

"Are you sure my mother is all right? She's very delicate."

I snorted laughter. Yeah. Delicate like a fine steel blade.

"I'm positive," I typed. My fingers hovered over the keyboard. I should warn him. But he might kill me for it.

I clenched my teeth. It didn't matter. A child's life was more important.

My fingers moved across the keyboard almost of their own volition. "Your mom tricked me. She pretended to be seriously injured and losing consciousness. I told her she had a granddaughter named Anna to give her something to live for. I'm sorry, I shouldn't have fallen for it. I told them never to mention her, and I think they'll comply. The name was the only detail I gave them."

The cursor blinked in place after I hit the Enter key, and I imagined Stemp dialling the number for a professional hit man. Or coming to hunt me down himself.

After a few moments the cursor moved again. "It's all right. That's not enough information to be dangerous. And my parents are masters of manipulation. You never had a chance."

I imagined his wintry smile as I read the last words, and sympathy twisted my heart in spite of myself. Poor Stemp. Brought up to be devious and suspicious. Tearing himself loose from his family and a pseudo-religion drummed into him since childhood. Believing his parents to be naïve and deluded at best; heartless manipulators at worst...

I swallowed hard and typed, "Thank you. That's all for now."

The text box vanished and I stowed the laptop back in my pack and shouldered it wearily.

Limping down the hill, I fought the undertow of worry. Surely Kane should be back soon with the truck.

What if something had happened at the roadblock? What if Skidmark had been wrong about all the terrorists being subdued there?

Or worse, what if Hellhound had been terribly injured and Kane was on the way to the hospital with him, unable to contact me?

My stomach twisted in knots of nauseated exhaustion.

I drew in a deep breath and let it out slowly. Stay calm. Go back to the tent and wait. If it was an emergency, Kane would call the commune's main line. If not, he'd come back to my tent when he was done.

A flash from the direction of the gate made my heart

lurch into rapid drumming.

Headlights.

I hurried along the road.

No. Only one headlight.

I drew my gun and faded into the trees at the side of the road.

The headlight drew closer, silver daggers of rain slashing through its bright beam. I caught the distinctive throaty whine of a hyperbike and realization dawned.

Kane.

I dashed out to the road and the headlight bobbled and swung sideways as Kane slammed on the brakes, skidding in the wet gravel.

He grabbed for his shoulder holster and I threw my hands up where he could see them, suddenly realizing that jumping out of the darkness at a guy suffering from battle fatigue was a really bad idea.

"It's Aydan!" I shouted. "Don't shoot! I'm an idiot, sorry."

He dropped his hand back to the handlebar. "It's all right. You can put your hands down now."

"Thanks." I wobbled over to the bike, my heart still hammering.

He wore no helmet, and I wondered whether he'd had to leave in a hurry or had simply been too exhausted to care. The rain plastered his hair to his head and even in my night vision his face was white with bone-deep fatigue.

"Thank God you're all right." He pulled me to him without dismounting, nearly crushing me in his embrace. "I was hoping it was just a radio malfunction when I didn't get a reply."

"It was. I could hear you but you didn't seem to be able

to hear me," I lied. "I tried to phone you but I'd broken both my phones. I'm glad you're all right, too." I clung to him for a moment before pulling away to survey him worriedly. "You are all right, aren't you?"

He hesitated before replying, "Yes. As all right as I'm going to be for a while."

Coldness that had nothing to do with rain crept down my back. "John, where's Arnie?"

He just looked at me, his eyes dark, his face etched with lines of pain and exhaustion.

"John!" My hand clenched on his wrist, a skeletal claw whitening over tendons taut as cables. "John, *where's Arnie?*"

CHAPTER 40

Kane's gaze searched my face like a child seeking refuge from a storm. "I don't know," he said.

"*What do you mean you don't know?*" My voice came out shrill and panicky.

Kane blinked and shook his head as though fighting to stay awake. "I don't know where he is," he repeated. "I assumed he'd be back at your tent by now. We loaded up the bodies and Orion said it was safe to approach the roadblock. Hellhound said something about looking for a cat and stayed behind here while I took Orion with me and dropped off the truck with the troops at the roadblock. They'll finish the cleanup and make sure Orion gets to the hospital. But I thought Hellhound would be at your tent by now."

"Oh..." I drew a breath, trying to calm my trembling. "Right, he was worried about Peaches. And I haven't been back to my tent. He's probably there."

"Well, mount up, then." Kane nodded at the seat behind him. "I'm done walking tonight. The commune members can just live with an unauthorized vehicle."

I slung my leg over the seat and wrapped my arms around him. As he guided the motorcycle expertly along the twisting path, I craned my neck to peer over his shoulder and switched to thermal-only.

My tent was dark and cold.

I slid off the bike, my breath catching in my throat. "John, where is he?" I cried as though Kane would somehow have acquired that knowledge in the past thirty seconds.

"I don't know, Aydan; did you try calling him?" he replied patiently.

"I can't, I fell on my phones and broke them and I don't have the numbers for his burner phones..." My voice climbed toward hysteria. I sucked in a breath and shoved my emotions back. "Sorry," I added, forcing myself back under control. "I'm not thinking straight. Too tired, too much adrenaline. Will you call him, please?"

Kane nodded and reached into his pocket. "Let's get out of the rain," he said, and herded me into my tent.

He pressed the speed dial and held the phone out so I could hear the ringing on the other end.

It rang over and over.

Kane laid a hand on my shoulder. "Don't panic. I'll try his other one."

He pressed the second speed dial button and turned the phone again so we could both listen.

Ring. Ring. Ring. Ring...

"Come on, Arnie, pick up!" I begged.

After twelve rings, Kane disconnected and we stared at each other in silence. A band of fear wound around my throat, coiling down to tighten my lungs and constrict my heart.

"What if Orion counted wrong?" My voice came out in a choked whisper. "What if there was another terrorist?"

"An MI6 agent wouldn't make a mistake like that," Kane said, but he didn't sound certain. He scrubbed his hands over his face. "All right, don't panic. We'll go to the bridge and start a search grid. That's where I saw him last."

"No, we don't have time for that! He could be anywhere; if he's hurt-"

"Aydan, we don't have a choice."

"Yes, we do!" I snapped. "Stay here in case he comes back. I'm going to ask Moonbeam to consult the Earth Spirit."

"Aydan." Kane's hands closed gently around my shoulders. "You're not thinking straight. There's no such thing as the Earth Spirit."

I shook myself loose. "I know that. But Moonbeam found a little lost boy once. Maybe she can find Arnie, too."

Kane's face softened, and I knew he'd indulge me. "All right," he said gently. "I'll start the search grid and you go and ask Moonbeam. Then you can join me in the search while she does... whatever she does. Take some phones so we can stay in contact."

I suddenly remembered Skidmark was out in the rain picking up brasses and thinking the danger was past.

Oh God, if there was another terrorist on the loose...

"I saw Skidmark wandering around earlier," I said, holding my voice steady with all my might. "Watch out for him, okay?"

"I will." He held me in his arms for a moment, stroking my hair. "We'll find Hellhound, Aydan. He's all right. Think good thoughts."

Heart pounding, I managed to return his embrace despite the sense of time ticking away. Then I pulled back and reached up to kiss him once, hard.

"Be safe," I admonished, and ducked out the tent flap to run for Moonbeam and Karma's tent.

As I dashed up their path, I realized I couldn't hear Karma snoring. My panting accelerated into little keening whimpers.

What if they were lying dead in there? What if the terrorist was going silently from tent to tent massacring the members in their sleep?

I flipped to thermal only and the sight of two heat signatures weakened my knees. Either alive or freshly dead.

My scratch at the tent flap was more like a frantic raking, and I hissed, "It's Aydan. Are you there?"

"Yes, of course." Karma's reassuring bass made me catch my breath in a sob of relief. "Come in. What's the matter?"

I shoved through the tent flap just as he lit a candle. Moonbeam's eyes widened at the sight of my face.

"What is it?" she demanded.

"We've lost Arnie!" At the horror in their faces, I clarified, "I mean, we can't find him. He said he was going to look for Peaches right before John left with the truck and now we can't raise him on the phone. Could Orion have been wrong about the number of terrorists?"

"No," Karma said firmly. "And even if he was, Skidmark would have known the correct number. Remember, there are surveillance cameras on the bridge and along the road. He would have done a count as they deployed."

"Thank God. I need to go back to the control room and look at your tracking screen, then."

"No need, dear," Moonbeam said, and reached under the mattress to withdraw a slim computer tablet. "We have a remote connection here."

"Oh." I dropped to my knees beside the mattress, partly to look at the screen and partly because my legs wouldn't hold me any longer. She worked rapidly for a few moments, and comprehension dawned. "So that's what Orion was doing in your tent the night of the Calling," I said. "He was looking me up on the tracker."

"Gold star, dear," Moonbeam murmured absently. "...here." She turned the screen toward me and jabbed a finger at the motionless dot east of the main building. "That's Blessed Soul Dream's bracelet."

Karma was already pulling a jacket on. "I'll come with you." He turned to Moonbeam. "Guide us." He pushed the radio earpiece into his ear and Moonbeam nodded and did the same, her gaze riveted to the screen.

I turned and ran.

Karma kept pace with me easily. My ankle jabbed with every step and my breath caught in sobs of pain and fear.

As we passed the main building, Karma reached out to tug my sleeve. "Go left," he said, and we crossed the open space and plunged into the undergrowth.

"Should be about fifty yards straight ahead," Karma panted, but I had already spotted the bulky figure lying on the ground.

"Arnie!" Tears mixed with the rain on my face as I charged toward him. *"Arnie!"*

He jerked as if woken from sleep but he didn't stand up. His torso looked oddly misshapen, as though he was holding his jacket tented over some wound too painful to touch.

"Hey, darlin', easy now," he warned as I fell to my knees beside him.

"Arnie, what's wrong?" I ran frantic hands over his head and shoulders.

"Nothin', darlin'... hey," he said as if noticing for the first time that I was sobbing with fear and exertion. He leaned up on one elbow, still moving slowing and carefully. "What's wrong? What happened?" He wrapped his free arm around me.

"I thought I lost you." Beyond dignity or even a modicum of self-control, I threw my arms around his neck and blubbered into his rain-soaked shoulder. "I thought... I lost... you."

"Shhh, darlin', I'm right here an' everythin's fine. I tried to call ya but I didn't get an answer. Kane said he'd left ya safe in the main buildin', so after we nailed that last guy I went to look for Peaches. I stopped by the buildin' for ya but ya were gone already. Sorry ya were scared. I figured I'd give Kane a chance to get back from droppin' off the truck an' then I was gonna call him an' let him know I'd be back in a bit."

"We tried to call you," I babbled, shivering uncontrollably in his embrace. "Why didn't you answer? Why are you lying on the ground?"

"Aw, darlin', I'm sorry." He kissed my forehead, a gentle touch of lips and whiskers. "I musta missed the vibration 'cause I had the phones in my jacket pocket an' I was usin' my jacket for this." He raised the jacket into the odd tented shape I'd seen earlier.

Smiling, he nodded toward it and I sucked in a quivering breath and managed to relinquish my hold on him long enough to lean in and peer underneath.

Laughter and tears choked me, and I pressed my forehead against his shoulder and gave in to both. When I was capable of speech again, I pulled out the phone and punched Kane's speed dial.

At his tense reply I said, "It's okay, John, I found him. You were right, he was just looking for Peaches. Go back to my tent and get some rest. We'll be along soon."

Several yards down the path, Karma caught my eye and melted into the forest with a smile.

Hellhound didn't even notice him. His enthralled gaze was still directed under his jacket.

I lifted a corner of the jacket again and smiled at the sight of Peaches and her brand-new family nestled safe and dry against his chest.

CHAPTER 41

"I'm really sorry, darlin'," Hellhound said for approximately the tenth time as we made our slow way toward the main building. He cradled Peaches and her kittens tented in his jacket, apparently oblivious to the rain soaking him to the skin.

"I really fucked up," he added. "If I hadn't shot Ratboy, none a' those assholes woulda attacked in the first place. An' then I just about gave ya a heart attack into the bargain. I'm really sorry," he finished again.

"It's okay, Arnie." I tightened my arm around him, partly to reassure myself that he was alive and partly to take some weight off my throbbing ankle. "If you hadn't shot Ratboy, who knows what he might have done to Nichele? He wasn't rational. He didn't want to negotiate, he just wanted to cause as much pain as possible. You likely would have had to shoot him no matter what."

Hellhound blew out a breath. "Yeah, you're prob'ly right. But I wasn't thinkin' straight. I saw him grab Peaches an' I just lost it." His arms curled protectively around the purring bundle. "What kinda fucked-up sicko'd wanna hurt a little pregnant cat?"

There wasn't a good answer to that, so I didn't offer one.

"When I found her, I thought she was hurt bad," he went on, reliving the moment with a shudder. "I was out in the woods walkin' an' callin', an' I heard this little meow. She was all curled up, soakin' wet an' shakin'. I got down real slow, didn't wanna scare her, but she never even moved, just kept lickin' herself an' her sides were goin' in an' out..." He walked on in silence for a few paces. "I was sorry I'd killed Ratboy then," he said flatly. "I wanted to wake him up from the dead an' make him suffer."

I shivered at that cold implacable voice. This was the part of him he'd never let me see. Even though I had known it was there, meeting the killer face to face chilled me.

"So I'm just as fuckin' sick as him," Hellhound finished, and the raw pain in his voice wrenched my heart.

"No, Arnie, you're not," I said softly. "Anybody who'd lie down in the rain to keep a cat and kittens dry-"

"Anybody who'd put an animal's life before a man's," he interrupted, "...is fucked up."

I said the only thing that came to my mind.

"That wasn't a man."

He grunted, but didn't argue. "So when I figured out she was havin' her kittens, I was afraid to move her," he went on. "She'd just finished gettin' everybody all cleaned up an' dried off when ya got there."

"Well, she's fine now, thanks to you, and so are her kittens," I said. "Let's put her in the cat house for tonight. If she wants them somewhere else she'll move them."

Inside the small room furnished with carpeted perches and cushions, we chose a spot tucked away in the corner. Hellhound crouched to bring his armload level with the padded basket and I lifted Peaches into it.

Squeaks from the tiny blind kittens made her trill an

anxious response, and I hurriedly transferred the motes of fur into the basket along with her. A couple of the other commune cats blinked sleepy eyes at us, and Peaches hissed a warning at one that approached too closely.

Hellhound stepped back, pulling on his jacket with a sigh of relief. "Thanks, darlin'," he said. "I'd'a been afraid to touch 'em. They're so little." He stared down at the basket, a wondering smile touching his lips. "They're no bigger'n my finger. Fuckin' amazin'." He passed a gentle hand over Peaches' deflated side. "Goodnight, little momma-cat. Take good care a' your babies."

We turned together for the door, and I slipped my hand into his. "You're a good cat-dad."

He chuckled. "That's the only kinda dad I ever wanna be." Then he sobered, watching me limp out the door. "That ankle looks bad, darlin'."

"It's pretty sore," I agreed. "I'll just lean on you a bit."

"I got a better idea." He grinned and turned his back on me, extending his hands behind him. "Hop on. How many years since ya had a piggy-back ride?"

I laughed. "You mean 'how many decades'." I linked my arms over his shoulders and hopped up. "Put me down when you get tired."

He wrapped his hands under my thighs and headed for the door. "Hell, darlin', I humped a hundred-pound ruck on marches just for fun. I can get ya to your tent without even breakin' a sweat."

I leaned down to nibble his ear. "Humping a ruck doesn't sound very sexy. You should hump me instead."

"Helluva plan, darlin'."

"But I'm going to need a rain check tonight." I laid my head on his shoulder with a sigh. "I'm so bagged and full of stale adrenaline I feel like I'm going to puke."

He patted my ass. "If ya puke down my neck you're gonna owe me big."

"Mm." I slid my hands down his chest. "I owe you big for this ride anyway. You'll have to write me an invoice."

"I'll get right on that."

We rounded the last bend in the path and I switched to thermal-only from force of habit, only to let out a whimper of sheer despair at the sight of my cold dark tent.

"What, darlin'?" Hellhound demanded.

"John's gone." My sluggish brain registered the heat signature in Orion's tent. "...oh, wait. Maybe that's him. Let me down."

I limped over to Orion's tent and scratched on the flap. "John? Is that you in there?"

"Yes." A moment later he poked his head outside, followed by his flashlight beam. "Don't stand out in the rain. Come in."

I beckoned to Hellhound and we both ducked into the tent.

"What are you doing in here?" I asked. "Did Orion want you to get something for him?"

"No." Kane stared down at the spot of light his flashlight made on the floor. "I'm going to sleep here tonight. You two can take the bed in your tent."

I glanced at Hellhound. He looked as unhappy as I felt.

"John..." I reached for his hand. "I know this might sound a little weird, but I really want both of you in my tent tonight. Not for..." Heat rose in my face. "I'm not asking for anything kinky, I just... I really need to have you both close. To know you're safe."

His face softened. "Aydan, I understand, but this will be

better." He met my gaze, his eyes dark hollows in his bone-white face. "I haven't slept in over forty-eight hours," he said gently. "I've been avoiding it because I know I'll have nightmares. When I do, I'll wake up punching. You could be seriously hurt. Just go to bed, the two of you, all right? We'll all sleep better that way."

"No." Hellhound's rasp held a note of finality. "Ya can take the cot in Aydan's tent an' we'll use the mattress if that's the way ya want it, but ya ain't goin' through this alone." He gripped Kane's shoulder. "Come on, Cap. Let's go."

Kane hesitated and I thought he'd refuse. Then he let out a breath and his shoulders sagged as though they couldn't bear the weight of his pain any longer.

"All right," he said quietly. "Thank you."

In my tent he pulled the mattress pad off the cot and laid it on the floor. At my raised eyebrow, he explained, "It's easier to start out on the floor than to fall out of bed later. Besides, the cot's too short."

I nodded, feeling as though I was swimming through syrup. Stifling a yawn, I took out one of the burner phones and began to dial.

"Who ya callin'?" Hellhound asked. "Ya know it's four AM, right?"

"I know, but this is important..." I shut up when Dave's anxious voice came on the line.

"Dave's Trucking, Dave speaking."

"Hi, Dave, it's Aydan-"

"What's wrong?" he interrupted. "Is Nichele okay? You need me to come out there?"

"Nothing's wrong, and yes, I need you to come. But not for a few hours," I added hurriedly as rustling and a thump emanated over the line.

"When? What's happening? Is Nichele okay?"

"Nichele's okay," I promised, hoping I wasn't lying. "But we had some activity here last night and I want her safe with you. If you could be here by..."

I hesitated, trying to force my exhausted brain into some useful calculation. Nichele never got up early at the best of times, and she'd been drugged.

"...ten o'clock," I decided. "And be ready to drag her out of here kicking and screaming if necessary."

"That sounds bad," he said worriedly.

"It could have been. It wasn't, and it won't be now, but..." I shut up before I could worry him any more. "Everything's fine and Nichele's safe, I promise," I said firmly. "I'll see you tomorrow at ten, okay?"

"'Kay."

I could tell he wanted to demand answers, but I was pretty sure he wouldn't.

I was right.

"See you tomorrow, then," he said, and hung up.

"There's a guy that ain't gonna sleep for the rest a' the night," Hellhound observed drowsily from the mattress.

"Yeah." I sighed and stowed the phone. "I feel a little guilty about that, but I just want Nichele out of here."

Kane had bedded down, too, and I knelt beside his pallet.

"Goodnight," I murmured. Looking down at his exhausted face on the pillow, I stroked his hair and leaned over to kiss him. "You're safe here. Don't worry about having nightmares. You won't hurt anyone. Just let it go."

"Thank you." He pressed my palm against his cheek and his eyelids slipped closed. "G'night..." The word trailed off into a mumble, and I tucked the blanket around his shoulders and rose.

Feeling a little odd about stripping with both of them in the tent, I turned off my flashlight and shivered out of my clothes in the darkness before sliding in next to Hellhound's warm bulk.

He tucked an arm around me and I laid my head on his chest, soaking up his body heat and taking comfort from the strong steady beat of his heart.

"Same goes for you, darlin'," he whispered. "Don't worry about havin' nightmares."

I let out a long breath, feeling sleep overtaking me already. "I never do... when you're... here," I mumbled. "G'nigh..."

It felt as though I had barely closed my eyes when a crash rocketed me up in bed, my heart trying to escape my chest. Beside me, Hellhound bolted up and flicked on his flashlight, capturing Kane's dazed white face on the opposite side of the tent. Blank-eyed, he flexed his fist, blood welling up from a shallow gash in his knuckles. The remains of the cot lay broken in the corner.

"John," I said softly. "Wake up. You're dreaming. It's just a dream. Wake up."

He blinked and drew a shaky breath. "Sorry." He blinked a few more times. "I'm awake." He grimaced. "I told you this wouldn't work. I'll go and sleep in the other tent."

"Nah, it's okay," Hellhound assured him. "We'll wake ya up a little sooner next time. Ya didn't start punchin' right away. Try it again."

Kane looked as though he would argue, but then he seemed to succumb to exhaustion. "Your funeral," he mumbled as his eyes dropped closed and he fell back on the pillow.

I had barely begun to dissipate the adrenaline and relax when he began to mutter in his sleep, the rustling of the blankets accompanying his struggles.

Rolling off the mattress as Hellhound turned the flashlight on again, I limped hurriedly across to stroke the hand that had already clenched into a fist.

"Wake up, John," I urged. "It's just a dream."

"Uh?" His eyes opened, staring up at me without recognition.

"Just a dream," I repeated.

"Oh." He blinked and shook his head. I knew he was fully awake when his eyes focused and flicked down over my naked body before jerking up to meet my eyes again.

"Sorry," he said. A flush rose on his neck. "Sorry. Go back to bed."

"Just move over next to me by the mattress," I urged. "You won't punch me; I'll wake you up before you do."

"No. I won't take that chance." He wrapped his arms over his chest.

"Please, John?" I shivered in the damp chilly air. "Otherwise I'll have to keep getting out of bed and it's cold out here."

"That's why I should be sleeping in the other tent," he argued.

"Come on, Cap, move over here," Hellhound said. "Aydan's freezin' her ass off. It'll be better for everybody if ya just move over."

Kane shook his head stubbornly and Hellhound blew out a breath. "Okay. You win, Cap. Come on back to bed, darlin'."

I hurried back to huddle gratefully next to Hellhound's warm body, and he pressed his lips to my ear. "Just wait'll he falls asleep again, an' I'll drag his mattress over. He's so bagged he won't even notice."

I cuddled closer. "Good plan. He gives lots of advance warning before he starts punching so we should be able to get him awake before he does any damage."

It only took a few minutes for Kane's breathing to slow and deepen again, and Hellhound rose quietly from the mattress. Some careful jockeying later, Kane lay stretched out next to my side of the mattress. He groaned and turned over, his hand falling across my arm. Then he stilled and his breathing deepened again.

Hellhound crept back under the blankets. "There, he's better already. See how he settled down soon's he touched ya? This's gonna be better for everybody. But d'ya want me to trade places with ya?" He waved a hand at his battered features. "It ain't gonna matter if he nails me."

I chuckled and cuddled closer to his warmth. "No, this is fine. I think it might be a bit of a shock for him if he woke up playing kissy-face with you."

Hellhound snorted laughter. "Helluva shock for both of us, I'd say. G'night, darlin'. Sleep tight."

I woke slowly, aching all over. A moment of claustrophobic panic seized me when I opened my eyes to find myself enclosed by mountains of blankets on both sides, but it dissipated rapidly when I recognized Kane and Hellhound under the mountains.

On my left, Hellhound's familiar quiet snoring lulled me back into relaxation, his arm draped warm and heavy over my hips. On my right, Kane slept in silence, his breathing deep and slow, his face still pale but peaceful. His arm lay across my ribs, and I suppressed a giggle at the thought of what they'd do if I managed to slip out and they woke up in each other's arms.

If I craned my neck, I could see Hellhound's wristwatch without sitting up. It read eight-fifteen, and I let out a long breath. Still another hour of sleep. Thank God. Between waking to soothe Kane's nightmares and being woken when Hellhound soothed mine, it had been a damn short night.

I was just closing my eyes again when Kane jerked and mumbled, his face twisting in agitation.

I stroked the hard knot of his clenched fist. "John," I whispered. "Wake up. It's just a dream."

His eyes flew open, dark and disoriented.

"Just a dream," I repeated.

"Oh." His fist opened, his eyelids drooping already. "Thanks."

A moment later his breathing slowed into sleep again and I relaxed. Beside me, Hellhound whispered, "Okay, darlin'?"

I turned to smile at his sleepy face on the pillow. "Okay. Go back to sleep."

"Mmhmm."

A moment later his snores resumed, and I drifted into warm oblivion.

I woke with a start to the sound of scratching at the tent flap. Kane bolted up in bed beside me, fists clenched, and Hellhound roused on my other side, leaning up on one elbow to gather me close with a protective arm.

Moonbeam's soft voice floated through the canvas. "Storm Cloud Dancer, it's Moonbeam Meadow Sky."

I gave my two bare-chested companions a resigned glance and received shrugs in return. Tucking the blankets around me, I called, "Come in."

Moonbeam stepped through the tent flap and stopped short at the sight of us. Then she smiled. "Good morning, dears. I just thought you'd want to know that Blaze Featherwind is up and planning to leave in an hour. I don't think she'll seek you out for some time yet, as she seems rather..." she hesitated. "...taken aback," she decided with a smile, "...about the state of her hair, her bed, her tent, and the weather in general."

I cocked an ear at the pattering of rain on canvas above us. "Ah. Right." I leaned against Hellhound's solid heat behind me and ran an appreciative hand over Kane's muscular back. "You know, this is the first time in four months I've woken up warm."

"Well, dear, now you know what it takes." Moonbeam's eyes twinkled conspiratorially.

"How's your arm?" I asked.

"Sore." Her fingertips floated over the neat bandage that swathed her forearm from wrist to elbow. "I can't believe I was foolish enough to reach through that broken glass." She gave a light shrug. "Silly old woman. Well, I just wanted to let you know about Blaze Featherwind."

I grabbed Hellhound's wrist and turned his watch toward me. "Right, so she'll be leaving at ten o'clock," I said, wondering whether Dave had called her or she had called him. Or if she had made other arrangements entirely. That would be bad. "Uh, do you know how she's planning to leave?" I asked.

"I understand her fiancé will be picking her up."

"Fiancé?" Hope warmed my veins. "Really?"

"That's what she said." Moonbeam smiled. "I see that's good news to you."

"Very." I grinned. "I'd better get dressed and see her off, then."

"I'll see you later," Moonbeam said, and withdrew, closing the tent flap behind her.

I flopped back on the mattress. "So that's taken care of. Thank God."

"What about you, darlin'?" Hellhound asked. "Will ya get to go home now?"

"God, I hope so," I breathed. "I was planning to call Stemp this morning and see if he'll finally let me go. Which reminds me, did either of you report to him about any of this?"

"Nah," Hellhound said. "Not unless he asks. I was never officially here."

"I gave him my final report on my last mission last night," Kane said. "Nothing since. And I don't think I will either unless he asks." He eyed our triple-wide bed with a wry twist to his mouth. "I see I was overruled last night."

"Yep. An' it worked out fine," Hellhound said complacently.

Kane got out of bed and stretched to his full height, muscles flexing and crackling. I watched the magnificent sight, feeling slightly uncomfortable about appreciating his well-filled black briefs and rippling muscles with Hellhound's naked bulk at my back.

Apparently Kane was uncomfortable, too. He dressed rapidly without looking at us and paused by the tent flap. "I'm going to take some leave time," he said to the floor. "I have several months built up and I need a chance to... unwind. To think. I'm going to call Stemp this morning and tell him. Then I'm going to get on that bike and take a road trip down through California. It's something I've wanted to do for a long time."

"That sounds like a good idea." I hesitated. "Maybe... you should think about calling Dr. Rawling, too."

He met my eyes. "I will. That will be my second call this morning."

"Hey, Cap," Hellhound said diffidently. "If ya need some time to yourself, I get it. But if ya want some company, that's a ride I been wantin' to take for a while, too."

Kane smiled, and I hadn't realized how much tension he'd been holding in his shoulders until they relaxed. "We always talked about it, didn't we?" he said. "But we never got around to it."

Hellhound grinned. "No time like the present. Just lemme swap that pansy-ass street-an'-trail bike for a Harley an' call Miz Lacey to look after Hooker a little longer, an' I'm ready to ride."

Kane turned to me. "Aydan, would you like to come, too? You could rent a bike in Victoria."

I hesitated. I wanted to go home. But would he be hurt if I declined?

Probably not. It sounded as though this was something they'd planned together long ago. Guy time. It would do them both good.

"Thanks, it sounds like a great trip, but I really just want to go home," I replied, knowing I'd said the right thing as soon as the words left my mouth.

"Just like old times." Kane straightened and a bit of the old sparkle returned to his eyes as he grinned at Hellhound. "Get up and get dressed, you hairy ugly bastard. We've got a highway calling us."

Hellhound threw him an exaggerated salute with an extended middle finger, and Kane laughed and ducked out the tent flap.

Hellhound let out a breath and I felt the tension leave his body.

I turned to face him. "Are you okay?"

"Yeah." He sank back on the pillow. "I was worried about him."

"Me, too. I was worried about both of you. And... this." I waved a hand at our state of undress. "I don't want to be a strain on your friendship."

"Well, yeah, this ended up kinda weird, but we'll figure it out, darlin'. An' I think this bike trip is gonna be good for him. He's been wound up too tight for too long."

"And you?" I touched his cheek.

"Me? Hell, I'm always okay."

I shook my head and kissed him. "No, you're always amazing. Come on, let's get dressed. I want to call Stemp and then go and see Nichele off."

CHAPTER 42

An hour later, Nichele fluttered beside her suitcase in the rain-drenched field. "Oh-em-gee, Aydan, I can't believe what a mess I am! I had a little party with Aurora last night..."

Beside me, Aurora flushed guiltily, but Nichele prattled on, "...and this morning I had the mother of all hangovers! I swear to God, Aydan, I hurt all over! And I can't find my clothes. Thank God my Valentino sneakers were under my bed. And I've got the worst bedhead *ever*; I can't believe how this wet weather wrecks your hair. I don't know how you lasted here all this time. And I haven't showered in two days!" She turned anxious eyes toward me. "I'm such a mess. What if Dave..."

"Dave will be so glad to see you he won't care if you're covered in pig shit," I assured her.

She wrinkled her nose. "Eeeuw, gross, girl! I'm going to make him take me straight to the Empress in Victoria and I'm going to shower for *days* and go to the spa, and oh-em-gee, look at my nails! A manicure, first thing..." She broke off. "Look, there he is! Oh-em-gee, there he is!"

She gripped my wrist hard enough to leave little half-moon nail indentations in my skin. "Ohmigod, Aydan, I can't believe I'm so nervous!"

"Relax. Take a breath." I pried her fingers loose, beginning to be infected by her nerves myself.

Dave's highway tractor rumbled into the field, bouncing over the uneven ground to pull to halt in front of us, the air brakes hissing. Dave swung down from the cab seconds after the wheels stopped turning and hurried toward us, looking as nervous as Nichele.

He bent to give her a quick hug and a peck on the lips. "Ready to go home, honey?" he asked, his voice cracking with false nonchalance.

Nichele cast her gaze down, clinging to his hand. "Um... no, not really..."

"Oh." Dave threw me a desperate look. "Well, um..."

"I was hoping..." Nichele gave him a quick glance from under her lashes. "...maybe you'd take me to the Empress Hotel in Victoria...?"

He brightened, already beginning to nod when she added, "...maybe... for an early honeymoon?"

"Uh..." A flood of crimson raced up his face to set his ears alight. "Did you say honeymoon?"

"Yes." She bit her lip, looking up at him with pink cheeks. "I mean... *Yes.*"

"Yes?" Comprehension burst onto his face in a grin wide enough to threaten his ears. He swept her up in a bear hug and I revelled in the sweetness of their embrace, grinning almost as widely as Dave.

When they finally pried themselves apart, I asked Nichele, "What changed your mind?"

She beamed at Aurora. "The Earth Spirit. And Aurora."

Aurora flushed, her smile bright.

Nichele went on, "She said if love is real, it'll never let you down. And even if it does, having your heart broken is

still not as bad as never being loved because you were afraid to try."

She turned to Dave. "So I want to try." She screwed her face into a ferocious scowl. "But if you cheat on me even once, we're done."

Dave's arm tightened around her. "Honey, if I was dumb enough to cheat on you, I'd deserve to be alone."

Nichele leaned into him, gazing up adoringly. "I love you."

He flushed. "I love you, too, honey."

I made a gagging noise. "Get out of here, you two; you're throwing me into diabetic shock."

"Don't be such a cynic, girl!" Nichele bounced over to throw her arms around me. "Maybe someday you'll find somebody-"

"Don't start!" I hugged her back. "Jeez, now you're going to be matchmaking as well as trying to turn me into a girl. I don't know, Nichele, there'd better be some beer in this for me somewhere."

"All you can drink," Dave spoke up gratefully as Nichele released me to hug Aurora. "Without you, I'd never have met Nichele."

She returned to his embrace and he folded his arms around her, giving me a significant look over her head. "And you know I'll do anything to take care of her," he added.

I stepped over to throw my arms around both of them one more time. "I know you will. Now get out of here."

A few minutes later I waved at the receding taillights of the highway tractor before dropping my hand with a sigh of relief.

"Thank you for what you did for Nichele," I said to Aurora. "I didn't spend enough time with her while she was here. I'm glad you were able to change her mind."

"I was happy to," she replied, and her voice didn't bother me a bit. Her eyes shone with innocent joy. "That's what we do here. We share the love of the Earth Spirit. Will you be staying with us? We'd love to have you live here permanently."

I sighed at the memory of my conversation with Stemp an hour earlier. New problems awaited me in Alberta, but at least they weren't likely to be life-threatening. And I'd have a warm dry bed and hot running water while I dealt with them.

The corners of my mouth tugged upward.

"Thanks, Aurora, but no..."

My farm beckoned, my heart yearning toward its peace and solitude. The slow life-affirming transition of winter to spring. The sweet aroma of moist fertile soil and new grass. The wide-open country that let my soul spread its wings to soar on the long prairie winds.

I drew a breath that felt as though my lungs had been unlocked for the first time in a year.

"No," I repeated, my smile widening. "I'm going home."

Book 10 is available!

Visit my Books page at dianehenders.com/books for progress
updates and announcements.

A Request

Thanks for reading!

If you enjoyed this book, I'd really appreciate it if you'd take a moment to review it online.

Here are some suggestions for the "star" ratings:
Five stars: Loved the book and can hardly wait for the next one.
Four stars: Liked the book and plan to read the next one.
Three stars: The book was okay. Might read the next one.
Two stars: Didn't like the book. Probably won't read the next one.
One star: Hated the book. Would never read another in the series.

You can help prospective readers by writing a few sentences about what you liked or disliked about the book.

Thanks for taking the time to do a review!

About Me

Before I started writing fiction, I had a checkered career: technical writer, computer geek, and interior designer. I'm good at two out of three of those. Fortunately, I had the sense to quit the one I sucked at (interior design).

When my mid-life crisis hit, I took up muay thai and started writing thrillers featuring a middle-aged female protagonist. ('Walter Mitty', you say? Nope, never heard of him.)

Writing and kicking the hell out of stuff seemed more productive than more typical mid-life-crisis activities like getting a divorce, buying a Harley Crossbones, and cruising across the country picking up men in sleazy bars; especially since it's winter most months of the year here in Canada.

It's much more comfortable to sit at my computer. And Harleys are expensive. Come to think of it, so are beer and gasoline.

Oh, and I still love my husband. There's that. So I stuck with the writing.

Diane Henders

And here's my "professional" bio, in case you need something more suitable for mixed company:

Diane Henders is the Kindle best-selling author of the NEVER SAY SPY series: Sexy thrillers packed with tension, laughs, profanity, and sometimes warm fuzzies.

The first book in the series, NEVER SAY SPY, has had over 450,000 downloads to date, and stayed on Kindle's 'Women Sleuths' Top 100 list for 60 consecutive months.

Diane enjoys target shooting, gardening, auto mechanics, painting (art, not walls), music, and martial arts; and loves food and drink almost as much as she loves her husband. They live in the wilds of British Columbia, Canada, where they get all the adrenaline rush they could ever want by growing fruit trees in bear country.

Want to know what else is roiling around in the cesspit of my mind? Drop by my blog and website at dianehenders.com, check out the extras, and don't forget to leave a comment in the guest book to say hi – I love hearing from you! Or you can connect with me on Facebook at:
https://www.facebook.com/authordianehenders.
See you there!

www.ingramcontent.com/pod-product-compliance
Lightning Source LLC
Chambersburg PA
CBHW030758260626
47169CB00001B/106

* 9 7 8 1 9 2 7 4 6 0 2 2 1 *